THE STRAY PITCH

Marilyn Bos

In 1950, it was hard for a woman to score.

Produced by Flat Sole Studio,
a division of Skywater Publishing Company,
398 Goodrich Avenue, St. Paul, MN 55102
www.flatsolestudio.com

Library of Congress Cataloging-in-Publication Data
Bos, Marilyn Janice.
    The stray pitch / by Marilyn Janice Bos.
    p. cm.
    ISBN 978-1-938237-02-7 (pbk.)
    ISBN 978-1-938237-03-4 (ebk.)
    1. Women private investigators—Fiction. 2. Baseball for
women—Fiction. 3. Baseball stories. [1. Iowa—History—20th
century—Fiction.] I. Title.
PS3602.O825S77 2013
813'.6—dc23   2012023532

Credits
Cover Art by Nancy Allan
Book Production by Flat Sole Studio

Acknowledgments
The author is very grateful to the following people who contributed to
this work: Zoē Barta for offering suggestions throughout the writing,
Jim Scheller for line editing, Nancy Allan for cover art, Linda Thurnau
for comments on the synopsis, Mary Logue for the final critique, and
to the members of our former mystery writers' group: Becky Bohan,
Pete Hautman, Mary Logue, Tom Rucker, George Sorenson, and
Deborah Woodworth.

THE STRAY PITCH

A Wendy Winkworth Mystery

WINKS BOOKS
Minneapolis

Cast of Characters

Wendy Winkworth	private investigator
Duane Shupe	police chief
Dan Robinson	police officer
Leroy Williams	unemployed barfly
Sid Dobrotka	local sportswriter
William Winkworth	Wendy's father
Mary Winkworth	Wendy's mother
Norris Winkworth	Wendy's brother
Jim Winkworth	Wendy's brother
Yegor (Yegg) Washington	league owner

The Star Spangled Girls Baseball League

Aurora, IL	Alices
Burton City, IA	Hornettes
Cedar Rapids, IA	Starlets
Davenport, IA	Sofies
Mankato, MN	Maulers
Waterloo, IA	Flickas

The Burton City Hornettes

(Roster of players during the 1950 season)

Pos	Name	Bats/Throws	Yrs in League
1B	Dinah (M&M) Timberlake	L/L	6
2B	Lorena (Lor) Willey	R/R	6
SS	Dorena (Dor) Willey	R/R	6
3B	Joanie Dober	R/R	4
C	Edaline (Eddie) McLaine	R/R	6
LF	Twyla Ziegler	L/L	3
CF	Connie Schulz	L/R	2
RF	Pepper McLaine	R/R	rookie
utility	Wendy (Winkie) Winkworth	R/R	rookie
utility/C	Helen Sanders	R/R	3
P	Roberta (Bobby) Bied	R/R	5
P	Kay (The Kid) Brock	L/L	rookie
P	Millicent (Milly) Tubbs	?/L	4
P	Loretta (Letta) Lorrimer	R/R	4
P	Molly Powell	L/L	rookie
P	Betty Jane Wadlow	R/R	rookie
manager	Clint Appling		

1.

I'm Private Investigator Wendy Winkworth, the dickless dick.

The evening of August 6, 1950, I was sitting in the Burton City, Iowa, ballpark, watching a game between teams of the Star-Spangled Girls Baseball League. I had gone there hoping the contest would raise my spirits. They were low, because, in the two months since I'd received my PI license, no jobs had come my way.

Betty Jane Wadlow, star pitcher for the Burton City Hornettes, was doing her best to elevate my mood. The first seven innings, she destroyed the Waterloo Flickas, uncorking wicked fastballs, mixing them with change ups and curves. After each of her fifteen strikeouts she posed on the mound, tossing her spun-gold hair, looking as confident as a model for Coca-Cola. How can you be that good-looking and that good too?

But in the eighth Betty Jane struggled with control. After walking the first two batters, she allowed a double and those first mistakes scored, spoiling the shutout. Eventually she got out of that inning, and, entering the ninth, the game still seemed well in hand, with the Hornettes ahead, 8-2.

The lead-off hitter for the Flickas grounded out, but then Betty Jane threw three straight balls to the next batter. Catcher Edaline (Eddie) McLaine] trotted to the mound. Betty Jane turned away from her, seemingly disdainful of what Eddie had to say. Battery mates not communicating: very bad. A stoic Eddie strode back to the plate. She adjusted her mask while the batter took practice swings and the umpire picked at his teeth.

The infielders started into their chatter.

Suddenly, before anyone was ready, Betty Jane uncorked a fastball that sailed over Eddie's head and crashed against the backstop, violently shaking the screen. The ump bellowed, "Wild pitch!" as Betty Jane wheeled and stared into centerfield.

The infielders shut up. In the bleachers, gasps hushed to murmurs. Manager Clint Appling burst from the dugout and headed toward the mound. Running for the clubhouse, Betty Jane banged his hand away. After an instant of astonishment, he motioned for centerfielder Kay Brock, also a relief pitcher, to take over. The young southpaw raced in happily. The Kid, as she was known, was boundlessly eager to pitch.

But ambition isn't everything (I'd found that out) and after Brock threw four straight fastballs nowhere near the strike zone, Appling signaled for the more experienced Letta Lorrimer to replace her. Drooping with failure, "The Kid" trotted to the dugout. Letta's speedy deliveries got the defense dancing on their toes and she obtained the final two outs.

On my way out of the park, if I'd looked to my left, I might have seen Betty Jane emerge from the clubhouse. Maybe I could have said something comforting to her, something so significant as to be life saving, but I don't know what it would have been.

I was running my PI office out of my home, a trailer on the outskirts of Iowa City, about 80 miles northwest of Burton City. Owen Ray Mandel, my mentor in the law enforcement program, had expected there'd be some small-time crime in a university town, enough to ease a twenty-four year old into the business. So far he'd been wrong.

At 7:00 the next morning, I dragged myself out of bed and opened the trailer door to sultriness. I grabbed the Iowa City Press

Citizen off the stoop and scanned the front page for the latest about the Korean War: General MacArthur said to be kowtowing to President Truman. I shifted my gaze to the far right hand column. It blared: "Pitcher Betty Jane Wadlow murdered in Burton City." I recoiled. Betty Jane was dead? The article said the body had been found on a bank of the Mississippi. She had been shot, the killer at large. As I reeled in disbelief the thought snuck through: what an opportunity if only the case came my way. Well, fat chance. And shameful to think of my needs before I felt proper grief.

I tossed the paper on the table and sank into my swiveler. Rotating the chair, I tried to put the tragedy on the backburner; there'd be time for mourning later. Right now, best get busy advertising my services by writing local businesses. While mailing those letters, I'd drop by the Iowa City police station to introduce myself. In fact, why not call the Burton City police right now and proclaim expertise in all things homicidal? No, too early for big lies. Better wait until 9:00, a decent hour for getting a story straight.

Outside, I heard two doors slam in rapid succession. Glancing out the window, I saw Hornettes Manager Clint Appling and another middle-aged man emerge from opposite sides of a dusty Burton City squad car. They moved over patchy grass to my door.

Perhaps my conclusion had been too hasty. It looked like the principals were coming to me.

2.

Four raps sounded on my door, ever more insistent. After shedding pj's and slipping into jeans, T-shirt, and moccasins, I opened the door to a fist ready to pound again. It belonged to a slim man with a crew cut and sunken cheeks, a nick in one. He was clad in a cadet blue pinstripe suit, smartly tailored, and a light blue tie with a pattern of darker squares. He wore a Homburg that stayed on his head.

"Wendy Winkworth. That you?" he asked brusquely.

"Yes!" I gestured the men inside.

"Police Chief Duane Shupe, Burton City," said the pinstriped fellow, pointing to a silver badge on his lapel. He removed his hat, too late for me to be impressed by his manners.

The other guy whom I'd recognized as Clint Appling, the Hornettes' manager, grabbed my hand and shook it desperately.

"Please." I motioned them to sit. Appling took the kitchen chair, Shupe rested his lean butt on the stool. He placed the Homburg on the kitchen table. I seated myself in the swiveler beside the table, the dick at her desk.

Appling was dressed in tan slacks and a blue T-shirt. He looked stuffed into that outer layer. The Hornettes uniform fit him the same way; the pants made him look bandy-legged. Nonetheless, of the two middle-aged men, the manager, even rumpled and unshaven, was the more appealing. With bronzed wrinkles and a dimple in his chin, he was kind of cute in a paunchy way. Once a noted major league catcher, now he managed the sixteen women who comprised the Burton City Hornettes, a member of the Star-Spangled Girls Baseball League (SSGBL), one of two women's associations established for morale purposes during World War II while many of the major league ballplayers were overseas doing their duty.

Chief Shupe extracted a cigar from a jacket pocket and chomped through its tip. He placed the tip on the table. I swiveled toward the kitchen counter (not far), got an ashtray and scooted it toward him. He halted its path but left the cigar tip where it was. He lit up and blew smoke while taking in the scene. I saw what he did: sparse furnishings, old appliances, a dented saucepan tilted on the stove, dirty Melmac dishes from last night's snack left out on the counter. "You read about the murder in my town last night?" the chief asked. He thumped the newspaper with a stubby finger.

I nodded. "Yeah, what a shame." Appling had blanched upon mention of the news.

Shupe continued in a raspy voice. "Happened down by the river, after a game. Miss Wadlow was shot twice, first from behind, in the shoulder, not fatal, then from the front, close-up, near-contact shooting, powder burns, through the heart. Instant death. A .32 did the job." He studied his wiry hands. He mumbled to them, "You like to work with the Burton City police on this?"

"Of course," I said, "seeings I currently have time available." Noting the chief's unease, and mine, I added, "Like some coffee?" I indicated the Folger's Instant jar on the table. Create a homey atmosphere. It wasn't hard to sense the chief's reluctance at having to hire a woman.

Appling nodded at my offer. Shupe's response was to puff on the cigar, the query not worth his attention.

I rose, ran water in the saucepan, took three mugs from the cupboard and set them on the table. "How'd you hear about me?" I asked.

Shupe cleared his throat. Looking for a place to spit, he decided against it. He swallowed and said, "It's Mr. Yegg Washington who wants to hire you. Know who he is?"

My insides smiled. "The team owner." And a powerful owner he was, also mixed up, big-time, in the rackets. What Mr. Washington said went for law in our part of the world.

"Not only does Mr. Washington own the Hornettes, but the whole darn petticoat league." Shupe spread his arms expansively to indicate the entire pleats and puckers sporting world.

"He picked the right detective," I assured. "In my brief career, I've nabbed an armed shooter and a number of burglars." Grade school had supplied those miscreants, both of whom had burst into tears when identified to the second grade teacher by their fellow classmate, the future dick. The gun was a loaded water pistol, the stolen item a chocolate bar - my chocolate bar.

"Wow," Shupe said without enthusiasm.

I reached for my notepad and pen. "So what have you got so far?"

"Main suspect is Dinah Timberlake, the first baseman."

I was shocked. "What's the deal there?" Like any fan, I followed the team day by day. Professional baseball is different from other sports in that they play every day. You figure you know the players from watching them on the field, reading statistics and interviews in the papers. Okay, so Dinah was blustery and seemed to think she was the whole team. But a killer?

Appling raised his head to utter his first words. "It ain't Dinah."

"No, not definitely, not yet," Shupe responded. "The killer painted the word, 'JUSt' on a boulder near the victim. Capital 'J-U-S', small 't'. Keep that to yourself. It's a convicting detail in case some lunatic shows up to confess and can't supply the fact."

I nodded. The water was boiling. I spooned coffee into each mug, poured the steaming liquid, stirred, slid the finished product toward the men. Appling blew on his and then sipped, bubbles remaining on his lips.

Shupe shifted on the stool. "Leave the spoon, it's too damn hot. Killer used red paint to write the word, crimson paint to be exact. Rubbed it on with a stick. A small jar of crimson was found at the scene. No fingerprints on it or on the stick. You keeping up with this?"

I leaned back in the swiveler. "I'm way ahead of you, got a few ideas of my own." I didn't, but I'm skillful at coming up with responses that stall potential oppressors.

"I bet you do," Shupe said dryly. He took a breath. "Early today, we found an oil paint box, artist's set no less, in Dinah's locker. All the paints were there except for the crimson. Dinah admits the paints are hers, got real offended when pressed. Damn strong gal." He smiled vaguely. "But the boys and I quieted her down." I guessed it had been a kick for the cop pack to subdue her.

"Forgive the language," he added, "you don't mind a little four-lettering, do you?"

"Shit and piss, no. I grew up with it. The family's got career cops coming out of the woodwork." Now that was a blatant lie. Most of my employed relatives are crooks.

The chief didn't bat an eye at my manly vocabulary but Appling blinked.

"We're searching Dinah's apartment now," Shupe resumed, "for the ball pendant necklace they say Betty Jane always wore. Not on the body. Description says pure gold, with a little gold baseball hanging on it." His wiry fingers manipulated the cigar. "Dinah's got a motive. Teammates say that two days before the murder, she put a gun to Betty Jane's head and threatened to pull the trigger. Betty Jane went bonkers with fear and passed out. Team says Dinah was jealous of the new girl on the block."

I nodded. At twenty-six, Betty Jane was older than most first year players, who tended to be in their late teens or early twenties. She had arrived in mid-season, unheralded, from a rural area in Montana. With her astonishing success, the Burton City Gazette had shifted its focus from Dinah, a bashing Man Mountain Dean type, to Betty Jane, equal star quality and much better looking. The huge Mountain Man had been a popular wrestler early in our century. "Please God, let it not be Dinah," Appling implored to the ceiling.

"We don't have enough yet for an arrest," Shupe soothed. "That's what Wendy is good for, to prove it."

I drew myself up. "The Winkworth Agency will conduct an independent investigation and, in the end, might not agree with you."

"Winkworth Agency?" Shupe snorted. "Who's that besides you and the broken down Nash outside?" He rolled his eyes. "Can't believe I'm sittin' here doing this."

Appling grunted, "Miss Winkworth sounds fair." In his abject state, he didn't seem up to dispute.

"Did Mr. Washington specifically name me?" I asked. Might as well know the strength of my position.

"He did," Shupe said, "probably because you're the only female dick around."

I knew different. There was Olive Shimp in Chicago. In her mid-thirties, she was damn tough, with years in the business. And why did the dick have to be female? Best not ask about that and get them to considering.

"Was Betty Jane seen after the game?"

"Not that we know of," Shupe said. "Body was discovered about 2:00 a.m. by a young couple looking for a make-out spot. Dead girl was still in uniform. Wore tennis shoes though. Baseball cleats make for hard walking."

"Really. So she didn't take time to change. She have on fresh makeup?"

"Don't know. Got a reason for asking?" He tapped cigar ash into the mug filled with coffee.

"I've been to some of the games she pitched," I said. "Noticed she always started out wearing heavy makeup - red lipstick, heavy rouge. It was smudged by the third inning, or totally worn off from lip chewing. But next inning she'd come out with freshly painted lips. Last night, if she hadn't applied new makeup, that'd indicate she was in a hurry."

"Clever intuiting," Shupe guessed.

"Betty Jane was upset over that wild pitch," Appling intervened. "Probably couldn't wait to get out of there."

"I was at the game last night," I said, hoping that would win me points.

With a so-what shrug, Shupe passed over that revelation. "Maybe she was afraid of someone at the ballpark or maybe she had a date down by the river. "

Tears welling, Appling said, "It seemed like that girl was sent to us from heaven. With her, we could have won the pennant. Whoever did this …" His fists curled and he rubbed his eyes.

"We'll get the sonofabitch," Shupe gruffed. "Coroner says death occurred between 10:30 last night and 2:00 this morning. Body's going to the big morgue in Des Moines. They got all kinds of advanced hocus-pocus that may narrow down the TOD."

"Good, good. TOD's important." What the heck was TOD? Oh, time of death. I kept nodding wisely while I processed.

With an index finger, I drew a circle in the oilcloth around a tiny hill of powdered milk from last night's Wheaties snack. I wanted them to think I was deep in thought. In truth, the imagined taste of succulent steak had overwhelmed my tongue. I seemed very close to eating red meat again.

"Please inform Mr. Washington that it's $35 a day plus expenses." Boy, that was a lot of money but the guy was rich and I'd see quickly just how much he needed me.

Shupe didn't flinch. "You'll be joining the team as a utility player."

"Oh, no, not possible," I protested. "The Hornettes are experts at their craft. They'd spot an amateur in a second. No, if I'm to infiltrate, it'll be as a ball-girl or locker room attendant."

"Nope. Mr. Washington's one stipulation is that you be a good enough ball player to join the team. His theory is, if you're on par with the girls, they'll share confidences with you. Otherwise he'll look elsewhere."

I was of short stature for an athlete, even a female one. As a child I'd dreamed - at seven or eight years old you don't know how big you'll get. I had stopped at five-four. But I played softball throughout high school, and in college joined pickup teams that had more enthusiasm than skill. I cleared my throat. "No problem. Only last week, I played both ends of a doubleheader." Wishful thinking.

"You know baseball rules?" Shupe asked with a smirk. "What's a suicide squeeze?"

I snapped out the situation. "Where the runner on third races for home with the pitch. Batter's supposed to bunt."

Shupe barely nodded. "When you went to those games, did you tell people you were a PI?"

"No. I don't think I'll be recognized. I sat high up in the bleachers with a pack of fans around me."

A pregnant pause, before Appling said, "Eddie McLaine's our chaperon and also our catcher. Her and I will cover for you."

Shupe put up a stalling hand. "No, Clint, you can't tell Eddie about this. Wendy's got to fend for herself. No one on the team can know she's a plant and that includes your girlfriend."

"Eddie is not my girlfriend," Appling countered in a tone sharper than he'd used so far. "It's only in her mind she thinks so."

"Hah!" Shupe snorted. "That's how it starts."

I interrupted what seemed a debatable point. "Did Betty Jane have any other enemies on the team?"

Appling shook his head. "Everybody loved her. And everybody including M&M, that's what we call Dinah, loved her pitching." Man Mountain for sure. I almost giggled as to how spot-on I was.

Appling shot a baleful look at Shupe. "Eddie McLaine is our catcher and our chaperon, nothing more. She's the one for you to talk to. She knows everything about the girls."

"Where were you last night, Mr. Appling?" I asked conversationally.

Shupe took that one. "He was with one of the ballplayers most of the night. A kid named Kay Brock. Kid was seriously upset by her bad performance in the game. Kay verifies it."

Kay Brock: centerfielder and last night's first, failed, reliever.

My tone continued to be polite. "Mr. Appling, what time did you leave Kay Brock?"

He shrugged. "I don't know. Maybe she does. It was late. Didn't matter at the time."

The Kid seemed a little young to hang around a guy old enough to be her father, but you never know where adulation of a wise mentor will lead. It had happened to me with Owen Ray Mandel. I decided against pressing the manager further because Shupe was answering for him anyhow. Instead I asked, "Mr. Appling, you ever see Betty Jane throw that bad a pitch?"

"No. Call me Clint." Appling gave me an appealing smile, the dimple contributing. Deadly weapons, dimples. "No, she never did. Unbelievable." He shook his head. "Control of that pea was her strongest asset. But it happens to the best of us. Sometimes even the best don't come on the field with their best stuff operating."

"Granted. When can I meet the team?"

"Game's cancelled today but we're holding practice tomorrow. A time for gathering is what Eddie calls it."

"Biblical," I said reverently.

Appling's nod outdid my piety. "Gotta keep going to get through this."

As I stood, so did they. "Clint," I said, "the crimson paint came from the locker room. No matter how distasteful, it looks like the killer might be a team member. And remember to keep my role to yourself. I don't want to end up as victim number two."

"Hah," Shupe said, "Mr. Washington wouldn't like that one bit." Moving pugnaciously toward the door, he swung around to say, "Miss Winkworth, don't screw up this assignment. What's important to Mr. Washington means an awful lot to Burton City, too."

And also to your career.

3.

To reduce chances of being identified as a local, I went to a beauty parlor and had my long curly brown hair cut short.

Then I drove to Burton City in my brown and white '39 Nash. Truth to tell, the auto was a bit on the rusty side. When gazing to the left of the accelerator I could see pavement rolling by.

I hoped that if Dinah Timberlake were guilty, she'd hold off confessing until I earned some dough collecting the proof.

Arriving 45 minutes early for the 9:00 a.m. appointment with the team, I parked by the entrance to Cranston Park, where the Hornettes played. I wanted to exercise off my jitters by walking the half-mile to the ballpark.

Known mainly as an arboretum, Cranston Park held a variety of trees and shrubbery. The ball field was tucked in the far southwest corner of the park. Beyond its outfield lay a cow pasture. Mooing serenaded afternoon games.

Singing "Take Me Out to the Ballgame" in time to my strides, I proceeded down a winding path, among shadows of great oaks, past sun-dappled ash trees and knobby junipers from Mexico. A plate on each tree identified its genus. The genus for Oak was "Quercus." I'd remember that in case a conversation with a naturalist ever lagged. At the base of each of the older trees a worn lollipop-shaped marker commemorated a dead soldier from World War I.

I enjoyed the fresh, embracing smells of the outdoors. The day was muggy and by the time I reached the ballpark, my cotton shirt was sticking to my skin. I wished I knew more than one verse to get me to that old ball game. Like bubblegum, the same words over and over had to last far beyond their first invigorating taste. Come to think of it, was there more than one verse?

I passed the large lot where a few cars were parked. One, a Buick, had a fierce black and yellow hornet painted on the driver's door. Somebody nearby just LOVES those Hornettes. Clint had told me to report directly onto the field, so, passing a boarded-up concession stand, I climbed steps to the first row of bleachers and went down other steps to a short wall, scaled that and jumped down onto the cinders bordering the field.

On the diamond, in chest protector and leg guards, Eddie McLaine was warming up left-hander Kay Brock.

I had landed close to the home team dugout. While studying the two players, I took a deep breath of ballpark air. The newly mown grass held the moist, heady smell of baseball. I gazed about. The outfield stretched before me. From home plate, it was 320 feet down the left field line, 360 to center and 297 to the right field fence where Dinah Timberlake aimed. In May, one of her homers had landed over the fence among the cattle. Startled, the creatures crashed through the wooden fence that marked the parking lot causing fans to flee the game and protect their cars while helping with the roundup. Sid Dobrotka, the local sportswriter, had labeled the incident, "The Stampede of the Fans."

At field level, Kay and Eddie appeared larger and more immediate than from the stands. At the sight of those athletic physiques slinging a baseball like it was a greased pebble, I felt a shiver of apprehension. First thing to do: hire someone to help me compete.

Kay Brock, Manager Appling's alibi, was a rookie, at seventeen the youngest Hornette, a short, stocky, cherub-faced girl who wore leather shoes oversized for her height. An outfielder when not pitching, she had replaced Betty Jane on the mound with unpromising results two nights ago.

Kay's rapid pitches and Eddie's leisurely return throws made for an irregular metronome of thumps. After an errant pitch rocketed off the edge of Eddie's outstretched glove and rebounded off the wall, it skittered my way. I fielded it handily and flipped it back to the catcher, dead on even if it did bounce twice before reaching her. Ball in hand, Eddie advanced toward me, saying, "No one allowed in here until the gates open."

I began to introduce myself as the latest Hornette, but just then Clint bounded from the dugout and did the honors himself. "Eddie, say hi to Wendy Winkworth, our new utility infielder."

"You kidding? With that throwing arm?" A heavy-boned woman in her early thirties, Eddie had faded freckles and dull red hair that spiked from underneath the backwards cap.

I took umbrage at the criticism. "I'm young, but I learn fast. A whole lot faster than older people. May I carry your mask for you, ma'am?"

Eddie shook her head, possibly to reject my offer, more likely to express disbelief. She looped the ball to Kay. "Rosemarie Hapsburg's supposed to be next in line on the infielder list," she said to Clint. "I don't get it. Why is this gal jumped ahead? This is getting crazier and crazier." Clint shuffled his feet.

"You bring your papers?" She addressed me.

What papers? "They're in the mail," I said smoothly.

"Clint, you get those papers in the files as quick as possible. I need to determine her experience so I can begin a training regimen." She turned back to me. "Winkie, let's get you outfitted for practice."

Already a nickname and not a flattering one. Eddie veered toward the gate beyond third base.

On the pitching rubber, Kay Brock smacked her glove and whined in an accent straight out of the Ozarks, "Where you goin'? I'm startin' tomorrow; I need lotsa practice."

"Oh, take a break," came the reply, "I'll be right back."

"Shoot," the kid pled. She added, "I'm a starter now," impressing herself if no one else. She tossed the ball straight up about a mile and, when, seconds later, it hurtled down, she caught it without an upward glance. Boy, was I overmatched.

Beyond the third base exit, the circular clubhouse was a one-story building with a brick base and high windows about two-thirds around. A few windows were set lower, probably indicating offices. Inside, Clint and Eddie proceeded down the corridor while I trailed behind. Their clattering spikes covered the sound of my sport shoes slapping against the cement.

We entered a large locker room replete with the odors of dampness and sweat that I recalled from high school, and moved down an aisle that fronted a line of lockers to my right. Passing a swinging door labeled "RESTROOM," we arrived at the "MANAGERS OFFICE." Clint unlocked that door and we stepped inside. To our left, a long, clouded glass window faced the lockers, at its center a splintery crack. Several group pictures of a bygone Boston Red Sox team and a single enlarged photo of that era's catcher, Clint Appling, were on the wall the other side of the door.

"Nice," I said, admiring.

With a grunt, Appling dropped into a folding chair near three outside windows with drawn shades. From this position he had a good view of the photos.

In the center of the room a blackboard with streaky chalk marks on its surface, sagged on one roller. A rack of folding chairs stood nearby. A wooden table, strewn with smudged typing paper and smeary liniment tubes, was pushed against the back wall. Next to a small refrigerator, a spittoon in the shape of a baseball mitt sat beyond the parameters of accurate aim, judging by the glutinous splatter around it.

The room held an unpleasant, dank scent.

Tossing her mitt toward the manager, Eddie clomped past two file cabinets to a huge cardboard box, its torn flaps flying out like broken wings. She rooted around in it and came up with a stained fielder's glove. Dangling it by fingertips, she presented it to me.

I shrank away. "Has that creature been sterilized?"

"Take it. Clint says the railroad lost your game stuff. You're in the bigs now, where being prepared is better than being clean." She shoved the glove into my hand. It had a slimy feel as though blood had recently been drained. "Funny thing about you," she said, "most of the gals bring along a favorite leather oil or a rosin bag or something to remind them of their main interest in life which is baseball. I don't see any of that with you. Guess you don't really care, do ya?"

Eddie stepped toward Appling and kicked him in the ankle. "Where'd you get this cutey? By her looks and lack of ability, I'd say bringing her here was your doing. Does Mr. Washington even know?"

Clint slid his feet under the chair. "He's the one who sent her. Says she's fast and can bunt."

"You'll be impressed by my hustle," I reinforced. I dug into my handbag. "Of course I got something with me that I carry everywhere. It's my pet brand of emery boards that I use for digging the dirt out of my spikes on muddy days." I held out three fingernail files.

Eddie screwed up her mouth.

Clint's voice rose in irritation. "If you don't believe me even after evidence that this girl lives and breathes baseball, you can just call up Mr. Washington."

"Aw, you know he can't be reached."

He whistled a sigh. "Skip it. Later on today we're getting a replacement for Betty Jane."

"He's giving us two players? Golly, he's all heart. Except ten like this won't replace one Betty Jane." I could see my baseball card was doomed to every bicycle spoke in town.

A clatter of cleats and Kay Brock burst into the office. "Hit me some bunts, Clint," she twanged, "I'm pitchin' tomorrow." Like he didn't know already.

He leapt up, spilling Eddie's mitt, and rushed out the door. He and Kay created a diminishing racket.

"Running out's your middle name," Eddie shouted after him.

"That kid's a bundle of nervous energy," I noted after the noise died.

"Agh, she's from the sticks, so what does she know? Got a pushy Dad. Man's a Simon Legree, all the time pushing her farther than she's ready for." She wheeled on me. "Where you from? You got that same ig-nerant accent that Kay does."

"It's not the twang, but the ideas behind it," I said with dignity. "And I got plenty of good ideas, ones that'll make the team better." Fortunately, like Chief Shupe, she didn't think enough of me to ask for details.

A pensive silence ensued before I said, "Arkansas. One of Mr. W's scouts saw me play." Although I didn't yet have any ideas to share, I had prepared a fake background. "The fella approached me after the game and offered me a Hornettes contract and the moola to get here."

Eddie poked my collarbone with an iron finger. "Okay, you're here and brought your sassiness with ya, but you watch yourself around the manager. Don't be attending any of his private meetings of which he has too many. Pretty girls, they'll be the death of this team." Realizing the implication, she colored.

I pounced. "You think that's what happened to Betty Jane? That she was involved with the manager? I can see he's very approachable. I liked him immediately."

Another steely finger punch, same place. "Ow," I said.

"Don't be implying that Betty Jane was … What's wrong with you, she's dead, for pity's sake. Have some respect."

I placed the ratty glove in front of my chest. "Sorry. I guess she was on my mind. I mean her passing was all we could talk about on the train, and with me coming to the very location where … I heard about her last pitch, that it was a doozy. A wild pitch, I mean."

Eddie's eyes widened and she stared past me as though again seeing that stray pitch sail over the hitter and smack into the backstop. Her muted reply was directed inward. "Her arm was hurting; Clint overusing her for the sake of the championship. I told him it was wrong but he never listens. The others don't like her pitching so much because they can't get their regular turns in. 'Course none of them is as good as Betty Jane, but still. Just before she uncorked that wild pitch I told her to take herself out; she looked all done in, all wound up inside, but no - " Her voice rose and she directed her comments to me. " - Betty Jane always acted like a superior being and see where it got her. Oh my God, forgive me God. What am I saying?" Her voice hardened. "And why am I unburdening to some Johnny-come-lately?"

There had been jealousy in her voice, not only directed at me, but also at the deceased pitcher.

"Darn it," she exploded. "That girl could pitch. On the days she was to start, you couldn't hold a conversation with her; her mind was so completely focused on the game. And on the mound, so graceful, her arm rising and falling so quick, the ball spinning toward the plate. Could she hit the corners, the black, you bet she could. And the curve, nobody writes about the curve, not even the sportswriter thinks it's important. But hers was the best; it sank hard. And she could aim a duster right at an uppity hitter's chest that'd tumble 'em to the turf." She lowered her head. "I'll never see it again." After waxing eloquent, she seemed to fall into despondency.

I didn't dare admit I'd seen Betty Jane pitch, when I was supposed to be laying down bunts and stealing bases in backwater country. For that moment, I regretted not being able to contribute a fan's two cents worth to Eddie's moving elegy.

The catcher snatched up her fallen mitt. "Even on the nights when Betty Jane didn't have her best stuff, the girl battled like the devil himself was her opponent." She charged from the office, leaving me somewhat breathless.

Hooking a finger under a frayed stitch on the sickly glove, I followed her onto the field. At home plate Clint was tapping bunts to Kay, down the first, then the third base line. Repeatedly the rookie broke off the mound, fielded the ball, rolled it back to the manager and scampered back to her original position.

Eddie approached Clint and swatted his rear with her thick hand. He paused, resting the end of the bat on the plate, leaning a hand on its knob. Gazing at her, his eyes cleared of baseball concentration and he broke into a grin. It was like the sun peeked out. I was startled by the display of affection. Were the swat and the earlier kick mere love taps? He spit a stream of tobacco away from her.

Eddie's voice became throaty. "Come on, Mr. Delicious. Let's get the ladies concentrating on the job at hand."

Later I decided that the sobriquet meant Delicious Apple-ing and lent further credence to the possibility that theirs was a very close relationship.

I trailed Clint and Eddie to the clubhouse door where they paused side by side, two squat forms of about the same height and build, reminding me of an old painting, an idealization of youth: a boy and girl in coveralls, with heart-shaped lips and cherry cheeks, sharing a bat, a ball, and a glove. Here they were, aged into a fortyish fellow with a paunchy middle, and a plain featured woman who was past her prime. I smiled, pretending that the two ached to hold hands but couldn't get game-battered fingers to entwine.

The smile faded when I recalled where I'd seen the picture. It had hung over the sink in the ramshackle farmhouse where I'd been raised. Still, at first the memory had been sweet.

4.

Kay hustled to catch up, and Clint accompanied the three of us into the locker room where Lorinda and Dorinda (known as Lor and Dor) Willey, identical twins who played second base and shortstop, stood half-naked in front of metallic green lockers near the entrance of the oblong gray room. Neither showed discomfort at Clint strolling by, after all, he had averted his eyes. I'd heard athletes had amazing peripheral vision so probably they all kept track of each other just fine. The Willeys' eyes spent their time flicking onto the new girl as one buttoned her uniform shirt while the other, in panties and bra, drew stirrup knee socks over bony ankles.

In their early thirties the twins were flat-chested and sinewy, with straight black hair. Their skin seemed filmed with infield dust even before they took the field. They had joined the team seven seasons ago, the inaugural year of the new league, at the same time as Eddie McLaine and Dinah Timberlake. I wondered if these old timers had special loyalty to each other from being on the roller coaster ride from the beginning.

Extremely popular during the war, attendance at most of the women's games was dwindling now that the conflict was over and real major leaguers like Ted Williams and Bob Feller were back. On days when Betty Jane pitched, attendance was strong. Now that she was gone, I doubted that would continue.

Eddie led me to a row of shelves stocked with supplies. "Winkie," she identified me, "we got to find a uniform that'll fit. I think a size 8 will do if we got one that runty." She delved into a pile of yellow and black, emerging with satin shorts, a wool shirt, a cap, all basically yellow, followed by an undershirt and stirrup socks, black, plus a pair of sanitary socks, white. Outstanding hornet attire. With separate snatches, I took the uniform parts she thrust at me.

"I'd rather you didn't call me 'Winkie'," I said good-naturedly. "The nickname's always been 'Spirit.'"

"High hopes there," she returned. "I'll call you what I want until you show me something. And wear your sport shoes today. Tomorrow we'll get you spikes if yours don't get here. Maybe a grade school team will have a pair they've grown out of."

It was no use challenging this woman. Carrying the attire, I left the office to seek a locker. Eddie stepped out after me and shouted, "Willeys, this is Winkie Wink. She's the new utility infielder."

"—worth," I supplemented.

The twins shot up as if goosed and withdrew behind an end locker where their whispers crackled like static electricity.

"I hope they don't consider me competition," I said. But I had felt the competitive fire, and took a deep breath to restrain my ambition.

"They're worried," Eddie thundered, "that you'll send one of 'em packing, because those ladies are losing their steam."

Well, so much for any special loyalties. Must be sad for the Willeys, having had stature and feeling their skills diminish, to hear another old-timer crowing about the decline.

Sensing Eddie at my heels, I followed the twins around the corner to another bank of lockers, clearly unused, each door uniformly opened a crack. The shower room loomed to the right of this darker area.

"Don't take any of these lockers," Eddie commanded. "They haven't been used since the league was young and flush, and we had twenty players. We're down to fourteen and only need the one side."

As I stuck out the hand of friendship to the Willeys, Eddie withdrew to the brightly lit side.

"Nice to meet ya," I said, smiling with good will. In sync, the pair gave me their backs. Before the rejection, I saw that one had a beauty mark under her left eye. That was number 29, Dor. Lor's skin, although equally gritty, was mole-free. Otherwise the two looked exactly alike.

"Perhaps we can have a game of catch later on," I said. "When you're free."

"Yah?" The rigid back of 29 doubted they'd ever be that emancipated.

Giving up on chumminess, I parked the Hornettes' cap on my head and carried my uniform separates back to the busy side. Three more team members had entered. They were Joanie Dober, the third baseman, and Twyla Ziegler and Pepper McLaine, outfielders. Pepper was Eddie's sister, as pretty as Eddie was plain. All wore frilly sunback dresses and high heels. Twyla wore eyeglasses, horn-rimmed with amber frames.

From behind, Eddie was biffing my shoulder. "See those three? Didn't anybody tell you we don't wear trousers in the Star-Spangled League?"

Oh-oh. In the thrill of employment, I'd forgotten about the league's dress code. "My last sundress got caught up in my motorcycle spokes. I'll purchase a replacement immediately."

"Winkie," she said resignedly. "You'll need more than a fast tongue to stay on this team."

"Winkie," Pepper echoed with a sneer. The chance to ridicule couldn't be passed up; like sister, like sister. And, sure, why not, Pepper had a nice peppy nickname.

I had selected clam diggers, that is, trousers that came just over the knee, and a white T-shirt for my first encounter with this, so far, least congenial of teams. To complete the ensemble, I had on white anklets and the sport shoes.

Joanie slapped at my hand and said, "Howdy. The fans think we're queer if we don't dress all femi-nine." She pulled Twyla toward her and slobbered a kiss on her forehead. In return, Twyla ruffled Joanie's pony-tailed hair.

"Stop that," Eddie instructed and they did.

I reflected on crime boss and league owner Yegg Washington's rules: heels, nylons, dresses, and Helena Rubenstein consulted on makeup tips. I could have used some of those. After the fashion expert guided the All-American Girls Baseball League, the other pro circuit that existed in larger cities, she had brought her charm school over to the Star-Spanglers.

Hornette players were filing into the locker room and milling about in their skirted finery. Eddie, Kay, and the Willeys were the only players already in uniform. I noticed that most of the girls wore their hair combed back in a tight pony-tail. Pepper's fiery red hair was permed and fluffy. My short brown locks held a natural curl.

Eddie hopped onto a long bench. "Get dressed quick," she instructed, "we're here to play baseball, not fool around."

At that, her sister, Pepper, tossed her tresses and her green eyes flashed. She went to her locker, her lips set in a pout. Didn't like big sister ordering people around when she was one of them. With minimal baseball skills, Pepper had probably joined the team through Eddie, and since she was a statuesque good-looker, maybe Clint hadn't objected too strongly.

Muted conversations began and through the murmuring someone pronounced the name of the player who was not there today and never would be again. There followed a collective release of sound so mournful that I was shaken.

"Can't believe it," someone followed up. Other comments included, "Who did it?" and "Who could do such a thing?"

"What do you care?" a harsh voice responded. "You hardly talked to her when she was alive."

Crashes came from the hall and the door burst open. Dinah Timberlake filled the space, hips and torso meeting without a waistline, complexion of lava rock. But her voice was squeaky-high, like a little girl's. "I been all night in jail 'cause one a you stole my crimson paint and killed Betty Jane with it." That wasn't exactly factual, but the accusatory tone was clear enough, especially when she took a bat from a carton and swung it against the wall. Everyone jumped as the weapon shattered, its head making a beeline for a corner. She hurled the jagged handle into the mesh that covered a window near the ceiling where it stuck and swayed high above us.

Clint peeked from his office. "M&M, we have a new ballplayer who couldn't possibly have taken your paint because she wasn't here. Wendy Winkle, step up and greet our first baseman. Wendy's gonna help out in a utility role. Wendy," he urged, "go shake hands with our own M&M girl." M&M: could it possibly mean a hard shell with sweet chocolate inside? Apparently Dinah felt the nickname was flattering because she didn't react with an additional at-bat.

I stuck out a hand from where I was.

Dinah focused on me and squeaked, "No way that shrimp makes up for Betty Jane."

"No, no way," Clint assured. "Our new pitcher's coming in tomorrow."

"Nice to meet you, too, M&M," I said. Queen Kong, like the king but not so furry.

"I'm sicka all youse." Dinah gritted, laying her cheek against a locker.

Eddie sidled toward her. "We're all sicka," she said while tentatively massaging the big monkey's smashing and hurling arm. Soon Dinah's shoulders began to heave and she burst into great wailing sobs.

Most of the other women returned to their business with neutral expressions. Kay Brock gripped my hand and shook it vigorously. "I'm Brock, you seen me in action. I'm a starter. Where ya from? I'm a Ozarks girl."

In an inspired moment, I said, "From Arkansas originally but I lived for a while in Sperry, Montana, where Betty Jane's from."

"Holy cats," Kay said, bug-eyed. "You know her?"

"Many's the time we took the field together. Terrible what happened to her."

"Gol!" She stared like I was a god. I had to keep in mind that this was a simple mountain lass and not get too thick into fabrication designed to impress.

Pepper stepped up. "Come on, kid, Winkie's lying to get in good. That's how new gals always are." She made a goofy face.

Dang. I had considered my fibbing skills second to none.

From beside Dinah, Eddie chided, "Pepper, you're constantly disagreeable." That was from the pot to the kettle, but I was grateful anyhow.

Pepper whispered into her sleeve, "Ugly old beetle."

On the field, Eddie did sort of look like a beetle, bug-eyed through the mask, and oval-bodied with the chest protector on.

Kay reached into an unlabelled locker near me. She lifted a worn leather glove off a hook and stood pondering it as though in a trance.

"Put that back," came a shout. Joanie swooped forward and banged the glove out of Kay's hand. "Bad luck to steal a dead person's stuff."

"Hey, I didn't mean …" Kay stared at the fallen glove.

Eddie sprang to us. "We can't let that locker sit empty. The police have searched and there's no more locker space so we have to empty it out and move on." She looked around to see how such a drastic utterance had been received. Even with some negativity, she didn't retreat. "The new girl's gotta take this locker."

"Hey, no," I said, "not if it was Betty Jane's, I don't gotta."

"There's lockers on the other side," Joanie offered.

"No! Not necessary," Eddie said, her voice breaking. She pulled a hanky from a shorts pocket and blew. "We're clearing Betty Jane's gear outta this locker right now. That player is lost to us. She no longer needs her earthly possessions. Get used to it." She grabbed some glove polisher off the high shelf and shoved it into Kay's pitching hand. "This is yours now." She turned away, fighting off tears.

"We're cursed," Pepper lamented like a gypsy.

Relief pitcher Letta edged her way forward. She spoke into her shirt in an embarrassed manner. "I'm all broke up about losing her. No way am I getting used to it, but gosh darn, she did have nice make-up, I always liked the color." She scooped several tubes of lipstick off the locker shelf.

Reverting to her avaricious self, Kay grabbed Betty Jane's yellow ball cap, grimy finger marks on its bill, and jammed it over her cornstalk hair. She retrieved the glove from the floor. Pounding it, she said, "I'll wear her gear tomorrow, in honor of her and you'll see, it'll bring good luck to me."

"Sacrilege," Twyla warned, but she was out-voted as, like coyotes on a dead moose, the girls moved forward, jostling each other in their eagerness to strip Betty Jane's shelf of brushes, shampoo, make-up, shoelaces, shoeshine kit, Band-Aids. Dinah got over her separate miff and shoved through the group to claim Betty Jane's cleats from the locker floor. "They're kinda small," she averred, "but I can cut the toes off and wear 'em for detasselin'."

When the looting was over, only a wooden crucifix remained on the high shelf. It was old and beat up, as though supplicating hands had caressed it over many years.

Suddenly Clint was among us, lofting high a Phillies Perfecto cigar box with one hand and tenderly patting Eddie's shoulder with the other. "Trouble is, Eddie, you're saying good-bye too quick," he said. "We got to spread out the adioses. I'm putting this leftover cross into this box where it'll serve as a memorial. I'll put it in a place of honor so that any and all can seek comfort from it." He took a shaky breath.

There was a lull before Eddie said, "You have a kind heart, Mr. Delicious, doesn't he, girls?"

The question drew a listless response from the others, but I blurted, "He sure does, Eddie."

Eddie gave me a skeptical look. "Cross didn't do Betty Jane that much good."

"Hey, look at the greenhorn's nose," Pepper yawped, pointing at me. "It's turning brown."

The players carried the spoils to their lockers. I was left with empty storage space. Even though I wasn't a real ballplayer, and thus wasn't subject to a real ballplayer's superstitions, I couldn't help but feel that bad luck was dancing a jig on my shoulder.

"Who took Betty Jane's name off this locker?" I asked Kay.

"I guess somebody thought she didn't need it no more," she said defensively.

And I guess that somebody was Kay. I moved on. "Didn't Betty Jane wear a pendant, a little baseball hanging from a necklace? Did you take that too?"

"I would never steal. Besides she wouldn't leave anything solid gold laying around here." She reached into her pocket to grab a pack of gum. "Dummy," she said under her breath, tearing into two pieces of Wrigley's Spearmint and stuffing them into her mouth.

Now that I had cemented that relationship, and seeing Clint standing in the office doorway, the sacred box under one arm, I approached Eddie to inquire if the manager normally hung around while the team was dressing.

She spun to face him. "The man's sense of propriety must have been wisk-broomed away by murder and grief." Had this most serious of chaperons just made a joke? But she wasn't smiling. I suspected that, preoccupied as she was with caretaking and designating, she hadn't noticed Clint's continued presence until I brought it to her attention. She stalked over, nudged him into the office. Her door slam after him sounded aggravated.

I changed into yellow shorts, banded with lustrous black, and a yellow blouse, black "Hornettes" scripted across the front, big black "82" on the back. A number that large didn't auger well for longevity unless I was a tight end in football. As I beheld my image in one of several full-length wall mirrors, I did look amazingly like a true Hornette, inseparable from the group. I gritted my teeth and gloried at looking as mean as a hornet. I stretched myself as high as I could.

I fisted my very own broken-in glove. This battle-scarred feller has stopped many a grounder, I trusted.

A Willey approached and said faint-voiced, "Time for a little game of catch?"

On the field, the ball came at me sneaky fast. A Willey had thrown at my head from a few yards away. I dove, skidded across dirt, then raced to where the missile had rolled to a stop. Returning, I tossed it to the other Willey. Reflexively, she hurled it at my head. Cringing, I stuck out the ratty glove, but missed. Like any good sport, I gestured thumbs up, raced to the ball and tossed it to the first Willey. As a child on the farm, I had caught plenty of apples fired at me by my brothers, and added to my skills by scooping up softball grounders in public school and college.

When the next zinger came, I stuck the glove in front of my face. The ball popped in with such force that the catch numbed my hand. I couldn't close my fingers around it, so it dropped. The Willeys' grins spread over their dirty faces.

Running after and retrieving that ball in my own special good-natured, sporting and suicidal way, I returned at a dragging pace as Clint approached. "Wendy, you ain't played in a while," he yelled, "gotta get those chops back. Take some laps around the field, slow and steady."

"Gosh, do I have to?" I cried with false regret. I ran up close to him. "Get me outa here before I die. Hustle me up an injury or something."

His eyes were kind with concern. "How's hamstring or a bad back?" he said, low-voiced. "Knees going out are also popular." He shouted, "You getting treatment for those knees?"

"Starting tomorrow," I screeched. From his trouser pocket, he pulled out five sourball candies and handed them over. "Suck on these. You'll feel better."

The rest of practice, I sucked in every way, on the candy and while running laps along the outfield fence, legs pumping to motivate those bad knees, arms windmilling while trying to avoid outfielders racing after fungoes, that is, a ball tossed in the air by a batter and struck with a long, thin, light-weight bat.

Twice I received exasperated looks after nearly plowing into someone, even though I had forewarned with, "Heads up!"

The real players took turns hitting the manager's pitches, as the real pitchers threw long distances and from bullpen mounds. Infielders gobbled up grounders, and, at one time or other, everybody practiced cut-offs and relays.

In the locker room after the exhausting session, Eddie placed a spice bottle of bay leaves in my hand.

"We having soup?" I quipped.

"This week you're in charge of laundry," she said. She pointed to a bin by the entrance. "After tomorrow's game, that box is gonna be filled with dirty uniforms, yours among them, and as the newest rookie, you're gonna take 'em down to the 24-Hour Whistle Clean Laundry on First Street. Give one bay leaf from that bottle to the laundry woman, she knows it goes in with the wash. It's good luck like a four-leaf clover, but we don't have time to hunt any of those up, so a bay leaf's just as good. Pick up the clean clothes at 8 o'clock tomorrow morning, bring 'em to the clubhouse, set 'em by the outside entrance on the north side of the building next to the concession stands. You do this for one week, just the home games of course. After your week is up, we go by the alphabet, I think Dober's next."

"After the game, yes boss."

"Sew your name on your uniform if you want the same one when they come back clean. And wash out your undies yourself. The league doesn't pay for clean undies."

Eddie wheeled away. Kay saw me standing next to the laundry bin and said, "Take the laundry box out the back door. It's shorter. Door's in the spare locker area." She pointed to where the Willeys had withdrawn to discuss my arrival. "That way's a lot shorter than lugging the whole load down the hall."

I thanked her.

She wasn't through. "The back door's always locked from the inside. You can't lock it from the outside. You gotta come back in and lock it and then you walk out the long way to the main door. After you've left the laundry box outside the back door. Then you gotta drive around and pick up the laundry box and—"

"I understand," I interrupted. Is it my lousy play that makes me look like a complete idiot in every subject?

On my way to shower, I checked for the door. It was behind a bench in the unused part of the locker room. This is my first job as a delivery woman, I thought as I took a fast shower.

When I left the building, nobody said good-bye. I was so tired that if I'd gone to the hotel where Yegg Washington had reserved a room in my name, I'd have fallen down on the doorstep. Instead, having developed a defensive limp, I hobbled a short distance from the ballpark to a stately shade tree, its branches spreading over smaller trees. I sank down beneath it, pulled a licorice twist from my handbag and chewed.

Four players strolled by. I waved and they stared as though I was the oddest sight. They meandered a short way onto the manicured lawn and set out luncheon supplies on a redwood picnic table. While eating they chatted, afterward breaking out the knitting needles. Heads bent conspiratorially, they confided while purling. Some smoked; I tried to pick up whiffs. I had quit two years earlier, but still longed for the fumes. I thought about butting into the group on the supposition that they were identifying suspects, but knew they'd clam up and hate me for my rookie interference. How I resented the cliquishness I was being paid to penetrate.

The Willeys had been merciless. They had the snobbery of confidence. Fat chance I'd replace either of them. Perhaps one day I'd have enough evidence to place them both in handcuffs, a delightful thought. Alongside Eddie McLaine. Revenge. I snorted. Dreamer.

On this first day, were there suspects besides Dinah Timberlake? Perhaps. Eddie for one. Her protectiveness of Mr. Delicious

Apple, whom she apparently considered her personal property. His relationship with Betty Jane deserved attention. And Eddie seemed rather hard-hearted about Betty Jane's death, offering up the dead girl's locker and personal effects.

Kay Brock: becoming a starter meant the world to The Kid from the Ozarks. An ambitious father was pushing her awfully hard, according to Eddie. Kay had met with the manager the night of the murder. I'd find out when that soiree had broken up. A nocturnal meeting with a man old enough to be her father implied hanky-panky. They grow up fast in the Ozarks, I knew that. I was from Arkansas where fending for yourself at an early age was a necessity. But could she kill? We shoot almost before we can walk down there. I was shooting and skinning squirrels in my tenth year.

I recalled, in Betty Jane's final game, how she had rebuffed Eddie and then turned to stare in Kay's direction after she'd thrown that wild pitch. That last glimpse of the slain pitcher remained etched in my mind.

Police Chief Shupe trusted Clint. I guessed they were friends from what I'd observed in the trailer. What would have been Clint's motive? Surely he wouldn't destroy his best chance at a pennant. I'd check out his alibi.

I was sitting beneath an elm tree banded "Ulmacae, order Urticales." Stalwart, sturdy, noble; the tree looked like it would last a long time on these grounds, unlike me. A lollipop marker at its base was labeled "Sam Brueck, died 1917." Isolated from the group, with the chatter of picnickers in the background, I spoke to the inscription. "Sam, wherever you are, do you know my dad? We shared some grand adventures, but I never knew how it would end. Does he say he'd like me down there with him?"

5.

I was twelve when I met my dad for the first time. My mom, two brothers and I lived on a hardscrabble farm: one cow, five hens, two apple trees, and a few struggling vegetables, located in the backwoods about eight miles from Lead Hill in northern Arkansas. A rutted dirt road that was pretty much obscured by weeds and thorns, and then a bumpy ride three-quarters of a mile brought you to our dilapidated farmhouse. Mrs. Taylor from the next place over drove in twice, but stopped visiting when she found little in the way of friendship offered by our taciturn mother.

Otherwise, no one visited except for Jed Thurston, who owned the grocery store in town. Each time his Hudson neared, the sound of the motor brought Mom running to the porch, hand gripping the screen door, ready to dash back inside if the visitor proved to be a dangerous critter. Once my brother Norris asked her who she was expecting that caused her to react in such a fashion.

"Your daddy, the rat man," she said accusingly as though Norris had produced Dad instead of the other way around. Such a response stifled further questioning, but made for much speculation among the offspring concerning that monster rodent, our Dad.

When the grocery man's copper-colored Hudson appeared around the last twist of road, Mom's face relaxed and she scurried to help him unload sacks of food that they placed in a line along the berm. Us kids watched, not helping because he didn't care for us, in fact could hardly look our way except to say go play somewhere else. We hated him, our immature minds realizing he was a threat.

One day while Mom was in the kitchen getting lemonade, Thurston cuffed fourteen-year-old Jim twice, for hovering too close. Even then, Jim had a soft, clingy, heart. Norris and I were hard cases; we kept a sullen distance away.

When the grocery bags were ready, Mom said to us, "Take these in and put what needs be in the icebox."

Then she'd climb into the car and off they'd go. A kind of panic set in seeing her head bob smaller and smaller within the Hudson's tiny rear window. Nothing riled me more than Norris's habit of jittering greasy fingers through his hair as he watched that tank-like vehicle carry our mother off. And yet, years later, in the first days of my lonely freshman year at college what I wouldn't have given for someone who mussed his hair in that exact same way.

Mom would be gone with Jed for three or four days, doing what she had to, in return for groceries and gifts. When she returned, it wasn't long before her gay mood was replaced by a mute sadness as though we dragged her down. Anyhow, she always came back to us. That is, until the last time.

After the sound of the Hudson died away, we picked up the sacks and toted them into the house where we attacked the candy immediately, leaving the staples for when we were really hungry. That was when my lust for licorice twists was born.

In Mom's absence the three of us did very well together. We saved squabbling for when she was present. Never fought when abandoned; we needed each other then.

It was a blistering hot summer evening in August when my father first appeared. I'd heard the distant hum of an engine and stepped from the barn. Mom was already on the porch, peering warily, and Jim, clutching her elbow, was shouting repeatedly, "Car coming!"

Norris,16, the master mechanic who kept our sickly truck out of the graveyard, appeared from under its hood and posed with thumbs hooked in pockets. He was in his gangster phase.

The vehicle approached smoothly with no hint of the backfire that was the Hudson's calling card. When at last it rounded the bend, Norris breathed, "Wowser, look at that."

A brand new Ford pickup, its gray coat polished as a mirror. A tarpaulin was stretched over the bed, laced on with rope. The truck rolled to a stop and a small man in faded jeans and a light tan jacket stepped out the driver's side. That was one cool guy, driving that shiny truck.

Mom had a different interpretation. With a shriek, she bumped Jim aside and fled indoors. Jim tumbled after her.

The man strutted around the truck. His hard blue eyes were riveted on the porch and its empty fluster. Fear was in the dust blowing up from the floor.

As he turned to view Norris, I marked the resemblance: both had high cheekbones and full lips. I stepped in front of the newcomer in case he intended to do my brother damage.

"Sweetie," the man said to me. He smelled like spittin' tobacco. He picked me up and extended a hand to Norris. "Remember me? I'm your daddy." He jiggled me a bit, then set me down. I stared, caught short by the liberty he'd taken.

Studying my brother, he let a smile spread.

"Norris my boy," he spoke in a roughened voice.

Norris's eyes glazed over and his hands fell to his sides.

The visitor, our daddy, pumped Norris' hand briskly. "You sure turned into a big fella," he said, even though Norris was small and compact like him.

"Where you been all this time?" Norris said.

Dad's mouth hardly opened. "Making a living for your sakes."

Norris spit off to the side.

"Good to be suspicious. Don't let it rule your life though." Dad moved at a brisk pace toward the house, leaving Norris and me gawking after. He leapt onto the porch and banged twice on the front door. "I know I got a son named James," he shouted. "Jimmy, you in there? Come on out, I need ya, sonny." He must indeed have been the rat-catching man because Jim appeared quickly, squeezing out the door. From the depths of the house, Mom emitted an anguished cry, but refused to show herself.

Norris and I hurried to join the drama. Dad took off his jacket and arranged it with deliberation over his shoulder. I believed he was giving Mom time to confront him directly. But when nothing but suffering silence came through the torn screen, he said, "Boys, I need you to help out tonight. You'll make good money doing it. Agreeable?" Neither brother responded, their eyes as blank as Orphan Annie's. Dad prodded, "Don't you got the guts for some grand adventure? Don't it get awful dreary stuck out here on this dirt-poor property with nothin' to do to advance yourselves in life?" He bent over the splintered porch railing and spat onto the weedy ground. I snickered. Dad had hit exactly upon my opinion of our existence. I just hadn't realized until that moment "dreary" was the exact term for it.

He encouraged, "I pay ten bucks each."

Norris jittered his hair leaving a fringe of black oil. Honestly, the way he dawdled to cover up nerves was almost more than I could bear.

"I'll take your money," he finally said, "but if you need my help, I want twenty bucks."

I blurted, "For ten dollars, I'll steer that truck."

Maybe the fact of kid sister jumping in did it, because Norris didn't push the raise again. Instead, gesturing to Jim, he clomped down the porch steps saying, "Let's go help the man out." Jim followed after casting a backward glance at the house.

Dad stepped to the screen door and shouted, "Mary, I'm claiming my sons but they'll be back by morning." A strangled cry ensued from within.

I grabbed Dad's sleeve as he moved toward the steps. "Hey," I said, "I volunteered first." As he regarded me, Mom screamed piercingly, like she was just inches away, flat up against the living room wall.

"You ain't taking her and leaving me alone here! You get inside the house, Wendy Louise!" The plea was like that of the crazed bird that I heard sometimes in the middle of the night, a terrible hunger that went right through the wood beams and deep into my stomach.

Dad removed my hand from his arm and said, "You mind your mama now."

I dragged myself inside and watched from a window as the pickup swooped a U-turn and drew away.

Next morning in early light, Dad dropped off the boys and sped away fast. Fully dressed (I'd stayed that way all night) I greeted my brothers. Each one waved ten dollars at me and withheld secrets. How I envied them and hated all three of the men, and Mom too, for leaving me out.

I begged Norris to put in a good word for me the next time.

"Leave man's work to men," he growled.

I punched his arm and he shoved me to the ground. I grabbed his ankle and bit until he wrested my jaw away. I kicked him in the shins twice, raced away, hoping to make the security of the hayloft. He hurled an apple, stinging the small of my back. Our mother, in her nightgown, was on the porch, screaming, "If I'm causing you to kill each other, I'll just get out!"

Several times more that August, Dad pulled up in the shiny pickup to claim my brothers, with no protest from Mom. But when he arrived one night in early fall, the boys weren't around. I'd noticed they'd been strangely subdued after the last "grand adventure." I put it down to the paper money becoming humdrum, like working part-time at the grocery and getting bored with stacking cans, which we never got the chance to do, because of how Jed Thurston hated us. And which we didn't need anyhow because we rarely had to buy supplies for school. Norris and Jim stole enough notebooks, No. 2 pencils, and watercolor paint boxes from the school's supply room to last our entire public school careers.

But now, Dad was saying to me, "How about it, honey? You wanta make some greenbacks?"

I was leaping for the truck before the question was finished. In the aftermath of my defection, there was no motherly shriek from within that rickety house. People said she was a bad mother and eventually sought an easier route in life, but on that particular occasion I like to think she was just out back.

The truck smelled of leather and tobacco smoke. My heart was thumping as we pulled onto the highway. He drove for a while, saying nothing. I withheld comment, feeling like any words to come out of my adolescent yap would be stupid and silly. When dusk came he switched on the headlights. The gray pickup rode more smoothly than you'd imagine, considering all the potholes in the road. We passed rocky terrain in hilly country, spindly fruit trees at roadside. Great depressions were gouged in the sides of low mountains, where water collected and cattle drank. After the sun glimmered its last, our headlights stitched a seam through the cloak of night.

With confidential emphasis, Dad filled me in on the plan. I was to help burgle a gun store in an unnamed town. My role was to be the most important part of the job. As he spoke, he studied me for reaction; my face grew stiff to mask fear. The clincher came when he grinned at me and said, "The boys got real scared last time. Do a job bad enough and you don't have to do it again." I took it that my brothers had been fired. I certainly did not want that fate to befall me.

"I ain't scared," I said, my voice trembly, "I ain't worried at all." It made me mad that my voice had betrayed me.

But he didn't seem to notice. "Gunstore's in the basement. You can slip through the window bars easy as grease."

Entering the sleeping town, he shut off the headlights and under a streetlight we coasted down a side street to a stop. We exited the truck into utter stillness. Moonlight cast a silver sheen on a large building, giving it the texture of a grand tomb. He led me to a shadowed, barred window and we crouched beside it. A gentle breeze stirred my hair and chilled my bare arms, although I suppose that was more from fear than anything.

The iron bars were set about six or seven inches apart. Feeling like a part of a team, I held the flashlight while he pried into the window's wooden frame with several digging tools. Finally, straining, he raised the groaning window.

I squiggled through the bars, feet first. Jim couldn't have got through, too big, I was positive. Dad's hold slid from my arms to grip my hands as I stretched full length against the inside wall. When he let go suddenly, the cold, pebbled wall grazed my arms and torso as I tumbled several inches to the floor.

"You okay, kiddo?" he whispered.

I picked myself up off the damp cement. "No problem, Dad," I said from within the ominous darkness.

"Good girl. Look to the right. Rifles are strung out on a rack. Bring over one at a time, hand it up. Go slow and careful. We got all night." Creeping in the intense blackness toward the rack of guns, the ugly feel of grit beneath my feet scared me and I rushed slam-bam into a solid piece of wood, perhaps the store counter. Reeling, I snatched a rifle and ran to the window. It was a comfort to see his small hands reach through the gloom and lift away the gun.

"Good girl," he crooned, and then in a firmer tone, "Cut out the racket though."

"Okay, I know the way now."

"Shh."

After the exchange of the fifth rifle, he said, "That's enough. We gotta go." Whether he heard something, sensed danger, or, as I like to think, was simply not a greedy man, I don't know.

At any rate, it was harder to get me out than in. After I reached my hands to him, he drew me up to where I could get hand and knee holds on the rough wall and help out a little. Sharp stones cut my arms and knees and one cheek got sliced.

Finally I was out and we ran, stooping, to the truck where he slid the last rifle under the tarpaulin. Scrambling into the cab, I felt tremendous relief hearing the thunks of the doors closing, and the engine exploding to a start.

A vehicle charged toward us, siren erupting, headlights snaring the truck in their gleam. The patrol car was screaming and blinking red. It screeched to a stop and a cop sprang out the passenger side and fired a handgun into the air. "Stop! Hands up. Stop!" he yelled.

The attack overwhelmed me and I sank below the window, looking to my father for survival instruction. Grimness was carved in his face and his eyes held an insane fire. Gripping the wheel, he stomped on the foot-feed and we lunged forward, clipping the police car, pitching the cop back against its door. I was thrown to the floorboard as we whipped around and sped away.

To our rear, weaponry popped. When we reached relative darkness and it seemed we had lost them, I scrambled up on the seat.

But on the highway the police were on our tail, bouncing over rises, disappearing down inclines only to bounce up again. A siren wailed closer and closer.

A bridge loomed to meet us, its silver railing briefly lit. We dinged the metal fence with the right rear fender and flew out of control across the road, crashing through a wooden support rail and becoming airborne. Time was suspended as we floated. A crazy sensation replaced my fear, of flying free of every restraint on earth. The sensation didn't last long. Out the side window I saw black water churning up to meet us and realized with great regret that I was about to die before I had done much of anything in life.

The truck hit the water with a jolting smack. I was flung into the dashboard, tossed against the seat back, bounced around. Water curled over us. But Dad had gotten his door open in mid-flight. He yanked me across the seat, out and down into icy suffocating water. We broke through to the surface and swam away from the flashing lights and gesticulating, shouting people on the bridge. My dad kept me close as he knifed through the inky water like the phantom of all water rats. That night he saved my life but my sense of reality was left to sink with the truck.

I can no longer conjure up that marvelous sensation of flying free of every earth-bound slump into which life had sunk me, but I remember the glee of it. A short-lived, crazy thrill to be sure, but one I long to re-create. I think I entered the PI business hoping for more of such life-threatening moments. Maybe I crave them.

6.

The next morning in Burton City, I bought two sundresses and a cheap pair of heels. That afternoon during practice, Manager Clint yelled from yards away, so everyone could hear, including fans who had come out early, "Winkie, I'm gonna sit you down because of that muscle strain in your throwing arm." My first reaction was disappointment that he had so quickly adopted Eddie's nickname.

"Oh phooey," I shouted back. What exactly had I done wrong for him to pull me out of circulation? Wasn't I jogging right either? Or was it because I'd run into that clumsy outfielder yesterday? The Willeys sniggered to each other. Chin up, I strode to the far end of the dugout and plunked down on the bench. Just because you're a fake doesn't mean you don't have feelings.

The sky was cloudless and parched as the rest of the team trotted in to take batting practice. In an hour we were to play the Cedar Rapids Starlets. It would be Kay's first game as a starter. Trotting past me wearing her lucky cap and glove, The Kid boasted, "Watch me how I knock 'em dead." She went to the stands behind first base, where she removed the cap and wiped her brow while speaking animatedly to an older, nutty-brown man in the front row, most likely her pushy daddy. He absorbed her comments with deep concentration, grinning, nodding, pleased as punch. Maybe she was the one in the family supplying the eatin' money.

Eddie poked my shoulder and informed me that I was to be batgirl for the day. "Regular kid didn't show up. Parents probably afraid she'd be murdered on sight. All you have to do is run out and pick up the bat pronto after the hitter tosses it away. Think you can handle that?" She moved away before I could request a Band-Aid to cover the pit she'd gouged in my shoulder.

After the crowd sang "The Star Spangled Banner" to accordion accompaniment, a thrill ran through me because there I was, standing on a playing field as a Burton City Hornette even if it did take an executive decision.

Once the game began, between dashing to the plate to retrieve used lumber, sliding it into the bat rack, and returning to kneel beside the dugout, I talked it up like any good reservist. "Come on, let's go, way to go," I chattered over and over until, after three innings, it got to be really tiresome, so I began sticking in lines from favorite poems: "Way to go, let's go babes, 'now 'neath the silver moon,' let's get a hit, yes, 'how my light is spent,' take it to 'em, babes, show 'em, show 'em, you show 'em." I was yammering at breakneck speed, wanting my teammates to catch the Spirit (my desired nickname) but not the words. That was before the top of the sixth when the Willeys stopped chattering and stillness descended heavily upon the field, leaving my nonsense utterly exposed. I worked hard on a coughing fit to shut me up.

When the team trotted to the bench after that half inning, Eddie loomed before me. "What are you running on about? What does silver moon mean? How about light spent, which you musta said a half-million times? You are a pain in the …"

Eddie had excellent hearing.

"Well," I stalled, "we're playing 'neath the silvery moon, aren't we, and thus the light is spent."

"You a college girl?"

I chose to ignore that proof of extreme ineptitude as one of the Willeys said, "We're shuttin' up out there, not going up against crap we can't be heard over."

Slow-moving Joanie ambled in from third base to contribute her two cents: "Looks like Winkie ain't no good at palaver either."

Eddie reacted sharply. "You don't worry about Winkie. Worry about yourself. Batter up!"

The first hitter, Twyla, headed toward the plate as I dropped into my crouch awaiting the next bat-fling. The inning didn't take long. All three outs came quickly.

That game I learned that the Hornettes were a team lost in sadness and fear, unable to muster any offense, and lamentable in the field. Led by starter Kay, who pitched the entire game—Clint being too dispirited to remove her—we were clobbered, 8-1. The only bright spot came in the sixth when Dinah bashed a home run into the cow pasture, producing a cheer from me that no one complained about. The next inning though, Pepper, her coiffed hair lifting in the breeze, fumbled a fly ball that rolled up her arm and into her sleeve. I longed to join in on the razzing, but knew better. I risk my luck only so far. As a result of that miscue, Clint got thrown out of the game for arguing too vociferously that the ball had stayed on Pepper's arm long enough to be ruled a catch. He looked relieved at the ejection; as the innings passed, his slouching mien said he didn't want to be there anyhow.

After the game, fans shed their tickets in the dirt and a Hornettes banner stuck out of a trashcan. Trudging by myself to the clubhouse, I spotted the local sportswriter, Sid Dobrotka, interviewing Dinah by the entrance. In mousey-squeak tones, she was saying, "One of them stole my crimson and blamed it on me." Swell. What was she thinking? Tomorrow the newspaper would have a story about infighting among the Hornettes. Actually, the next day when nothing appeared, it made Dobrotka a company man.

The reporter was a sharp-featured young man in a checkered shirt, light green trousers, and wingtips, thick with dust. Seeing me, he stopped scribbling and jabbed the pencil my direction. "Hey, new girl. Hold up. I want to talk to you." He moved to intercept, leaving Dinah scowling at her abandonment.

Evading the scribe, I yelled over my shoulder, "Later, thank you," and fled down the clubhouse corridor, not sure what I'd tell such a clever man who, at least in his articles, knew an awfully lot about Burton City sporting life. After I'd cut him off, I realized that the guy might actually be someone worth interviewing.

There was little talk in the locker room. Most of the women stripped and went straight into the other area to shower. The office was dark, Clint nowhere in sight. Probably went home directly after being tossed and was in an easy chair glugging a beer while thumbing through French postcards. Beside her locker, Kay lifted Betty Jane's cap off her straw hair and placed it over her heart. She stepped to my locker (formerly Betty Jane's) and laid the cap on the high shelf, placing the creased glove beside it. "Giving it back," she said. "Fall down seven times, get up eight. My pop told me that when he kissed me goodbye at the depot."

"Yup," I said, not convinced her old man was the best source of wisdom.

"Pop was here tonight," she went on, "but I saw him leave early. Disappointed."

"Oh."

"I couldn't have faced him anyhow."

"Tell him the pay's the same," I quipped.

Eddie climbed onto a long bench and clapped her hands. She waited until the whole burned-out crew was eyeing her with irritation before she spoke. "Girls, we never surrender, we always come back. We played horrible tonight but we'll get the spark back. We do our best when weighted down with adversity."

"Musta had a good week," a Willey muttered.

Towels covering her, Dinah splashed around the corner from the showers. "How about jailbird Pepper?" she said. "She don't do nothing and gets away with it, thanks to the chaperon."

The room fell silent. Eddie jumped off the bench and jerked aggressively toward the big gal. "You watch your words, M&M."

Pepper flapped her lashes and her mouth. "Flippin' wide sleeves, a ball can get trapped in them."

"Yeah, if you're a dodo bird to start out with," Dinah said with a vigorous headshake that caused water to fly off her wet head.

Bobby Beid, a pitcher I hadn't yet spoken to, mumbled from behind a hand, "Rosemarie Hapsburg should be on the team. If it wasn't for Pepper there'd be room."

To forestall my name being added to the list of Rosemarie inhibiters, I asked Dinah where Pepper got that cute nickname.

"None of your business," Eddie snapped. Dinah took a teensy step toward the catcher/chaperon. She said, "Winkie wants to know what asshole thing your sis done to earn that name. Guess we all wonder how Pepper can even be on the team, considerin'."

A flush bloomed on Eddie's neck. "You are the absolute dinah-saur!"

"Oh yeah?" Dinah's fist shot forward and caught Eddie in the mouth. Several girls hollered when the catcher went down grunting as her shoulder brushed the bench.

"Whoo-hah," Dinah piped, waving her arms. Towels fell from her body, revealing that she vied with King Kong for furriest. "That's for insulting me and for bringing a no-talent jailbird onto the team. And for the crimson too if you stole that."

A Willey shot forward and shoved Pepper. Reacting quickly, Pepper was all over her, flailing and scratching until the Willey's knees wobbled and she went down.

Bracing palms against bench, Eddie struggled to her feet. "Everybody cool it," she gasped.

The other Willey rabbit-punched Pepper and Joanie flung herself upon that Willey, both of them collapsing to the floor, writhing to shake loose of each other. Three more girls piled on, cussing and flailing. Observing, I took this to be one of those baseball scrums where everybody gets a punch in and nobody gets hurt. What had set them off? Possibilities: the murder of a star, the suspect another star, resentment over Eddie getting the incompetent Pepper on the team, not to mention a humiliating loss, perhaps the straw that broke the camel's back.

Not wanting to enter the fray, I skirted the warriors and made for the exit. Clad only in my slip, I figured in the late night I could make it to the car where I had a spare key taped inside the front fender and extra trousers and shirts in the trunk.

Unfortunately, a swaying, naked Dinah blocked my path to fresh air. Edging past her, I touched her arm in empathy and said, "Now isn't this the silliest …" She snatched a plug of my hair and spun me to the floor. It happened so fast I had no chance to display any clever moves of which I had a limited supply anyhow, in this crowd. She didn't wave her arms and roar afterward, so it must have been a victory unworthy of the beast. "No winkle gets up close less I say," she muttered.

I crawled for the door. Arriving, I got to my feet, grasped the knob and shook my head to clear the cobwebs. A final glance back showed piles of females littered about the room, squealing as they slapped and mostly hit air.

I opened the door to discover freedom barred by a stranger, a gangly woman in her early twenties. All awkward arms and legs, she stumbled backward to make space for me.

Eddie broke through the skirmishes to snarl at the apparition, "Scoot on outa here, girl. No fans allowed back here."

"I'm Tubbs (or Dobbs)," the stranger said. I didn't quite get the name because of background racket. The unlucky girl retreated further until she encountered the corridor wall.

"What's going on?" she asked in a small voice.

I marked the baseball glove clutched in one hand and a plastic satchel in the other. I turned toward the room. "I think Betty Jane's replacement has arrived."

Eddie's fists were clenched, ready to go another round. "Oh. Oh, yeah," she said. She whirled to address the combatants. "Stop it, you STOP IT! You're giving a bad impression to our newest member!"

Letta flung herself off Pepper who sat thoughtfully massaging a knee. Others quieted and activity slowed.

Eddie pivoted toward the new girl. "Come in, don't dawdle. We're just working off steam after a tough loss. Get used to it. I'm Eddie and I'm in charge. Grab a locker. I'll find you a uniform. Try it on, make sure it fits, report back here tomorrow at 1:00 for practice." Tubbs/Dobbs didn't stir and her expression remained wary.

After Eddie had stalked off to acquire a spare costume, the new girl peered into the room. "Come in, come in. Don't be afraid," I whispered, probably sounding like Igor the hunchback. The newest Hornette stepped in. She was at least six feet tall and looked to weigh about 140.

Eddie had reached the office door when she stopped to proclaim, "There's lots of stealing going on, so slip a padlock on your locker real quick." I stored that information, because Kay had offered something similar.

Shortly Eddie returned with uniform parts. The new girl received them as she tippy-toed along the bank of lockers. In the aftermath of battle, players drifted aimlessly, Twyla being the exception. She greeted the lanky arrival with a cheery, "Hi ya." The poor thing was so grateful she dropped satchel and glove, stuck out both hands and shook one of Twyla's frantically. When she again moved forward, she stumbled over her luggage. Skinny and awkward, this gal had better have an awfully good fastball.

Most of the players had completed changing and were applying lipstick, mascara and eyeliner while gazing into hand mirrors, afterward squeezing into open-toed pumps. Big Dinah donned an out-of-fashion button-front dress with a gigantic bow at the collar. After adding tiny pearl earrings that got lost on her lobes, she clapped on a dated thistle bumper hat.

"There a carnival in town?" Pepper asked very seriously, also very softly, receiving a stern, "Don't start anything," from Eddie. Fortunately Dinah didn't hear the dig, and everyone else ignored it because Pepper seemed a poor bargain to try to shush.

On her way out, Dinah elbowed past Tubbs/Dobbs, observing, "You got too small shoulders for the pros."

The new girl plodded on; in searching for an empty locker she encountered only padlocks. "These lockers are all filled," Eddie finally advised wearily, "so go around to the other side, there's plenty of empty lockers there, take one of them." The new arrival managed to crank her rubbery body into motion and disappear around the corner. How she would brace up enough to uncork a pitch, I had no idea.

Relieved to no longer be the center of attention, I donned a flowery new dress, stepped into heels, combed my hair, fastened my necklace. Before leaving, players were spritzing on perfume from a large bottle by the door. So far I was passing that up. The Perfecto in memorium cigar box was placed next to the perfume bottle. I'd keep that old rugged cross in mind for prayer in case things got even worse.

One by one, players cleared out. It was a mark of the team's alienation that only Joanie and Twyla and the Willey twins left in pairs. With locker room talk decreasing, I heard tiny snivels coming from the other side.

Around the corner, she was seated on a bench, sniffling. I sat down beside her. "Hey, don't cry," I said. "On this team the only way to go is up."

In the late evening, this portion of the locker room lay within a dim echo of light from the other side. From the shower room's archway a faint light also flowed, casting shadows upon our area.

The new girl stared needfully at me. "I thought they'd be glad to see me, but I came fifty miles for this?"

"Where you from?"

"Kahoka. Missouri."

"Don't worry about the less than welcoming reception. We're grieving over Betty Jane's death as well as getting beat real bad tonight. It'll be better tomorrow."

"None of it's my fault."

"I know, I know."

An anxious smile overcame her sniffles.

The other side had become quiet and I assumed the last player had left.

All the locker doors in this area stood open one exact inch. Hold that position, lockers, some bossy someone had dictated, guess who.

"You'll find plenty of spots for your gear on this side," I said. "Can I give you a ride to where you're staying?"

"Naw, my car's in the lot. I'm staying with relatives, but I drove here right off, hoping I'd catch part of the game. Guess I lucked out that it was over." From her satchel she extracted batting gloves, cleats, leather oil, and lastly a beat-up wallet that she flipped open to the windows section. "Here's my sister and her kids and my granddad that I'm staying with." They were gaunt people too. She thumbed further. "And this is my folks and here's my Uncle Fudge …" On she went, pic after pic of dumb shucks. They could have been my relatives, the common forebears: Raggedy Ann and Andy.

Her sense of well-being restored, the newest Hornette stretched and caught my ear with an ungainly arm. How she'd make it to the mound without felling teammates, I didn't know.

She sighed. "I'm gonna sit awhile. I've dreamt of this day for a long time."

"I didn't get your name."

"Millicent Tubbs."

"I'll call you Milly. No one's permitted a three-syllable name in the bigs."

After she gave me a grateful look for being let in on the inside dope, I said, "I'm 'Winks' Winkworth, utility infielder." A gal named "Winks" sounded bigger and faster than a "Winkie," which seemed awfully close to "Dinky." We shook hands. She had a limp grip.

Suddenly the area was plunged into darkness when the lights on the other side went out with a sharp click, leaving only the dim glow from the shower room. Tubbs grabbed me and stiffened more than enough to provide the resistance needed to throw a pitch.

Bearing her weight, I was to my feet when Joanie's merry face peeked around one of the shadowy corners. "Oh, excuse me, young lovers. Have a sexy evening." She blew us a kiss and vanished to the other side. It took a few scampering steps for her to snap the light back on and then the hall door banged, swallowing her hooting laughter.

Millicent and I released each other.

"Our teammates are sensitive to implication," I said.

Millicent brightened. "What's her name? She's real cute." She started to follow Joanie out.

"Hold on," I cautioned, "she's already got a best friend."

"Oh, too bad." She did an about face and sized me up. "How about you? Wanna wrestle?"

Making tracks to the other side, I said, "As second choice? No thanks, I have my pride. I have to be considered the fairest of them all."

At the locker room exit I saw the laundry bin, overflowing with dirty uniforms, the bay leaf jar lying on top. Oh, this is too much. After such a grand exit line, I hated going back into Millicent's area to take the container out the back way, but I did because it was shorter and I was tired. When I re-entered the unused area, Tubbs was holding her uniform parts and approaching the bank of empty lockers.

"I'm going out this door," I said very business-like. "You lock it after I leave, you got that?"

"Yuh, sure," she said.

The lock was a deadbolt. I unlocked the turn piece, opened the door and exited into a refreshing breeze.

Bin in my arms, I backed up and shoved the door closed with my butt. That was when it occurred to me that, as the newest rookie, Millicent should have the honor of hauling the dirty clothes to the laundry. I thought seriously of going back in and delivering an order that she'd surely obey without question. But she'd already looked so done in that I thought any more instructions, like how to get to the laundry place and what to do with the bay leaf, might put her right back on the road to Kahoka.

So I set down the bin and trotted off to retrieve my car. After driving it along the narrow back way with access to the loading zone, I hoisted the bin onto the front seat. Minutes later, I arrived at the cleaners. A spry older lady accepted everything without comment, including the laying on of bay leaf.

Courtesy of Yegg Washington, I was staying in a spacious, well-appointed room at the Hotel Burton City. Each Monday the big boss was to deposit a check in the bank account that I had hastily opened.

In early morning, I awoke to the phone's jangle. Police Chief Duane Shupe's voice boomed through the receiver. "Get to the ballpark quick. There's been another death. In the locker room."

"What? Who?"

"A ballplayer. Funny thing is, nobody knows exactly who."

"She got beat up so bad nobody could recognize her?"

"Not the case. Get here fast." The way the receiver clattered, he had dropped it from a great height.

Two police cars were parked outside the clubhouse under gray morning light. At 6:12 a.m., I entered the locker room. By a bench on the far side of the locker room, Eddie pointed at me and accused, "That's the one I told you about. She was with her last."

She was addressing a quartet of cops, including Chief Shupe, who stood near the shower arch. To his left, Manager Clint averted his gaze from the long naked body that lay on its right side just inside the shower room, head resting on the raised sill of the archway, mouth open. The one eye visible was open and staring.

"Her name is Millicent Tubbs," I said quietly.

A cop scribbled, hesitated and said, "One 'l'?'"

"Two," Shupe said. "Apparently Millicent slipped and cracked her head."

He lifted the corpse's bony head and turned it slightly for me to see. "You ever see that many brains before, not on the dinner table?"

Blood and a bit of gray matter had flowed onto the cement sill. I noted a gash to Tubbs' left temple, some blood and grayish matter clotting in the skimpy brown hair. The chief gestured at tile flooring where a pink bar of Lava soap lay. "Slipped, fell, hit her head. Janitor found her about 5:30 this morning. Shower nearest the door was still running."

"Why would she shower?" I said. "She hadn't played in a game and was going directly to her relatives in town."

Eddie was looking at me oddly. Why would the chief show me the wound? Why would I ask an intelligent question? The conundrum caused her speech to slow. "I suppose because she wanted to hit the sack without bothering relatives. I mean, it was very late."

"Check," I said. "Stupid question. I'll just shut up."

"Back door was unlocked," Shupe said. "We got some smudged fingerprints off the inside knob, nothing useable on the outside."

Well, yeah, butts don't leave prints.

I stared at the door. "The prints might be mine. I left by that way. I told Millicent to lock up after me. Maybe she didn't do it fast enough and someone got in or maybe someone knocked later and she let them in."

"God, you're a help," Shupe said. "Why didn't you lock the door behind you? With a murder a couple nights ago, anybody would think to keep the doors locked."

"Door locks from inside. I told Millicent to be sure and lock it after I went out."

"Goddam, never trust civilians. Report to the station tomorrow to have your prints taken." He clapped his hands. "Clint, you and Miss McLaine can go. This player stays behind for questioning."

Clint blinked to show he was conscious but out of it. Eddie led him out by the hand. In retreating, she studied me.

After they left, Shupe and I moved to the bench where Tubbs' dress and underwear lay neatly folded. The other flatfeet remained by the showers, ogling the body.

"When's the coroner coming?" I said, hard-voiced. "After he's done, you can cover the body."

"Squeamish, huh?" Shupe heckled.

"Not hardly." Suddenly I was in a dither, hating cops. Recently so many folks had suggested I wasn't up to the task at hand, no matter the task. I'd held in my resentment long enough. "Chief, are you in charge of your ghoulish pals over there, or are they rooting around in the graveyard all on their own?" Getting some sense, I spoke more reasonably, "What clues are those coppers gathering from ogling the body?"

Shupe slid away from me on the bench and chose not to reply. The coppers shifted their attention to me.

I took a deep breath to regain my sense of self - stable, sure. No longer was I the cowering kid who'd see her brother beaten nearly unconscious by a jailhouse guard, and let's not even think on my dad's fate.

I glanced around the area. Tubbs' uniform parts lay scattered on the floor. All of the locker doors remained equally ajar except one. It was closed. "That's different," I said. I slipped on rubber gloves taken from my handbag. Crossing to that locker, I opened it. In a back corner lay several jagged scraps of material, none bigger than an eighth of an inch. Cardboard, plastic, or leather, it was dim back there and I couldn't tell.

"Bag the stuff that's in this locker," I ordered one of the cops. "Wear gloves while you're doing it."

The pouty fellow inquired of Shupe, "Me?" I could guess his problem. What was this little peanut doing, issuing orders to officers with badges?

Shupe was beside me. I stepped aside to allow him a look inside the locker. "Do it," he instructed the cop. "She's a ballplayer. So far she knows the team better'n we do."

"All these lockers were standing open when I left here last night," I said. "Were they searched after Betty Jane's murder?"

Shupe glared at the offending locker. "At that time, none of them showed any sign of use. This is probably no more than Millicent picking out a locker, then closing it without thinking before she stuck her equipment inside."

"After placing crumbs in it?"

Shupe examined the leather flakes that the cop held forward. "That stuff looks years old," he said, "left there from some past sporting event." The young cop seemed ready to brush his hands of inconsequential debris until Shupe added, "Bag it." He leveled his black button eyes on me. "Mr. Washington sends a pitching replacement, right away she dies, but there's no indication of foul play, except an outside door was left unlocked, damn it. Did Millicent seem upset or frightened about anything when you talked to her?"

"She was unnerved by the antics of this crazy team, so I don't think she'd have opened that door to a stranger's knock. If she locked it in the first place. I suppose it could have been an accident. She could have slipped in the shower. She was awkward as heck. But if she finished showering and was on her way out, why hadn't she shut off the water?"

"She's yards long. Slipped while washing off, skidded trying to stay up and fell full length to the doorway. Looks like hitting her head on the stoop was what killed her."

It didn't look like a mere slip and skid to me. Even from Tubbs' considerable height, she could hardly have struck with enough force to eject brain matter.

But right then there was no use sharing expertise with Shupe when I was stupid enough to leave a door unlocked, so I moved on to inform the chief of after-game events, including Dinah calling Pepper a jailbird. I left out Tubbs' come-on, because cops don't appreciate that kind of lifestyle.

I crossed to the cop pack and they gave way, allowing me to detour around the body into the shower room, which consisted of seven showerheads evenly spaced along the wall. I spent some time scrutinizing the area for blood, in case she'd been killed elsewhere and dragged to the entry. No blood evidence. Of course, a running shower could have washed it down the drain.

I returned to the bench where Shupe had seated himself. Digging into Tubbs' satchel, I brought up and flipped open her wallet to the photo windows. A basically toothless Ma Raggedy grinned out, oblivious to tragedy. I passed Tubbs' driver's license to Shupe.

Continuing to inspect the room, I spotted a few more scraps of leather, and what looked like a small oval photo partially stuck under a bench leg. Squatting, I raised the bench enough to slide out the portrait. It was about an inch high and three-quarters of an inch wide. The headshot was of a pale, smirking young man in a dark suit coat, a stiff white collar poking out. The haircut and style of the coat were from an earlier age. The fellow looked to be a city boy, not one of the Raggedy clan. Quickly to my side, the gloved cop retrieved the photo and placed it beside the wallet on the bench. His eyes sought Shupe's for approval.

"Millicent Tubbs showed me lots of photos," I said. "This wasn't one of them."

"Locker room's had many lives," Shupe opined. "We'll never identify this guy. Probably been lying on the floor for years."

"How often does the janitor clean this side?"

"Clint says this side hasn't been used in two years, but that the janitor mops it about every two weeks, give or take, Clint didn't really know."

"Might mean the photo was dropped recently. Does the janitor have a criminal record?"

"You're fishing." Shupe sighed and his jaw loosened. "We're checking him out. Name's Darrell Moeller. He's at the station waiting for me. Shaken up about finding the body." He spoke to the kowtowing cop. "Put the photo in the evidence bag with the leather scraps. We'll see if Tubbs' folks recognize an ancestor. Add Millicent's clothes and her belongings too. And bag the leather bits that are on the floor. Scoop everything up that's in here. It's all evidence." He was proud to be the professional saying that.

7.

I returned to the hotel and tried to nap, but was so on edge with thrill, plus fear I'd fail at this, my first sleuthing attempt, that the God of Dreams didn't dare approach. What had I got myself into? A crime boss, maybe a veritable godfather, was paying me good, laundered crime money to solve a murder, now possibly two murders. Oh, you sap, resigning is impossible, so best gird your loins and go get 'em. Or him. Or her. My eyes remained wide open, staring at the ceiling.

I recalled that, as a kid, I decided I could tell, after the fact, which of my classmates was doomed to die young. The skin's sheen, the angelic paleness, bones about to push through, a faraway look in their eyes: the death look, come from glimpsing the other side. Perry had it in high school and, at twenty-one, fell off a Navy ship at sea. And Shirley, dwindling away in class week after week before she was removed. Of course, as an adult, I don't believe such nonsense, although in thinking back, I had witnessed the signs on Millicent Tubbs.

At 10:00 a.m., I picked up four wrapped packages of clean, pressed uniforms and delivered them to the specified clubhouse door.

At the police station, I waited until my fingerprints were compared to the ones on the doorknob and found to match. Shupe fumed as though Tubbs' death was my fault. Under the circumstances, I almost agreed. I should have assigned her the laundry basket.

The chief spoke to me in restrained tones. "Who do you think you are? I'll tell you who. This is just a tomboy phase you're going through. After you brilliantly solve this crime, you can retire while you're on top and concentrate on your brilliant baseball career."

"Really," I said, my eyes stinging with the sarcasm. "The 'tomboy PI.' I've been called worse." I couldn't keep up the ice-queen act and my temper got the best of me. "You can go to hell."

That evening's game had been cancelled, but practice, "gathering time" in Eddie's words, was still on.

Entering the locker room forty-five minutes late, I found a distraught team, and not strictly because of Millicent's death. The police had returned in early morning and demanded everyone open her locker. After the search, personal belongings had been left strewn on benches. Players wanted be reassured by Clint but, "he's in such a bad mood," Joanie said, "We're afraid to tell him how scared we are."

"I'll talk to him on behalf of the team," I said. "The police questioned me last night because I was the last person they know about who talked to Millicent." I glanced toward Clint's office. The shade was down, indicating he was in. The shade being drawn in front of the frosted glass added to manager's propriety, but who did it fool? That crack in the glass afforded a peephole should anyone be interested enough to raise the shade.

Eddie was seated by the office door, pulling baseballs out of a pail, rubbing them down with mud. "Surely the girls aren't suspected of anything," she said when I approached. "Male paws rummaging through everything. I can't believe this is happening."

"It's disturbing all right," I said, "but with nothing to hide, we have nothing to fear. I had a cousin who suffered a mysterious death on her property. Detectives were suspicious. They searched everywhere, including the rabbit hutch and the puma compound. No dice. Just routine, they said afterward." I was pretty good at creating commentary that made me fascinating. "Big cats, too," I said, shaking my head in awe.

"You don't help matters one bit," Eddie said darkly, "and the manager kicked me out, so don't even look like you're going in there."

I nodded agreeably. "I'll just check and see if my glove is here yet. It's important to team effort that I use my own glove." By the time I'd finished I was in the office, closing the door before the Grand Poobah could effect a counter-action.

After nodding at Clint, who sat slouched in his favorite folding chair munching on a hot dog, probably a cold one, I played tug and release with the shade until it shot up exposing the clouded glass. Paper had been wadded into the jagged crack. I poked it out the other side. "Seen much lately?" I said, pointing at the hole.

"That plug there again?" The manager's face had a lost-soul look. "Somebody needs a joke. They gotta keep loose out there. Long time ago I applied to Mr. Washington to have that glass replaced but nothing's been done so far." He shrugged helplessly.

"Strange, considering the interest he's taking in more recent doings. You see anything through this hole after the game last night?"

"Whaddaya mean? After I was given the boot, I went home."

I peered through the small opening. I wondered if Eddie had arranged for her locker to be directly in front of the crack or if the opening had been carved after her installation.

In the locker room, girls were changing clothes to either side of the catcher, but Eddie was the central attraction. I watched as she sensuously stripped, then struck a seductive pose. Did she think Clint was watching, or, knowing I was with him, was the peep show for me, to warn me off the manager? Had she seen my silhouette through the glass?

Yanking the shade down, I brushed my hands of window grit. "Well," I said, voice full of implication.

"You got a dirty mind." Clint drew a pious breath. Standing, he straightened and the paunch disappeared for the moment. Too soon he exhaled and flaccidity returned. He went to the desk, unscrewed the cap of a liniment tube, and lifting his shirt, exposed a jungle of curly hairs. What now? First a girl show, then a boy show?

"Get your kicks where you find 'em, Winkie with the suspicious mind," he said. He dabbed a yellow blob on his chest. Energetic scratching became a one-finger massage of whatever liniment hadn't splatted to the floor.

"Thanks for doing that," I said, "because it makes me want to ask how often the janitor cleans in here. Oh, scratch that, in favor of telling me why M&M calls Pepper a jailbird."

Recent events, along with my barging in had worn our leader down. "Because she did eight months in a women's reformatory out west. Before she became a Hornette."

"Why didn't you tell me that before? For what? A violent crime?"

"Well, it's no secret. Everybody knows. Pepper was just helping out her man. Trouble is, he robbed stores and she assisted. They got caught. When Eddie brought Pepper here, we both laid down the law to her and she understands she's got this one chance, and she should cool it."

"Were guns involved in the store robberies?"

"The boyfriend carried a rifle. Yeah, she had one along, but it wasn't loaded."

"Stupid. Why carry if you're not willing to shoot."

He looked uncertain.

"Does she keep in touch with the guy?"

"Nah, he's in the slammer out west while she's here in Iowa."

"Well, there are the mails."

"She swore she's through with him."

"What about Yegg Washington's pure-as-a-virgin baseball league? Are convicted felons allowed on these teams?"

He waved a cautionary finger. "No, and don't you tell. Eddie wanted her sister on the team where she could watch out for her and I went along with it. I'd do anything for my sidekick but date her, because she's supported me like no one else. Her and Pepper live together in town and room together on the road."

I was not deterred by Eddie's good works on behalf of blood kin. "M&M knows about Pepper's record, so I assume the whole team knows."

"Yeah, way before yesterday. About a month ago, before the second game of the Waterloo series, I was coming down the hall when I heard all hell breaking loose inside the locker room. Okay, Eddie handles the spats, but she was still out in the parking lot, so I went in by myself. Pepper was yelling bloody murder and slapping whoever was nearest and pointing to a mirror where 'Pepper's a jailbird' was written in red lipstick, crazy writing that ran down the mirror and onto the wall." Clint took an audible breath. "A minute later Eddie walks in and when she saw it, she was ready to …"

In the pause, I supplied the word. "Kill? Eddie does get a mite testy when her little sister is concerned. Could Betty Jane have written the accusation?"

"What? Come on. Why would she? They were best friends, knew each other off and on for years. Pepper even went to bat for Betty Jane making the team."

"Did Eddie know Betty Jane before she came on the team?"

"Nah, Pepper and Betty Jane met after Pepper was grown up and out on her own. Look, I didn't want this job in the first place, but I was in a shit can of debt and needed it. I'm doing my level best now that I'm here. And I'm proud to say that whoever wrote that crap on the mirror, it never went outside the locker room. Not after Eddie warned that whoever told would be out of a job. Not even Sid Dobrotka knows, which, with his nosing around is a credit to our team's spriggy core."

"And to Eddie's threat," I added. "Spriggy core" stopped me, but I got the drift. It meant something like "spiky loyalty to the very core." Later I decide the phrase was a rough rendering of "esprit de corps."

And Sid Dobrotka might have found out about Pepper's record, but chose not to print because he too was infected with spriggy core; it sounded like something that might be contagious. I recalled a passing thought: that Dobrotka, the company man, might be worth interviewing.

Clint went to the refrigerator, flipped open a beer and lifted it to his lips.

I pressed. "Who has it in for Pepper?"

The manager came to me and dropped three sourballs into my hand, after which he glugged for a while. Emerging wet-lipped, dimple glistening, he said, "Nobody. Well, some of the girls don't much care for her."

"Who's that?"

"Easier saying who she runs with, Joanie and Twyla, that's about it, except for Eddie and that's not by choice."

I stored the intelligence in favor of a new subject. "Eddie said there was trouble with theft on the team."

Clint's voice rose in aggravation. "Oh, for craw's sake, just some gals admiring each others' stuff, and presto, someone borrows some little thing, lipstick or two-bit jewelry, or a plastic comb, and forgets about returning it. One time Betty Jane made a big deal out of her drinking glass being gone. She could raise a ruckus about any little thing because she was the star. Most of the other girls just shrugged off losing a cheap pin or whatever and started keeping their stuff padlocked up. What the heck, Eddie and me let it go too. Not worth the trouble."

But it was to Eddie; she'd warned Millicent Tubbs to secure her locker.

"I don't have no idea why Mr. Washington hired you when Betty Jane's awful passing has nothing to do with our team," he went on. "He's never interfered with league policy before." "I bet Mr. Washington realizes the police can handle some aspects of the crime, but can't delve into the inner workings of a women's ball club as well as an insider can. And that's me, hired to do the job. You'd like the killer apprehended, wouldn't you? Even if it's a team member?"

"Which it's not." His eyes pled that supposition.

I'd given Yegg Washington's active involvement in the case a lot of thought. I never expected to meet the great man. Indeed, I wondered if there really was a larger-than-life individual named Yegg Washington who, the story went, operated his businesses from a large-roomed mansion in a hoity-toity part of Milwaukee. Rumor had it that this mythical figure was a major racketeer who operated gambling syndicates and dealt in extortion. A sinister creature, who for some reason chose to fund a women's baseball league. Did it mean he had a spark of decency in him? I wasn't likely to solve that question.

Clint interrupted my musings. "You'll see. The police will find out Betty Jane's death had nothing to do with us, that she was killed by a - I don't know - a bum traveling through who came upon her by the river, alone, in the dark, and wanted her gold necklace or to take her by force."

"No evidence of rape, and now we have the likelihood that another pitcher has been murdered."

Not wanting to discuss that dread possibility, Clint moved to the door where he paused to regard me, not with the affection reserved for real ballplayers. "Listen," he said, "at night I cry for Betty Jane and for that other girl I never met who died accidental, but come daylight I coach baseball and nothing's getting in the way of that, not you or anybody else. And," his voice steadied, "today you have to work out with the team because Eddie's real leery of you. And don't let her catch you out at nothing, because there'll be trouble and you'll find out she's the smartest cookie you ever had the bad luck to meet up with."

8.

I hurried through the vacated locker room, down the hallway and onto the field. On baseball time, I trotted everywhere as though Eddie's breath were hot in my ear.

A few of the players stood outside the home dugout. Others were huddled in small groups in the outfield, talking amongst themselves. I didn't spot Eddie. Practice was going forward despite Millicent Tubbs' demise. After all, no one had known the dead girl, thus she had made no contribution, even though she'd definitely made an impression.

"I'm afraid to go out on the field," Twyla said as I walked up. She pushed her glasses up her nose. "Somebody might shoot me from the stands."

"We're in peril," girlfriend Joanie agreed.

Lor Willey seconded the opinion. "Nobody wants any part of baseball today. I want to be in bed with a sheet covering over me."

"Dead already," Joanie cracked.

Lor feigned punching Joanie. "Look for yourselves," she said. "Nobody's doing nothing today." Standing as still as statues, the players on the field presented easy targets. Running sprints, dodging, would have been better. With that in mind, I shifted my feet, bobbed my head, and then settled down, not wanting to betray the tough-guy image that, as yet, only I recognized.

"New girl joins us, sees M&M acting like a maniac," Letta said. She's so upset she trips and falls, bonks her head against concrete and expires forthwith." Letta had a New York accent. She dropped final 'r's' and punched out certain consonants.

"It was an accident," Pepper said, sounding unsure.

"World record for in and out," Joanie cracked.

"Team's jinxed," Pepper said.

"Why do you think?" I inserted.

"God's revenge for letting you on the team," Pepper answered.

Kay hustled in from the outfield. "Anybody see my bat? I can't find it nowhere." The silence that followed lasted longer than necessary.

Finally Joanie said, "A bat could have conked Tubbs in the head."

"Criminy, it was an accident!" Dor exclaimed. "Although with our luck, who knows?"

"Where'd you leave the bat?" I asked Kay. I tugged at her arm. "Come on, let's retrace your steps."

Accompanying me, she wailed, "I looked all over."

I walked her toward the outfield, as much to get the anxious girl away from the doomsayers as anything.

Well down the foul line in left field, Kay spotted the bat lying among weeds. Trampling down foliage to retrieve it, she called back, "Oh, yeah. I slung it here after I lost yesterday," like the concern was all in my mind. Nonetheless, she was relieved far beyond finding a favorite slab of ash. For a moment she stood caressing the bat tenderly before we moved to rejoin the group by the dugout. Once there, she took short practice swings and cuddled it like other kids did their dolls or teddy bears.

At the sight of the bat, Pepper exclaimed, "There, see, nothing to be scared about."

The players teased each other with comments like, "You were white with fear."

"You were whiter."

During the razzing, I drew Pepper aside and spoke in low tones. "Betty Jane's death must have hit you real hard. I hear you were best friends for years, that you practically got her on the Hornettes."

She popped her bubble gum and made a goofy face. "I got her a tryout is all. Her daddy wanted it, begged me to put in a good word for her. The least I could do."

"Betty Jane must have been grateful."

"Never said. Got better'n me and made more useful friends, like Sid, the writer. He always gave her a big play in the papers. I didn't care. I'm used to being on my own."

Odd. Of all the girls, Pepper seemed the least independent, being pretty much controlled by her sister, the heavy-handed chaperon.

I saw movement within the shadowy dugout before Dinah Timberlake's bulk emerged. "Is that li'l ol' Winnie Winkle?" she spouted.

Then, addressing me properly, "Wendy Winkworth," the big girl hurled herself onto the field. Something about not being identified as a cartoon character, or a stunted person, put me on notice. The fact that she was grinning broadly to show how much she adored me was downright scary. "You're invited over to my house Monday night to see my art. I only invite people I like," she guaranteed. "A course, my latest paintings don't have no crimson in 'em thanks to some bitch of a witch." The happy face vanished and in its place came a scowl directed at the other players. Stiffening, they studied the ads on the weathered left field fence trying to decide between Ipana and Pepsodent for their teeth. "Don't forget, eight o'clock Monday night," my prospective hostess continued before breaking into singsong with, "I'll be expecting you." The ear-to-ear smile was back, saying I could do no wrong.

I saw Kay mouthing, "No, no," not really necessary, considering a previous encounter with M&M had left me writhing on locker room cement. Besides, Monday was only three days away. Not enough time for me to catch up on all the things I wanted to accomplish before I left this life.

"Thanks, M&M," I said, "but I'll have to check my social calendar. Kinda hard on the rookies, aren't you? Put a gun to Betty Jane's head? Why? She prefer Rembrandt over the moderns?"

Dinah issued a squeal of protest. "Gun was a kid's toy I bought at the dime store. She took it the wrong way. What a touchy broad."

"It's over with," Dor declared, "and none of Winkie's business anyhow."

"Don't know about that," Letta demurred. "We don't want this girl going nuts when her funning time comes. Like Betty Jane did."

I forced a chuckle. "Funning. What's that?"

Kay spoke up. "Initiation rites. Every rookie goes through it. They got a whole bag of tricks to level at you." She picked at a speck of dust on her bat.

"Betty Jane failed her funning?" I asked.

"Looka here," Dinah said, smacking the step a good one. "I'm invitin' Winkie over to my house. You all will be there too. It'll make us a team again, bring us outta the doldrums and on back to our spriggy core." I marked the gravitas in the declaration. My assassination was to be a seminal moment for the team, like the Gettysburg address had been for the North.

No one appeared puzzled by the term "spriggy core." Must be common usage among this gang of merry-makers.

Letta was evaluating me. Was I a one-for-all teammate? "Winkie's heard something about that particular funning from an outsider," she said. "If we're filling her in on what actually happened, let's do it in the dugout where we're safer."

"Count me out," Twyla said firmly. "I'm not reliving that funning. It wasn't fun."

"Don't leave," Joanie urged, going to her pal and slipping an arm around her. "We have to hear what they say. It'd be just like them to blame it on us."

"I'll stay and I won't let them," Pepper said stoutly.

"What's all this mistrust about?" I asked.

"It's about them being dykes," Pepper said, "and some of present company not liking it one dang bit."

"Who do you mean?" I played the dummy.

"None of your business," Dor said. Second time she'd made that clear.

"Why? After all, I am a teammate."

Twyla slipped from Joanie's gentle hold. "I'm not staying," she announced. "What we did to Betty Jane still makes me sick." She walked slowly toward the clubhouse, perhaps expecting her partner to follow, but after taking a tentative step, Joanie followed the rest of us into the gloom of the dugout. I chose the bench while Dinah posed nearby, arms crossed like Bunyan the woodsman. The Willeys stood, listing toward each other, while Joanie, Kay, Letta and Pepper sat on the steps.

Dor waited until we had settled before saying in her flat-as-the-prairie voice, "We gave Betty Jane a trial and found her guilty, that's it."

"Not that any rookie is ever found innocent," Kay observed.

"Guilty of what?" I said.

"Being snotty," Lor said. After pausing to assemble other crimes, she added, "and really selfish."

"She was the hub in our wheel," Kay asserted. "Now the spokes don't turn no more."

"I turn the spokes," Dinah said.

"Sure, since now," Kay amended hastily. "But I mean before, when both of you were …"

"I carry the team on my back. Always did. End of subject." Dinah was pouting.

"What happened during the funning," I asked, "to make you turn on each other like this?" I gave "funning" the same religious intonation as the others did. Sort of like saying "baptismal event." But when only baleful silence ensued, I added, "Maybe it'd take the sting off to sit down and discuss it among friends."

"Like hell, among friends," Dinah sneered. "All you framing me."

Dor pursed her lips and frowned deeply. Her eyes became slits in an all out effort to bunch up those brain cells, get them sparking against each other.

Letta didn't wait. After clearing her throat, she stood up and became a storyteller. "We told Betty Jane it was going to be a hike. We started out when it was almost dark. We sang the team song, which you should learn the words of, Winkie."

I nodded. I had heard the team song. "All for one," was prominent in the lyric, you might say it dominated; you might say that's all there was, except for "One for all." The tune also was not deep.

When no one objected to Letta's narration, she resumed, "We hiked to the cemetery and brought Betty Jane in the back way where tombstones are broken up and sticking out of high weeds every which way. It was pretty dark by the time we got there. The moon was full and it lit up those gray stones. I thought Betty Jane was only pretending to be scared, like the rest of us."

"She was fluttering her hands out," Kay affirmed," and saying, 'Oooh,' over and over like we all was."

"You was the nervous one, Kid," Dor said, "tripping over that slanty old stone practically got you running for home."

Everyone guffawed as Kay reddened. "It was buried in the brambles. None of you would a seen it either."

"Matter of fact," Letta said, "I think it was Betty Jane who helped you up. Right after that the wind blew up and slammed my hair over my eyes so I couldn't see a darn thing."

"Whoo, that's God's truth," Lor said, and laid her head against Dor's chest. Sis drew her closer.

"What happened next?" I asked.

"We came upon a metal bench," Letta continued. "The seat was covered with lichen and had rusty stains on it like dripped blood. It was perfect. M&M signaled for us to stop." I glanced at Dinah. She had a most obstinate expression like she was going to bear up under this tortuous tale no matter what lies were told.

Letta went on. "M&M stated like a judge does, 'Betty Jane, we have brought you here today for you to face the court of public opinion.' She pulled out a rolled up paper like always and as soon as she started unwinding it and reading off the charges, Betty Jane started yelling about how we couldn't treat her like that, and she broke for freedom. Some of us jumped on her and pulled her down. Betty Jane wasn't thick with muscle but it took three, four of us to hold onto her. She was very strong. She was kicking and cussing until M&M biffed her a good one in the head and told her to take it like a good sport. Betty Jane kind of sagged. M&M commanded her to arise and go thereforth to the bloody bench and sit herself down in the defendant's chair."

Letta's tone darkened. "All rookies go through this. Betty Jane thought she was too good for it, but she was wrong. It's tradition."

"You'll get the same, Winkie," Lor inserted. "We'll do it different next time."

No need to plan for that. I'd be out of here by then, I fervently hoped.

"We took a vote like we always do," Letta said.

"Voting went real quick," Kay said. "Then we chanted, 'Guilty as charged,' like they did to me earlier this summer."

"Let's wrap this up quick." Lor spoke urgently. "I want to go hit a few. Eddie's on the field now, she'll be all over us in a minute. Besides it's ungodly hot in here."

"Dinah pulled the gun from her bag of tricks and pressed it to Betty Jane's head." Letta spoke dramatically. "She said, very regally, 'You, Betty Jane Wadlow, are going to die right here and now unless you drop your stuck-up attitude and act like a teammate should.'"

Dinah broke her silence to speak with deep grievance. "Yeah, blame it on me."

"We all went along," Kay modified.

Letta shook her head. "We expected Betty Jane to laugh and say something like, 'You silly girls, is that all there is to this?' and therewith apologize for being such a smarty pants."

Kay broke in. "Instead Betty Jane's head started shaking and her eyes teared up." The Kid's eyes misted. Sitting with elbows on knees, she leaned forward and laid her head in her hands.

"Aw, you couldn't see nothing shaking, it was too dark," Dor sneered. "Probably your knees were still shaking from falling over that stone."

Maintaining a portentous tone, Letta continued. "Betty Jane stayed that way for the longest time …"

"Yeah, maybe two seconds," Lor broke in.

"I don't care," Letta said. "It seemed like forever. It wasn't turning out like it was supposed to. She didn't relax or repent of anything like she was supposed to."

"Why didn't you say, 'enough, let's go home?'" I asked.

"Face it," Lor said, "it was a kick to see her taken down a peg or two. I mean, she won games, sure, but she never hung around after, never kidded around or celebrated with us. She was always out the door fast, hardly spoke to no one."

"Kept to herself, never was one for all," Dor augmented. "It was fun this one time to see her really scared."

"She was the icy one, never showed no nerves," Kay said.

"Besides M&M's the one who runs these funnings, not us," Lor said.

"Shut up, all you!" Dinah squalled. "You hated her just like me!" Frustrated, she shoved the closest body, that of Lor, into her sister. Lor stumbled and fell up the steps. Dor wavered but retained her footing.

I feared another dog pile might form, with Dinah coming out on top, but one shove seemed to satisfy the mighty M&M. She backed away and regrouped.

While Lor was muttering imprecations from her sprawled position on the steps, I prodded, "What happened next?"

Dinah lumbered up the steps past the downed one. Mouth puffing in aggravation, she stood gazing at the ballplayers on the field, who, at Eddie's urging, had started running laps. The big girl sat down hard on the top step. "Betty Jane give out with a little cry and her head jerked back. Her eyeballs rolled back in her head and she began to slide off the bench. She passed out. Lucky I was right there to catch her before she broke a bone or two, because then where would that have left us?"

"You saved the day," I said.

Kay spread large hands over her child's face. "You left out that she throwed up. At the same time her head come up and her eyes rolled back, some yellow stuff dribbled out of her mouth, I'll never forget that. The sight of such a great pitcher so done in."

Lor cuffed Kay on the side of her head. "Shut up, thumbsucker."

"M&M," I said, "could I have a look at your sack of initiation goodies? It might help me prepare for my funning."

"Too late. Cops took it. Part of the plan to nail me."

The others drooped, all except Pepper, who blurted, "If Eddie'd been there, she'd never have let it go that far."

"That's why we don't invite her," Letta snarled.

"A couple days after I put that toy to her head, she was shot dead," Dinah burst out. "How you think I feel about that?"

"How the hell you think we feel about it?" was Dor's reply.

9.

At 9:00 the next morning, Pepper showed up for practice wearing pistol earrings. "Defensive measure," she said, "meaning don't mess with me."

When Eddie came onto the field, she was jingling a bunch of whistles on knotted strings. "Put one of these around your neck," she ordered, "if you're in danger, give it a toot and the rest of us will come running."

As we proceeded through warm-up drills, the whistles bounced against chests and chins. Disgusted, Joanie stuck hers in a shorts pocket, whereupon a penknife popped out. She shoved that back in with the whistle. Later sliding into second base, she claimed knife and whistle burn.

The rest of us ended up holding the whistles in our mouths where they chirped as we ran, fielded, and swung. The ballpark soon became aviary alive. Before she caught on, Eddie ran back and forth trying to spot where a victim had fallen injured or dead.

After Joanie sustained a toot for an unbelievable length of time, a competition started about who could blow the longest and loudest. In frustration, Eddie rushed to a light pole and beat on it with a bat, after which we were instructed to turn in our whistles.

What do you do when faced with something terrible over which you have no control? You have a laugh.

During practice, I got enough exercise to feel my limbs getting stronger and complaining less. That night we lost the game to Cedar Rapids. Most of the sparse crowd wandered off early, after the Starlets got six runs ahead. I rode the bench in silence.

Afterward, I couldn't find the bay leaf jar. Sabotage. At the 24-Hour Whistle Clean Laundry, I handed over the dirty clothes with the explanation that we were searching for a real four-leaf clover to improve our luck. "When we find one, it'll have to be returned after each washing," I advised. "Those things are unbelievably scarce."

The laundress kept a straight face.

10.

I needed a break so I used the off day to travel twelve miles south to Mediapolis, home of ninety-eight sleepy people, one grain elevator, and Dave Madison, a friend who furnished delicious meals and perfunctory sex. The proximity of his farm to Burton City explains why I had often gone to Hornettes' games. Sometimes Dave came with, but more often he stayed on the farm and read or did chores. To get to his place, I drove past flat fields cut in rectangles, and squares of various greens, each homestead surrounded by barbed wire with clumps of trees serving as windbreak.

Pulling into Dave's gravel driveway, I shut down the motor and opened the door to let the breezes in. I was attired in pink shorts and halter, pink anklets and brand new sport shoes.

In jeans and work shirt, Dave sauntered out of the large white frame house. At thirty-five he was built like a plank, wide and flat in front, slim from the side. Serenity had been forced upon him by his wife's death, of cancer, two years earlier. In the aftermath, he had renounced his lawyering career as sleazy and unethical. Now he happily worked the land they had purchased as a hobby farm.

Dave and I had met at a bowling competition, brought together from mutual need: his wife's death and my leaving my PI mentor Owen Mandel, not to mention my initial loneliness, compounded by failure to get established in Iowa City. And, to put it crassly, as a lawyer Dave had had important contacts and I saw that his influence might lead to jobs. It was simple: I needed work, he needed me. At the time, I didn't catch on that this was what my mother had done: attach herself to a man, love not required, for her own selfish purposes.

And Dave had his charms. He enjoyed the oddity of me breaking ground as a female PI.

I loved the irony of his life. He'd been raised in an upper class environment, had graduated from Harvard; the man existed in a level of sophistication that I could only dream of.

He worked hard at keeping low key, but there was usually tension around his mouth and I'd catch him squinting anxiously through wire-rimmed spectacles.

As he came down the front steps of the large clapboard house, Annie and Mike, black lab and German shepherd, kept pace, bobbling around his legs. The animals were easily spooked, so each visit it was necessary for us to get re-acquainted. Drawling, "Howdy, dawgs," to set their rears quivering, I brushed Dave's cheek with my lips and he placed an arm around my shoulders. Except for calling to say that at last I was employed, we had not spoken in a week. We liked it that way, or I did, preferring to be close for a short time, then running for the hills so I wouldn't actually get snared. It was difficult to discern Dave's wishes in that respect, since reticence was his way of life. In any event, I had too much to accomplish to think of forever with Dave Madison. Right now, he was a welcome distraction from my all-consuming ambition.

After we touched, Dave moved in and hugged. He said, "How's my little private investigator?"

"I need you," I said to his responsive eyes, "to hit me some grounders."

He became poker-faced. "You're kidding."

I reached into the car and drew out a bat and ball. "Afterward, we can play catch. You have a glove? All guys do, right? From your childhood?"

"You're usually so hungry," he said, "I thought you'd want to eat right away."

"No Dave, hunger must wait. Right now I need better baseball skills. Fast."

Registering my determination, he said, "I'll put the salad away. But really, accepting a job that calls for playing on a professional team. Was that wise?"

Well, maybe not too, but this was not the time for a seminar on the subject, so I said, "Come on, I'm making good money and paying off bills while investigating the murder of a great player. So help me out."

He made a face. "I believe I have a glove."

"Good deal." I stepped back several paces and looped the ball to him underhand. He caught it adroitly for a defunct lawyer and ballooned it toward me. A dog raced over and snatched it.

"Oh, Annie, very good," I praised, wrestling it from her spit-laden mouth.

Dave strode to the house with one of the dogs crowding him. The other remained beside me, breathing hot air on the hand that clutched the ball. I tossed tiny pop-ups to myself until the two returned with the upright one carrying a glove that looked brand new, reminding me again that Dave was the kind who prepared for all emergencies. I'd have to ask if he'd once been an Eagle Scout.

In the game of catch, the ball quickly became a slobbery mess as competition grew keen between human and animal. Better than actual game conditions, really.

As we played, throws that got through burned harder and harder until my hand prickled through the glove. We were really firing when one of my shots caromed off Dave's throwing hand.

"Oops, Dave." As I trotted to him, he hurled the glove to the ground and, bending over, stuck his hand between his knees. The dogs had gone hell-bent after the ball.

"Wendy," he said through his teeth, "Aren't you afraid you'll hurt yourself doing this?"

"Nah, I'm getting it down. Say, how about hitting me some grounders? And could I borrow your glove? Mine is paper-thin. As you say, I might get hurt," I said with a smile.

He booted his glove my way and picked up the bat. I pried the slick ball from Annie's jaws. We spread out on the lawn. Turned out, the dogs loved batted balls too. But after Dave got the swing of it, he didn't spare me and I fumbled some of the harder hit grounders. Still, by the end of the session I felt progress had been made, mostly by the dogs.

Good humor thus restored, the four of us walked together up the handsome steps Dave had crafted, into the farmhouse and dining room. The cherry wood table was covered with a lace spread and set with china plates. After washing up, he fed the dogs in the den and shut the door on them. With a chef's flourish, he produced the centerpiece from the kitchen - a mounded marvel of a salad - chopped lettuce, tomatoes, radishes, carrots, onions, all from the garden, and topped with his own recipe for buttermilk dressing.

I plunked myself into the fancy chair he held for me and guided a linen napkin over my knees. It was so beautiful that he had made lunch. Even at that, I couldn't keep my mind on my blessings. Between bites of salad, I prattled on about the investigation: Jailbird Pepper, her past exposed by an anonymous teammate, and Betty Jane's "funning," so scary she lost her ice cool and her dinner and fainted. And Millicent Tubbs' suspicious accident three nights ago. I didn't mention that I'd left the door to the murder scene unlocked. Didn't want to hear any more of "How stupid can you get?"

By the living room archway hung a painting of a white table on a manicured lawn, a vase of roses at its center. Two wrought iron chairs turned outward waited for people outside the picture. I doubted I would be one of the pair who strolled side by side over that perfect lawn. The house was a living testament to Dave's deceased wife. What she had selected and decorated remained. He had loved her and still did, I knew without asking.

During my visits there were no pictures of the late lamented set around, but once I discovered a studio portrait in a bedroom drawer (I am not a part-time snoop). He and she, blond, good cheekbones, were smiling formally, heads tilted to each other, and not a blemish between them, thanks to the studio's airbrush. His furrowed squint was missing although I imagined that it lurked.

After consuming the salad, we repaired to the living room and sat on the flowered sofa, her choice, of course. He bent and kissed me. Reaching around, he unsnapped my halter and, with a lustful cry, yanked it off.

I cautioned, "Not here, let's do it in private."

He pulled me to my feet. "Hurry," he said, dashing upstairs. Once the oven was lit, it sometimes heated up too fast, if you catch my drift. In the spare room, the iron-frame double bed was sheeted, no spread. The windows had shades but no curtains. Her presence was not here. No one had bothered with this room, which was as dusty as the Hornettes' infield, except for the bed.

Dave stripped while I hurried to the bathroom and inserted my diaphragm. "Come on," he urged. I hit the bed. He slid over me and the whole thing was over fast.

He rolled off, crowing, "Baby, we did it."

I said, "We?"

"What? You didn't come?"

"It was a little fast, wasn't it? A little foreplay might be nice."

"We could do it again."

"Nah, that's okay." Didn't work the first time, why would the second be different?

At 5:04, after we had snacked on crackers and cheese, I threw my baseball gear onto the back seat of the Nash. I took his glove up front with me.

I was eager to leave. The smell of hay rolled in as, with friendly squeezes, we prepared to part for another week. "You're sure you don't mind lending the mitt to me?" I asked, climbing into the Nash.

"No, go ahead, take it. That thing you're using is disgusting. I know mine will be a mess when I get it back, if I ever do see it again."

"Thanks, honey." I shut the door and revved the engine. By the steps the dogs, tongues flopping, tails wagging, awaited their master.

Speeding down the road back to Burton City, I assessed my day off: got in some baseball practice, liked the food, liked the dogs, liked having a friend, even though he wasn't much good in the sack. There was almost nothing in the sex for me, except having sex made me feel grown-up. So far, I figured that's how sex was: the guy talked purty and did nice things for you and you paid him back by acting obliging about what he desired.

Five miles down the road, I sniffled some over Dave and me, and over leaving what passed for security in my life. I was also relieved at having escaped it.

11.

Sunday morning dawned under a vivid blue sky. Heat rose from the sidewalk as I entered the Burton City police station. Three rotund cops I recognized from Tubbs' death scene, along with Chief Shupe, lounged around a glass coffeemaker bubbling vigorously on top of a table stove. The room smelled of burnt coffee. A plate of plain donuts and some Baby Ruth bars rested near the pot.

"Mornin', chief," I said, "you follow up on the info about Pepper McLaine? Does she have a record?"

He gestured me away. "Yep, in Helena, Montana. Clint told me about the 'jailbird' mirror thing some time ago. Contact me when you got news I don't have." He brushed his hands of crumbs and me, slopped coffee into a mug and headed for a rear door. I followed as he moved down a short hallway and entered a dark office that had the blinds closed.

"Why didn't you tell me you already knew? Should have been the first thing for me to know," I said. I was angrier at him for withholding than at Appling. After all, being a lawman, he knew the importance of past criminal activity. "Does Pepper have an alibi for Betty Jane's death?"

"She was with the two bull dykes."

"Who's that?" I asked.

"There's more than two? Joanie Dober and Twyla Ziegler are the ones I mean."

"Where was Pepper when Millicent Tubbs met her end?"

"Where was anybody?" he responded. "And who cares, it was probably an unfortunate accident." He paused to let his opinion sink in. "According to her sister, Pepper was home in bed. The only other players with alibis for that entire period, 10:00 p.m. to, say, 2:00 a.m., are the homely twins. So thank the Lord, all the blood relatives are alibied."

"Joanie was the last player to leave the locker room. Maybe she saw somebody on the way out." It had occurred to me that Joanie might have returned for a sexual encounter with the enthusiastic Millicent where something went totally haywire. Farfetched. From what I'd seen of Joanie and Twyla, they were devoted to each other.

"We interviewed Joanie," Shupe said. "She confirmed she shut the lights out on you and Millicent, thought it was goddam humorous. Bunch of Gracie Allens on that team."

"Uh-huh. Did Millicent's relatives identify the old photo of the young man?"

"Nope, didn't recognize him. That picture, a few shreds of leather, and the painted rock near where Betty Jane met her end constitute our entire evidence bag. When you get yours filled, tote it on in."

"Knife pricks roll right off me, Chief," I said. But they do accumulate in my resentment bag. "What's the status of Dinah Timberlake? Are you still going after her for Betty Jane's murder?"

His enthusiasm had cooled on that subject. "We don't have enough evidence to hold her. Any one of them could have picked up that paint jar."

I went on firmly. "I need to be kept up to date by the police chief who's supposed to be working with me."

"Let it go. The McLaine girl didn't have anything to do with this. She's kept under wraps by her sister."

Seeking a diversion from the slow burn I was doing, I gazed around the chief's office. It was a place for remembrance. On the hardwood desk, a handsome box displayed five colorful medals. A wall held a rack of rifles from World War II: M1 carbine, M16, FLN, and a sterling SMG.

Seeking to impress a man, a requirement for all women and beasts, I said, "I see you have an M1 Garand. That's a terrific weapon. Best rifle in the war. Eight bullets to a clip. Fires as fast as you can pull the trigger. Clip ejects, you jam another one in. Whoo-ee, dead Nips galore. Or Krauts as the case may be."

I waited for Shupe to reveal which theater of war he'd fought in, but he seemed struck speechless.

I could have rambled on about the other guns but figured I'd wait until he digested the fact that a little female-gal might have a knowledge of weaponry. Being in the rifle trade, my dad liked to talk guns, and it pleased him if I recognized the different types. That interest has stuck with me.

On the wall tacked to poster board was a photo of a group of soldiers posing with M1s. In the middle of the front row knelt a younger, fiercer Sergeant Shupe. The current Chief Shupe went to the armchair behind the desk, and indicated that I too should rest my bones, which I did, on a metal folding chair.

"Impressive exhibit," I commented. I was offended that his interpretation of my attempt at equality meant letting me unfold that chair. Changing times had their complications.

He lowered his coffee mug behind the desk where I couldn't see. A drawer was slid open and I heard the brief slosh of liquid.

"I doubt you'll ever earn your stripes by fighting for your country," he observed, bringing the mug up and sniffing it pleasurably.

"An occasional nip is justified," I declared, "because you fought for your country. Like in the movies."

Poised with the cup, he stared. "Okay, Sherlock, figure this out. " Opening a second drawer, he produced a wrinkled sack and dumped its contents on the desk. Two necklaces, a brooch, a ring, a pair of earrings, and a heart bracelet made tinkling sounds as they hit. I checked for a gold baseball necklace. No luck there.

"So?" I reacted, "a bunch of jewelry."

"Cheap stuff, most of it. Trinkets stolen from the Hornette girls. Clint reported the thefts about a month ago after Betty Jane raised a stink over something she'd lost, a drinking glass as I recall. The one expensive item here is the black onyx ring, stolen from … " He uncrumpled a penciled list that he took from the sack. "… pitcher Roberta Bied."

"Where was this found?"

"In a Hornette girl's locker when we searched after Millicent's death."

"Whose locker?"

"Can't you guess? Aren't you gals good at intuiting?"

"Cut the crap."

He inhaled vigorously. "Eddie McLaine."

"Really."

He took a long swallow, thumped the mug down. "Now I got to waste my time questioning Eddie over a bunch of mostly junky jewelry. And I gotta be subtle about it because Clint likes her, not in any romantic sense, but because she's been a major help to him."

"Does Clint know she's a thief?"

"Not as far as I know."

"Why would Eddie steal? She's good at her job and the team accepts her as their leader. Has she confessed?"

"Doesn't know we have the booty, but you can bet she's missing it. The motive is most likely plain and simple kleptomania. Unlikeliest people are kleptos, Wendy. They feel worthless and rejected and - unloved." It seemed difficult for him to reveal such a sensual word, even in its negative form. "The woman's got a crush on Clint. He's what she wants most and can't have."

"So she purloins trinkets as a substitute? Hardly comes out even, at least in weight. Look here, I have to be present during her questioning."

"Can't let her know you're a PI."

The floorboards creaked as a pudgy cop with a baby face, button nose and chubby cheeks entered. "Chief, what you want to do with Leroy Williams? Release him?"

"Leroy Williams? Who's that?" I asked.

"Betty Jane's cousin, a traveling man, that is to say, a drifter," Shupe said. "We been at him all night with no luck. You want to try? Use the pretty girl approach?"

"Ah, the old subtlety ploy," I said. "My specialty. You suspect him of killing her?"

"We found a will where she named him next of kin. Not likely that her wealth amounts to much, but Cousin Leroy is a small-time hood, shoplifting, penny ante stuff so you know pennies mean something to him. Served time in Montana for his crimes. Montana is where Pepper served her time, and Betty Jane's originally from there too. Leroy moved to Burton City shortly after Betty Jane came on board. He's unemployed. Claims he was in the Elite Café the night she died." Shupe stressed the first syllable of 'Elite,' pronouncing it like the letter 'E,' and saying 'lite' as 'light.'

"Cousin Leroy says the barkeep will back him up," he continued. "Leroy practically lives in the Elite. I know the place well; Clint and me and some of the fellas play darts there every Monday night, and I've seen Leroy wandering around with a drink in his hand. The Saturday night Betty Jane bit the dust, the barman said the bar was crowded. Cousin Leroy could have slipped out, done the dirty deed and been back before anybody knew he was gone."

I absorbed that before issuing the familiar complaint. "Why didn't you contact me about Leroy Williams' arrest?"

"Letting you concentrate on your theories." The edge to his speech told me he was rankled over my continuing dissatisfaction.

Shupe shoved a coffee mug at the young cop. "Go fill this up." The flatfoot, "Fisher," by nameplate, complied.

No one asked if I might like a jolt. My resentment bag was ready to spill over.

Shupe took enough time getting a cigar going that Fisher was back with the steaming mug, setting it on the desk and remaining close by. Shupe sipped, leaned back, puffed. Satisfied momentarily, he said, "Leroy William's neighbors say they recognized Betty Jane sneaking into his rooming house after dark and sneaking out at first light. They say they saw this eight, ten times. So what's your opinion of a deadbeat and a baseball heroine shacking up together?" He exhaled a cloud of smoke.

"Is he a cousin or is it a lie? She's not going to bed down with a cousin." I was almost shouting. My image of Betty Jane wouldn't allow for that.

"Take it easy, Sherlock, how do you know? We don't know how the girl thought."

"What I know is that you've got a drifter you'd like to pin a murder on. Less trouble than charging a local."

The young cop shifted his feet. "I bet you ain't from around here neither."

Shupe rose noisily and moved toward the door while offering an explanation for my presence. "Officer Fisher, Miss Winkworth here is one of the Hornette ball players. She's got an attitude like they all do, being competitive by nature. This one wants to help out the police, but she's got such a chip on her shoulder, I don't know how effective she'll be. Why she's acting so disagreeable, I don't know."

At times like this I can't recall why I'm on the law's side, except that being a dick is exciting and normally you don't go to jail if you're caught at it.

"Well," Shupe was going on, "we'll give her a chance at Leroy. If nothing comes of it, we'll let him go."

The chief signaled to me to follow and we filed down the hallway to a windowless cubicle smelling of mold and sweat. A vacant-eyed Leroy Williams had pushed himself back in a metal chair. From first sight I couldn't take my eyes off him. Strikingly handsome, even in his bedraggled state, he had a squarish face with a beautifully formed chin, wavy blonde hair and a blocky body, heavily muscled in the shoulders. He was barefoot and clad in striped prison shorts, his torso bare and damp with sweat. A slender hand held a cigarette.

A burly cop, "Robinson" on his badge, smirked as he watched me drink in the suspect. "You got another one for me to entertain?" he inquired of Shupe.

"Nope. What we got here is a member of the Hornettes baseball team, like Betty Jane was."

"The Whore-nets?" Robinson said and added, "is that with a 'W'?" so I'd not miss the inference. I was revolted. I really hate cops, and all males sometimes.

Shupe ignored the insult. "Miss Winkworth is gonna talk to Mr. Williams about his cousin, Miss Wadlow, and her days with the team." He confronted the prisoner. "Be respectful, bub, or Officer Robinson'll give you what for."

With no indication he'd heard, Leroy reached to the table, picked up a half-eaten Baby Ruth bar, bit and chewed.

Now I was being denied not only a hot cuppa but a candy bar, too, when it seemed common hospitality afforded to others, miscreant or not. Face it, Winks. To make this place go, they need cops, suspects and criminals. What they darn well don't need is a female PI.

"Officer Robinson, report any success to me," Shupe said. He and the kid cop departed the room.

I took a step back, placed my palms against the wall and pushed off quickly in Leroy's direction. In Owen Ray Mandel's training class, this was termed "gathering momentum" and I was trying it out for the first time with a real suspect. "Leroy," I said, drawing up short, "you are in big trouble." He stared at me. I sweetened the attack. "Bet you wish you were home in bed." A vision came, of Adonis lounging atop the covers. I did dress him in pajama bottoms, gold, with fringe. "How well did you know your cousin?"

"Didn't hardly know her but you can't tell this flatfoot nothing."

Robinson's flat feet stirred and he punched Leroy in the gut. My fantasy man folded. The candy sailed from his hand and slapped against the grubby floor.

"Enough of that," I snapped at Robinson. "You're job is to watch and report, not interact."

"So sorry," the goon sneered. "My short fuse got the best of me. I can't control it, could happen again."

I picked up the biggest piece of candy and returned it to Leroy's hand. My mistake. Probably the worst thing I could do was to return a candy bar to a man who'd just been belly-punched. He must have realized that because he let it slip through his fingers.

My father was never far from my mind in such circumstances. When he was led, handcuffed, into the visitor's room of the Harrison jail, I had tried to avoid seeing his smallness, the gray pallor, the purple bruise on his cheek, but most of all his shame at being there.

The blow had amended Leroy's story. Thin-voiced, he said, "Betty Jane and I might have got together once in a while for the sake of family."

"According to witnesses, you overnighted with her," I said. "What were you trying to do? Keep the offspring in the family?"

He drew himself up and the dead eyes came alive. "If we'd of made babies, they'd a been strong and beautiful like she was."

The declaration brought him out of his trance and rocked me. Even Robinson was silent for an instant before blowing an offended breath.

I shook my head and smiled. "I'd sure liked to have seen them."

There had been such fire in the prisoner's eyes, but they dulled and became disinterested again.

Further questioning proved futile with Leroy giving one-syllable responses as though he had spent all his energy on that single statement. For my part, I learned from that one passionate outburst that Leroy Williams had cared mightily for Betty Jane Wadlow.

Returning to Chief Shupe's office, I spoke to him about taking a look at Betty Jane's apartment. Handing over the key, he agreed with one proviso. "Tomorrow an expert from Des Moines is coming so absolutely do not disturb anything. You have to account to Mr. Yegg Washington and he's hard on those who slip up. And for Christ sake, lock up when you leave." He shuffled papers angrily on his desk. "You gotta watch those ballplayers more closely. Don't let anyone else die over there. So far I'm not impressed with your work or your manner."

Nor I with yours. I picked up his coffee mug and took a slug, tasting the bitter alcohol going down. "Thanks. After dealing with you I needed that." I slammed the cup down, splashing liquid on his desk. "I work for Mr. Washington, not you," I stated. "He's heads above you in power. You withhold information, you're asking for trouble and you'll darn well get it."

12.

I called Clint and begged off appearing at the game that afternoon. "You have the fresh laundry and you don't need me, and beside, this case has reached a critical point where I need to remain available."

He decided the official reason for my absence would be a doctor's consultation, something mysteriously feminine that a manager might not feel comfortable explaining to the team.

At the corner of Jefferson and 2nd St., I bought a copy of the Burton City Gazette from a boy vendor, and took it into Dinty's Diner where I devoured two greasy burgers as I read. Chief Duane Shupe was quoted as saying they were following a number of leads and looking for witnesses to account for Betty Jane's whereabouts during the three and a half hours between the end of the game and when her body was found.

In Sid Dobrotka's column, a eulogy: "Betty Jane Wadlow entered our sports scene like a comet from the heavens and left it as a comet does, in one devastating flash. In her last game as a Hornette, she seemed to lose focus, but even at that, Betty Jane was better than most." Not while flinging a wild pitch, I critiqued. Dobrotka's summing up seemed like raving hyperbole.

I left the newspaper on the counter for any diner who wanted to know the greasy latest.

It was just after noon and the sun was high as I walked to my Nash past Minnie the wooden Indian, who had survived a gaudy paint job to pose in front of Byers Cigar Store.

As I drove to Betty Jane's apartment, the Nash, even with its windows cranked, was a pocket of heat. The apartment house sat partway up a steep hill among other run-down two-story dwellings. On the first floor of her building, a window shade had been drawn. Two wooden planters sat on the porch ledge with petunias trailing wildly over them. The yards in the neighborhood were tiny, but grass and weeds made up for it by unbridled growth upward. In the August heat everything grew ragged and uncontrolled.

I entered the lobby. A runner, chewed by rot, covered the stairway to second floor. The area smelled of wet wood and muddy rubber from transients hauling boxes of belongings up and down steps.

Betty Jane's apartment was to my immediate right. Using the key Shupe had given me, I opened the door, stepped in, and stood listening. From the street a child's yell, the hum and fade of a car. Heavy footsteps overhead.

On my left an open door led to a bedroom where a yellow bureau stood. The kitchen was straight ahead.

The dingy brown living room contained only a threadbare davenport and a rickety-looking coffee table. Aware that most of the baseball girls rented furnished or bought used, I hadn't realized how used, and how much that took away from the prestige of the job.

Two built-in wall shelves were empty, nothing decorative positioned for pretty effect.

It occurred to me that Betty Jane hadn't really lived there, but with her gorgeous punk cousin and she kept the address for propriety's sake. I was no prude, but I was young and assumed my sports heroes lived exemplary lives with no room for a sexual relationship with blood kin and a petty criminal to boot, regardless of the heart's desires.

I explored the kitchen. The bare refrigerator had been unplugged. No use wasting electricity on a dead tenant. One package of Twinkies in the cupboard, nothing else.

In addition to the yellow bureau, the bedroom contained a single bed, sheeted, the pillow uncased. I raised the top mattress and checked underneath. I went to the bureau and opened the top drawer. A few pieces of cotton underwear lay there: bras, panties, a slip still in the package with a Sears receipt. A thin washrag and three towels were piled neatly on top of an old gray towel, hand-sewn, flimsy, with hens and chicks the subjects of red cross-stitching. Attracted by the cunningly cute, was she? Bought cheap from the Salvation Army, or preserved as a memento? If you were from Sperry, Montana, you were thrifty and practical, never becoming the sophisticate that Helena Rubenstein aspired for you.

The bras were size 36. Wow. Betty Jane was a beautiful woman, and muscular, but from the stands she hadn't looked that large. I sighted down my blouse. Mine were anthills in comparison. I despaired of having the stuff even to practice alongside the big girls. For me, Charles Atlas would have been more help than Helena.

I removed the dry goods and set them on the bed. I pulled the drawer completely out and checked its underside for taped envelopes bearing significant clues. I followed suit with the other five drawers. They were empty, inside and underneath.

I dragged the bureau away from the wall to see if there was writing behind it. My mother had a small safe in her room and wrote the padlock combination on the wall. Norris discovered it and occasionally "borrowed" a dollar from the repository.

I was feeling a little weird about the lack of habitation when I saw a newspaper propped against a bureau leg. The two-week-old paper was folded to an article by Sid Dobrotka about the previous day's game. I remembered that game. It had been one of Betty Jane's rare struggling times with Dinah Timberlake's double in the last of the ninth bringing home the winning run. Dobrotka had concentrated his words on the pitcher, her never-say-die attitude, the grim slog back to the mound after each hit whistled through. According to Mr. Local Sportsman, Betty Jane had demonstrated the doggedness of a grunt infantryman, stopping just short of saying that such courage was why we won the war. One sentence dismissed Dinah's homer as what was expected, ho-hum. M&M had envied Betty Jane with good reason. The comely pitcher had relegated the freakish slugger to second banana in the press. A gun to the temple must have felt satisfying, even in jest. "JUSt" had been written beside the victim's body. "JUST" meaning "deserved, a fair punishment?"

Next I searched the walk-in closet where five hangers hung from hooks on the back wall. From one draped an elegant silk dress with a red pattern of lines and circles. I felt the slick pockets. I smelled the armpits. No odor of drycleaning.

Beneath the dress sat a pair of black three-inch heels, hosiery folded across them. Ah, now I understood. This was the booth where Betty Jane shed the costume of average woman to become—Local Paragon!

The bathroom was next, just off the bedroom. As I worked, I admired my professional thoroughness. I peered into the toilet tank, reached behind it. Nothing taped there.

Opening the medicine chest, I found Betty Jane's personal domain. Packs of hair color, dribbly makeup jars, tubes of lipstick, rouge, mascara, eyebrow pencils, face powder, littered the cabinet. Betty Jane never took the field without makeup on. Blue eye shadow, cheeks with none too subtle dabs of rouge, gaudy bright lipstick. Overdone, like an actress on the stage. She probably dolled up for her other public appearances too. Going to the grocer, shopping, whatever. Mask up!

Between us, the contrast was obvious. I scrubbed my face in the morning, applied a bit of lipstick, and never thought of it again all day, uh-huh.

Three medicine bottles, two Bayer Aspirin, and a larger bottle lying on its side, probably tipped over by the cops as they snooped.

Had headaches, did she? I guessed life as a local idol meant a lot of pressure for a small town girl.

I took the medicine bottles out one at a time, shaking each as I rocked on my heels and assessed. Empty shelves, a few things in drawers and closet. Full medicine cabinet. This place seemed merely a makeup repair station. Like other tenants in the forlorn building, this woman was just passing through.

I set the large medicine bottle upright, in doing so there was no rattle of pills or slosh of liquid. I unscrewed the cap. Inside was a rolled-up piece of newsprint. I drew it out, unscrolled it: a yellowed news photo of Betty Jane. An ink scrawl in the upper right corner identified the source as, "Sperry Journal 7/14/40." The four-by-five picture was scissored neatly around the edges, but dog-eared and discolored as though she couldn't get enough of handling it. In the full body shot, Betty Jane posed on the mound, blonde hair upswept, right arm bent, ball hidden behind her hip. In the bloom of youth, vibrant, alive. Hey, stop it. Baseball longa, vita brevis. The caption read, "Betty Jane Wadlow, Sweet 16, the Strikeout Queen." The photo was grainy and not awfully focused, but ten years later, control and power still leapt from the page. In my mind's eye, the image transformed itself into the mature Betty Jane, poised to let fly from the mound of the Cranston Park diamond. Now why would she store that in a medicine bottle?

I examined the photo more closely. The profile was fuzzy. I went to the living room, to the picture window and pulled up the shade to scrutinize the jaw line. The girl in the photo had a Ted Williams jaw, strong and stubborn. But Betty Jane's slightly receding jaw was that of a Joe DiMaggio.

I glanced away, squeezed my eyes shut until I saw stars. When I looked again, I saw the same image as before. For sure, these were two different people. Was it possible? Whose mistake was it? Or, more than a mistake, a deception?

But whose? Who was Sperry's Betty Jane Wadlow? Or, more to the point, who was ours?

13.

After parking in front of the Gazette building, I got Sid Dobrotka's office number from the receptionist and raced up two flights. The newsroom featured a central open space and several connecting offices. The floor shook with the rumble of presses turning. Typewriters clacked and there was the brittle smell of newsprint.

A wall clock read 3:45. Ten minutes earlier I had left the dead pitcher's apartment. If Shupe missed the photo, he might be tempted to reprimand, but by then everyone would know that our Betty Jane was not Sperry's Betty Jane.

As I was getting my bearings and in the process avoiding a couple of fast-moving reporters, Sid Dobrotka came weaving through the busyness. Grasping my hand, he said, "Wendy, isn't it? Ballplayer? Finally coming to see me? I got interviews set up for days but I'll fit you in."

He dropped my hand, turned and hurried out of the fray. From behind I could see that his shoes still looked dusty. We took a sharp right into a small office, SPORTS, in black, arced across the upper half of the wood and glass door. A sparkling clean window looked out upon the Mississippi where a loaded barge inched by.

He directed me to an armchair while settling himself in a swiveler by a roll-top desk. He zipped paper out of a monstrous Underwood typewriter and inserted a new sheet. "First of all let's get your bio."

"Sid, take a look at this." I handed him the curled photograph.

He spread it out, scanned it. "So, an old picture of Betty Jane. What am I supposed to do with it? The other day on the field, you went by me mighty fast. And Clint doesn't have much to say about you." He laid the picture on his desk where it immediately scrolled up tight. He placed his nicely formed hands on the typing keys. "Where you from? Who'd you play for last?"

"Sid, look closely at that picture, please. Caption says it's Betty Jane ten years ago. It's not."

He snatched up the photo, smoothed it out. His expression went from irritated to interested. He shook his head. "This is not Betty Jane."

"The chin's wrong and the posture, too. Betty Jane was somewhat round-shouldered, wasn't she, and this girl's shoulders are more squared off."

He grabbed the phone and spoke into it. "Eleanor, get me the Sperry Journal in Montana. Head sportswriter there. Mention my name." He replaced the receiver. "They'll know me, I've got a reputation. Although it might not have spread that far." Inquisitive hazel eyes upon me, he flashed a grin and ran a hand through his thatch of sandy hair. He was quick, good-looking. Ambition had produced an eager beaver along with some rough edges. Sid wore a white shirt, at the open throat a button hung by a thread, and gabardine trousers with frayed saddle-stitched seams.

"While we're waiting," he said, "fill me in about who Wendy Winkworth is."

I divulged the story of my athletic history, totally concocted, of course. "I played on a softball team in Milwaukee for a while. For the company where I worked, a brassiere factory owned by Yegg Washington. Part of Washington Industries. You know Mr. Washington?"

"Well, sure, everybody does, he owns this league. I don't know a bra-stitching softball team though."

This man said "bra" right out without blushing; that made him more interesting.

He seized the phone when it rang. A voice boomed, "That Sid Dobrotka?" At the volume of sound, Sid jerked the receiver away from his ear, then jammed the speaker up to his lips and sent a return bellow. "Yep, in the flesh."

"This is Mike Hanel of the Sperry Journal, in case you didn't know."

"Recognized your blast of hot air right away." Sid covered the receiver and asided, "Cheekiest guy in journalism class." He flapped the hand away, playing the phone like Rudy Vallee did the megaphone. "Mikey, what you doing out in the wilds of Montana?"

"And you stuck in the cornfields? Doesn't fit either. Thought you'd be on the Chicago Tribune by now."

Sid's tone sobered. "Thought by this time I'd be outa here myself."

"Yeah, well we'll both make it big some day."

Another covering flap along with an assessment: "One of us will anyhow." Again the trans-state shout: "Mike, I called because we got a girl athlete here who got killed last week. Pitched for the local Hornettes team, in the Star-Spangled League for ladies. Ever hear of it?"

"Vaguely. Don't know any specifics, though."

"Dead girl's name was Betty Jane Wadlow. Claimed to be from Sperry. You familiar with that name?"

There was a pause, and when Mike came back on, his voice stumbled. Sid pressed the phone to his ear so I could no longer hear.

Finally he said, "Yeah? Betty Jane Wadlow?" The receiver went silent and so did he, placing the phone against his chest while he decided how best to present the bad news for my delicate sensibilities.

"Just tell me," I said.

In a voice of doom, he said, "They had a Betty Jane Wadlow out there. A high school pitcher so good she pitched on the boy's team.

She died in a car crash when she was seventeen, her senior year in high school. Big funeral."

Sid restored the phone to his ear. "Mike, send me everything you got on the dead girl, will you?"

"Ask if any Wadlows still live there," I said. The idea was to get a line on our deceased pitcher's true identity.

Sid complied, relaying Mike's answers in spasms to me.

"… parents moved away after their only child was killed … heartbroken … pulled up stakes and were out of there …"

Once more into the phone, Sid shouted, "You're right, it's sad, very sad. Mike, let's keep in touch. Let me know what happens in your sorry excuse for a sports scene, and I'll do the same from mine."

After fond farewell noises and an abrupt disconnect, Sid swiveled toward me and queried rapid-fire, "Where'd you come across that photo? Do the police know about it?"

"Maybe not. I found it in her apartment. It was rolled up in a bottle. I headed here right off because I know you're the sports authority in this town."

He grinned and nodded. "In this office, flattery will get you somewhere. Why were you in her apartment?" The questioning had become a reporter's probing so abruptly that I was caught short because, in my excitement, I hadn't thought to cover my tracks.

"Well," I stalled, fully expecting an answer to flow forth. I wasn't surprised when it did. "I live right upstairs, yeah," I began. You'd think this guy would show some gratitude for being handed a major scoop. With a pretty shrug, I continued, "I wanted something personal of hers is all. She was my hero. So, going by today, I tried her door and it was unlocked. It happens, cops forgetting to lock up." A little revenge there. "Anyhow, I went in. It's what we did all the time back in the bayou when I was a kid. We were all very good friends in the bayou."

It seemed that the explanation went over because the reporter grabbed the phone. "Let's find out who Burton City's star pitcher was. Eleanor, get me Police Chief Duane Shupe."

When Sid spoke again it was with a playful cast. "You ever try to say 'Chief Shupe' fast, four times in a row?"

"Chief Shupe, Chief Shoof," I responded and giggled.

"See, it sounds like a hay fever allergy." He opened a scuffed cigarette case and offered me a Camel. I shook my head. The nail went into his mouth where it drooped until he flipped it up with his lips and lit a match to it. Exhaling, he said, "Mr. Washington ever come by to check out those brassieres?"

"Not when I was there. Did he come to Burton City to investigate the scene before financing the league?"

"Nope. Sent three representatives with foreign names. People you wouldn't want to disagree with. I looked over my shoulder the whole two days they were here." He paused, perhaps picturing the three lugs. "No one knows much about Mr. Washington. An old foreign guy I ran into told me that Yegg was a star soccer player when he was a boy, overseas, somewhere in southern Russia. Said he could do everything and then some on the field. But as he grew up he got into crime and did pretty well at that, too, offing people left and right. In no time Mr. Yegg Washington had become king of the rackets there in south Russia."

"That's his reputation here too," I said, "according to the rumors." In my experience, people like to build up a man who has a slightly nefarious reputation until he's the biggest and baddest, not even human any more. A modern day fairy tale, serving as a warning to all.

"'Washington' is a funny last name for a Russki," I went on. "Odd first name though. Means 'burglar' or 'thief,' doesn't it? Appropriate."

"Oh, Yegg's a nickname. His name's really 'Yegor.'"

"That's an odd one, too."

"No doubt changed his surname when he immigrated. Wanted to be the ultimate American. 'Yegor' is Russian. I imagine he stuck with that as a tie to the old country. What I've heard is that he wants to buy into the St. Louis Cardinals but the major league commissioner and his staff caught the stench of blood on his breath and want no part of him, at least not yet. It's my belief he created this league to show the big boys that he can run a sports business honest and aboveboard when he has to."

"Mmmm," I said. A connection appeared: Yegg's plans were at risk because of Betty Jane's murder. The commish might think that a major crime boss had something to do with it. So, Wendy Winkworth to the rescue, an insider hired to clear it up fast.

"Mmmm," I said again and became aware that Sid was studying me shrewdly.

"Betty Jane's pitching brought in the crowds," I said. "Now that she's gone and the team is losing games, people are staying home."

"Yep, you might be unemployed soon." He gave my shoulder a pat, tore his eyes away from my bosom, stood and strolled to the window, where he gazed down upon the barge that was in about the same position as before. He stuck his hands in his pockets, pulling his trousers tight. Cute butt. When he turned to focus on my lower parts, I found I had crossed my legs so a little thigh was showing. After an instant of profound interest, his eyes raised and met mine.

"The women's leagues are going belly up," he said. "The soldiers are home now, and a lot of the players went back to being housewives again. And TV doesn't help by showing big league games. Too bad."

The phone rang and he grabbed it. "Chief Shupe, Chief Shupe." I suppose he spoke rapidly with impeccable enunciation to prove he could do it. "Sid Dobrotka here. Duane, you got a mistaken identity on the Wadlow body. It's not who we think. You better fingerprint that corpse before it goes under."

As I slipped out, I gave Sid the trademark wink that I believed my name implied. Fluttering a couple of fingers, I mouthed, "See you."

He responded happily with a return wink, followed by lips forming words that looked like, "What's your game, really?"

14.

Assuming Cousin Leroy had been released from custody, I found him right where Shupe said he'd be: perched on a barstool in the Elite Café. The long narrow restaurant, actually a dirty shabby bar, was located on South Main St., across from the CB and Q railroad and its ear-splitting locomotives. Beyond the tracks flowed the mighty Mississippi.

In the late afternoon light, the neon sign on the café's plate glass window blinked, "Tables for Ladies." Just inside the entrance, two huge fans blasted my hair to my skull and tried to pull it out the other side. Tables and chairs cluttered the floor with booths along the sides. A separate area in back held three pool tables and Shupe's favorite recreation, dartboards.

At the bar, Leroy Williams sat holding a beer, his thumb rubbing circles through the moisture on the glass. The other hand lay in a potato chip bag. I slid onto the stool next to him. He kept his eyes where they were.

Seated at the far end of the bar, a grizzled man with raw eyes nursed his medicine while a skinny-wristed bartender toweled the same spot on the counter over and over, puzzling out, I suppose, why a lady would pass up a chance to sit at a table and instead join a barfly at the counter. Considering Leroy's gorgeous looks this was not a poser for me.

"Leroy Williams, how you doing?" I said. "Remember me? We met in the jailhouse."

His eyes shifted and recognition dawned. "Go away."

"Not yet. The cops and I made an interesting discovery. The real Betty Jane Wadlow died in a car crash nine years ago. So who's the imposter, your cousin the athlete?"

"Oh, Jesus." He expelled air, leaving his striking features wobbly. The hand in the potato chip bag dragged out some salty scraps and forgot them on the counter.

I pressed. "The cops will insist on knowing who she really was. Tell me before they get their teeth into you and we'll take them on together."

His hands collapsed in his lap. He bent forward and began rocking lower and lower until his forehead hit the counter.

"Whoa there, Leroy," I said. "Don't hurt your nice head." The sound of flesh and bone hitting the counter had been sickening, like a melon conked with a hammer. The customer at the end of the bar jumped up and, leaving his glass teetering with beer slopping over, hurried through the fan blast out the door. The barkeep threw down his cleaning rag and strode to the jukebox. He jammed in a nickel and "Goodnight Irene" blared. Returning, he snatched the cleaning rag and mopped up the spilled beer, then used the same cloth to dry a freshly washed glass.

"Don't take this too hard," I whispered to my bar mate, "but if the dead woman's prints are on record anywhere in these forty-eight states the cops will find out who she was."

"Oh, Jesus, fingerprints." Leroy's desperation was such that I knew somewhere her prints were on file.

The bartender confronted me. "You ordering or driving him to suicide?" He was holding the formerly clean glass now streaked with foam from the polishing rag.

"A beer and bring him a refill," I ordered. "Don't put mine in that glass. I want a clean one." I slapped a dollar on the counter.

Moving with the barkeep along the wooden counter, I asked if he'd been working the night Betty Jane was killed.

"I was. Why?"

"You remember if Leroy was here? I'm a friend of the family. I need to know if he's in trouble."

After busying himself with the order, the bartender returned to Leroy, plunking two beers down and sweeping the empty and my dollar away. "He was here, moaning to customers who didn't want to hear about how he didn't have enough cash to buy a car and afford gas and repairs, too. A couple times before, I kicked him out for hassling people, but that night, I was too busy to bother. He was here till 1:00 a.m. closing, even a little after that because he made a buck by sweeping up."

"What time did he leave?"

"Between 1:15 and 1:30? I don't know. He kinda drifted off somewhere in there. I told all this to the cops. Why don't you check with them as to what trouble he's in? And hire him a lawyer while you're at it."

"Good idea. Thanks."

Our conversation was carried on as though Leroy weren't right there, which is what most drunks come down to, ignored unless they're bouncing heads, theirs or others, off a bar top.

"Cops gotta nail somebody and Leroy looks ripe for the deed." The barkeep sounded sick over that deal.

A siren whooped toward us. "Leroy," I said biffing the ex-con's arm, "last chance." The whining blare sputtered before cutting off. 'Tell me her real name and we'll take on the blue boys together."

He raised his head blearily and looked toward the door. I winced seeing the red mark where his forehead had hit the bar. He was glugging beer as Chief Shupe and Officer Robinson burst through the door and, after a few pounding steps, seized him.

"You're busted." Robinson made it official.

Leroy ducked off the stool with the edge of the glass pressed to his lips, beer trickling down his front. Shupe pushed him against the wall, placed an arm against his collarbone and drove his chin up.

"Who was she, creep?" the chief snarled. "I spent all night hammering at you, I'm not doing that shit again. It's truth-telling time right now."

Wind nearly cut off, Leroy let go of the glass and rasped, "Lois Magic … her name … Lois Magic."

Officer Robinson shoved Leroy into the backseat of the patrol car. When I attempted to climb in beside him, Shupe gripped my arm. "You want to come along, drive your Nash in."

I jerked my arm free. "I softened him up so he'd tell her name."

"Getting strangled helped. We follow procedure here. The officer drives, I sit behind him with the prisoner. You want to join, follow along in your chariot."

Officer Robinson pleaded my case. "I don't know, Chief. This gal's got a way with the guy. If he's our man, she might soft-talk him into a confession. Much as I'd like to beat the hell outta him, of course." He scowled at me.

Shupe pondered. "Bad procedure to let anyone in the squad car unless they're under arrest."

"I could spit on the sidewalk or jay-walk," I said.

"Fine. You armed?" He sounded fed up.

From my handbag, I took the .38 and handed it over. Shupe made way and I climbed in the backseat next to Leroy, whose eyes were as dazed as a deer's in headlights. In the arrest, his shirt had been yanked apart, buttons ripped off. His neck was red and splotches ran down to his collarbone.

Shupe got in front, on the passenger side. Before the boss was seated, Robinson rocketed the car from the curb. When we finished swaying, I said to Leroy, "Why did Lois Magic call herself Betty Jane Wadlow?"

He worked on clearing his throat. The words, when they emerged, were croaks. "Team don't take cons unless they're like Pepper." He swallowed and felt his throat. "I mean, kin to the chaperon."

"Betty Jane, I mean Lois. She was a convict too?" I said.

Leroy gave the barest of nods.

Twisting, Shupe crossed his arms over the seat back and nuzzled his chin against them. "Should have guessed, what with all the perverted activity that goes on with that team."

"Right," I said, "and that's only the manager."

Shupe ignored my wisecrack. "Boy, are you acquainted with Pepper McLaine?"

Leroy resumed, only to me. "Lois and Pepper was in the reformatory in Helena, Montana. They played on the softball team there. Plotted on how to get Lois a tryout for the Hornettes and decided the best way was for her to change who she was."

"How did Lois find out about Betty Jane?"

"Prison library. She read an article about a young girl tragically killed in a car crash. She boned up on accounts of ballgames the real Betty Jane pitched in."

"For that you let the police knock you around?" I said. "I mean, she's gone now. Why continue to protect her real name?"

His eyes beseeched me to believe. "I never wanted the good people of Iowa to know she was a convict. The name Betty Jean Wadlow is magic around here."

"Yeah, Lois was magic, too," I quipped, then told myself to stop with the wisecracks because they weren't going over in this crowd.

"Now, boy, tell us about Lois Magic and how you fit with her." Shupe leaned farther over the seat back to catch Leroy's yet softer words.

"I met Betty Jane - Lois - before she was sentenced to reformatory, when she was out on bail in Kalispell. It was in the court building where she was awaiting for trial. Charge was petty theft, she never committed nothing major, neither did I, ever. That day I was out on probation and reporting in. She was alone, her folks didn't show then or later neither. After she done her time and before she made the Hornettes, we got married." He puffed up in offense. "She was still going by 'Lois Magic' at the time. So now you know we were married and not first cousins at all. She was my beautiful wife."

I asked him why they didn't say they were married when she was alive.

"We kept our marriage a secret because, with all the press she was getting, my name could lead to her real identity. I won't ever change how I think of her. Betty Jane was her name for when we had our best times and she'll always be Betty Jane to me."

"I'll always think of her as Betty Jane, too," I comforted. I laid a hand on top of his long slender ones that were resting, cuffed, in his lap. His skin was sticky with beer and potato chips.

"I found a photo of the real Betty Jane among your Betty Jane's things," I said.

He rolled his eyes. "I know that picture. She pulled it out all the time, wore it thin with handling. Painting herself up, she'd worry if she looked like the real one good enough. I always made the same joke, that she used so much decoration, who's to say if she did or didn't."

So the "painting up" was to disguise, as I had thought earlier.

The patrol car careened around a corner. I clutched the door handle and Leroy tipped into the window glass before we lurched to a stop in front of the police station.

The humid early evening had turned to dusk. The darkening street was deserted. The streetlights came on.

Shupe pulled Leroy out of the vehicle and resumed grilling him. "She left her savings to you, $301.46 in a savings account. Now you can buy some wheels, can't you, boy, and even have cash left over for gas. That why you killed her? You have a fight about her financing a car for you? Lose your temper when she refused? Or did she find another man with a job and prospects? Was she about to throw you over like the worthless nothing you are?"

Leroy shivered and groaned.

Shupe lowered his voice. "The folks that live next to you say they heard a man and woman brawling in your room, between 3:00 and 4:00 the afternoon before she was shot. Bet that was you and her, boy. What you fighting about? Where's the gun you used to shut the bitch up?"

Shupe shoved Leroy toward the station entrance and he and Robinson bumped him repeatedly into the building. The two cops couldn't wait to get the prisoner into the third degree room.

At that moment, Leroy reminded me of my brother, Norris, also not awfully able to fend for himself. Years ago, in suffering a cop's thumping, Norris had clammed up and been clobbered almost into unconsciousness.

I watched from the silent, shadowy street knowing I'd had my day. At the least, they'd charge him with obstructing justice. Leroy was in for a long, tough night. But that was the first I'd heard about a man and woman "brawling." Did that mean a simple spat or an actual knockdown, drag-out? Damn that Shupe for withholding information again. And what was that about another man? Was the chief just fishing?

Betty Jane had saved her pay, had made a will. Unusual for a 26-year-old. Had she felt threatened, seen something like this coming?

15.

Sid's column the next morning broke the news. By the time the Hornettes gathered in the clubhouse that afternoon, everyone knew that the woman known as Betty Jane was a fraud. The Willeys said they had known something was off the whole time. Eddie took pains to prove non-complicity by saying she had called the reformatory right after Pepper recommended Betty Jane and inquired if there was a convict in residence by that name. There wasn't.

"I know my sister." she averred, "she's always been intensely loyal to her friends. I scolded her about making a mistake, and there will be no more said about it to anyone, by any member of this team if you like this job."

A slight flush spreading over her cheeks, Pepper kept her mouth shut for once.

Nobody on the team mentioned missing me at the game the day before, except in regard to the laundry not being done. With scads of Tabu perfume sprayed on uniforms and into the air, the locker room soon became filled with bouquets of sweetness and stale sweat. I got scowly glances and a few "Ew's," straight into my face, but I forgave the reaction. In addition to everything else, our weakest starter, Kay, was due to pitch that day against the Aurora Alices.

Right before the game, I called Chief Shupe from the lobby phone. To his brusque, "Shupe here," I snapped, "What's this about

Leroy and a woman fighting in his apartment? I need to be told this stuff first hand, not hear it secondhand by accident. Also, was there another man in Betty Jane's life?"

He tried to spoof his way out of it. "Oh, it's nothing. There was some kind of squabbling going on but I made up about the other man. The car thing has validity though. One of Leroy's biggest gripes was about not having wheels."

"Odd that someone as young as Betty Jane would make out a will. Almost as if she was afraid something like this would happen."

"Lots of young people see to taking care of their responsibilities. Maybe not where you come from."

Was that a dig at my cornpone accent? Boy, did I hate his guts.

He kept at it. "You're a greenhorn, Wendy. You don't know investigative procedure. You should stand back, observe, absorb, gain some goddam expertise before you go popping off. "

I boiled over. "Shut up, Shupe. I'm tired of listening to your crap. Let's get to it. Leroy and Betty Jane fought …"

He spoke slowly, patiently, as if to a nitwit from the hills. "Leroy admitted they argued, about sex. He wanted a quick lay, she didn't. Save herself for the game I guess. Did you know women did that too?"

"No, but I can tell it's important to the case." I could not work with this man. Opting for a life of crime might bring better companions. But, until and unless I formed the notorious Winks gang, I'd better communicate with a little more civility. "I want daily reports," I demanded. "Let's set a time for daily meetings."

"Before we do, you might be interested in this: Betty Jane's remains are back from Des Moines forensics. You interested in the results?"

"Of course."

He spoke in a stilted voice, as if reading. "1. First bullet hit her in the back. 2. Second shot was fired at close range, penetrated her heart causing fatal damage. 3. Slugs were .32s. 4. No trace evidence under fingernails." He loosened his delivery. "The victim was close up to the killer when that second shot stopped her permanently. 5. TOD between 10:30 p.m. and 2:00 a.m., nothing new there."

After recording key words in my notebook, I muttered, "That's that," and raised my voice to say, "Thank you."

"You might consider sharing your plans with us, too," he responded, "instead of going to Sid Dobrotka first with the photograph and then confronting Leroy Williams all by your lonesome. Some fuckin' teamwork mentality you got."

He had a point. "I hear ya," I said.

There was a pause while we both took deep breaths.

Then he said, "The stolen jewelry. We let Eddie McLaine twist in the wind long enough. Also there's Betty Jane's missing drinking glass to account for. Tonight we're bringing Eddie in for an interview. Be here at 7:00 if you want to listen in. That sound like I'm cooperating with Mr. Washington's girl Friday?"

Ignoring the provocation, or rather, filing it for later, I said, "What excuse will we give to account for my presence?"

"You won't exactly be in the same room with her."

That afternoon, Kay pitched erratically for three innings before relievers took over. The Kid had a super fast ball but couldn't control it. In the 5th inning, center fielder Connie Shulz rifled a throw directly into Eddie's mitt, nailing a runner at home. The brilliant play didn't matter; we lost 10-3.

At 7:00 p.m. I pressed a large highball glass to the wall adjoining Shupe's office. This was Burton City PD's latest technology for listening in.

At first Eddie spoke so faintly I could hardly hear. Right off she admitted the theft, said she'd been on tenterhooks about the whereabouts of the jewelry sack, but since it had gone missing directly after the police search, she figured they had confiscated it. She had pumped Clint for information, but he acted like a dummy.

Although Clint and Shupe were good buddies, throwing darts together in the Elite Café on Monday nights, I figured the chief had not confided in the manager. Perhaps he felt that Clint was too involved with Eddie, owing her team-wise and to some extent, personally, too.

When Shupe roared, "Speak up. We can hardly hear you," I suppose Eddie was to assume he was using the royal we. Fortunately he didn't ask that she address loud comments to the wall.

She raised her voice. "I took the trinkets on different occasions, as an example to the girls, to show how unimportant such trinkets are. My girls are not to be spending hard earned money on trifles that break or wear out. Food, clothing, shelter, that's what we spend our earnings on. Not everyone has a sugar daddy. And I was right. They got over missing the junk easily enough. It was only when somebody stole Betty Jane's drinking glass that she made a major crime of it. Betty Jane insisted that the theft be investigated. Big deal from a big shot." Contempt was in her voice. "So after that, we reported all the thefts so nobody would think I was favoring one girl over the others."

"Where is the drinking glass?"

"I don't know. I did not take that glass. It was a ten-cent glass, for heaven's sake. She bought another one right away, anyhow."

The chief segued smoothly. "Why'd you take the crimson paint? Was Dinah spending too much money on her art?"

"No! I don't know. I don't know anything about that."

"Hmm." After letting the denial settle, Shupe said, "The jewelry wasn't in your locker when we searched right after Betty Jane's murder. When and why did you put it in there?"

She gave her nose a lengthy blow. I could picture the hanky being twisted into weeping nostrils. "The day before Millicent Tubbs died," she said. "Unlucky me. I was going to leave it out in the locker room, to give it back."

"Why?"

"It is not Christian to steal."

"Where did you keep it before then?"

"In my home."

Poor troubled woman, hired to lead a bunch of fractious girls by example while bound up in her own frustrations. In the end, Shupe released her after a warning not to skip town. Fat chance, what with Clint, the girls, the game, and her criminal sister apparently her only interests in life. Before she left, Shupe advised that he might bring charges later, because of the one expensive item, the onyx ring, but he'd wait until the season was over to decide. If that happened, she could plead guilty and possibly get off with paying a fine.

As soon as she was gone, Shupe bustled into my listening room and relieved me of the large tumbler, placing it on the technological shelf next to headphones, a fingerprint kit, a Brownie Hawkeye flash camera, and a police radio.

He summed up the interview. "That pitiful lady is going home alone with only a low-life sister for comfort. Pining for Clint like she does, and with all the pressure on her, no wonder she's unbalanced. Watch out you don't get into that situation, Wendy. I mean, you're too goddam sensitive for this kind of dangerous life. It's fuckin' hard even for us men." He became expansive. "You're a good-looking gal. Bet you'll be snatched up by some rich farmer before this case is over."

"Doubt it. This PI's main man is Yegg Washington. I got a real crush on him."

His lips tightened. Coming from me, that name seemed to offend.

Since I'd heard nothing more from any Hornette about reporting for funning duty at Dinah's that Monday night, I headed straight home after the interview. The next day in the locker room, no one mentioned the party I had neglected to attend so I assumed my initiation rites had been tabled until everything had settled down.

That evening, after a second loss to the Alices of which I took no part, I went back to the hotel and settled in bed with a pack of licorice twists and a Coca-Cola. To sleep, not a chance, but perchance to analyze. I was a better dick than Shupe was a cop, I knew that much. I had discovered the photo that he and his minions had missed. I was not so sure about Eddie, though. In many ways a noble woman, she was so frustrated with her existence that she sought revenge by stealing trinkets from her charges. Her big mistake was stealing the onyx ring, because that made the crime a felony. A lesson in jewelry appraisal might be in order if she was bent on continuing in that fashion.

16.

We lost all three games to the Alices. That made five defeats in a row since Betty Jane's death.

Eddie assigned the laundry to the next in line, Joanie Dober, after announcing that I was simply too undependable. The bay leaf jar had mysteriously returned and I put on my saddest face when handing it to Joanie.

The team's batgirl was back, her mother explaining she'd been down with the flu. With that, I was left with no duties at all. I was glad. "Do a job bad enough and you won't have to do it again," as Dad had said of my brothers.

The day after the third game, ten days after her death, the mortal remains of Betty Jean Wadlow, nee Lois Magic, were laid to rest in a graveside ceremony.

There was no church service preceding the burial, which was held on a hot, steamy afternoon. Betty Jane hadn't specified a religion in her Hornette records, although, recalling the antique cross now lodged in the in memorium cigar box, she must at least have been interested.

Leroy Williams was not let out of jail to attend. "As the suspect, he'd probably be torn to bits," Shupe justified. Although most townsfolk seemed willing to postpone a lynching party until all the facts were in, there had been several vengeful letters sent in anonymity to the newspaper.

The Gazette had confirmed Sid's initial article, reporting Betty Jane's real name and that Leroy was her husband. Now that she was gone, it didn't seem to matter to fans that their favorite player had served a wee bit of time in a distant state for what must have been a minor offense. Fears among the community that a murderer might still be at large seemed to have diminished with Leroy's incarceration.

A sizable crowd wearing dark clothing and severe expressions attended the interment. An anonymous donor had sent a cashiers check for $688, earmarked "for the casket of Lois Magic." Team members speculated as to who the donor might be and decided on Fred Hamff, an avid fan who never missed a home game. Mr. Hamff, owner of Hamff Iron Works, was a voluble man whose cheeks were rosy from the heat of his fiery furnaces. Twyla said it was unlike Fred to give and not claim credit. He bragged of every good turn: Salvation Army, Community Chest, Masons, etc.

"Although donating a specific amount does sound like ol' frugal Fred," said Twyla's sweetheart, Joanie.

"Okay. If not him, who?" asked Letta.

When approached, Fred Hamff accepted thank you's with noncommittal gracefulness. Whoever the donor, the money was used to purchase a fine oak casket lined with tucked and rolled velvet.

Bused to the cemetery, we Hornettes alighted like flowing black birds into the humid morning. A few clouds patched the sky, barely able to hold their own in the heat. Eddie was poised and dignified, but dark splotches under her eyes suggested she had cried. For herself or Betty Jane? Hard to tell.

Center fielder Connie attended with her husband, a tall, lanky soldier in a smartly pressed uniform, under orders to go to Korea. The pair was holding hands when Connie asked Eddie if she might say a few words during the ceremony.

Before Eddie could reply, Pepper latched onto the notion. "Yep, as her best friend I want to say stuff too."

Ignoring Pepper, Eddie addressed Connie firmly. "No, you can not speak. Clint and I will speak for all of us today. If you'd asked me earlier so I could run through your lines, then maybe, but I'm not up to enduring any off the cuff remarks." That seemed a pretty severe reaction to a simple request, but it was also meant for Pepper, who might have blurted out anything. Hearing that, Pepper gave the ground a good stomp. Connie's husband reacted differently, tenderly touching his wife's face and tucking a stray hair behind her ear.

Eddie fled to join Clint. He looked devastated, his creased face weighted with grief.

"Gosh dang it," Pepper said after the two leaders had retreated a few yards down the path, "I wanted to tell the world about our lifelong friendship."

"Not true," I said. "You first met Betty Jane as Lois Magic in jail last year. Isn't that right?"

"Oh," she said, "I suppose. What do you say to this: I heard two cops in the café this morning, going on about you and Sid, how you're as thick as thieves."

"Really?" I said. "Interesting. Is it true about Betty Jane's dad asking you to get her a tryout with the Hornettes?"

She snapped her gum. "You bet it is. Day I got out of prison in Helena, he introduced himself and asked for the favor. I had no problem granting it because I loved her like a sister."

"Uh-huh." It was hard to believe Pepper about anything, much less love and sisters. "Is Betty Jane's father here today?"

She gave a cursory glance around. "You kidding? They couldn't stand to have a thief for a daughter. Her parents ran out on her. I think they worked for the circus, had to travel all over to make a living. I don't think Betty Jane knew or cared where they were when she got out. They had writ her off and vi-sa-versa." She folded another stick of Juicy Fruit gum into her mouth and broke it in vigorously.

"That day when her old man asked me for help," she said, "must a been 'cause he wanted to give her one last chance be on the straight and narrow. Like Eddie prides herself doing with me. I mean, who needs it?" She spat the last statement venomously. All in all, I didn't know whether to believe a girl who lied as easily as I did.

Seven of the heftier ballplayers, Dinah included, carried the casket, four on one side, three on Dinah's side. Floating down the cemetery path, they swooped the box onto a platform beside the open grave. Even though they made the task look easy, six of the seven said later that the expensive box was so heavy it was a struggle to keep ahold of the brass railing. The seventh simply flexed her muscles.

The team moved to sit in wooden folding chairs that had been set graveside. A Protestant minister spoke a prayer and then Clint mounted the steps to the podium, adjusted the microphone and stammered, "She w-w-wahr wonderful pitcher and f-f-friend." He broke into sobs until Eddie reached up and guided him off the platform. Taking his place, she lowered the microphone a bit, and with eyes wide and black, delivered a ringing eulogy, her tones echoing over the sloping hills where mourners stood swaying slightly and shifting their feet. In closing she said, "Our dear departed teammate, Betty Jane Wadlow, or …" An attempt to recall the birth name failed. "… transformed a bunch of average ball players into a championship unit, in ability, in spirit, and in record. We wish she could have taken us all the way." To which those assembled uttered a collective, "Ahh."

Afterward, the Hornettes rose almost as one, to tremble our way through the team song, the rendition of which I prefer not to describe.

A simple marker, pictured the evening before in the Gazette, would indicate the grave:

BETTY JANE WADLOW
nee Lois Magic
1924-1950
SAFE AT HOME

The reception was held in the cavernous Burton City Armory. Connie and Letta had finished setting out the buffet when I arrived. The eats had been catered by the local bakery: ham and cheese on fresh bakery buns, baked beans, potato chips, and cole slaw. Two bowls of lemon jello spotted with black licorice drops. A huge cake with a yellow and black Hornette logo decorating it.

"Wow," Joanie said, viewing the feast. "Makes you almost want to die."

A good crowd attended, including most of our ballplayers and a few young women I assumed were from other league teams. There were scads of card tables set about, wooden folding chairs at each.

Concerned they'd run out of food early and this being a favorite meal, I immediately filled a plate. Adding globs of mustard, my favorite condiment, I dove in. Finishing that, I sliced off a large piece of cake. I looked away when biting into a portion of hornet leg. All was washed down with Dr. Peppers in the stagnant heat.

Chairs were plentiful, but most of the attendees preferred to mill, although exceptions were some hefty men in dark suits who overloaded their plates and sat together at a corner table. After dining off a white tablecloth, they exited, not stopping to chat with anyone. One got the sense that they considered themselves elite, pronounced the correct way.

Throughout the room, a strong hum of conversation prevailed, the usual release that follows a funeral. Most of the Hornettes stayed grouped together like one giant human cactus, prickly to well-meaning townspeople who tried to crash. Mostly shy girls from farm country, they didn't socialize very well. The exception, Pepper, on the other side of the room, had slipped her hand through the arm of a cowpoke-type.

I spotted Clint shoveling down potato chips. I sauntered over to ask who those very private dark-suited men were.

"It's the entire league office," he responded proudly. "Every one of them shook my hand. Mr. Washington ordered them to be here for this and they'd be served a nice lunch and good drinks. They put a spray of roses on the casket. The card says 'From the League.' I'm gonna keep that card. She was a great pitcher. They knew her value."

Quite a mouthful from a mouth that was full. I asked when the team was getting another pitcher.

"Mr. Washington hasn't said. After making sure her memory was honored, he probably thought his job was done and went on a vacation." That sounded cynical.

Probably the extreme show of respect for the slain pitcher was meant to be a show for the major league commissioner. Now that was cynical, too.

On a lighter note, I asked Clint what Dinah's nickname, M&M, stood for. "It's probably not the candy."

"She thinks it is, but, well, I can't control what the team thinks is all in fun."

"You're stalling; I won't tell, I promise." I crossed my heart.

He looked around warily, to see if Dinah was nearby, but she remained stuck in the cactus. "Stands for Man Mountain Dean, the Man and Mountain part," he said. "Joanie thought it up." He shook a finger. "If Dinah finds out there'll be big trouble."

"It'll mean Maim and Maul, then," I laughed.

"It's no joking matter." As several fans approached, Clint's eyes warmed painfully and he tried to become an upbeat, forward-looking leader. "Watcha say, fellas," he said to their gruff greetings. Clint was all about publicity; could put on a happy face when required. I backed away to let the well-wishers in. I drifted over toward Fred Hamff, and when the crowd parted, I stepped forth to thank him for the lovely casket.

"Hey, pretty girl, if I did it, I don't want any credit for it." The corpulent iron works magnate made a grand gesture that ended with an arm sweeping behind, trying to goose me.

"None of that now," I said, waggling a finger and jumping back.

Next I made myself known to Sid. He was interviewing Kay but when he spotted me, he abandoned the youngster and crossed to me.

We interviewed each other. Every conversation with the sportswriter seemed like a mutual quest for information. How alike we were in that respect. I led with "What's the latest, Sid?"

"What do you hear from the locker room?" he countered.

"We're not winning."

"Yeah, that about says it all. I sent a picture of our Betty Jane to Sperry and Mike says he showed it around. Nobody recognized her, so she lied about being from there. Contacting the reformatory is my next step. They'll have a record of her hometown, I hope. I can't get to Leroy Williams. He's stashed in solitary. The chief wants whatever he says to remain private for the trial."

"Leroy hire a good lawyer?"

"Haven't heard if he even got one. Hasn't been charged yet and can't pay for counsel anyhow."

"I don't think the guy's much interested in his defense or anything else since she went out of his life."

"Hmm. Undying love." He examined me. "So you're from down south. You sure sound like it."

"Right. The bayou. Excuse me, I see somebody I know." No use submitting my biography from birth to present day until I concocted it.

I had recognized a muscular young Negro woman off by herself, stowing away ham and cheese on a bun with almost as much gusto as I had. Her presence today, among the fair-skinned, indicated she had guts. I knew who she was: the only Negro player in the league and its best catcher, bar none including Eddie. She played for the Davenport Sofies.

I went to her and said, "You're Betty Gibson, aren't you?"

"Bet I am," she said. She took a mammoth bite of sandwich and chewed for a while. Then she said, "You look familiar too."

Batgirl duties, no doubt. "I'm an infielder with the Hornettes, currently hobbled by injury."

"Tough," she said, not sympathetically.

"Something particular about Betty Jane bring you here today?"

"Why? Something wrong with it?" Her sharp response caused me to maintain an especially pleasant expression. I wasn't awfully surprised by the instant hostility - her presence in the league had brought some brutal remarks from the stands. If teammates objected to her excellence, I hadn't heard one way or another. My demented grin must have won her over, or maybe she needed to unload her grief on someone. Either way, she said, "Betty Jane stuck up for me once. After a game, her and me came out of the clubhouse about the same time. A guy was waiting for me. I recognized him; we'd exchanged pleasantries the night before at a church social. This time, after I shrugged him off, he grabbed aholt of my arm and was real strong 'bout wanting me to go off with him. Betty Jane came over and asked him politely to scat along outta there. He said something real crude back to her and she got a look in her eyes that said she might have to hurt him. He laughed at her and yanked my arm in a ownership way and when he wouldn't let go, she delivered him a real haymaker. Boy, did he go down hard. She kicked him a couple in the shins. He let loose a stream of cussin' and slunk off. A couple of the Hornettes were standing around with their boy friends. They saw all of it but didn't do nothing. Betty Jane stuck up for me. I'll never forget it."

"Yes," I breathed. "That's Betty Jane in a nutshell, that's exactly how she was." I was bluffing, of course, but the incident did fit my idea of the dead woman exactly. For the first time in this miserable case that image was verified: Betty Jane was brave and stalwart. She could control situations on and off the field. She was not any sort of a divisive element.

Afterward I drove to Dave's. With self-improvement utmost in mind, I immediately took baseball and glove from the Nash and insisted we shut the dogs in the house and then play catch. After he reluctantly agreed, I burned them in. He showed his disinterest by lobbing the ball back with all the power of a butterfly.

A half hour later, after getting in a few good at-bats off his wimpy pitches, I socked a mighty blow that landed in the cornfield. He refused to chase after it so I retrieved it myself, thinking of it as endurance training. Afterward, to appease him, we went to the bowling lanes in town. There we'd always been evenly matched, which meant I usually made sure Dave won.

On the lanes, my competitive nature irritated him. As my score moved steadily ahead of his, I suppose I could have rolled a few into the gutter but I didn't. Something about being around the strong, agile Hornette women, who played with intensity even while losing, didn't allow me to let up.

Even when I didn't get a strike, but settled for a spare, Dave got more and more grim, neck clenching before each of roll. Talk about intensity. Between frames during the third game, he said in a clipped voice, "I don't mind if you beat me but not this badly."

I posed, ball in hand. "What do you mean?"

"I mean, not only do you have to win, but you have to win big. It's from being around those Amazons."

Leaning forward, I released the ball. It missed the head pin completely. "Gosh darn, Dave, you're spoiling my concentration." I poked his arm and grinned.

"Your sassy mouth doesn't become you either."

"You never complain when you're winning."

Lips clamped, he hot-rodded me in his Continental back to the farm while I kept my arms folded tight across my chest, praying we wouldn't crash. When we arrived with a screeching halt, I headed straight from his car to mine. The baseball equipment, including his glove, lay beside my overnight bag in the back seat.

He trailed after, his attitude moderating. "Okay, I played stupid ball of various sorts with you. Now come on inside and I'll feed you. You owe me a second act. I bet it turns out better than the first one."

"You mean the jumping into bed part? This hardly counts as good foreplay, bud." Slamming my door, I said through the open window, "Until you can come my way a little, and appreciate what I'm doing."

"So it's to be tit for tat, huh," he said sullenly.

I gunned the engine and reversed out of the driveway, spinning gravel on the way. In the rearview, Dave's face, contorted and powder white, was lost in the dust.

Speeding away I felt as if I had slid off the plastic seat and was floating in space, rising into the wild horse latitudes where there was nothing to hang onto.

17.

At 5:00 the next morning, the sound of a mop thwacking against cement greeted me as I approached the Hornettes' locker room. Janitor Darrell Moeller, a slight, gimlet-eyed man, confronted me, mop at the ready. The floor beyond him was washed down.

"Not one step farther," he warned.

To my right, a storage closet stood open, the weaponry of cleaning aligned in a row: brooms, mops, a shovel, various size vacuums and brushes. Standing by for touch-up were feather dusters in a bucket.

I gushed, "I said to my teammates, gotta meet this wonderful cleaning man even if I have to get up before the cock crows. They say you discovered the body. Well, you'd never know there was one, the way you spiffed up the area." I paused to marvel, and added confidentially, "Must have been awful messy."

He slapped his forehead, setting keys jangling that were hooked to his belt. "That lady left puddles of blood and hair and even a chunk of scalp. But the worst part was the brains. This job's been a no-go from the beginning. Lipstick!" He paused for effect. I recoiled in empathy. "Last July, they left it running down a mirror onto the wall. I scrubbed hard, but you can still see the stains. Those are marks that will never come off."

I peered where he pointed, but saw no blemishes. "Sad," I said agreeably. "It's the state of young people nowadays." Since I had heard enough cranky oldsters say that, the opinion flowed off my tongue.

"Slobs!" he barked. "Whoa, that's far enough." Leaning toward the mirror, I jumped a little and straightened up.

He relaxed a tad, saying, "You on the team?"

"Yes, but I just arrived so I don't make messes yet. Most the time, I just sit in my car awaitin' the call, haven't even unpacked the lipstick." Fortunately at that early hour I wore no makeup. "Say, some time ago, did you come across a photo of a young man on the unused side of this room? It would have been near where the body was. A friend lost it and wanted me to ask. She thought she might have dropped it over there a while back."

"Nobody uses that side. What was she doing over there anyhow?"

I shrugged. "She's young and adventurous."

"It's not there or I'd have spotted it. Warn her not to go over there any more, except taking the route to the showers and then no wandering. There's enough work without that side added to it."

I firmed my stance. "You sure you didn't just mop over the picture and let it lay? Kinda aggravated, were you, about some girl's carelessness? Where's the lost and found box?"

He grinned evilly. "It stays empty. Whatever I find goes in the trash." A ponderous silence descended.

Finally he said, "You leaving?"

I shattered his hopes by asking, "You clean the manager's office regularly?"

"Why is that your business?"

"For my health. If I'm ever invited in there, I have to wonder if it's … uh, quite sterile."

He let out a howl. "Appling is a slob. I don't bother going into that pig sty except when the fat lady nags."

"Uh-huh, uh-huh." I backed into the hall while keeping an eye out for a fuming janitor. My mind was on the cleaning tools in the broom closet. One of those implements could have been used to kill Millicent Tubbs. Far-fetched, considering that a recent inquest had ruled Millicent's death accidental, no evidence presented to the contrary. Still, I wondered if Chief Shupe had thought to examine the shovel, for instance, for blood traces.

As far as the janitor was concerned, it was a cinch he wouldn't rescue a lost snapshot left in a forbidden area by some trespassing numbskull. I wasn't sure what one tiny picture could mean to my murder case.

That day the team was notified that Millicent Tubbs' body was to begin its trip back to Missouri for burial. On a warm gray afternoon that held the strong possibility of rain, we assembled at the ball field for a rehearsal of a short ceremony that Eddie made up on the spot, to honor a deceased player who otherwise would be sent off alone.

Afterward, the team loaded into several players' cars and we drove to the depot, in uniform, with our bats. Clint arrived in the Buick with the hornet painted on the door. Aha, I had found the owner of the picturesque Buick. I could have guessed, because Clint never overlooked a chance for publicity.

As mortuary employees brought forth Millicent's box from the hearse, the team formed two smart lines opposing each other, eight to a side for the ceremony of the casket. At Eddie's command, "Raise ash with your right hands, trademark facing the departed!" we formed an arch with our ash-made bats under which the casket passed. As honorary bats-man, it was Clint's duty to swat the backside of the casket as it emerged from our arch. With that swat, the late Millicent Tubbs officially became Milly Tubbs, an official member of the Burton City Hornettes.

Immediately afterward, someone whispered, "I saw lightning," and the team made an ignominious retreat because every ballplayer is terrified of lightning. That was okay; the remains were practically on board the boxcar anyhow.

Okay, so the ceremony was a little goofy, but it was done with the utmost sincerity. You don't mock Mister Death.

Sid took multiple photos, none of us fleeing, of course, and the best appeared in the next edition which thrilled Clint, the hound for promoting the team.

The team went on the road for three games against the tough Davenport Sophies. Neck and neck with us for third place, the way we were going, they'd soon pass us. That first afternoon, the small crowd sat glumly as though they had come only to evaluate our mood.

Riding the bench, I watched as side-armer Molly Powell and a dismal troop of relievers failed to get more than a couple of outs. In addition the Willeys slow-handled a couple grounders. We lost, 10-6.

Trotting onto the field a couple hours before the third game, (we'd also lost the second) I saw Sid Dobrotka behind the batting cage interviewing Dinah. Sid rarely travelled out of town to cover a women's series. There must not have been a threshing bee or horseshoe toss in Burton City that weekend.

Dinah was yammering at the sportswriter that "One a them witches made it look like I done it," the repeat of a theme that Sid, being the company man, would never print. In response, he soothed, "Oh, Dinah, I don't hardly think so." Not wishing to interrupt and be granted the patented M&M glower, I sprinted toward the outfield as humid breezes stuck to my skin.

Kay and three other players were chatting it up near the outfield fence. Not working out, Eddie would soon put a stop to that. I looked around for the chaperon to see if I dared join them in slothfulness. No sign of her. Sprinting toward the four, I saw that the talk was not friendly. Joanie, Twyla, and Pepper had Kay pressed back against the fence.

I was fed up with those cliquey girls needling the rookies, me included. On the bus trip to Davenport, Joanie had hotfooted my tennis shoe as I napped, to the delight of the old-timers. Okay,

Yegg Washington, I'm submitting a bill for a new pair of leather Naturalizer street shoes.

Kay was peering over Joanie's shoulder in a wordless appeal for help. The other three turned to see who held her attention. Seeing it was only me and not the big bad chaperon, they parted and made room.

"Winkie, we're filling the kid in about M&M," Pepper said. "How she's the biggest cunt-chaser in the league."

Twyla echoed. "Dinah loves rookie pussy."

"Speaking from experience, Twy?" I cracked. In attacking the girl's sexual orientation, I was placing her on the defensive. Star-Spangled League rules dictated that team members must be heterosexual, and not an over supply of that.

Twyla fiddled with her glove. "I'm just supporting Pepper," she said mutedly, "everybody knows she likes guys."

"Yeah, the tomcatters just love me," Pepper said. "Wisht I found one wanting to see me a second time."

"Meow, meow," Joanie said. "Your problem is you got bad taste in gender."

Pepper gave her a mock shove.

Kay piped up. "They're kidding, ain't they, Winkie, about M&M? It ain't true, is it?"

"Probably not."

"It is too true," Pepper said. "I'm scared for you rookies. It's not only M&M, it's all the old-timers looking to catch you alone for immoral purposes." Pepper pinched Kay's cheek. The Kid shrank and tears formed.

"Oh, come on," I said, mightily irritated.

"Let up, Pep," Joanie said, "can't you see the kid's going to cry?"

Eyes cruel, face flushed, Pepper swatted at Kay, slightly brushing her crotch. The action shocked the perpetrator as much as it did the rest of us and she jammed the offending hand into a shorts pocket. Reflexively Kay covered her private parts.

"That's not funny," Joanie said, shoving Pepper backwards into the fence. Hitting with a thud, Pepper rebounded, freed the pocketed fist and wrestled Joanie to the ground.

A familiar voice came from behind. "Get up. Stop that!"

They stopped punching. "Which you want?" Joanie smart-mouthed, gazing up at Eddie, "Get up or stop that getting up?"

The chaperon ignored the semantic by-play. "Pepper, you're taking things too far again."

Pepper got to her feet and opened her mouth to sass. Eddie waited for the first hint of sound before striking an openhanded blow across her sister's face. Wild anger flared in Pepper's eyes. Everyone stared in shock and time seemed to stand still for a few seconds.

Then Joanie and Twyla spun away and raced after a popup that had been fungo-hit by Bobby Bied. When they spotted one of the other outfielders circling under it, they slackened their pace but remained well away from our zone of contention.

"Come on, Kay, let's leave Pepper to feel herself up," I said. "Maybe she'll find out what sex she really is." I disliked sinking to Pepper's level, but wanted to observe any more outsized reactions from the redhead, and from her supposed keeper. But neither responded. Instead, as Kay and I scooted, I heard Eddie ask Pepper what Winkie had meant by that.

Slowing to a walk, I assessed the situation. The lesbian thread, now extended to Dinah and half the team, according to Pepper. Almost certainly false. Joanie, Twyla, and Pepper had alibied each other for the night of Betty Jane's death. Had they formed a protective society of three, a straight with two curvatures? Perhaps they stuck together because each, for different reasons, was on the outs with society.

Kay and I reached the foul line. There we halted and I said, "Next time walk away or punch them out."

"I can't," she wailed.

"Why not?" This was a strong kid who could have leveled any one of the tormentors.

"Because everybody here seems like big people. Older, smarter, I mean."

"You're not that much younger," I said, but at seventeen and a loser, I could see why she'd see it that way.

I left Kay to play catch with Connie, one of the more tolerant veterans what with her soldier husband destined for Korea.

In late afternoon, the sun was peeking out as I hustled toward the batting cage. Several players waited in a ragged line, wiping hands on blouses, gripping and ungripping their bats to get the feel. In turn each woman stepped to the plate, took three swings against Clint's flat easy pitches and got out of there so as many as possible could get their cuts in.

Sid approached as I extracted my 30-ounce piece of lumber from the rack and short-chopped the air. Clad in western denims and an iron-creased checkered shirt, he looked as fresh as a loaf of bakery bread.

Used to seeing him in frayed outfits, I said, "You're looking sharp. New threads?"

"Yep, I was getting awfully shabby." He smiled and I felt a tingle course through me. Spotting the gleam of fun in my eyes, he beamed back. I glanced away, feeling somewhat put upon. I mean, there I was, vulnerable after breaking off with Dave, and already another guy was taking advantage, with a new wardrobe and fun-loving hazel eyes and a come-hither smile. How did he know I was ready? Simple. By my "come on baby" attitude, of course.

I sought diversion. On the mound, Clint pitched a floater to Dinah, who sent the ball on a far and away ride. The few Davenport fans that had come out early gasped with apprehension.

"What a beautiful swing Dinah's got," Sid said. "Amazing reflexes. She whips it around so fast and with all that power. Too bad she's not a man."

"Huh?" I couldn't let that go. As a woman doing a job normally reserved for a man, I got irritated easily.

"Hey," he spotted the warning sign, "don't take offense. I only meant women's sports aren't where the action is. At the rate I'm going, I'll never get hired by a major paper." He showed his palms. "Now don't get your dander up. I enjoy watching the girls play. Really." Sid was pouring oil on troubled waters before they even got to churning.

"Shortening the base paths from ninety feet to sixty-eight and moving the pitcher's mound in closer makes the game as fast as the men's. Yep, the Hornettes are able enough, present company possibly excepted. The game's just not significant in the eyes of those who count. Pay's low too, working for the Gazette. Cost a bundle for these new duds, but worth it if the lady is impressed." He rocked on his heels until I acknowledged with a nod. The cocky grin returned.

"Didja know I'm official scorekeeper for home games? Bring in extra shekels that way."

I knew that already. In Burton City, leaning from the dugout, I had spotted him in the fourth row behind home plate, signaling with a scorecard to the PA announcer: hit or error, passed ball, wild pitch, or some other necessary ruling.

"Wendy Winkworth." The name sounded desirable the way he pronounced it. "I've decided to do a feature on you. 'Utility player with remote prospects has dreams too.' What's the name of the brassiere company team you played for?"

"The Brassiere Company Bouncers," I improvised instantaneously, maybe a little too fast. Darn my sense of humor.

"Uh-huh, uh-huh." His approval of the ridiculous came instantly. He took a small notebook from his shirt pocket and pressed it to his lips to keep from snickering. Drat, if he'd wanted to appreciate my little rib-tickler, he should have burst into honest laughter and then waited for a serious response.

He scribbled. "Be a terrific article. I'm writing it all down."

I believed I knew my man. Wouldn't be surprised if he checked out the team's name as soon as he got to a phone. I'd be a lot more surprised if there were such a team, but that sort of luck was for lottery winners, not me. Let's face it, if push came to shove, Sid's ambition might override any other interest he had in me.

That slip of mine was a harbinger of disaster if I continued to pass myself off as a ballplayer. I needed a profession where there was no expert around to question my credentials. I'd work on it.

18.

When it was my turn to hit, I struck each of Clint's three pitches sharply, sending the first two down the third base line and his final easy toss through the pitcher's box so he had to jump. That was the best I'd done, maybe because I was still jacked up from the dispute in centerfield.

"Way to go, Winkie," chirped Connie from the sideline.

Jogging in from the outfield, Eddie gestured for Kay to meet her in the bullpen down the first base line. In about two hours, the kid was to make her second start. If it began as badly as the first, I knew Clint would have her out of there fast. Already reliever Letta Lorrimer was throwing to reserve catcher Helen Sanders near the outfield fence.

I intercepted Clint as he trotted off the field, and said, "You see how much I've improved? I might have come in incompetent, but I've sure toughened up. So when do I get into a game?"

He didn't slow his pace, indeed tried to move right past me. "Sorry, Winkie, but I gotta put a winning team on the field. If we ever get ten runs ahead, I'll think of substituting you. For right now, your place is on the bench, cheering on the others."

"Darn," I griped, "I might as well be married." He tried to shove a sourball in my hand but I wouldn't be appeased.

Hustling past on her way to the bullpen, Eddie said, "Think about it, you got anyone feels that strong for you."

"Hey!" I dashed in front of her. "I'm part of the team too, so stop making fun."

Her lips parted. She was astonished that a miserable peon like me would challenge her. With a "Humph," she bumped me going by.

Absorbed in indignation, I stood for a while watching Kay's pitches thudding into Eddie's glove.

That poor kid had about as much chance at a win as I did becoming an All-Star. Her pitching motion was effortful, as if she were shot-putting an 8-pound ball. The baseball had little movement and no spin. The cockiness Kay once had was gone, the Alices' slugfest in her previous start had seen to that.

Eddie rose off her haunches and trudged to Clint, who was chawing and spitting, no doubt deep in his own worry. She poked him and they shared a confidence behind her mitt. Watching the two leaders, Kay pounded her glove and hunched her shoulders.

I began stretching. Kay trotted over. "Watchyer doing? Looks weird."

"Warming up my muscles."

"Hah. Why bother? You won't get off the bench."

"Hey, twerp, I saved you from the mean girls and this is how you say thanks?" I gave my neck an aggravated jerk and felt a sharp pain.

Seeing I was hurtfully upset, she said, "Thanks for rescuing me out there."

I faced her. "No problem. Betty Jane would have done the same."

"Nah she wouldn't. She stayed to herself mostly."

"All you know. In the old days she was a tiger when someone was in distress." I would remind myself of Betty Jane's saintliness whenever possible. So I wouldn't forget.

"You're real smart, ain't you?" she said.

"Those gals acted awful," I said, "but everybody has their bad days. It's the price for being human."

"I'd sure like to be as brainy as you are."

Well sure, who wouldn't? But this kid, The Kid, needed to lighten up, laugh and share some jokes with somebody friendly. The neck pain had eased. I began massaging the index finger of my throwing hand, which was still sore from jamming a knuckle when I dived after one of Dave's piddling tosses that last time we were together. Bobbing my eyebrows, I said lightly, "Watch. These are motions that strengthen the three muscle groups in the pitching hand. When I pull," I yanked a finger, "those muscles stretch despite themselves. They don't want to, but I make 'em. When I twist," I twisted the finger, "agh, that hurt some, but it strengthens, and soon enough these fingers become strong as steel." I supplemented with a few finger flutters as if tapping a cigar. I shook the hand out because it was beginning to tingle. "The old circulation," I said with phony wisdom. "Sure feels good when blood starts flowing again."

"You're kidding me like they did."

"Do I look funny?" I waggled my eyebrows and imagined how funny I looked.

She shook out her pitching arm and massaged her fingers, afterward twisting the index digit excruciatingly hard. She did not cry out as I had.

"Whoa," I cautioned. "These exercises can be dangerous for amateurs."

"I'm a pro. I can do them right now better than you."

"Okay," I said. At this point, I didn't think letting her know I was kidding was the best plan.

Eddie had returned from her discussion with Clint. Flicking her glove, she called for Kay to get back to work. The Kid trotted back to the bullpen mound. Eddie folded her mitt against a sizable thigh and squatted with a groan. A lot of wear and tear went into a catcher's knees.

"All right, babes," she thumped the mitt, "put it here baby, right in here."

Kay stood rooted, the ball resting in the dirt, as she pulled on a finger, twisting and rubbing it before moving to the next finger and repeating the treatment.

"You milking a cow?" Eddie said, "pick up the ball and pitch it."

Kay snatched up the horsehide, reared back and let fly a zinger that smacked into the catcher's mitt without Eddie being ready. She expelled a "Whoops," and fell over backwards.

From a distance, Clint shouted, "Thought you said she didn't have it."

I sauntered nearer to take credit in case The Kid threw like that twice in a row.

Eddie bounced onto her haunches and fired the ball back. She stood and went to get her mask. Donning it, she shook out her curls to preserve that Star-Spangled comeliness. "Do that again, Kid," she said, resuming the squat.

Meanwhile, after depositing the ball on the ground, Kay was lengthening, twisting and yanking the various fingers and, lastly, shaking out her arm. "The ol' circulation," she clarified wisely to me.

I nodded with authority. The Kid seized the ball and with the swiftest of windups, hurled it at Eddie's target. A doozy of a pitch; it rocked the sturdy catcher back on her heels, but this time she was prepared and didn't do a gymnastic flip.

Coming on the run, Clint exploded, "Jumpin' Jehosaphat," as tobacco juice squirted out his mouth.

"Baby, oh baby," Eddie exulted. "Baby, baby, BABY!"

Kay's lip curled, and her eyes snapped with something like contempt for the ignorant battery-mate.

"Fling that ol' pea, Kid," I yelled. "Fast as you can with Winks backing you up."

That night the Hornettes were on the field practically forever, what with our young pitcher engaging in mysterious rites before every pitch. The game went on so long that the chattery Willeys in the infield and Eddie behind the plate could barely croak encouragement during the almost endless late innings. Settling back on their heels, our outfielders grew very bored awaiting each pitch and made four errors born of inattention. But that worked both ways as Kay struck out eight flat-footed Sofie batters. En route, she walked one and allowed four hits before we nailed our second victory in the last nine games, 5-2.

In the early innings the Hornettes came off the field eyeing me and muttering amongst themselves. As Kay's success compounded inning by inning, silence descended along the bench, of awe edged with fear. Hearing Connie run through an entire Hail Mary, and Joanie imitating Connie with,"Hail Winkie full of shit," before dropping out, I responded by crossing a leg, jiggling the foot and popping my bubble gum.

After the final out, Eddie pumped my hand. "Nice bullshitting," she said, cracking a faint smile, and with that the others loosened up and soon were hollering and flinging themselves on each other in celebration of the win.

In Sid's interview afterward, Kay didn't mention me.

19

While the rest of the team was showering, Eddie slipped into a cotton dress with ruffled trim on the pockets, dark silk stockings and the customary high heels. She pranced off to the visiting manager's quarters. A half-hour later, when she returned flushed and contented it was obvious something was up. Whether she had confessed her kleptomania to him and he understood and taken her using old scorecards and chew tobacco pouches as mattress, I could only speculate and not sure I even wanted to.

In the locker room, she invited The Kid out to celebrate. At the door she hesitated. "Yeah, Winkie, you come too. I don't know what happened out there but I'm about to find out."

Kay told me that I had to get perfumed up, "like everybody else does." In each locker room, home and visitor, a large scent bottle labeled Tabu, was set near the door. I had been avoiding it except when doused by bad-tempered or prank-loving teammates. I didn't want my aroma getting where I was going three seconds before I did. Now, with Eddie at my elbow, I had no choice. Just a sprinkle of the stuff brought a tickle to my nose and made me want to sneeze.

"Don't take the whole bottle," Eddie instructed dryly and strode on ahead.

Watching her gain distance, Kay said, "We gotta smell Star-Spangly. It's Eddie's law and what a bore. My pop says you can tell by a woman's ripe smell if she's a hard worker and that's the only kind worth, uh, courtin'." After a pause she went on. "Eddie keeps her perfume private but I seen it. It's real pricy May-Wee parfum from Paree. That means 'but yes' in French, but no, it ain't for us ordinary folks."

So the victorious pitcher, catcher, and catalyst went in heels and frocks to the restaurant in the Tamarack Hotel where we were staying. Being asked out by the chaperon was special because it meant you didn't have to be in at curfew. On the road, the girls were required to be in their rooms one-half hour after showering. Tonight the extra hours of freedom would involve an interrogation, that much I knew. Best of luck, Madam Inquisitor. You'll need it.

The cozy restaurant was lit by three low-wattage bulbs in a crystal chandelier. Newly painted tan walls blended with the carpeting. We had our choice of table, since only one other couple was dining that night.

An impassive Negro waiter in twill trousers and matching shirt glided toward us, a white towel draped over an arm. At our table, he produced a kitchen match and lit the candlestick that was its centerpiece.

According to the menu, the establishment served only top quality canned vegetables. Although spaghetti was on special, we passed it up to order a couple of burgers apiece plus side salads with French dressing and large Coca-colas. In addition, Eddie ordered a Manhattan. Yegg Washington had dictated that players of drinking age might have only one glass of wine when dining out. Obviously Eddie saw herself as special and not merely one of the girls.

Now that Eddie seemed more tolerant of me, I decide to dig a bit. "It's marvelous how well the team gets along," I said. "Thanks to you, Eddie, for getting us all working together."

"Tonight you mean. Otherwise this group is a mess of conflicting personalities. It's a heckuva hard job I got right now."

"All the more credit to you. It was worse though, wasn't it, when Betty Jane was here? I mean, M&M being jealous and sticking a gun to her head and all that. Must have been hard for you to hear about."

"Darn that M&M. If I'd a been there it never would of happened. Normally funning brings out camaraderie but it sure didn't that time." The waiter delivered our orders and, after lighting a Tareyton, Eddie alternated drags with sips of the Manhattan. She bit into her burger and chewed many times before deciding what, if anything she wanted to add to the conversation. Finally she said, "There was only that one time. Mostly Betty Jane and M&M kept their distance. You must have noticed that we separate the rookies from the veterans."

"Uh-huh. We yannigans have the lockers farthest from the door, away from the old-timers like M&M and the Willeys."

She nodded. "Keeps the sweet young things away from the vets and their advanced ideas. About girls and I don't mean Pepper. She likes men as well as the next gal does."

"Yes, ma'am. Appreciate it."

Kay broke into the conversation. "Gimmee a nail, will ya, pardner?"

"Just one," Eddie said, handing over a cigarette. "After each win you get one." Kay stuck the smoke in her mouth but seemed reluctant to ask for a light. One step at a time. She rolled the cigarette between thumb and index finger and studied it before saying, "Another time Betty Jane and M&M really got into it was after a game where Betty Jane didn't pitch but we won anyhow. So here comes M&M sashaying down the aisle into the rookie section. I seen her coming and scooped up my Injun beads off the bench 'cause the aisle's way too narrow for M&M's swagger after she wins a game. She slugged a homer in the ninth."

Eddie had flinched at the mention of jewelry. I pretended I didn't notice.

"Eighth," she corrected, "and I'd not be telling stories to recent arrivals if I were you."

"Too late, Eddie," I said. "Besides I'm a Hornette, just like you."

She rolled her eyes "Not by golly like me." She swizzled the stick in her Manhattan.

But Kay wasn't to be stifled on her victory night. "Betty Jane was all dressed up and ready to cut out real quick like she always did. She was fastening that gold baseball necklace around her neck when M&M come up to her and said something like, 'Didn't need you out there today, my little pitcher pal.' That stopped everything. I swear Betty Jane came undone with that necklace pressed at her throat. She didn't have it hooked shut. She glared right through M&M. She said somethin' like, 'My gigantic first base fr-r-iend.' Betty Jane rolled her 'r's like a radio announcer so most everything she said sounded important. 'My GIGANTIC fir-r-st base fr-r-iend,'" Kay repeated, enjoying the attention, "'I don't need to sweat out ther-r-re on the field every day to make a heck of a lot mor-r-re money than you do.'"

Eddie gave a vigorous headshake and shoved a hand forward like a cop stopping traffic. "Hold it right there. The thing about money drove M&M nuts like it would any one of us. She snatched the necklace right off Betty Jane's neck and threw it against the lockers. She said a couple of nasty things. Betty Jane just stood and watched because she knew she had it coming. Betty Jane knew money was a sore point since no one's sure who's paid what, so, with no more sass she picked up the necklace, hooked it on, and walked out. End of story."

Not to Kay, who said, "We're supposed to be paid by seniority."

"Yeah, sure, but that's naïve, Kid," Eddie said. "There are plenty of under-the-table deals made with the most popular players. M&M's a star who's paid plenty, I bet, but the way Betty Jane taunted her, people kind of resented it, because how could she know what M&M made? Betty Jane had an arrogant streak. She just knew she was the most important one on the team and therefore made more money than the rest of us. I doubt it was true, but what do I know?" Her tone changed to bitterness. "I'm not important enough to be told about the salaries."

Kay bit off a hunk of sandwich and chewed. She said, "Once Betty Jane told me she didn't really need the money because her family was filthy rich. In fact they was so busy raking it in they didn't have time to come see her pitch. I felt sorry for her sometimes when she got moody; I thought it was because of her missing her kin."

"But her husband was here with her," I said.

"Didn't make no difference 'cause no one knew about him." Kay picked up her cigarette. "My pop comes to see me whenever he can."

"He here tonight?"

"Huh-uh. He wrote after that first game I started. Told me he was pretty upset I pitched so bad. Said maybe I should come back home and not waste any more of his time. He'll be happy now I won one. Always gotta prove myself to him. He's a tough son of a gun, except I'm glad he raised me to be a winner. Up to me to follow through on it and be one."

Eddie rolled her eyes. She tore a match off a book. "You gonna smoke that or just play with it?"

Kay stuck the fag in her mouth. She dragged until it was lit, blew out smoke and tried not to cough.

"What else did Betty Jane say about her family?" I asked.

She coughed once, drank some Coke. "That's about all, I guess." She examined me. "You didn't really know Betty Jane in Sperry, did you? Because maybe she wasn't never there, was she?"

"I admit I fudged on that, to get in good with the team."

Eddie sniffed, "Typical rookie." She lit a fresh cigarette off her old one, then made more progress on the Manhattan. "To me, Betty Jane acted like a poor girl who made good all of a sudden. Spending all that money on a gold necklace when she should have been saving for the future. She was rude. At our publicity dinners, she'd leave right after she ate, never staying around to hobnob like Clint and I have to do. Her folks weren't at the funeral, were they? Pepper says Betty Jane hadn't spoken to them since she went to jail. She told Pepper that they were filthy rich, too. Probably wishful thinking, like Pepper does sometimes. I have my sister reading Karen Horney, the psychologist, to improve her sense of self-worth. Stay away from that book, Winkie, you don't need it. You already got an over-supply of ego."

Don't read it yourself, I thought but didn't say.

"Wendy! How are you?" The amiable voice at my ear belonged to Sid Dobrotka. I smiled and nodded at him. Eddie bumped her chair over to make room for the one Sid was cramming in beside mine. Sliding into it, he stuck a Camel between his lips.

"Whoo-ee, talk about favoritism," Eddie said. "The two of us just pitched a four-hitter and Sid's serenading Miss Cutesy."

"You had your interview earlier," the sportswriter responded. His good humor faded. "I couldn't help overhearing what you said about Betty Jane. I found her to be very accommodating. Every inch a lady."

Eddie hooted. "Maybe you had a little too much personal interest." Her eyes caught mine. Eddie wanted me to note the sexual implication. Her tongue had loosened, maybe the result of drink.

Sid ignored her comment. "Betty Jane was a professional, above all the squabbling and horseplay that goes on. She arrived at the ballpark with her game face on and never let nobody put her down." The double negative reminded me that Sid often used bad grammar when with real ballplayers, something he never did with me.

"You're right," Eddie was saying. "She wore a mask from the time she walked into the locker room until she rushed off after the game. No outside crap ever got to her."

"Until right before she died," I qualified.

"Yeah, she was inconsistent in a couple of those later games. But that was because her arm was sore from Clint pitching her too much."

I had learned it was no use trying to change the beefy catcher's mind. Once she squatted on an idée fixe, she kept it warm.

"Sid," she went on, "What do you hear about the murder investigation?"

"Nothing new. The police believe they've caught the guy."

"What a relief. The girls are nervous that some fiend is going to creep through their windows and throttle them."

Kay looked kind of uneasy at that.

Trying to get the most out of the team chaperon while she was feeling talkative, I asked how Betty Jane got along with the manager.

"Why's that your business?" Eddie shot back.

"Betty Jane liked Clint," Sid said. "Sometimes after games she'd meet with him to go over various strategies."

"Strategies," Eddie brayed, "like how to get her panties off. Betty Jane had a cheap prettiness to her. She used entirely too much make-up."

"She was entirely too pretty and too blonde," Sid laughed.

Eddie stared at him. "She huddled with Clint after games. What do you expect from a young woman who desires … fatherly advice? Shoot, who'd believe that." She fixed Kay with a shrewd look.

Kay reacted. "Clint uses his after-hours time to work with the less experienced players, to our great benefit." The message sounded rehearsed, like she was preaching the party line.

"Clint's a skirt-chaser, pure and simple," Eddie stated.

"Geez, I didn't mean to get you started," Sid said.

"Eddie's got a soft spot for Clint, don't you, chaperon?" I said. "I saw that the first time we met."

"Don't act sorry for me," she said angrily. She uttered a despairing laugh. "I don't have any hope of making our relationship permanent. Clint is too much of a free spirit."

To me, the man looked hounded by the murder of his star pitcher and her replacement's untimely demise, not to mention by the chaperon.

Eddie used the moment to challenge me. "What I'm wondering more and more is why Clint keeps you around. He's never invited you to join his select group of dewy-skinned blondies, even though you're cute enough to qualify, and you sure as heck aren't a ball player."

"She's off and running," Sid groaned.

Select group of - ? I'd ponder that later. For now, I needed to offer an explanation for my presence on the team.

I thunked my Coke down on the table. "Eddie McLaine, you are partially correct. I am only a part-time ball player. Mr. Yegg

Washington, the esteemed owner of the Star-Spangled League, hired me, for I am primarily a psychologist and an expert in kinesiology." Fearing skepticism on the part of the unschooled, I offered a definition. "Kinesiology has to do with the spotting of bodily stress. I possess a double doctorate in both subjects."

"A Ph.DD," Sid murmured. "And so young." He pressed a pencil to quivering lips.

"Yes," I continued, "Mr. Washington was a star soccer player in his youth, so he knew the Hornettes would be down and depressed after the murder of their star pitcher. Consequently he hired me to infiltrate the team and, using the methods of my training, elevate team spirits and raise players' hopes for a positive future."

"How you doing so far?" Eddie asked.

I drew myself up. "Tonight, with Kay, you saw one result."

Sid uttered a strangled, "It's all true, I checked her out." With his astonishing verification, Eddie had no leg to stand on and so she withdrew into moody contemplation. I wasn't worried about Kay; she was already mine to mold.

I gave the table a single rap. "Okay," I said, "now that you know, you can't tell anyone. If the players find out, they'll clam up on me and I won't get anything accomplished. Keep in mind that it's Mr. Washington who signs our paychecks, and he insists on it being this way." Realistically I doubted the secret would be kept for long, but I hoped the three of them would stay mum for a little while. Anyhow, if I were to be exposed it was better to be as a psychologist and the other thing, rather than a PI.

"Hey!" Eddie yipped. "Joanie and Twyla are peeking around the corner. Those dykes are supposed to be in their room. Pepper said she'd keep track and tell me if they weren't."

We followed her gimlet-eyed gaze past a doorway into a dark hall. She rose, knocking her chair into Sid's. He caught and set it upright.

Kay shot out of her seat. "Let's go pound 'em, pardner." She wobbled in her heels.

"I'll handle it," Eddie said. "You save your pitching arm."

Hearing the raised voices, the two other diners, middle-aged men in suits, glanced over.

"Steady yourself, Kay," Eddie warned. "We are Star-Spangled girls and people are watching. We will walk very stately over to that doorway and when we rush the hall, I'll corral those babes while you provide backup. You can shove a little if necessary."

With an athletic stride, Eddie traversed the floor, Kay tottering after. I admired Eddie's balance in heels. I imagined her training for hours to be the perfect poster gal for the Star-Spangled League. At the door, The Kid slipped out of her pumps, then the twosome disappeared into a black void. Almost immediately there was scuffling, punctuated by an offended cry that sounded like Twyla.

The two male diners rose and sneaked up on the doorway.

Sid spoke with authority. "Leave the ladies be. They're professional baseball players. They have their spats but they sure don't need an audience."

The customers hesitated before peering into the hall.

Sid covered my hand with his. "Wendy Winkworth, Private Investigator from Iowa City. Yep, I've been doing some fishing west of the Mississippi." He gestured to the waiter who was poised beside the two kibitzers, order book in hand, in case refreshment was needed between rounds.

"A burger and a beer," Sid called. He asked me if I'd like dessert.

"A piece of apple pie ala mode, please." Visualizing a fight always makes me hungry. The waiter nodded, and retreated through the doorway at a measured pace. From the hall, shrill voices ceased for the time of his passage.

"Are you going to expose me?" I asked.

"Course not. I mean Mr. Washington hired you to investigate the murder, didn't he?"

"Yes, he did," I said, squeezing his hand. "I don't know why he chose me, what with Olive Shimp in Chicago. She has lots more experience than me and she has to be a better ballplayer."

"He hired the best, I'm sure," Sid said gallantly.

The two spectators drew back as Joanie and Twyla, with Eddie and Kay close behind, hurried out of the restaurant, Star-Spangled composure restored if you blurred your eyes to Joanie's shredded hosiery and Twyla's eyeglasses hanging off an ear.

In the calm that followed their exit, I asked Sid about Eddie's fascination with Clint's love life. "What's with her? Is she nuts, or could Clint be leading on some of the younger girls?"

"Oh, it's all in her mind. Clint flirts with every female, age nine to ninety; it's his style. It doesn't go further than that, I'm sure." He didn't sound so sure.

"Did you know he's got a peephole in his office window that lets him look directly out at Eddie while she's dressing?"

"She probably put that hole there herself." Sid shifted uneasily.

Always it's the woman who does the seducing. From what I'd seen, in this case it might be.

"About Betty Jane," I said, "you must have seen her at parties and in other situations where she could let her hair down. What was she like off the field?"

He took a moment deciding what to reveal. "She made obligatory appearances at parties and fund raisers. The girls are told show up, look good, be polite, not get too involved. She showed up, said what she had to, and ducked out early. People thought she was standoffish, that she thought she was better than the others, like Eddie said. Once I heard Eddie urging her to stay. After all she was the star. People wanted to get to know her better. Her reaction: steely silence and then she left anyhow. Couldn't wait to get home to Leroy, I guess." He shrugged. "How do you figure a good-looker like her taking up with such a loser?"

"Guess you haven't noticed he's pretty good-looking himself. Also, from what I hear, her parents ran out on her about the same time Leroy came on scene. Perfect timing for him. She needed someone and he snagged her at the right moment."

"Maybe it's just that losers hang with losers."

"She was no loser!"

"At the time they met, is what I mean."

My statement had sounded quite hot, and called for a new subject. "What I can't figure out is that wild pitch. What if Betty Jane was throwing at someone in the stands?"

"She'd never disrupt a ballgame. She wasn't unstable or nuts. In fact, she was one of the most down-to-earth ballplayers I ever met, male or female. Most of that bunch are superstitious. They freak out if they forget to touch the foul line when they come off the field or skip eating fried chicken on days they pitch. Never saw any of that with Betty Jane."

"You sit in the stands near where she threw that pitch, don't you?" I said. It's the PI's curse: suspect everyone, even would-be boyfriends.

Sid turned sad and thoughtful at my implication. His response, when it came, was small-voiced, like a child. "Could be she was throwing at me, God knows, I've entertained the possibility. Because I had let her down. The thought haunts me. Betty Jane came to me right before she pitched her next-to-last game, four days before her murder. Said she'd been followed home from the ballpark the night before, about a mile, by a man in a suit and tie who appeared silver-haired under the glow of the streetlight. She got frightened and ran the last couple blocks, made it inside safely."

"Why didn't you say something before now? That might have been the killer."

I'd gotten loud and the two male diners looked up, one saying, "What's going on now?"

Sid waved them off as he leaned toward me and whispered, "Because I only found out yesterday that you were a PI."

"Oops, sorry. Did Betty Jane tell the cops?"

The two eavesdroppers relaxed back in their seats.

"Don't think so. Knowing her shady background, I bet she stayed away from cops. After her death, I told Shupe about the guy but he didn't want to hear."

"How come? Because he already had Dinah, or Leroy, picked out as the killer?"

"No. Worse. Because that guy she saw was no killer of this type murder. The description she gave matched one of three rough-looking types who were at a couple of the games. If those guys had shot her, it would have been with a Tommy gun from the side window of a sleek black limousine."

I felt a chill in my chest and took several swallows of Coke but since it was icy too, the chilliness spread. I shivered. "You mean those men are gangsters? Chief Shupe might not want to hear, if Yegg Washington's thugs were involved."

Sid barely nodded. He took a last bite of burger and wiped his mouth. "I noticed them because they were dressed different from the other fans, in expensive, tailored suits."

"She could have been throwing at them."

"They weren't there that last night. I'd have seen them, dressed to kill as they were, pardon the expression. They usually sat two rows in front of me and a little to my left."

"Have they been back since she died?"

"No. Why walk into a murder investigation?"

"Maybe Leroy was mixed up in the rackets or …" I hesitated giving voice to the ugly possibility. "Maybe some of the players are throwing games for the mob."

"You kidding? Girls' baseball, who'd care?"

"You're so big-hearted about my temporary career choice," I said. "But, okay, I concede the point. What if Leroy crossed the mob and the silver-haired fella tailed his wife to intimidate him? Wonder if she told Leroy."

Still with my hand in his, Sid leaned forward. "Don't go ahead with this. Don't stumble into something that's dangerous for you, and it might get back to Mr. Washington that what I said led to a whole investigation. He might do me in or at least ruin my career." I withdrew my hand. Sid was brash but not brave. Not like my dad who had set new standards in that quality.

"I told Betty Jane those guys were employed by the league owner, Mr. Yegor 'Yegg' Washington, a thug in his own right, and that she should take a cab home for a while. I believed then and still do that the stalker was a lovesick or star-struck hood, out for a little extra-curricular activity.

"Needless to say," he went on, "the news that the guy was a hood unsettled her and her start that night was really rocky. I figured she was dwelling on the guy, afraid he'd return. I discovered the three men's names were Kramer, Surdick, and Katz. Kramer was the one who followed her."

I had no desire to cross Yegg Washington either. He had hired me. Had he suspected his own man of doing the job and was I supposed to confirm it? There were stories of Washington associates double-crossing the boss and ending up sprawled by a barber's chair with their torsos bullet-stitched.

As we left the restaurant, one of the curious suits asked for my autograph on a napkin. Sid gave him his, too, although he hadn't been asked for it.

20.

Kay had insisted on being my roommate on road trips, so when I returned to the Hornettes' floor, I found Eddie sending my present roomie, Connie, down the hall to stay with Molly as Kay moved in with me. This was to provide more opportunity for Double Doc Winkie to work her magic.

Later, listening drowsily to The Kid's snores from the next bed, I tried to imagine what the powerful criminal Yegg Washington would look like.

Would he be tall, suave, and graceful with an aquiline face like George Raft or short, wide, and lumpy, with a puss like a bulldog, namely Edward G. Robinson? As I drifted into sleep, I did recognize the man who appeared at the head of a long metal table in an ugly gray room. Not the mighty Washington but my small wiry dad. He sat, resting his elbows on a shiny black table, a purple bruise marking his cheek. He was examining a carpenter's file before presenting it to the little girl who sat across from him.

Jolted awake, I shook off the image. After a moment, the flash of my dad joined me through the smoke of a campfire, and returned me to memories of our brief time together.

Dad and I were four days in the woods following the gun store robbery that went sour. Once, far off, we heard men's voices. He pushed me down and jumped on top of me, his fists pressed to my gummy head, the pistol in his belt gouging my hip. We scrunched under a log as far as we could get. The posse tromped by so close we could hear their plans for us: "Skin 'em alive. Rip their legs off." But we were small people, and dirty. We blended right in with that log.

The first three days we lived on beef jerky that my dad brought, and wild persimmons that fell ripe and juicy that September. The fourth morning we crept into a garden by a farmhouse and stuffed our pockets with green beans. Hurrying back to the woods, we heard a heavy motor and watched the top of a yellow school bus glide above corn rows down an unseen road to a distant world that right then I wouldn't have wanted to join.

Retreating into thick woods, we sat by a pond while he devoured most of the beans while I, more excited than hungry, chewed on a few.

After he was done, he held out a handful of beans and asked, "You sure you had enough, honey?" I took them. Feeling their rough unappetizing texture, I didn't want to return the gift as though ungrateful. An instant later, I felt a scrape against my hand and looked to see that the beans were gone and he was munching on them. After spitting out some stems, he said, "If it's yours and you ain't watching it, then it's mine. In this life, you'd do well to heed that philosophy." I teared up and right away he handed me two or three more beans that I popped in my mouth.

Breaking into a whiskery grin, he said, "You're a good girl, but you got to learn to guard what's yours."

That was the only advice I got from Dad. Mostly when he spoke, it concerned guns. He loved talking guns, the Springfields we'd taken in the robbery for instance. "I hate losing them sticks," he grumped. "They'd a brought us three squares for a month." He waxed poetic about the Springfield '03. "A Mauser knock-off. Bolt action, holds five rounds. Uses full size centerfire rifle cartridges. Whoo-ee, one of those guys blows a great big hole in a varmint." And so it went, as I learned the caliber and optimum use of each weapon we'd stolen.

Dad's gun knowledge went down a lot easier than those beans. He never mentioned the drowned pickup truck. Guess he knew how to acquire another without too much fuss.

He talked survival. In his oversized pockets, he carried a flashlight, knife, matches, beef jerky. Those deep pockets were survival kits. He was determined to survive.

Dad carried a compass and we zigzagged southeast from the pond, moving past tall, thick-trunked trees with catalpa-like leaves. During the journey, he pointed out landmarks, two logs in the shape of a cross, distinctive rock formations, in case we had to retrace our steps. He didn't say where we were heading and I, picturing our destination as "safety," didn't think to ask.

At the edge of the woods we came upon a decrepit old shed. About twenty yards farther on, a ribbon of road appeared over a hill and snaked along before disappearing beyond another rise. I recognized that familiar stretch of highway and only then realized he was going to ditch me.

"That's the road we come in on," he said. "You run down there, hitch a ride to Lead Hill. It'll be about five mile to your left. You get there, you know where the house is from Lead Hill?"

Stunned, I couldn't reply.

"It's eight mile east from Lead Hill," he persisted. "Ask somebody in town."

"I know where it is, but I don't want to go." I hooked thumbs through belt loops.

"You done good. I love ya but you're better off with your mom. Take care of her for me. I know you'll be the one to clear the way in the wilderness." He grabbed my shoulders and pulled me close, so those last words came out a little muffled, but I think that's what he said. He was smelly and filthy, and scratchy with a bristling growth of beard, but in that final tight embrace, he was my shining hero. To my mind, Dad was Mercury, the winged god, and the green beans and pond water were his ambrosia and nectar.

He spun me around and pushed me toward the road. "Now get going. Git!" he emphasized. Tears stinging, I flung myself forward and ran as fast as I could, not looking back.

At the highway, I stared to the right and didn't look back to see if he was watching. Probably he split right away. It was his style to materialize, get what he wanted, and vanish. When an old pickup came putting along I put my thumb out and it stopped.

"You lost, little girl?" the driver, a skinny old lady, asked. I could have punched her I was so angry, but instead I climbed in. She squinted at my face and wrinkled her nose. I must have looked a sight and smelled worse.

"Drop me in Lead Hill," I commanded, absorbing some heady farm smells within the vehicle. As we pulled out, I looked to where he had been but he was gone.

After twenty minutes with no words exchanged, she dropped me off at the Phillips station on Main Street where Don, the attendant, was pumping gas into a Chevy. He didn't glance up, and young Mrs. Criner, coming from the market with a tall grocery bag under each arm and a brood of kids trailing, had enough stress without worrying about whose grubby little girl stood alone in the street.

I started walking toward home and in about ten minutes a car of fashionable ladies stopped and gave me a ride to our secret road. About a half hour later I was slogging past the broken gate of our property and through the back door of the house. It was dark inside, and silent. I had never felt so alone.

He saved my life, he hid me, he said he loved me, and yet he left me. He was instrumental in making me who I am: chronically suspicious, and a damn good PI.

I swore I'd never be that vulnerable again.

21.

The Hornettes continued the road trip, splitting games with the Waterloo Flickas, then returning home for a day off. The next evening in our ballpark, Kay won again, shutting out the Aurora Alices.

Showering afterward, I asked Eddie if I was still a utility infielder after the revelation of my true life's work.

"Especially upon hearing that," she declared.

"Before the season ends, I have to play in a game."

"Are you tetched?" She raised one eyebrow really high.

"Gee whiz," I said. "I'm so totally awed by brow control. How do you do it? Practice in front of a mirror?"

She turned away, not willing to divulge, so I splashed over to Kay, who had recently become very gracious to her own personal genie.

"Roomie, how about I sit in on your confab with Clint tonight?"

She averted her eyes. "We're not doing it tonight or any other for you."

"But I'd love to partake of his professional expertise. Besides," my voice hardened, "you owe me."

"I know I do, but this ain't nothing interesting. When we do meet, all we do is go on and on about stats and charts, stats and charts. You'd be bored out."

I stuffed myself into a sundress and went to ask permission of the old pontificator himself.

His office door was ajar and when I pushed it farther open, I saw him bent over a cluttered desk, rooting among papers. A gold bauble glinted in his hand before he heard me and stuffed it into a shirt pocket. A bit of gold chain hung out before he shoved that in too. It had to be Betty Jane's baseball necklace.

"Yep, yep," he said, sounding like a small dog. "What's up, Winkie?"

"Watcha got there, Clint?" I asked.

As I closed in, his thick hand moved to cover the pocket.

"What's in there, Clint?" I said. His free hand brought out a flock of sourballs from a pants pocket and offered them to me. "There's a lemon one in there," he enticed. I knocked the offering away.

He stiffened, letting the candy drop, his eyes fixed on something behind me. I followed his gaze and saw Eddie looming in the doorway.

"You damn double-doc," she blurted, and then addressed him, "You making eyes at her now?"

"Geez, Eddie," I said, "the door was open. I'm innocent as a newborn."

"You got it all wrong," Clint explained further. "I was sympathizing, on account of how little Winkie can't get into a game."

Eddie measured us with cold eyes. "Grab your jacket, Clint," she said. "Let's go home. Winkie, you get out of here before they shut off the lights in the parking lot."

"You betcha."

Eddie plucked Clint's Hornettes' jacket off a chair back, pitched it to him and guided him out by the elbow. She snapped the office light off leaving me in darkness. I wended my way along the locker room aisle, dimly lit from the high windows, into the hallway where a nightlight burned. I couldn't let Clint escape; hoped he didn't try to ditch the necklace in grass or gravel.

The parking lot lights were indeed shut down. As soon as fans left, the management did this to save pennies. Kramer, Surdick, and Katz must be impressed.

The moon had slipped behind a cloud, leaving the expanse quite dark. I followed the pair, catching snippets of Eddie's soothing words (how nice she was when they were alone) and Clint's rumbling responses (he also had settled down.) Off by themselves, they were behaving like best buddies.

The couple paused beside Clint's Buick. The big hornet painted on the driver's door was recognizable by dim streetlight. Eddie pressed herself into Clint and kissed him passionately. He broke free and grappled for the car door handle. With his entry, the ceiling light blinked on and off.

"I'll see you to your car," he said gruffly through the open window.

"Thanks, Mr. Delicious. What time you gonna be at the field tomorrow?"

"You'll know when I get there."

I was a little disappointed they weren't both leaving in the Buick. I imagined a passionate tryst in some remote lover's lane. Headlights on, Clint drove alongside Eddie until she reached her Chrysler. Then he sped up out of the lot. She spun tires in exiting and took the same left turn.

Two vehicles remained in the lot. One was mine, near the entrance. The other was at the far end, near the cow pasture. Someone was in that auto, a someone who started the motor and rolled the car forward. As it passed, I saw it was Pepper's Chevy, taillights winking and vanishing as she also turned left.

I needed to get to Clint and check his pocket. I didn't believe he'd toss the necklace out the window with Eddie following so closely. Another possibility: he'd leave it in his car. Since I knew where he lived, on Fairfax, a street perpendicular to Main, I decided my best bet was to get to his home first by taking the back alley route.

I swung out of the lot, turned left, then right onto the first side road, turning left a half block later into an alley. It was about 11:30. Each side street I came to I buzzed across; allowable since there was not much traffic that late at night. I flew from one alley to the next, passing sheds, garages, tipped garbage cans, weaving around a barking dog, bumping over some poorly maintained surfaces. Once I screeched to a stop, almost colliding with a speeding car on the boulevard. "Idiot!" its driver bellowed, whizzing by. The way some people drive, almost as recklessly as I do.

Three blocks more and I sped past Main Street, took a right up Pine and two blocks later, swung another right onto Fairfax, Clint's street. As I turned, I saw two cars approaching from the opposite direction. "I win," I whispered. Killing my lights and the engine, I coasted to a stop about three houses down and across the street from his residence. Clint and Eddie pulled up on his side of the street and both popped out of their cars at virtually the same instant. He waited while she walked toward him.

I switched off the ceiling light so no one would see me as I slipped out of my vehicle.

Large trees lined the road and I crept in their shadows toward the pair, who stood beside the Buick. I needed to catch Clint alone, before he escaped indoors.

"No, Eddie," I heard him say firmly. "You can't come in."

"Okay, some other night." Her tone became inviting, amorous. "We're both too anxious right now. I want it to be special too, Mr. Delicious." She turned, hips swinging, jumped into her car and sped off.

I made a short dash and ended up right across the street. I hid behind a thick-trunked oak, as Clint strolled up the walk to his house. I was about to make my move when another car entered the block from Main Street. I crouched down and waited. Pepper's Chevy drew up behind the Buick. Clint saw her coming and broke into a trot toward his front door. He dug into a trouser pocket, presumably for keys. He almost made it into the house, but the long-legged girl caught up as he was fitting a key into the door.

"Clint," she shouted, "I got something you'll wanta see."

"What the hell you doing here? Get outa here or Eddie'll think we're fooling around."

She reached out her arms to him. "No, really, this you gotta hear about."

He paused. His hand dropped away from the key in the lock. "We can talk in my car." He turned her around and gave her a push. She kept going toward the Buick. The moment her back was turned, he reached into his shirt pocket, pulled out the necklace and flung it about ten yards onto the lawn. In the moonlight the chain sparkled like Christmas tinsel through its graceful twisting journey. Relieved of the item, he enjoyed a rear view of Pepper swishing in tight skirt and heels.

He followed her into the Buick's front seat as a light came on in the house next door.

In the car, Pepper grabbed him around the neck and kissed him. She refused to let up, clutching him even as he struggled. It wasn't long before he gave in, reaching for her and nuzzling her flowing hair. Shortly, there was heavy petting going on in the vehicle.

From the corner of an eye I glimpsed movement. A blocky figure was creeping toward my hiding place. I shrank back and sank behind some prickly bushes. Eddie crept by, so near I could see the pores on her face, and the intense look in her eyes as she focused on the Buick. She inched across the street, slowly, slowly, until she crouched beneath Clint's open window. In the car, the two were wrapped around each other like peppermint stripes on a sourball.

Eddie reared up and punched Clint. He cried out in surprise. She flung open the driver's door.

He scooted down in the seat until his head hit the seat back. Eddie leapt into the car, landed on him and bumped over him to pounce on Pepper who was pressed against the passenger door.

"I thought you were Winkie," Eddie screamed. Pepper clamored out of the car and fell onto the grass. Eddie managed to stay in the car as Clint zipped out the driver's side. Leaning against his open door, he shook himself like a shaggy dog.

Eddie screamed at her sister, "After all I've done for you!"

"You tore my blouse," Pepper complained from somewhere below. She stood up. Poised by the far side of the car, Pepper was everyman's pin-up, a Rita Hayworth in a low cut, ruffled blouse, big bosomed, red-lipped, velvety, sultry.

A police car took the corner on two wheels, turret light blinking red. It rode up the curb before squalling to a stop. Chief Shupe leapt out and made for the combatants. "What's going on here?" he shouted. "Neighbors reported a ruckus, physical contact made, car entering the street without lights, someone lurking in the bushes." He glanced across the street, trying to spot the lurker. I stopped breathing.

Eddie scooted over the driver's seat and exited to stand beside Clint. He fiddled with his shirt collar.

"What are you hiding?" she squawked and yanked the collar aside. A red hickey was visible.

"You two-timing S.O.B.!" she cried, her face distorting with grief. "I saved myself for you. I've taken cold showers because of you and I find you with my sister in this horny hairnet of a Buick. Hairy hornet! To think I respected our relationship."

She was still berating Clint when I rose from the briar patch and started across the street. Shupe whirled and drew his pistol. "Oh, Wendy, it's only you." He sounded disappointed.

"You think you could have him next?" Eddie screamed at me. "Orgy, one after another. Fresh fawns leaping around this man. They're so hot for him they come out of the bushes."

"I'm not here for fun," I said with dignity. "Chief, Clint had what I think is Betty Jane's gold necklace. He tossed it onto the lawn. Over there."

I moved around the Buick and headed onto the grass. Shupe followed after warning the others to stay put and not move a goddam muscle. The necklace was easy to find with the help of Shupe's flashlight. I picked the trinket up and handed it to the chief who secured it in an evidence bag. In the meantime, no one had made a break, although Pepper was looking antsy.

"Clint and I were just having some fun," she whined. "Is that a crime?"

"What am I supposed to do?" Clint pled his case. "All day with those fresh fawns leaping. "

"Shut up!" Eddie screamed.

Clint sank against the Buick's front fender. He dug into a pocket, presumably hunting for a pacifying sourball. He came up empty.

Shupe sympathized. "Hey, buddy, thumbs up. Three women at once. What is it, the dimple?"

"I dunno," Clint said, shaking his head, hair flopping weakly. "Everybody wants me. I feel a little used up."

"You were trying to hide Betty Jane's necklace," I accused.

Clint gestured in Pepper's direction. "I think she left it on my desk."

Pepper yawped defiance. Clint's accusation had come out of the blue and made everyone hesitate.

Shupe recovered first, speaking in low even tones to quell further outcries. "Everybody's coming to the station so we get this straightened out."

He phoned for backup and a cop car quickly drove in, Officer Robinson at the wheel. By that time, the neighbors were out on the street, chattering excitedly about the fuss.

En route to his squad car with Clint, Shupe barked, "Whoever's frickin' Nash that is that's parked on the yellow at the end of the block is gonna get ticketed if she don't move it right away."

Clint climbed in beside Shupe in one squad car; the sisters were chauffered by Robinson in the other. I drove my Nash.

In Shupe's office, I waited while the chief rolled a stogie between his palms, stuck it in his mouth and clamped down. With Yegg Washington somewhere out there watching, evaluating, we both were under a fair amount of pressure.

Pointing at the photograph of his rifle company, Shupe said, "I miss those guys. Back then you knew the difference between good and evil."

Hearing him comment on the picture allowed me to reflect a bit. This man was one of the millions of ordinary men who had saved the world.

After getting the cigar going, he said, "We'll quiz the three stooges in a couple minutes," he said, "but first I want to bring you up to date, of course I do. We had to release Leroy Williams. Again. Damn, I know he's guilty but we can't break his alibi. Got four patrons of the Elite Café, plus the counterman, who swear he was there that night, at least until 1:15 in the morning. Not much time for him to race two-and-a-half miles down to the river and dispatch his wife before 2:00 which is when the body was found. I believe he sneaked out earlier in the evening and was back before anyone noticed. Anyhow, he's ordered to stay in town. Moved out of his old place and into a room over the café. Used the name, 'Billy Leroy' to register. Isn't he clever?"

"Exceedingly." I blinked, my eyes stinging from the smoke. "You ask him if he's afraid of the mob?"

"Oh, can that crap. Sid told me about Washington's guy following Betty Jane home, trying to strike up an acquaintance. It's just some hanger on, wants to say he knows a famous lady, and if he gets lucky, maybe in the Biblical sense."

"Might be worth checking the guy out. Sid says he's a hood."

"Baloney. Not everybody Mr. Washington sends out is a hood. Some are respectable businessmen."

This old soldier wasn't about to invade that particular Tommy gun nest.

"Hear you interviewed the janitor," he said. "What'd you get from him? He a suspect for Millicent's accidental death?"

"No," I said, "but I found cleaning tools, one of which could have been used to deck Millicent. I suppose you've checked them for blood evidence?"

"Part of the job. Not a speck on any of them." I must have looked disappointed, because he said, "Don't let it get to you. You'll learn that, in this job some you win and some you don't."

I grabbed a donut, got silly, waving it in the air and saying, "Some you win and some you do-nut." I took a big bite to complete the shtick.

Even with my true roles of psychologist and kinesiologist known to Eddie, Chief Shupe didn't let me sit in on her questioning. Once again I pressed the large tumbler to the wall of the adjoining room. Leaving out a portion of the histrionics, I'll report the essence of her statement.

"Hands to yourself, bud," she said as she was guided in by Officer Robinson.

"Don't worry about that, lady."

Right off, she informed the chief that all the players on the team, including the fake one, were out to seduce Clint, because he was the most virile man in the world. "Dear God," she exploded, "the man is only human. He can only hold out for so long." This evening, she had bade her fella sweet dreams, but following her suspicions that he was seeing someone else, she doubled back to catch him, only to discover that it was her very own sis betraying her.

"I don't get it," Shupe said. "What's this guy got to make you so dotty about him? Maybe you don't know it, but a hole in the chin is actually a birth defect like hemophilia or Huntington's chorea. Leaving out the mutation, the guy's just a middle-aged sap like the rest of us."

"You might not get it, but Pepper gets it. Winkie gets it," she countered. "The young gals he entertains after hours get it. You're jealous. If you didn't curse every third word, maybe you could get a date too."

She went on about Clint spending time alone with some of the girls, for instance Kay or Betty Jane, or in groups, Joanie, Twyla, and Connie added, the door bolted and shades drawn.

Shupe interrupted. "When did you steal the gold necklace? Same time you took jewelry from teammates? Did you leave it on Clint's desk to make him pay attention to you?"

"No, I didn't, and I didn't steal Dinah's red paint either. Or kill Betty Jane, in case you'll ask that next."

"I haven't asked, so why offer?" He waited a respectful interval before continuing. "Where were you the night she was killed?"

"Playing in a baseball game, in case you forgot. After the game I stayed to commune with the girls, those who were available that is, and then I went home and hit the sack. So did the others, I'm sure."

"Most of them did, supposedly. Not your sister and her pals." Eddie didn't respond.

"What do you know about the gold necklace?" Shupe pursued the truth. "Clint thinks Pepper left it. How would she have come by it?"

"Ask her."

A pause while he regrouped. "Tell me the names of all the girls who meet with Clint, I mean besides Kay, Joanie, Twyla, and Connie. Who else?"

She thought. "That's about it, but Kay's only seventeen, I mean, of course Clint doesn't do anything with her, but still it's just the idea of what she might be thinking, and him being so irresistible. Oh God, forget I said anything; I can't think straight with all this pressing on me." Not to worry. Even though she had been speaking to the Chief of Police, Clint was Shupe's darts buddy and would remain innocent until proven innocent.

Eddie was dismissed and told to head home. When Pepper was brought in, I reversed position and shifted the tumbler to my other ear.

Shupe started with, "Clint said you left the gold baseball on his desk and he was going to give it back to you." Clint had evidently been questioned in the squad car.

"I didn't have nothing to do with it!" Pepper responded. "Clint's a liar. He's a dirty old man who can't get it up, flabby old chicken skin hanging off their arms. I was only at his house because he told me he wanted me to come over right after the game. Okay, maybe I didn't hear him right, I was on the way out at the time, but when I got there, he got fresh right away. I went along with it, after all, he is the manager."

"Is that a negative where the necklace is concerned?"

"Why you picking on me? I was out with Joanie and Twyla the night Betty Jane got it. Lay off!"

"When I start picking on you, you'll know it."

"You can't do enough to make me do anything," she bragged.

Further inquiry elicited that Pepper had known about Betty Jane's marriage to Leroy Williams, but kept it secret because the lovebirds wanted it that way. Hey, reformatory mates are loyal as hell. Pepper added that Leroy's incredible good looks were negated by a weak chin. "Watch it wobble like white Jello when he's scared. And Betty Jane told me that he can't get it up either."

Pepper was released to Officer Robinson with the order to "Keep her in jail overnight, until we see if we got enough to press charges."

That produced a wail: "You call my sister, she'll never let that happen!" I waited until I heard the door close and agitated footsteps retreat down the hall, before entering Shupe's office through a side door.

"How can you hold Pepper without charge?" I complained.

He didn't bother to glance up. "What were you doing out there in the middle of the night?"

It was futile debating the niceties of the law, so, while he devoured a Hershey bar, I explained the evening's circumstances, begun by seeing Clint pocket the gold piece.

Shupe listened while chewing. When I finished my tale, he said, "After grilling those babes, I could use a few of these." He unwrapped another Hershey, took a giant bite. "I'm forgetting my manners; have one yourself."

I had become one of the law-enforcement gang. I chose a Snickers. The warm melt went down easy. I went to sit near the window. After all, I was there merely to observe.

Robinson produced Clint. He was not cuffed and I assumed Pepper and Eddie hadn't been either, otherwise there would have been a stink raised about that. The gray-faced manager sank into a metal chair close by the desk. He accepted my presence without surprise or comment. He and Shupe focused on each other for several seconds, the chief's face softening as they reinforced their bond.

Shupe said, "You found the necklace on your desk after the game. Go ahead from there."

"Well," Clint eyed me, "I thought Pepper had left it because she liked shocking people. I can see now I was wrong. A couple times before tonight, she came on to me pretty strong and I told her, no thank you, you think I'm crazy enough to get mixed up with you when your sister's after me too?"

Shupe made a disagreeable face at the very thought. "You said all that to her?"

"Pretty much I made it clear. Tonight was different. I was tired, my defenses were down." He bent forward, plunked his elbows on the desk and groaned.

Shupe slapped the desk. "Clint, why'd you take this job anyhow? I know you needed the money, but, shit, you could have worked the popcorn stand or boiled up hot dogs. This way, sure you're staying in the frickin' game, but you're getting manhandled by a bunch of hot chicks."

Clint didn't answer and Shupe didn't push him. I considered that Clint had the necklace and tried to blame someone else, which threw suspicion right back on him.

"Did you take that necklace off Betty Jane's body?" I asked.

The two men looked up sharply.

Clint sputtered, "I got an alibi for that night."

"Come on. What would you and Kay Brock have to talk about for the bulk of the evening?"

"Hold on," Shupe cautioned.

I faced the chief. "These people are not scintillating conversationalists. All I can think of that'd entertain them for hours is sex. Maybe I'm underestimating them. Maybe they discussed art, literature, physics, but I think not."

"You don't know baseball," Clint justified. "There's plenty to talk about."

"Let up, Wendy," Shupe warned. "Clint didn't kill that girl."

"Oh, were you there?" I whirled to confront the manager. "What do you do in your private meetings with the players?"

"Stats and charts."

"Don't insult our intelligence!" I looked to Shupe for support but he was focused on sliding a desk drawer back and forth, probably thinking about the bottle inside.

I gave up for the moment. My best bet for answers was to find out for myself.

Shupe pushed back his chair and stood. He yawned, stretched at length, and dismissed Clint. "Get outa here, buddy. Go on home and don't let none of those broads indoors. I'll see you Monday night at darts."

"What?" I objected. "You keep Pepper in jail and the man with the necklace goes free?"

"Lay off. I know my people. Clint's not gonna run. She might."

Driving home in the early morning, I took stock. There seemed no truth to Pepper's assertion that Clint had told her to report for after-hours duty. From what I'd witnessed, she had been the instigator. Clint had implied Pepper left the necklace to create a rift between him and her sister. But why would Pepper kill Betty Jane? They had been friends, and the pitcher owed the temperamental outfielder for getting her on the team.

To acquire the necklace, Pepper would have had to kill Betty Jane or at least be an accomplice. Why would she do that?

22.

The next morning Pepper was released to Eddie.

That afternoon, Kay pitched ninth inning relief to preserve a 5-4 victory against the Alices. There seemed no limit to her arm's resilience, at least in Clint's estimation. Starter Nancy Grant picked up the win. When feeling really cocky on the mound, Kay added the Groucho finger flutter and popping eyebrows to her pitching ritual. I held my breath for fear people would recognize the goofiness for what it was, but no one seemed to catch on. As Burton City's latest sensation, The Kid was loved by the crowd and lovingly written about in Sid's column, to the exclusion of one large first basewoman.

In the clubhouse before the game, Pepper was brazen about her conquest of Clint. "I got what she can't have," the reference to "she" being apparent. The team hated Pepper's gloating. On the practice field when the inept outfielder's back was turned, a ball fired by Letta struck her in the butt. Eddie saw but did nothing.

Clint had Band-Aided the hickey and made sure the vinyl tape stayed there until the evidence disappeared. In the meantime, he curried Eddie's favor, saying, "I'm not bragging, I'm not proud of this," but she refused to play the forgiveness game. The rift made for much awkwardness in the clubhouse.

"Kay." I caught up with the young pitcher after the game. "Is today the day I'm invited to your post-game wrap-up with Clint?"

"No, not never. Don't keep at me about that."

"Aren't I your best genie?"

"Genies don't want return favors. Besides you're only a lucky charm, not no genie. Clint says I don't have to believe in magic, that I'm good enough without it."

How demeaning to go from genie to lucky charm. Of course Clint was right about the source of Kay's talent, but this was not a moment to pursue that truth. The Kid avoided further discussion by bumping up against Letta and the two engaged in a spate of shoulder jabs and grunts.

I donned skirt and blouse and slipped on my new one-inch Naturalizer heels. In fact, the entire outfit was new. With Sid making a competition of it, a lady had to keep up. And Yegg was paying.

As I dressed, I couldn't shake the desire to know what was happening in those closed- door meetings. If Clint wouldn't allow me into his fresh-fawn-aleaping group, it was up to me to infiltrate.

I left the locker room as Kay was braying to Dinah, "I got power and speed, and everything else between."

"Hot shots get justly reaped in deserts," Dinah lectured, a mangling of "reaping just desserts," I translated. I should have been issued a ballplayers' dictionary along with the uniform.

Eddie and Dinah exited the locker room ahead of me, taking a right toward the parking lot. I headed the other way, toward the lobby, where Clint, still in uniform, was inserting pennies into a peanut vending machine. Several fans chatting with him made room for me.

I stepped up close to him and said, "Manager, I don't want to scare the fans, but I don't feel so good. Been hawking up the green stuff like mad. Hope it's not catching." I coughed toward one of the devotees who had leaned in to overhear. He peeled off fast. Clint let go of the little salt-clouded door and also retreated.

Now that I had some space, I cupped my hands and whispered, "I'm not really sick. I just want to talk in private. Eddie suspects you of carrying on with some of the girls. Let's clear up the rumors before they spread any farther." I allowed my eyes to wander toward the fans who were still hovering.

"Where'd you hear that?" Clint responded. "Oh, I get it. She told that to Shupe, didn't she? Eddie thinks if I so much as look at another woman I'm doing her wrong. One night after the All-Star game last year doesn't give her sole rights to me."

"Huh? Why you must have been fabulous for her to want a repeat so bad." I examined Clint - mournful eyes, grizzled whiskers, chin dusted with salt, wrinkled shirt, counterbalanced by one dimple and multiple sourballs. I guessed some girls could find him sexy. Five nights ago after Kay's first win, I'd been convinced that this fella and Eddie had had sex when she emerged from his office looking positively starry-eyed. I felt sorry for her if a squeeze to the tush and a few tender maunderings had that effect.

Clint blurted, "A long time ago I was married and I don't want to be depended on again. I'd fail at it this time too, and she'd run out on me like before."

"I don't know. Eddie seems more the stand-your-ground type."

He lifted the vending machine door and a few peanuts dropped into his paw. He stuck another coin in the slot and more peanuts rolled out. He popped all of them into his mouth. As he spoke, a few trickled back out. "I'm mad at you. You really got on me yesterday in front of Duane. Too bad because I was beginning to think of you as a real Hornette. That's all gone now." He sagged and his mouth drooped.

Good grief, what a master psychologist. I gave him my most awed look. "Okay, coach, I'll behave myself. How about if I sit at your knee and absorb your after-game wisdom?"

"Post-game's only for ballplayers, so no. And don't threaten me with the law, me and Duane Shupe have hoisted more than a few down at the Elite. He knows I'm just an old fart settin' by the cracker barrel spinnin' my tall tales."

Since I was getting nowhere in making this ballplayer shake in his sanitary socks, I switched tactics. "You should go check the parking lot right now because last I saw of Kay, she was getting pretty sassy with M&M and the Mountain was looking grim enough to pound The Kid right down into the gravel."

He whirled. "Jeez, why didn't you tell me?" He lumbered off a bit stiffly, but the gait still showed what a kick it was for him to be at the old ballpark.

The hangers-on ambled after with beers in hand.

I headed to the locker room, hoping all the players had left. Lately everyone cleared out in a hurry, what with Tubbs having died in there and camaraderie not at its height. But Molly and Letta lingered. I rushed to them, saying breathlessly, "Fight in the parking lot. Clint needs our help." A quick pat to their hair-dos and off they skeddadled.

I waited until they were down the hall, then tried Clint's office door. Locked. I took picks from my handbag, probed and manipulated for some seconds until the lock gave. Growing up with burglars had its advantages. I stuck my bag, lock picks inside, in my locker.

I entered the office, bolted the door and drew the long shade.

I moved to the huge cardboard equipment box that sat against the wall. I needed to empty it, but where to stow the junk to clear space for me? In such a messy room, I didn't think a few more gloves, bats and shoes would be noticed if strewn casually around, but on closer inspection, it seemed that most of the clutter consisted of ragged stacks of sports magazines and comic books, scorecards, sourball wrappers, smeary tapes, hot dog wrappers, and gigantic dust bunnies.

Yanking out file drawers, I discovered two that contained only a single squished liniment tube, a rosin bag, and a few packs of nail files. If this man were here a few more years, he'd have all the drawers emptied and their contents spread about the room. I stuffed those drawers with six ancient oil-sodden gloves and three pairs of broken-spike shoes. I hung a 1930s catcher's mask on a wooden coat tree near the door and covered it with a torn team jacket labeled "Civets," and some old ball caps. That left five cracked bats that I set behind the file cabinets.

I climbed into the empty box, drew my legs up to my stomach and closed the flaps over me. I took cellophane tape from my pocket and attached long strips to the flaps to hold them down. In that I succeeded pretty well, although, when finished, I could still see a limited portion of the ceiling. Hadn't noticed those high cobwebs right above; if they fell, the box and I would be netted.

I took my switchblade and cut a tiny slit in each long side of the carton, one with a view of Clint's chair and desk, the other revealing a tiny portion of the window shade and a little of the area near the door. I'd have to rely on moans and squeals for the rest of it.

I'd be safe unless someone peered directly into an opening, but if Eddie were correct, they'd be too busy to notice.

Hearing people approach, I scooched down onto the gritty cardboard surface and became still. A key turned in the lock, the door opened, and a rush of footsteps entered.

"Hey, Clint, you see that fight between the fans and Letta?" I heard Twyla's voice say. "She busted right through them and one shoved her back. It happened right by your painted hornet."

"Not good publicity," Clint moped.

"I was only trying to help," Letta said. "Winkie told us you were in trouble."

"Winkie's an odd one," Molly said. "Real jumpy."

"People say she's been to college. That makes you iffy." No response. Apparently no one knew what to say to that.

The door banged shut and the bolt was shot. Metal folding chairs were squawked open and moved about.

"Grease me up, Clint," Twyla said. A minute later, "Oh, that feels so good."

"Do me too," Joanie exclaimed. The thought of a stack of buttered bodies made my stomach queasy and I had no way to confirm or deny the activity through any of the slits.

"A place to go free of Eddie." It was Connie, a married Christian woman, in there with the heathens.

"Eddie's right near, right now. I just know," Kay said nervously.

"Well, the shade's down, so we're safe," Connie said.

Clint appeared in my view and sat down at his desk. "Let's forget about Eddie. We played a great game today," he said through a chaw. He spat and the spittoon pinged. "But not perfect. Joanie, don't be afraid to smack that catcher hard sliding in, and be happy doing it. A bump and a bruise is your reward if you score."

My nose was filling up, well on the way to dripping. I resisted the urge to sneeze. What a time to discover I had allergies.

"Yep, girls," Clint was nattering on. "Do your best to show you're the boss." He spat. My goodness, five spittoon pings resulted from that one effort. As he grinned toothily in the other direction, I heard a solid shot of spit and spittoon colliding. "Beautiful aim, Kay," someone gushed. Before I could deal with that, a brown wad sailed right past my hole. Others were spitting. Was this simply a sit-and-spit session kept secret from the bogey-woman?

"Hey, Clint," Joanie said, "you see Eddie stripping right in front of the crack in the glass? What an ugly sight. I bet right now she's got her ear up to that crack, trying to hear what we're up to."

"Let's not rag on Eddie," Clint said touchily.

"Let's peek behind the shade and catch her in the act," Molly said.

"Let's not," Connie said. "Let's leave her be and let her wish she was in here herself."

Too late, there was a woosh of footsteps toward my box and firm hands were laid on from both sides and my cardboard residence was jerked away from the wall, ripping the tape that held my refuge together. I made myself very small and wished I had Betty Jane's iron cross to ward them off with. A couple stronger tugs and Kay said, very near my ear, "Oof, this is heavy. What you got in here?" With people yanking from opposite sides, the tape came unstuck even more. I reached for the cellophane and painstakingly separated a strip. Extending my arm, I tried to patch a flap cross-wise, but the gap only widened further. I stopped when I saw that applied pressure was making it worse. I could now glimpse an arm through the ever-expanding opening.

"Please, girls," Connie pled, "don't mess with the shade. We know she's out there."

Joanie giggled, then squalled, "Oh, Clint, don't touch me there!"

From across the room, Clint barked, "Shut up!"

"Hey," Kay shouted excitedly, "there's a new shoe in this box. It's a Naturalizer, like Winkie's got. Gee, I always wanted a pair like that." Her hand burrowed past the flap and grabbed the toe of my shoe. She shrieked, "Ooh, there's a foot inside this shoe. It's a dead body in here!"

A low despairing wail came from Clint and immediately the room was filled with the screaming meemies of a world gone mad. "Another one! Not again," terrified people wailed. I parted the flaps and, with noble bearing, rose from the coffin. Total silence. Rubbing a left leg muscle cramp and snuffling back mucous, I said, "I suppose you're wondering what I'm doing in here."

"Beat her silly and after that …" Joanie snarled. The players fanned out. In their panic, some had spilled tobacco juice down their fronts.

"Before you do something you'll regret," I said, "you should know that I am not only a ballplayer, but also a practicing psychologist sent here by Mr. Yegg Washington to study childish behavior. You'd best let me get on with the job."

On his feet, Clint spat, missing the spittoon by a yard. "It's okay," he said, "we know she was acting under orders."

"… mop the floor with you," Joanie finished her threat. She was always slow until she got going.

The commotion brought pounding to the door. "Let me in, Clint," Eddie shouted, "I'll save whoever needs it."

"Gimmee a minute," Clint shouted, "until I get things in order,"

"Since when? Open this door right now!"

Glancing around, Clint said, "So many women and nowhere to hide."

Twyla tore off her juice-stained T-shirt and slipped it on, back to front. In the effort her eyeglasses were wrested off and landed on the floor.

"Mother of God," Connie moaned, "with all this racket, Eddie's got every reason to break in."

"Oh, she can't bust the door down," Joanie said reassuringly.

"She can get M&M to help," Twyla said.

"Oh boy," several voices chorused.

"First thing we do is talk this over," I said. "What was all the greasing up about?"

Now the door was being kicked.

"You mean the liniment?" Connie pointed at three spent tubes on the floor. "Clint rubbed Twyla's arm. She had a muscle strain, and then Joanie's calf ached. Why, what did you think?" She sounded offended.

"Pepper says Winkie's working with the cops. One time she saw her coming out of the police station with the Chief of Police," Joanie said.

"So shut up in front of Winkie," Twyla said. She put on her glasses.

I squared my shoulders, high-stepped out of the box and strode through the women to the door.

As Joanie backed away to let me past, she said, "Don't open that door under threat of death." She pulled off her stained T-shirt and patted her sweaty face with a sleeve.

"We have to tell Eddie what's going on in here," I said. "It's only a tobacco chawing session. After she hears the truth, she'll probably be relieved and think it's a fun thing."

"Eddie doesn't want fun," Joanie said. "She wants to think we're orgying around with her vee-rile man." She gave Clint an apologetic grin for making light of his vee-rility.

"Eddie was born to fuss and fume," Clint said. "We're letting her."

"You're unbelievable, the whole bunch of you," I crabbed. "We have to clear this up right now."

"The heck we do," Joanie said.

I laid a hand on the doorknob. No one prevented me. I withdrew the hand. No sense walking into a knockout punch from the other side. Inhaling deeply, I exhaled in like manner and opened the door just a sliver. Eddie's sturdy form was pressed against the doorframe, one eye peering around the corner.

"Hi ya, chaperon," I said, voice high and tight as a fastball, "come join us for the hijinks. You won't believe what they're doing in here. They're spittin' tobaccy." The eye narrowed. "Yeah, really, I know, it's a silly thing for grownups to be doing." I giggled.

Eddie's baleful orb scouted the area in back of me. She said darkly, "Twyla, you have your shirt on backwards."

Speaking of shirts, I hoped Joanie had put hers back on. Whatever Eddie saw when the eye continued to rove, its pupil widened and a teardrop rolled down her cheek.

"You scummy girls," she cried. "It's awful being left out every time." She slammed the door and her steps echoed as she fled the locker room. I faced the players, who were mashed together in defense. "I'll explain in more detail later on."

Joanie, in her bra, slipped the T-shirt back on. No doubt seeing Joanie half-clothed justified Eddie's perception of wickedness in that room. The other three girls, brown stain on their blouses, stayed dressed, wanting to retain their modesty around Clint. For the two lesbians, that didn't seem to matter.

Now that the door was closed and Eddie a bad memory, the women relaxed. Joanie sank into a chair and stretched her legs onto another chair. "Whew," she said, "This is something to write home about."

"I guess you're all eyes and no touching," I said to Clint. I sounded defeated.

"I taught every last one of them to spit. It's baseball, " he said proudly, "and it got Eddie talking to me again, didn't it?"

"It's the pretense, tormenting her with it." I asked Kay, "Is this what you were doing the night Betty Jane was killed?"

She nodded. "We was spittin' and talkin' baseball and about life."

"Baseball is as big as life," Clint said. "It's been around a long time. Long before The Kid's pushy daddy comes along and tells her she's no good because she lost one game. Whee-ew. She needed somebody who knew better to be with her that night."

Besides an almost all-nighter with Kay would really tick off Eddie. That seemed Clint's modus operandi: tormenting his pursuer to make her want him even more. He chose younger girls to hang with, those who didn't know enough to judge him. Cute, wise, he'd lead them down the path to success. Along the way, he'd get his ego stroked, but that was it.

"My pop ain't so bad. He's all for me now," Kay said.

Joanie blew a raspberry.

I asked if Betty Jane had been in on the spittin' sessions.

"I tried with Betty Jane, but she wasn't a natural born spitter," Clint said. "She was slow getting the chaw wadded just right before letting fly. Only came to group once, never came back. Embarrassed to not be the best, I guess. But a couple times I worked with her alone where people wouldn't laugh. I think she would have come back to us if she'd only had the chance."

"I can't imagine proud, contained Betty Jane spitting. It's so disgusting," I said.

Twyla made a derisive noise. "You kidding? She was an ex-con, wasn't she? Mostly she was gosh-darned tough."

"Spitting is disgusting. That's why I love it," Joanie averred. "Besides we get back at Eddie for all the stupid rules. With her being a chain-smoker, she never smells it on us."

When does the conspiracy of silence go too far? Did Eddie murder the star pitcher believing those solo hours Betty Jane spent with Clint were for sex? And maybe they were. Only one participant was available to say they weren't.

Clint rotated his jaw before saying, "You blew our secret, Winkie. But you may have trouble getting Eddie to believe you." He adopted an avuncular tone. "Anyway, we gotta forgive the Winkster, don't we, girls." He gazed around benignly. The girls didn't look very forgiving; once more their expressions had become stormy.

Clint turned on the charm. "Let's be big about this. In fact, let's vote Winkie into our group after she gives her word she won't say any more to non-members than she's blabbed already. And she's gotta learn to spit." He asided to me, "It's called co-opting, stick with me on this."

"She's with the cops," Twyla warned again. "And if she's not, she's a rat fink."

"Winkie aids the police as a psychological consultant only," Clint said. "Chief Shupe's always been one to keep up on the latest techniques." Rooting into a back pocket he withdrew a bag of Red Man and dangled it in front of me. "Whaddaya say, Winkie? Want to leave here in one piece?"

"Let's have a vote," Joanie said.

I talked fast. Anything to prevent a popular vote that would land me on my duff in the parking lot. "Before accepting your kind offer I must reveal my diagnosis of what's bothering this team." I paused. This was bad. I was drawing a blank. Working with this team was shrinking my brain.

Joanie let out another raspberry, but I couldn't let more evidence of skepticism stop me. I had to conjure up something.

"Being present today has been very revealing." I started slowly, speaking loudly with great, and false, confidence. An idea flashed. I picked up speed. "What we're experiencing here is a variant of the famous battle known as Custer's Last Stand. Yes. What this team has fallen ill with is a familiar psychological syndrome, common to upright, tightly knit sports organizations. We professionals term it the 'S'BLISS.' That's an acronym for the Sittin' Bull Last Indian Stand Syndrome. The 'S'BLISS,'" I sighed, as though longing for an earlier time when sport was simpler.

"It's challenging to describe the symptoms to the laity," I went on, gaining confidence, "because the laity, that's you, often take umbrage at such complicated diagnoses, but I'll give it a whirl anyhow. It's where a figure, known as Custer, or Eddie in this instance, tries to dominate an entire people, you being the people."

Kay already knew I claimed to be a psychologist, but I eyed the other girls, wary of their reaction. That was the best piece of fiction I could think of at a moment's notice, but who ever heard of an acronym with an apostrophe? I said with less fervor, "I will provide you with a vocabulary list."

All the players were slack-jawed from being drubbed with big words. Joanie's eyes were half closed and she was rubbing her nose sleepily. Since she seemed more attuned to the ridiculous than the others, I feared saying anything more that might rouse her, but it was Twyla who stepped forward and grabbed the pack of Red Man from Clint. After pressing it into my hand, she stepped back, extended her right hand with palm forward, and intoned, "How, Injun Winkie."

23.

Two hours later, Sid called me at the hotel. After talking in circles for a while, he finally got around to inviting me to have a coffee at the Elite Café. Although I'm generally sure of myself on first dates, I did change outfits twice before deciding on a newly purchased aqua blue faille-ribbed dress with bolero jacket. Didn't want the man looking better than me. It had been an exciting day where, hopefully, some suspicions about me had been snuffed by snuff. Even though I was going on a first date, I anticipated a more relaxing time than I'd had so far today.

Before leaving the hotel room, I checked my teeth in the bathroom mirror, looking for brown juice residue. Not yet over my chawing high, I swallowed a Sen-sen tablet.

In the café, Benny Goodman was playing on the jukebox. A tall couple foxtrotted to the music in the space they had created by pushing a table up to an already scuffed wall. On an early Saturday evening, only a few people were there, most clustered at the bar in front of a dark mural of sailing ships and nicotine-stained clouds. Many of the women wore haltertop sun suits, so I was totally overdressed.

The neon sign blinked red through the plate glass window as Sid rose from a corner table and pulled out a chair. I waved a greeting before stopping to ask the barman if Leroy was in the place. He pointed to the counter where an open potato chip bag lay. "Was here a minute ago."

I thanked him and moved to join Sid.

The sharp-featured reporter with the intense hazel eyes said, "Nice to see you, Wendy. You look very nice."

Keeping my mouth closed in favor of a modest smile, I took the chair he offered. He was dressed in a brown suit and white shirt. Sedate, well tailored, he and I were strangers to bar fashions that night. He slid me in and seated himself around the corner.

"Two coffees," he instructed the waitress, who wore an apron on which was inscribed, "Elite," in flowing script.

"And a burger for me, please," I said. I explained to Sid, "I haven't eaten." Actually, I needed grease to pacify the roiling stomach juices.

"Sorry, I should have asked," my date said. "A burger for the lady and I'll have one too."

"With ketchup and pickles and an order of French fries," I added. The waitress looked at Sid for verification.

"Ditto," he confirmed, "make that a double order." Scribbling, the woman backed away.

Sid fumbled a Camel from a pack in his shirt pocket. His hand trembled as he lit it. Ditto when he reached for the napkin box. Was Sid nervous? Maybe he didn't date that often, what with being consumed with activities designed to get him on the sports staff of the Chicago Tribune. He ripped a napkin yanking it out of the holder. Setting the pieces in front of him, he spoke while playing at patching them together.

"I thought you should know, several weeks before Betty Jane died, there were some weird happenings with the team. I don't know if they had anything to do with her death."

"Fill me in." I felt he was talking business to get comfortable, and was happy he'd selected a topic of interest and not sports or food or clothes.

He flicked an ash into the cardboard ashtray. "I don't want to say Eddie's wrong about Betty Jane having a sore arm, but I think whatever was bothering her was more mental than physical. I think it started in mid-July, in Des Plaines, Illinois, when the Hornettes played an exhibition game there, because when the team arrived home, Betty Jane said something to me that was totally out of character for her."

The waitress brought our coffee mugs. Sid grabbed his and drank. "Oh, hot," he sputtered. He screwed up his lips and banged down the mug. Fumbling for his notepad, "check my notes," he seemed on edge, napkin shredded, mouth seared, eyes pink with tears. The man was too highly strung for me.

He continued talking, albeit in a constricted tone. "So you'll understand what I'm about to tell you, I'll give a little background on Betty Jane. Highly talented athletes typically have little tolerance for players who can't keep up and consequently might hold them back. With Betty Jane, case in point was the Willeys. Lor and Dor are inadequate, as you can probably tell and Betty Jane really took it to them. You can bet they didn't much appreciate a rookie trying to knock their brittle pegs out from under them." He paused to study me. "How well do you know the Willeys?"

The sound in the restaurant increased with the arrival of more patrons.

I leaned closer. "Well enough," I said. "At first they saw me as the new utility infielder and a threat. Later, after giving me a taste of hard ball, they got over their fear real fast."

Sid smiled. Hearing of my ineptitude relaxed him. "Once during a home game," he said, "Dor skidded trying to field a ground ball, and fell on her stomach. Betty Jane yelled from the mound, 'You playing ball or eating grass?' People in the stands got a kick out of that. It was the way she pronounced 'grass' that made it especially funny. She rolled the 'r' like an actress. I wondered if she hadn't done some acting, she was so pretty and all. And then to find out her real name was 'Magic,' which sounds like a stage name, and with all that makeup she smeared on - " His eyes pierced mine. "I prefer women with a natural look."

I smiled demurely and tabled my decision about nervous men, this one in particular. Good looks and compliments can't be easily dismissed.

He resumed, "I don't think Betty Jane realized how much she frightened the Willeys. I mean, if they aren't re-signed at season's end they won't have much to fall back on."

"Okay, so Betty Jane went for the kill when she pitched, but that's what she was supposed to do. Was she like that all the time?"

"I don't know. I didn't know her that well. But when it came to baseball, she only saw the dream of a game executed perfectly."

Our order arrived as I asked what had happened in Des Plaines.

"I can't be sure of what it meant." Sid took an exploratory bite of his burger to avoid burning his tongue any further. Satisfied, he took a bigger bite and between chews said, "When she got off the bus from Des Plaines, she sought me out and said, here I quote word for word, 'There's nobody here plays as good as the Willeys or tries as hard. Be sure you print that.'

"I said, 'But you gotta be kidding.' Boy, did she get upset, so I backed off fast and pretended to go along with her. I resolved to find out why, after weeks of lambasting them, she turned around 180 degrees. So for the next couple days, I dug and dug, irritating more than one Hornette and discovering nothing. I went back to her and said something like, 'You sound so bitter about the Willeys, so what's the real story?' Her reply was absolutely painful: 'Don't worry about how I sound, you just print my words.'"

I shook my head. "The hood following Betty Jane home must have made her even more anxious." I blotted my forehead with a napkin. I had become unpleasantly hot, as though the evil juices were triumphing. I'd nibbled at one fry but hadn't yet tasted the burger because Sid's tale had been engrossing. "Wish I'd known about this sooner," I said. "It may be relevant to the case."

He grimaced. "Hard to know what's relevant. I figured this for one more thing added to the Willeys' sneaky way of operating, that they had found something to hold over her, like maybe she had violated one of Eddie's code-of-conduct rules. Now, with no more arrests and Leroy a free man, I believe the detective ought to know about anything unusual."

"About three weeks before the murder, in mid-July, someone wrote with red lip-stick, 'Pepper's a jailbird,' on the mirror in the team locker room."

'Yeah," he replied, "I knew about that the day after. Clint told me. He trusted me to keep it quiet. Knew I wouldn't print an anonymous slur."

I wasn't surprised Sid had been informed. I felt Clint had been less than forthright when he insisted the incident had been kept from the reporter.

"When was the Des Plaines game in relation to the mirror writing?" I asked. "Before or after?"

Sid finished his food and wiped his lips with a whole napkin. Absorbed in the mystery, he had become his old assured self. "The 'jailbird' sign was maybe three days before Des Plaines. I'm sure of that, because it seemed like one weird thing after another."

Frowning, I considered. "Betty Jane must have been upset by that mirror message because whoever found out about Pepper's criminal past could have discovered hers too."

"And maybe the Willeys did find out and were blackmailing her. It's their style. They're notorious for sticking their noses in where they don't belong. Clint says that they give him the creeps. Now that's not for the general public."

"No, no problem there. Hmm, the creeps give Clint the willies. And vice-versa."

He didn't crack a smile, dang it. Perhaps that witticism was already much repeated.

He said, "The team records are on file in Clint's office. I suppose the twins could have snuck in and searched through them. But I doubt Pepper's police record would be there. Eddie would have made sure it wasn't."

"I'm not so sure Eddie has access, because she doesn't know about salaries."

He shook his head. "Nonetheless Clint would never put that incarceration stuff on record. Wouldn't dare, because of league policy."

"Right," I said. "If the Willeys lip-sticked that message and then traced Betty Jane to the reformatory alongside Pepper, they'd have had leverage to force her into saying nice things about them. Only how would they accomplish that?"

"Eating again, Sid?" Two brawny men in dirty work clothes had appeared and the ruddier one continued. "Saw you stuffing your face at the hotel and here you are eating again. You can sure put it away for a little fella."

"Yeah, Bob, yeah." Sid waved a hand dismissively while his eyes remained fastened on me. The men glanced too, before taking the hint and moving through smoke and the increasingly raucous Saturday night crowd to the far end of the bar. A pall of blue cigarette smoke had accumulated overhead.

To be heard, I leaned closer to Sid. "Yegg Washington would have kicked Betty Jane off the team if he knew she was a con, despite her being the star."

"Ironic, isn't it, with his terrible reputation. And Pepper would be gone, and Clint and Eddie, too, for bringing ex-cons onto the team. The Star-Spangled League has got to appear pristine-pure so major league baseball will let Washington buy into a real big league team."

"That's what I've heard, but let's move on. You said Washington came from overseas. You recall the name of the country?"

"Yep, I'm not a sports-writing ignoramus, you know. He's from the Ukraine, born to wandering, some say fleeing, parents. Came to the U.S. in '33 when he was about thirty-five. May have brought henchmen with him. I imagine when Stalin seized power he and Yegor, known to us as 'Yegg', had their differences, Uncle Joe not liking competition in savagery. Washington passed through several countries to get here. We know he spent time in Ankara, Turkey, on his way our fair shores."

"How did such a monster get admitted to the U.S. in the first place?"

"Influence, or bought his way in. There's plenty of under-the-table deals and we know he had cash because as soon as he got off the boat, he started in with racketeering: numbers, gun running, gambling, extortion and the like."

"At least he's done one good thing by buying into this league and giving the girls a chance. And he hired me, I don't know why, when he could have gone for Olive Shimp out of Chicago."

Sid shrugged. "Maybe he tried and she turned him down. I believe it was your address that got you hired, the likelihood you'd be familiar with the team. He might even have found out that you attended some of the games."

I shivered. "Spooky. I don't want to dwell on that."

Voice and hands trembling, he teased, "The weeds of crime bear bitter fruit."

I smiled. "Sort of biblical, or did The Shadow say it?"

Neither of us knew and we both had a chuckle.

"Is your hamburger tasty?" he asked.

I broke away from trying to recall the source of the "bitter fruit" adage to comment, "Excellent." Finishing the last flakes of bun, I said, "Will you join me for some pie? Apple, please, with a scoop of vanilla."

My man nodded. "I believe I will."

24.

The waitress hadn't yet brought the apple pie when Leroy Williams slunk by, head down, like a committed benchwarmer. He squeezed into the spot at the bar where the potato chip bag lay.

I yelled above the electric fans, juke box and the jabber. "Hey Leroy, join us. We'll buy you a drink." Betty Jane's widower looked wasted. Black circled his expressive eyes and his face had a greenish pallor, even adjusting for the lighting. He seemed to hold a sorrow beyond grief. Or maybe it was guilt.

"Catch the waitress, will you Sid, and order Leroy a beer?"

"This is our first date," he objected. "Just the two of us." When I showed no sign of relenting, he signaled the waitress and pointed to his glass.

Leroy meandered over and plunked down next to me, across from Sid. "A shot and a beer," he said.

Sid signaled the waitress again.

I hooked my heels over the chair rung. With the most tender of expressions, I allowed my hand to "accidentally" graze the widower's shoulder. Gentle personal contact reinforces the detective's connection with others. Sid stiffened. Obviously he didn't understand detective work. "Buddy mine," I began, "how you doing? Must be tough without Betty Jane."

He gave me a "what do you know about it" scowl. Turning to Sid, he said, "You buying me a shot and a beer?"

"Done," Sid assured him.

I tapped the ex-con's hand. "Leroy, I need to know how your wife got along with the Willeys. Reason I ask is because they been saying things about her, unseemly things, considering she's passed on."

He leaned toward me. His breath was rank. "She hated them. They're awful ballplayers and thieves besides."

"What do you mean?"

The waitress delivered the drinks to Sid who slid them into Leroy's eager grasp. The ex-con managed the shot in one toss, then guzzled the beer, liquid trickling down his chin. He set the glass down half empty.

His weepy eyes settled on Sid. "Gotta smoke?" The reporter tapped a Camel from his pack. Leroy shoveled it into his mouth and Sid lit it with a silver lighter. "Purchased this today," he confided. "Ronson."

"Elegant," I said with a bit of an internal gloat - there he goes again, spending to impress me.

"The Willeys. Thieves," I reminded Leroy.

Smoke spinning, he said, "Dirty old biddies broke into her locker and stole her drinking glass. They're supposed to be teammates, all for one and all that crap but you'd never know it."

"Why did she think it was the Willeys who took it?"

"She saw them sneaking peeks at her locker and whispering together. Next morning the padlock's smashed and the drinking glass is gone. Two and two makes four. So at noon she goes to the five and dime and buys a new lock and a glass like the one that was stole. Back in the locker room, she hands them the glass. 'Now each of you has one,' she says, 'Hope you're happy.'"

"How did they react?"

"Stupid grin times two."

"Didn't protest at all?"

"Didn't dare. She'd a killed 'em. I mean with words. Right after that, they found out what her real name was."

"Wow." All at once I knew the connection. The glass carried her fingerprints, the prints of a felon. The Willeys didn't seem bright enough to put glass and prints together but maybe career jeopardy had kicked a few brain cells into gear. Only how had they gone about matching the prints with reformatory records?

"When did the theft happen, before or after the 'jailbird' sign about Pepper?"

"The next day was when they stole the glass. I know because that morning started off real bad with Pepper getting mixed up and calling Betty Jane 'Lois' in front of the whole team."

Another piece of the puzzle snapped into place. The Willeys, constantly on alert to be one up on those who threatened them, suspected Betty Jane of being someone else after Pepper called her by a different name.

"After that," Leroy despaired, "it seemed like trouble just chased Betty Jane until it caught up to her out there on the river bank. Nothing nobody could do." He shrugged.

I sipped my coffee before asking, "How'd the team react when they heard Betty Jane addressed by another name?"

"She told me that for a second the place went cemetery silent. Then Eddie told everybody to get out on the field which they did, except not Pepper because Eddie held her back."

He drank the rest of his beer and belched. "That night Pepper told us that her sis was stone-cold serious wanting to know what that other name was about. Pepper said she told Eddie she was still upset about the 'jailbird' sign the day before and she kept remembering her prison days and a con named Lois who reminded her of Betty Jane. Said Eddie bought it, no problem, but," Leroy's voice trailed off, "I dunno. Eddie knows how fidgety Pepper gets when she's lying."

I reflected, "Pepper does make goofy faces when she's telling lies. Did Eddie know about Betty Jane's record prior to that?"

Leroy didn't render an opinion, perhaps he hadn't the stamina. "After Pepper left, Betty Jane got real teary and said to me, 'Bet if something went wrong you'd hit the road fast.' She liked to tease me that way but sometimes I thought she meant it. I mean, that's an insult, right?"

"Oh, I'm sure not." But she knew you better than I do. I asked how Betty Jane and Pepper got along.

He slurred the answer. "Jus' perfec'." Leroy was becoming tipsy.

"Words say one thing while tone says the opposite," I said. Sid nodded slightly. His pencil and notepad at the ready, he wasn't writing.

Leroy's speech faltered. "I'm too beat to know what I'm sayin'." He placed the shot and beer glasses in front of Sid. "Fill 'em up, will ya? It'll help get my thoughts together."

Sid glanced at me. "A date with you is kind of hard on the wallet."

"I insist on getting the next round," I said, knowing that in gentlemanly company women didn't do that.

"No, no, just kidding. My pleasure," my date came through. He gestured to the waitress but this time she was occupied with the swelling crowd and didn't respond. A second server, buxom, harried, had arrived, drifting through the smoky haze. The hot crowded room, the cigarette fog, and my chawing experience were not a good combination. Not to mention the greasy food. My stomach was starting a revolt and I began to feel shaky and disconnected. If I reached to touch Sid would he really be there? I drained my water glass and rubbed its dew against my forehead.

Sid pushed back his chair. "I'll have to go order at the bar. You want anything, Wendy?"

"Just some water, please."

"Are you okay? You do look kind of pale. It's the smoky atmosphere."

After Sid had waded into the din, Leroy shoved his face close to mine and whispered, "Pepper brought Betty Jane down." The statement seemed surreal.

"What? Say again?"

Leroy's face wavered. "It's Pepper's fault them two toad-faces found out who Betty Jane was. Now my darlin's life is over and mine is fucked up for always."

"What's the connection between the Willeys, Betty Jane's real name, and her murder?"

"I dunno. Is there one?" He looked vaguely interested.

I moved on. "Your former neighbors said you and your wife were fighting right before her last game."

"Screw them. We had a squabble. The cops pounded on me about it. It was about sex, okay? I wanted it, she didn't. Jesus, you're just like the cops. I should shut up. Where's that booze?" He writhed in the chair.

"You need a friend, Leroy, and you've got a good one in me," I said with all the sincerity I could muster, God forgive me.

Sid was back with the ex-con's order and a large glass of water. "Go easy with this," he counseled, thumping it down. "Just take sips." I drank as Sid set Leroy's beverages in front of him.

In the time it took me to swallow a few sips of water, Leroy had finished the shot and the beer. "Question," I said. "Who was the silver-haired man who followed your wife home?"

Leroy began rubbing a rhythm into the table like a drummer using soft brushes on a blues tune. "Just a guy. Happens when you're famous. Didn't have the guts to go right up and ask her out."

"Leroy, the guy's a gangster. His name's Kramer. Do you know him? Did you work with him where something went wrong and he got back at you by harassing your wife?"

"Sure, pin more dirt on me. Sure, you're my buddy."

"I want to help you, Leroy, but I need the truth to work with." Pepper was right about this man; his fine looks were diminished by the weak chin. I averted my eyes to its quivering. I didn't want to feel pity for him right then.

Sid was staring at the café entrance and I followed his gaze. There stood Dave Madison, farmer and former boyfriend, making long-armed motions at me.

"I think that fellow knows you," Sid said.

"Yes, we're acquainted." I was surprised because, since Dave retired from his law practice, he rarely went anywhere except to the general store in Mediapolis and the bowling lanes with me. Tonight he was dressed in a gray suit and tie, not the jeans and plaid shirt of the committed agrarian. He looked like the lawyer he had been, except you couldn't have inserted a legal brief into his balled fists.

Wide frame bumping patrons aside, at our table he clamped a proprietary hand upon my shoulder. "Wendy, I stopped at your hotel and the clerk said you might be in this place, but I hardly believed him because I understood you always went to bed early to save yourself for the next day's practice." Dave paused to breathe.

I flexed my shoulder to rid it of the hand. "Let's do introductions," I said. "This is an out-of-town friend, Dave Madison, and Dave, these are two friends from in town, Sid Dobrotka and Leroy Williams."

"Billy Leroy," Leroy muttered.

Sid waved his wallet. "Siddown. Order something. I got a couple bucks left."

Dave sized him up. "You're paying for Wendy?" He bounced out the remaining chair, between Sid and Leroy, across the table from me. Gripping the chair back, he studied the two good-looking men I was with. His condemning eyes said I was a loose hussy floozy tramp. He yanked the chair out, took a napkin and brushed off the seat before sitting down.

"I always pay for my date," Sid informed, "and any of her acquaintances who happen by."

Dave snapped, "Wendy, do you consider this fellow to be your date?"

"Dave, stop cross-examining me. Really."

Blearily, Leroy watched us go back and forth from the nest of his hand.

I pulled a napkin from the holder and took a pencil from my handbag. "While you-all get caught up, I'm going to make a list of pertinent events that preceded Betty Jane's murder. Contribute if you like, but I warn you, I'm looking for facts only, no emotions allowed. Oh, nuts, my pencil went right through this flimsy napkin!" I tossed the wipe into the air and it floated to the table. "Sid, may I borrow a page from your notepad?" Wordlessly he handed over the whole tablet.

Dave screeched his chair back, in doing so, he swung an elbow out and jostled Leroy's beer. Leroy scowled murderously at him and pulled the drink to his chest. Raised in gentlemanly circumstances, Dave said, "Excuse me," as Sid asked, "What do you do, Dave? I'm the sportswriter for the Gazette. If you ever need a table, give me a call. I can get you one even if the place is as jammed up as it is tonight."

Dave's nostrils flared. Where he came from, anyone boasting an occupational title without being prodded was looked down upon. "I am a farmer," he proclaimed, "and proud of it." He banged out of his seat and, swooping past Leroy, bent toward me. "What have you been doing, Wendy? You smell like a field of tobacco plants. How long have you been in this dive?"

"Listen, mister," I gave it back, "I don't remember inviting you into this dive."

Sid also retaliated. "Everything smells like smoke in here. What's your problem anyhow?"

I picked up Sid's notepad and read aloud from it. I hadn't actually written anything, distracted by the present company, so I drew upon memory. "1. About the middle of July the 'jailbird' sign goes up on the mirror. 2. Next day Pepper calls Betty Jane 'Lois.' 3. That night, the Willeys steal Betty Jane's drinking glass. 4. Several days later, Des Plaines happens and Betty Jane returns home praising the Willeys." I paused, awaiting contributions. There were none.

"I came all this way to see you," Dave exclaimed. "The least you can do is …" He grunted trying to snatch the notepad from my hand.

"Who do you think you are?" I jerked the pad away and it flew backward from my hand.

Sid half rose from his chair to intercept. The pad brushed by his palm and fell to the floor.

"Really, Mr. Madison," Sid said, sinking back, "we were having a very fine time before you showed up."

I kicked off my shoes, got up and stooped to retrieve them. While under the table I picked up the notepad and tucked it up my sleeve. I had no intention of returning it to Sid, not yet anyhow. Rising, I bade my gents a good evening and cut my way in stocking feet through fascinated customers and out the door. There was more than enough testosterone at our table for me.

As I retreated, I heard Leroy say, "Can't nobody order me another beer?"

Out in the fresh air, I looked through the picture window, afraid I might see an outright brawl over li'l old me. Not to happen. Sid and Dave were both on their feet, eyeing each other. They exchanged a few words, pulled back their chairs slowly and sat down again. Leroy was staring into his beer glass, just as I'd left him. Then, unbelievably, Dave waved to the waitress as though to place an order.

25.

The Hotel Burton City was three blocks away. After donning footwear in the lobby, I climbed the winding staircase to my room. I sat at the kneehole desk paging through Sid's notepad, to find out if he'd had valuable information he'd neglected to tell me. Nothing, although one otherwise empty page was revealing in that it had "Wendy" written and underlined three times. I had made an impression. Another page provided a neatly printed vocabulary list - epistomology, analemma, elipse, makhovic, neibelungen. Goodness. Neibelungen were in operas, weren't they? Was Sid interested in something other than sports? I'd have to find a dictionary to keep up with him.

The rest of the pad was blank although pages had been removed.

I stripped off my nylons, their soles gray with sidewalk grime. I spread out on the double bed that was so big not a finger or toe reached over the sides. This is the life, I exulted, let no one take it from me.

Hotel Burton City was built of brick and Bedford stone in the Renaissance Revival style. The proud natives called the nine-story structure, "The Little Hilton." I adored my capacious room, paid for by one Mr. Yegg Washington, big-time criminal, way ahead of my dad in that respect, although my old man had quite a reputation at the local level.

I loved returning to the hotel after a hard day's floundering on the diamond to be greeted by fluffy clean towels, starched sheets, and the snugly made bed that maid service provided. I could ring room service at 3:00 a.m. if I wanted, for a deluxe macaroni and cheese dinner with orange rolls and a Coke, although I never did, too expensive even with my substantial per diem. Still it was a comfort to know that if I ever had to hole up, I wouldn't starve.

I slid off the bed, padded across the room and removed stationery from a desk drawer that glided out like it had been greased. Thick carpeting and heavy drapery made the room virtually noiseless.

Sitting on the bed, I jotted down the previously recounted events of the case and added two more: 5. In late July, the gangster Kramer followed BJ home. 6. Three days before her murder, BJ's funning included a toy gun rite that caused her to upchuck and pass out.

"Shit," I said, sad for what my hero had endured in her last days.

Before the game the following afternoon I played easy toss with Kay. This was a habit she insisted upon because, previously, one of her warm-up pitches had landed in the stands and she had lost that game. You can never be too superstitious in baseball. Now the first thing Kay touched coming onto the field had to be a ball rubbed by me. Then we'd play catch for exactly five good throws, a pre-ritual that made the magic of THE ritual especially potent.

"Ready to win another one?" I inquired after the third leisurely toss. Even though The Kid had pitched nine innings two days ago and an inning yesterday, Clint was starting her again. "If she can go three, I'll pull her out," Clint promised, "but I need somebody in there who can WIN." Eddie greeted his decision in stony silence.

The Kid pondered the ball. "A lot's happened," she said, "since Betty Jane passed on. Can you believe I was so hard up for a win that I wore her cap and glove for luck? Shoot, you make your own luck, don'tcha, Winkie baby?"

"Sure do, infant gal." Recently The Kid had no shortage of gall. She should be told that she was feeding off my mumbo-jumbo as she had once snacked on Betty Jane's gear, but who was up for doing that? Not me. The truth might ruin her pitching. Better for my mission if I just shut up and play catch.

"Your pop here?" I asked.

"Yup, but I'll see him after, not before. When I talk to him before a game, I lose." Kay's scheduled mound appearance attracted a large crowd, although it didn't hurt that this was also Dr. Pepper Day, the first thousand fans getting a free drink. Already giant paper cups teetered in the hands of small children who raced up and down bleacher steps.

Our opponents, the Waterloo Flickas, were in third place in the six-team league, one game ahead of us. After Kay and the rest of the starting nine took the field, Sid came down from the stands and joined me on the bench.

"Had a good time last night after you left," he said. "That Dave's an interesting character. Too old for you though. You call him yet?"

"Not yet," I said, like I was thinking it over, but I knew Dave wasn't anybody I wanted.

"Too bad you didn't hang around," he said. "You would have seen Leroy get absolutely skunked. He was so drunk he started recounting the murder as though he'd been there. Said just before the fatal bullet he imagined his wife imploring the killer, 'Why you doing this?'"

"Did you ask him who he imagined the killer was?"

"I did. 'Was that you she was begging?' I asked. Leroy hemmed and hawed and finally admitted he was just being morbid, imagining her last moments to suit himself. He didn't kill her, Wendy. He was just so completely potted last night. Poor guy, he's totally destroyed by her death."

"The reason I didn't stay," I said, "was I didn't want to come between the friendship you three boys were forming."

Sid pulled out a scorecard and examined it. He seemed oblivious to my moodiness. "Clint's pitching Kay too much," he grumbled.

With that concern being mutual, I lost my indignation. There'd be time later to ruminate on Leroy's drunken story. Right now I'd best concentrate on the game in case Clint put me in. Fat chance.

The bottom of the first inning, Dinah ran in from her position and plunked down beside Sid. Since I had thought I was already sitting right next to him, I had to make room fast. Even so, space was tight, what with her large bosom heaving with every intake.

"What you courtin' Winkie Winkle for?" she queried. "She can't hit or catch. Guess that won't stop her being writ up in your newsrag though."

Sid chuckled. "Newsrag. That's clever." He twisted and thumped her on the bicep. "You're unique, M&M. Not like other girls."

Dinah beamed. "You think so, Sid?"

"Absolutely. You're more like a man." This "compliment" was not taken well. Dinah leapt to her feet, and in striding past, gave my ankle a hefty kick.

As the big girl heaved her intimidating self out of the dugout, I cradled the hurt, observing to Sid, "I took that one for you."

"What did I say?" questioned Sid, but expected no answer because he was absorbed in annotating details on his scorecard. As official scorekeeper, Sid had his own way of recording the batting order:

Dober, 5
??Lor W, 4
Eddie Mc, 2
Timberlake, 3
Ziegler, 7
Brock, 1 (although a pitcher, Kay was a good hitter and batted sixth)
??Dor W, 6
Schulz, 8
Pepper Mc, 9

"What are the question marks for, in front of the Willeys' names?" I asked.

"They like to entertain themselves by changing their middle infield positions and sneaking it past people. You can't really see Dor's identifying mole from here, or from the stands. Of course, I spotted the funny business immediately, from watching their mannerisms. The one is forever touching her mole. The other leaves her face alone in favor of digging into her left ear. I don't nail them for the deception because they're equally clumsy in either position. Let 'em have their fun. I record their plays accurately and neither one ever complains."

As a baseball neophyte, I wondered if Sid was pulling my leg. But Mr. Sincere Sportswriter would never do such a thing, would he? I'd keep an eagle eye on the Willeys to find out.

No score when in the fourth our leadoff hitter, Joanie Dober, limped to the plate. Not injured, she always just poked along until something worthy of notice occurred.

With the first pitch, Joanie's crippled manner changed and, back foot leaving the dirt, she lashed out and lined a single past short. With Lor Willey next up (supposedly), Joanie danced off the bag, so unnerving the Flicka's pitcher, Markham, that the southpaw tried twice, unsuccessfully, to pick her off.

"Who they are off the field shows in how they play the game," Sid explained in teacherly fashion. "See how Joanie studies Markham?" The base runner was shuffling her feet almost faster than the eye could follow, her head never moving, eyes riveted on the pitcher. "Joanie's fast but more than that, she's smart."

On the fifth pitch to Lor, Joanie lit out for second, drawing a throw, but making the steal.

Sid elucidated. "When Markham is gonna pitch to the plate, she turns a fraction more toward the catcher. Means Joanie can take off earlier in the windup knowing the throw won't be to first base."

I studied Sid's face, the brightness of his eyes, the joy he got from analyzing the scene. I felt a jolt of inner happiness. Was this man the one for me? Or was it only that I was captivated by a master of his trade?

Facing a 3 and 2 count, Lor wiggled the bat, nervously awaiting the next pitch.

"Probably a hitter's pitch," Sid said, "but she's so darn overeager." The aging twin swung late, striking out. "It also doesn't help that she has the reflexes of a turtle."

Tossing aside the bat, Lor clomped down the dugout steps, her moleless face dull and expressionless.

With Eddie at bat, Sid slipped an arm around me. I lifted it away. "Not while I'm working, or hoping to." He had the good sense not to comment.

At bat, Eddie displayed a patience not in evidence otherwise. Broad butt wiggling, she eyed each delivery, waiting for exactly the right pitch. Between deliveries, she whacked her spikes clean of dirt. After fouling off a number of pitches, she drew a walk.

Runners on first and second, one out, Dinah swaggered to the plate. She kissed her bat, tapped the plate three times, twitched her shoulders, cracked her neck and stood in. The crowd's little kid shrillness erupted and Dr. Pepper spewed skyward. With the count 1 and 0, Dinah swung, obliterating the air but not much of the ball. She flied out to centerfield, whereupon there was a distinct reduction in soda shower.

Next up, Twyla held the bat high and punched a single to right, filling the bases. Kay then doubled and, with the fans roaring and Clint waving mad circles from the third base coaching box, we scored the first three of many runs that day.

Beside me, Sid yelled, "The Kid can do it!"

Before the bottom of the fifth, he rose intending to return to the stands. Before he left, I asked for a favor - make a certain phone call and charge it to me. Yegg Washington would reimburse the cost. Sid gave me a searching glance, but knew from my tone that the request was important and he agreed. He departed with a swagger that told me he knew I was watching

At the end of the bench nearest the outfield sat the Willeys. On the diamond, their chatter was part of the game, but upon trotting in they sat close together, apart from teammates, guzzling from the water dipper.

Heads darting, the twins studied the game, the bench and even the stands; you felt nothing got by them. Baseball is an exacting business where results are there for all to see. Like the PI business, success and failure are clearcut: a murderer is nabbed or walks free; a hit or an out, a completed play or an error, nothing in between. When it's all you care about and all you know, your life is at stake.

My dad's philosophy was in the air. "If it's yours and you ain't watching it, then it's mine." There would always be someone eager to take away what was yours. I knew the double-dealing Willeys held answers, so, in preparing to take them on, I dwelled not on a game that was safely in hand, but on stirring things up, to make the pair as frightened of me as they had been of Betty Jane, before Des Plaines.

The phone call from Sid would give them added incentive to come after me. They topped my list of suspects, but I couldn't figure out a motive. They'd had Betty Jane where they wanted her, making effusive, and false, statements about their abilities to the press. Maybe something had happened to again make her a threat and they had killed her. If my plan worked, if I could scare them enough to ignite their violent instincts and make them come after me, I'd snatch those metaphorical green beans right out of their hands.

26.

"We won, no thanks to you," I yelled at the Willeys as they ran from the field at game's end.

We had blasted the Flickas 12-5. Kay pitched seven innings before Clint sat her down to save her arm. He gave the ball to Letta who promptly allowed four runs. Clint left her out there to "persevere through adversity," Eddie's much-repeated phrase awkwardly echoed by the manager.

The win moved us into a third place tie with the Flickas.

At my denigrating comment, the Willeys pulled up and Lor said, "You call yourself a psychologist? Ain't they supposed to help people?"

"You two are beyond help in this game."

Several other Hornettes approached. Dinah sing-songed, "The Willeys hit with toothpicks."

Joanie joined in. "You gals got the worst hands since my last lover."

But levelheaded Connie advised, "Careful that Winkie doesn't draw you into a fight."

"Let's not blame Winkie for everything," Joanie said. Surprising since mostly she did.

The Willeys took off for the clubhouse.

Sensing it was also time for me to slip away, I moved to follow, but as soon as my back was turned, someone shoved and then tripped me. I went down hard.

"So sorry, puffball." Letta's malicious face gazed down. "Gimmee your hand, lemmee me help you up." No chance, lintball. After crawling a few inches on my hands and knees, I was on my feet sprinting for sanctuary. Laughter rose behind me.

In the clubhouse, I found the Willeys beside their lockers, greeting me with frozen backs. I spoke over the clatter of spikes coming down the hall. "Lucky for you Betty Jane's gone 'cause she sure had your number."

Dor whirled to face me, her elbow striking a locker. Rubbing it, she said, "You having a bad day, Twinkie? Back off or I'll show you a worse one than you ever knowed."

Lor echoed the sentiment. "Got some nerve, can't field for shit yourself."

"Don't have to," I retorted, "I'm a registered psychologist slash kinesiologist." I had practiced my title until it rolled off the tongue.

We faced off about four feet apart, Dor seething with anger, Lor looking tired and downcast. Dor was the dangerous one. "Betty Jane and us was best friends," she said. "Ask your buddy, Sid, if you don't believe me."

Sid's affection for me was well known, thanks to his telling everyone.

"I know what you had on Betty Jane. I know what you blackmailed her with," I said. I brought up a hand, formed the fingers around an imaginary glass and pretended to drink. I added sound. "Glug, glug. I know it happened in Des Plaines." What I didn't know was how the Willeys linked the glass's fingerprints to Betty Jane's criminal record.

The pantomime had the desired effect. "Don't say nothing, Dor," Lor squealed. "It'll go straight to the cops."

"I'm not stupid," Dor responded. She spoke at me, every syllable a threat, "Better stop now, Winkie, 'cause we got charms you cannot see."

Merry team members burst into the room. Fortunately Eddie led the pack. There'd be no pummeling with her around. Dor began removing her blouse while pinning me in her fiercest glare. I withdrew to the rookie area near the chipped back wall and watched as the twins donned faded blue skirts and white cotton blouses stained yellow under the arms. I couldn't deny that I had pity for these women who were doomed to lose their beloved way of life whether or not I started the process.

A thunderous banging sounded on the locker room door and a substantial male voice called out, "Telegram for Miss Susan Hamburger." Sid's phone call come to fruition.

"No one here by that name," Eddie shouted.

"I'll take it," I said, galloping past her. "It's for a close relative."

I opened the door a crack and snatched the envelope. "Thanks," I said brightly, closing the door fast before the young man could study his hand with no tip in it.

Back at my locker, I was aware that curious eyes were upon me, but the attention I most welcomed was that of the Willeys.

"What you up to?" Kay said narrowly. Seeing I wasn't about to confide, she sniffed, "Oh well, big deal."

I made a grand flourish of opening the telegram and throwing back my head in anguish before I even read its contents. Got to remember to scan bad news before reacting. I clutched the paper to my bosom.

Several players were on me like flies on honey, with expressions of avid concern: "What's going on, Winkie? Is it bad?"

"The worst," I muttered. I moved through other teammates who were celebrating the win with snaps of garter belt at exposed nipples. Fearful of being hit by an errant, or more likely, deliberate, swipe, I dodged toward the Willeys. Closing in, I let the message flutter from my hand. "Oh, no," I said frantically, but too late, Dor scooped it up faster than she'd fielded any grounder that season. She drank in the message that read, "To Susan Hamburger, Infielder, Burton City

Hornettes. Your gramma is dying. Come quick. Your loving uncle, Ferdy."

I grabbed ineffectually at the paper. "Gimmee that," I wailed. "It's private."

Dor stuck it behind her back. "This yours?"

"Please, my grammy is sick and needs me."

Her grin spread. She returned the telegram to my trembling hand. "There you go, Susie," she crowed.

As I stumbled away, shaken and teary-eyed, I heard Dor say gleefully, "First she's a ballplayer, then she ain't. Now she ain't even her. Another one pretending to be somebody they aren't."

The next afternoon from the bench, I observed infield practice. Dinah and Joanie were at the corners, the Willeys at second and short, Eddie behind the plate. I admired their hands, so graceful in coaxing the ball to go where they directed, and their bodies, capable of stretching in such elastic ways, although in slow motion where the Willeys were concerned.

But the Hornettes lost that game, 3-2, and sank in mood and in the standings. Lor dropped a throw in the sixth although no runs scored as a result. The team gave it to her pretty good afterward. I stayed out of it.

I didn't know how the Willeys would react to my riding them, but I took care not to shower alone. No problem there; since Tubbs' death, there were never fewer than three girls taking showers.

At night I made sure my hotel room door was secured both by lock and chain guard. I expected they might want to search my room for information as to who I really was, or maybe they'd just jump to the next step and try to kill me.

The following evening the game was rained out. As lightning zigzagged and thunder rumbled, and with downpours periodically crashing against the Nash's windshield, I staked out the Willey bungalow. If the twins meant to try anything, it was easier to follow them than remain in my room as a sitting duck.

That soggy night the pair stayed dry inside.

We lost both ends of a double-header the next afternoon. That night, I returned to the Willey household and parked down the street. After three hours of observing an unoccupied porch, illuminated by a dim glow through a window shade, the thrill was long gone and my mind began drifting. As usual, when a stakeout became tedious, I got to thinking about my dad.

27.

About a month after our "campout" in the woods, Dad was arrested for theft and sentenced to four years in the county jail. Our family didn't attend the trial, which was held in Harrison, 33 miles from our farm. Too far for our ancient truck to travel and too expensive for gas anyhow. I forget exactly what it was the authorities said he stole. In our family, the story is that he stole so much you couldn't keep track and it would demean his reputation to specify.

At home in our living room, my brother, Norris, slumped in his easy chair while Jim and I sat cross-legged on the floor. They listened as I read the newspaper article about Dad's sentencing. When I finished, Norris tapped his jaw with a comic book and said, "Bastard got himself caught, now it's up to us to go to the trouble of saving him."

"Being shut in will kill Dad," I said.

"I believe it will," Jim agreed solemnly. A weird equanimity had replaced his youthful jumpiness since he'd taken to attending revival meetings.

I pictured my bearded Dad roaming the woods, so intent on evading capture that he stuck his pistol in his belt for all to see.

One day, soon after Dad started serving his sentence, Norris was waiting for me when I got home from school. "We'll be taking a trip on Saturday," he stated. "Going to visit our daddy." He was slouched in the easy chair, a cup of coffee at his side.

My heart did a flip-flop. "Who's going?"

"You and me and Jim. The whole family. I saved up."

Mom had left two months earlier to live with the grocer so she wasn't family any more. She had stayed away pretty long this time and I was seriously considering whether she might be gone for good. As it happened, the bags of groceries she and her lover placed at roadside the day of her departure had to last forever.

Conflicting emotions erupted at the prospect of seeing Dad again. "No, I won't go. One line up, one slant down, one line up, circle!" I blurted. After all, he had left me by a road to fend for myself.

"Why not just say 'no' and leave it at that?" Norris said. "Like usual, you're being difficult, and different, too, calling him 'Dad,' when the rest of the world says, 'Daddy.'"

I shook my head vehemently because I called him "Dad" to show how special he was to me. (I called my mother, "Mom." The usual soft and cuddly "Mama" was not for me.)

Stuffing a Twinkie in his mouth, a black-garbed Jim joined us from the kitchen. After his conversion, in honor of his newfound righteousness, he wore only black and developed a straight-legged, rigid walk. Occasionally he spoke in tongues to the delight of his fellow rabid flock-members. But he still loved sugar.

Mouth forming a knothole, he spoke tonelessly around the cup cake. "Daddy's gonna try to escape."

"See you don't mention that to your bible-beating friends," Norris growled. "Look here, Daddy needs our help. The whole family gots a part. You too, Wendy. He's real happy you're doing good in school."

"Yeah? How's he know that?"

"Word travels, like how we know he needs us."

The praise from behind bars, even second or third hand, made my heart swell. But I remained contrary. "Why should I help? He ditched me last time."

"He didn't ditch you, you'd be in reform school right now. Besides he says only you can do the job."

"Must be something small then," I figured. Of course I committed to Dad once I heard that only I could fill the bill.

Come Saturday, I rode between my brothers as Norris coaxed our sickly truck toward Harrison. As we travelled, dry fall air blew dust into our faces through the open windows. Insects clicked against the windshield and vaulted away, smearing their insides on the glass. The brick jail was on the edge of town, surrounded by barbed wire fencing and swirling dirt.

I wore jeans, the cuffs rolled up twice, and a scruffy plaid shirt with sleeves so long they swallowed my hands. The shirt was courtesy of Jim after he switched to black. Earlier Norris had taped a slim 6-inch carpenter's file to my lower left arm.

After parking by the jail's front door, Norris lifted me down from the truck. My job for the day was to act utterly incapable of movement or thought except with the aid of my dear oldest brother. Scrawny, with deep-set eyes, Norris had embarked upon a career as a night burglar. He looked in need of a meal, but his full lips were set to discourage any offer of charity.

Two armed guards in tan uniforms met us outside the jailhouse door. The one with muddy yellow eyes jeered, "What a mangy crew." Norris gave us false names on the sign-in sheet: Billy, Freddie, and Toots were Dad's children come to visit. Our home address was in Missouri. Don't remember the town he wrote down. "We don't want 'em hounding us after he gets away," was the way he had explained it.

The guards escorted us to a dank holding room where we were searched. Dragon Eyes patted down, thumped was more like it, my brothers. I drew the second guard, a big-nosed, sweaty man in a wrinkled uniform and crooked tie. He searched me with a distracted air as though his mind dwelt on more pleasant pastimes. As his hands wiped down my upper arms, coming close to the file, I twisted away and said, "Gotta use the bafroom QUICK." I wiggled my right hand out from under the flannel sleeve and trustingly offered it to him.

"Okay, come on," he grumped. He took the hand, clammy with fear, and we trotted side by side to the toilet, his long shoes matching my tiny treads step for step. "Some daddy you got to put you through this," he groused. I smiled winsomely at his concerned face gazing down. He waited outside while I went into the ladies' toilet. When I emerged, he had forgotten about searching me further and the file was still up my sleeve. If I hadn't been so frightened, I'd have felt contempt for such a dumb cop.

The visitors' room was small. Over the years, cleanser, sweat and stomach trouble had made for a variety of stinks. Handcuffs hanging from hooks decorated the wall. Most of the furniture was gouged and grimy, except for one table that was brand new, glossily black. That was our goal; we needed that table because Dad had discovered narrow ledges at each corner of the underside.

"Daddy's quick to spot a weakness," Norris noted on the trip in. "He's a sly ol' bastard."

Jim added, "After he flees, I'll bet the cops check that table forevermore."

Two other visitors were already waiting for their men, a fortyish woman with an enameled face, and a windburned old man, who, I was shocked to see, was seated at our table. Clutching a large creased hanky, he hacked and spit into it. Jim, imposing in his shiny black suit, strode stiff-legged toward him. My brother bent down and stuck his broken teeth right up to the man's snotty nose. In a dire voice, he proclaimed, "This here table is reserved for our family in the name of Lord God and the Holy Ghost." He grinned like a demon. The man stopped hacking and furrowed his brow. He slid from the chair and sat at one of the other tables. He opened the crusty handkerchief, and blew.

Dad and two other convicts were brought in. Dressed in faded green, their hands cuffed, they wore leg irons, the chains chinking like the skeletons in a horror movie I saw once.

The two guards, Dragon Eyes and Dumb Cop, sat the prisoners down at their respective tables. Dad took the end chair across from me. I was seated next to Norris who was between me and Jim, the three of us on the same side.

Dad looked older. His shoulders were more rounded and gray speckled his close-cropped hair.

The guards withdrew and stood beside the door, hands clasped behind their backs.

Dad smiled at me and said strongly, (at least his voice hadn't changed) "How's my honey?" His face was ashen and puffy. I shut my eyes at the sight of a raw purple bruise on one cheek.

"Look at me," he coaxed, "it's okay, I ain't dead yet." Speaking to the guards, he said, "I'm scaring my little girl. Can I hug her to show her I ain't dead yet?"

"On no account. Stay still," Dragon Eyes warned.

"Your hands got to stay cuffed," Dumb Cop explained.

"Kiss her then?" Dad struggled against the ankle chains to rise and lean across the table.

"Siddown or you go back to your cell!"

Norris steepled his hands to cover nose and mouth. "Daddy," he wailed, "you look awful sick."

On cue, Daddy sobbed, "Aw, how I miss my dear children." I was so nervous my knees went wobbly because that was the signal for our plan to begin.

Jim fixed baleful eyes upon Dragon Eyes. My dark brother intoned, "Deliver me speedily out of their net for Thou art my strength." Gasping, he spasmed to his feet. His head jerked back and arms flailed. A second spasm sent a hand striking his mop of unwashed hair and coming out with an Alkaseltzer tablet he had hidden there. As he crumpled to the floor, he put out a hand to break the fall, while the other slipped the tablet into his mouth. His head lolled to one side as foam coated his lips. Kicking, writhing, he remembered to let his tongue dangle. Black Jim was half-Christian and half con man that day.

All of a sudden, my fear was gone. I had an essential part to play.

The guards were making confused moves as Norris knelt to aid Jim. Dragon Eyes waved his pistol and yelled, "Watch 'em, they're faking."

"Help, my boy is having a fit," Dad cried. Bracing cuffed hands on the table he raised himself to his feet. "Get his tongue out. Keep it out or he'll choke himself to death. Roll him on his side. Oh, my poor sick boy."

Dad was chinking around the table. Dragon Eyes holstered the gun and, drawing his billy, rushed forward. He grabbed Dad by the waistband while thrashing at his manacled ankles. Dad screamed and collapsed, falling with cuffed hands under him. Backing away, Dragon Eyes tried to stuff the club in his holster but found the gun already in residence. His voice climbed, "Stay put all of you."

"Help me," he roared at Dumb Cop, but that fool was stuck in place, yammering, "Hands up, hands up."

Dragon Eyes' billy club clattered to the floor. He drew his pistol and swung it in arcs around the room.

The other convicts raised their cuffed hands while the female visitor started in on an extended whine.

Dragon Eyes stutter-stepped to Jim and put a foot on my stricken brother's back.

From his kneeling position, Norris said, "Get offa him, he's sick." He pushed the guard's leg hard enough to make the guy lift it and set the foot on the floor. Dragon Eyes leveled the gun at Norris. Norris raised his hands and slid away. "Easy, easy does it there, King," he said over Jim's continuous moans.

I didn't have the file any more.

But, glancing around, I saw one of the other convicts wink at me, slowly and deliberately, and my heart stopped for an instant. I knew he had seen me hide the file. When the convict maintained his silence, I decided that the wink must have been in allegiance to the Winkworth name which was well known among the criminal class in northern Arkansas.

Dragon Eyes went to Dad and, gripping him by the cuffs, dragged him out. "Watch 'em," he ordered the other cop. Haltingly Dumb Cop brought out his police special.

"Nobody gets hurt," he said thinly, "if nobody moves. Think it over."

The woman stopped whining and touched her enamel complexion for breakage. The visitor with the snotty handkerchief started hacking again.

Dragon Eyes came back to escort the other prisoners out. When he returned again, he found Norris and me kneeling and cooing beside our fallen brother. Jim's eyes were wide and dazed, his face was shiny with sweat. Foam was caked on his lips. Dragon Eyes tapped Norris on the shoulder and led him away. In about fifteen minutes, an ambulance sirened in for Jim, who twitched as they took him away on a stretcher.

Dumb Cop walked me to the holding room. Through the wall, we heard thumps and cries that Dumb Cop attempted to mask with loud speech. "I got a little girl just like you," he nearly shouted. "She's a sweetie, I bet you are too."

I recognized the anguished cries. Rushing to the door I flung it open. Norris lay in the corridor; Dragon Eyes was beating on him with fists. "That's my brother there," I screamed. Dumb Cop yanked me back into the room and kicked the door shut. "Why don't you help us?" I pleaded.

"I can't, I can't," he babbled. "Think of something else. Your brother will be all right. He's just getting a lesson not to talk back. My daughter likes dolls and tea parties. Teacups and saucers and a teapot. They sit around a little round table, her and her dolls. I'll bring a doll for you next time you come. You'd like that, would you? Wouldn't you like that?"

"I don't play with fuckin' dolls!"

Somewhat shocked, the dummy reproached with, "Well, you're no nice little girl."

My chin was quivering and I was ready to break into wild tears when the door opened and Dragon Eyes shoved Norris in. My brother staggered but stayed on his feet. His nose was bleeding; actually it was broken. The evil dragon allowed the corners of his mouth to curl up. "Shoving an officer of the law ain't healthy," he said. "You're free to go, both of you. Get out now." He spat on the floor.

Norris drove me home. He cussed each blob of blood let loose on a grease rag. The next day we returned to Harrison to pick up Jim from the hospital. The nurse gave us pamphlets on epileptic seizures, their cause, recognition, and treatment, but nothing on how to deal with rage.

I never saw Dumb Cop again, except doing his worthless shuffle in my nightmares.

28.

In my car on the Willey stakeout, memory folded me in its heavy blanket and I dozed. Creaking sounds awakened me. Brushing aside imaginary fuzz, I peered out. The twins, in T-shirts and shorts, were moving stealthily down porch steps, heading for their beater of an automobile. Soon the roar of an unmuffled engine split the calm and headlights cut a bright path down the road. So much for stealth.

Beneath a slivered moon, I followed with headlights off, my recent M.O. At 2:40 a.m., sleeping homes and foliage beside the street blended into a shadowed border.

The Willeys thundered past the gates to Cranston Park and continued down the winding road to the ball field. Parking around a curve, I glimpsed them in near darkness, scampering from their car, dodging trees, scaling the ballpark wall by a shuttered gift stand. I followed over the wall and, staying close to the border, saw them running for the clubhouse. With effort, one twin boosted the other through Clint's office window. This foray had to be planned because Clint always locked his windows to keep Eddie out. Beyond the shade, a flashlight came on and darted around.

I crouched beneath the window which was set about six feet from the ground. In the office, metal was screeched against metal. The twins were searching the files. Lor spoke in her paper-doll voice.

"There's no Winkie here. Lookie, Wadlow, next comes Willey. No Winkie between."

"Dope-us," Dor's fog-horn replied. "Look for Winkworth. It comes after Willey."

Furious scrabbling of papers, accompanied by afflicted sighs. "Nope, so there. We're the last ones in the records."

"Who is she? Wait, try Hamburger. You know how to spell that? Should with all them you put away."

Moments later: "Nope." Not a morsel. The searcher hit the file drawer a vicious shot.

"So who is she with no records?" Dor said. "Eddie always makes us have a file so she can plan for our training. She was as surprised as anybody when Winkie turned out to be a psychologist and that extra thing. We gotta keep hunting. If Winkie's really a 'Hamburger,' it means she's a fake there too. If she's a fake there, and she's already fake as a ballplayer, then she's a fake other places too."

"She might even of killed the real Winkie and stole her college degrees," Lor said hopefully.

"That'd be the best thing. Then they wouldn't believe anything she said about us. We gotta search her room for evidence she's a Hamburger."

"Oh, not tonight. I'm too tired."

"Okay. But we gotta keep searching in this office long as we're here."

Silence ensued for a long period. I stepped to one side of the window and froze against the wall.

Inside, the rustling of papers began again, interspersed with a series of crashes. I figured the files were being upended.

"Lookie!" Dor expelled.

"What? Oh." They had discovered something and I needed to know what.

I looked around. The window was too high for me. There was a metal garbage can several yards away. Overturning it slowly, I intercepted a bottle as it clinked out. I waited for reaction from within the office, but hushed discussion continued with no evidence of having heard.

I carried the can to the window and placed it upside down with infinite care. The rim was badly dented so no matter how I adjusted the container, it wouldn't sit level to the ground. I stopped trying and listened. Nothing changed within the room.

I gripped the windowsill and pulled myself up onto the wobbly can. Parting the shade, I leaned in a couple inches. On their knees by the far wall, the pair huddled over a dark object. Their flashlight caught one of them waving a small object. Even with only a hint of light, I knew it was a gun.

I regretted leaving my pistol in the Nash. In shorts and T-shirts, the two had seemed unarmed.

The garbage can tottered beneath my feet. My support became even less secure as I sought to regain control. The can swayed, it tipped, it actually rocked. I hoisted myself onto the sill and leaned slightly through the window. The can fell away and clattered to the ground. I lost my last shred of balance and tumbled into the room. I landed hard on my left shoulder.

The Willeys sprang to their feet and ran into each other. One dropped the flashlight but the other hung onto the gun. I'm a goner now, I thought, especially if the armed one was Dor because she had already been measuring me for road kill. I rose slowly, keeping my hands out to show I meant no harm. The Willey raised the revolver and located me dead center, but then she swung the weapon up toward the ceiling. I sprang for a folding chair and hurled it. It caught her arm and the gun spun away and skidded across the floor.

The two of us pounced but I was first on it, covering it with my body, grabbing hold of it. She hit me a glancing blow, but I managed to stagger to my feet. I pointed the gun at her and she stopped being fierce. It was Dor; I saw the facial mole. On all fours, Lor was no threat. Being exposed as a burglar was already too much for her.

The flashlight's thin beam was all that lit the room. Backing to the door, keeping the pair in view, I turned on the overhead switch.

Papers, liniment tubes, and ancient, oil-encrusted gloves spilled from two overturned file cabinets.

I broke open the revolver. It was a .32 Smith and Wessen, the same caliber as the firearm that killed Betty Jane. No bullets in the chamber. Closing it, I addressed Lor. "You find this here or bring it with?"

"Don't answer," Dor said. "It's none a her business," but too late, the terrified Lor whimpered, "In here, in that."

She pointed to a briefcase that lay on its side near the sagging blackboard. They had knocked over the spittoon and I kicked it aside for a better look at the case. Old and scuffed, it had a thin metal handle that looked uncomfortable to hold; probably the original leather grip had worn through years ago. The gray leather of the case was scaly in places where smooth brown material showed through.

I rubbed at some dry, flaking bits of leather; they came off easily in my hand. I knew where I'd seen their like - in an unused locker and on the floor near where Millicent Tubbs had met her end.

Breaking my concentration, Dor yelled, "Let's go." Lor shot from her crouch and together the pair lunged toward the door and ran into each other again. "Dang it," Dor shouted and pushed Lor out the door. She followed, slamming the door behind her and they both took off. I didn't go after them. I'd had one triumph over Dor, didn't want to risk another. Besides I knew where they'd be in the morning.

After I heard the locker room door slam, I slid the bolt on the office door and drew the long shade fronting the lockers. I moved to the window to watch for their flight, but saw nothing. When I heard the distant sputter and roar of their car, I waited until it faded away entirely, then shut the window and locked it. Now the night was soundless. I raised the revolver to the light and examined it. There was a bit of discoloration on the butt that might be blood. This weapon would go to the technician. Perhaps Millicent's blood was embedded in the butt. With the evidence of the flaked leather bits, there was a strong possibility that she had been murdered too. I laid the revolver on Clint's desk and set the old case beside the gun. I was right about the harsh grip on the case; it left a thin white line across my fingers. Without a doubt, this case had been in the locker Millicent Tubbs had chosen, maybe with the gun in it.

I skirted the overturned files. Behind their original position was dust around a space on the floor that exactly fit the dimensions of the briefcase. I might have spotted it several days ago when I'd hidden the cracked bats, except I had been occupied with other things at the time. The briefcase must have been hidden there after the ball-charm necklace turned up, because that had resulted in a third search by Chief Shupe's minions, the first two happening after each death. Did this evidence implicate a ballplayer, or even Clint, in Millicent's death?

I opened the case by its latch and ran my hand the length of the compartment. The inner cardboard backing felt slightly moist and tiny bits of grit stuck to my fingers. Deep in a corner, I touched something small and metallic, and brought out a silver heart-shaped locket, about one-and-a-half inches high and an inch wide, engraved with sunflowers, the kind I'd call a grandmother's locket, meant to be pinned to a lady's dress. Forty or fifty years ago, this particular style had been in fashion. I held it to the light where it displayed more than a few nicks and scratches. Despite the damage, it was expensive, I judged with Sears-Roebuck expertise. Concerned that the fragile clasp might break, I gently worked it open. An oval photo portrait of a pretty young woman wearing a high-necked dress with mutton sleeves and a frilly collar gazed out of the past. There was an empty space for a photo on the other side of the opened heart. The matching oval picture of a young man dressed in his finery, had been wedged under a bench leg near Millicent Tubbs' fallen uniform.

Were the contents of this battered case a reason for murder? Had the locket been part of a larger cache of antique jewelry and had it been missed in haste by the killer?

I wound the ornament in a hot dog wrapper from Clint's desk after licking spots of mustard off the other side. After all, I hadn't eaten in hours and mustard is my favorite condiment. I stuck the wrapped locket in my pocket. Delving once more into the briefcase, I located a cloth label and raised it. Fringed and faded with wear, it read, "ANTILOP DERI DUKKANI, ANKARA, TURKIYE," in a language an Iowa ballplayer didn't often get to see. Below that was the translation, "ANTELOPE LEATHER STORE, ANKARA, TURKEY."

That brought me up short. Sid had said that Yegg Washington had lived in Ankara for a while. Staring at the faded label, I wished the store's location would fade away entirely. Chief Shupe wouldn't be thrilled by this find either.

The possibility loomed that the killer was one of Washington's henchmen. If so, how had he gained access to the locker room? Hard to get in and out of here without someone unlocking a window or door from the inside. It was hard to imagine a thug strolling through the locker room.

An urge to vacate the room swept over me. The space seemed filled with Washington's evil power. I reached for the briefcase and revolver, snapped off the room light, and slipped out the door, closing it soundlessly. I was holding the empty gun at the ready, as if this were a situation where death was preferable to capture.

Outside, the weather had turned cooler. In my car, driving fast, I worked at regaining composure. No longer were the Willeys my prime suspects. They'd employed their usual M.O., trying to find something they could use as blackmail. Treacherous and despicable, but not murderous until further notice.

The Willeys' jalopy was back in front of their house. I climbed the front steps shouting, "Open up, crooks. Neighbors, you live next to crooks!"

Aware that the Willeys might, in panic, try to dispatch me, I held my .38 close to my chest.

The door burst open and I was yanked inside. I stiff-armed the ladies aside and entered the living room. I made for a threadbare davenport.

Dor blundered after, Lor fluttering behind.

"Why ain't you in the files?" Lor complained around her sister's shoulder.

Dor answered for me. "'Cause she's a cop like Cousin Ernie. That .38 makes her one."

My gun waved them to chairs, but they refused to obey and huddled together in symbiotic intimacy. As a child, I remember two old maid sisters sashaying down Main Street, arm on arm. No matter how hot the day, they wore the same frayed tan coats and headscarves tied tightly around fruity or flowery hats. Norris made fun of them and Jim went along until he converted, after which he maintained a pious superiority over ridicule and old ladies. We'd heard that one of them had the opportunity to marry, but instead chose to remain with her sister. Easier, I suppose, not to have to seek outside companionship when you were lonely. Sometimes I wish I had a twin.

I spoke out of the corner of my mouth. "I carry a gun because, when patients refuse my help, I have to get tough."

Lor nodded. "Yup, talks like Cousin Ernie, don't she?"

"Yep, she's a cop, all right. One of them underground ones."

While they deliberated all the tunneling it took to earn my keep, I checked out the living room, aware of a musty smell, as though the furnishings had come from basements or attics. In addition to the ancient davenport there were two torn armchairs with cardboard boxes serving as end tables.

I spoke over the debate. "Isn't this your seventh year with the Hornettes? Why don't you lay out a few doilies and settle in?"

"Job's one season at a time," Dor offered.

You can't change these types, I thought, then caught myself because I'd been the unsettled type too.

"You followed us here but we followed you first," Dor said. "We know where you live, in that fancy downtown hotel. Who's paying for that? The police, I bet. How'd you like the other girls to know you're riding high on the hog while the rest of us are struggling?"

"You vandalized Clint's office," I stated.

"If she tells we'll blame her, say we were trying to stop her," Dor said. "Clint'll believe us. She's only a rookie."

"I caught you with a gun. Plus, this isn't the first time you've stolen stuff - stole Betty Jane's glass from her locker and found out her real name from the fingerprints, didn't you? Was Cousin Ernie a help? Where's his beat? Des Plaines, Illinois?"

"Ernie's beat is in the big city, Chicago, so there. Before he came to Des Plaines to see us play, he says, 'Get aholt of something with her prints on it, I'll check it out for ya.' I gave the glass to him before the first game and by the third game, he had found out who she really was. We gave him a hint, look where Pepper was 'cause they was such pals. Sure enough, her prints were in that Montana hoosegow, right next to jailbird Pepper's. Big shot star Betty Jane Wadlow was really dirty jailbird Lois Magic, no different from lowlife Pepper."

"'Jailbird,'" I repeated. "You wrote on the mirror didn't you, about Pepper being a jailbird."

"Did it after we listened in on Eddie warning her she'd go back to jail if she didn't straighten up," Dor said proudly.

"What was she doing that Eddie didn't like?" I asked.

Lor pawed at her sister's arm. "Shut up, Dor."

"No I won't. Pepper was going against every rule in the book, out with those deviates every night, all night."

"Listen to me," I said. "I can be extremely forgiving of those who repent their evil ways because us doctors are required from training camp on to be merciful. So you wrote those ugly words and you stole a drinking glass. Those are minor crimes, but tonight you broke in and trashed an office. Those are felonies, girls, punishable by prison terms. As for the revolver, I'll ask again, is it yours?"

"It's not ours," Lor said.

"Yes it is," Dor said. "You can't charge us with stealing that."

"Tell the truth, sis," Lor begged. "Winkie's trying to be nice."

"Old cop trick. She's not on file so we know she's not a real Hornette," said the other.

I didn't get what difference my being in the files made.

"Let's get on with it," I said impatiently. "Last time I saw my Hornettes' file, it was in that pile of papers on Clint's desk. What with you tossing stuff all over the place, I can't say where it is now."

Lor sagged. Face buried in hands, she blurted, "Oh, Dor, she says she's a psycho, and if she is we're cooked, but if she's a cop, we're cooked too." She summed up brokenly. "Either way we're cooked."

Dor's voice was bitter. "The only thing that'd save us now is if we join Clint's sex parties. He'd speak up for us then, you betcha."

"But," Lor protested, "you already said we're not the type to do that."

"Don't count on sex partying to save you," I broke in. "I mean, has Clint ever made a pass at you the whole time you've been Hornettes? I bet not."

"We got too high morals for him," Dor responded, but Lor's cheeks were puffing until she exploded, "I bet he did too! One game after we got rained out, I went to his office to get some sourballs and he's looking me up and down in that kindly way of his and he says, 'Darlin', here's some sweets, and your shoes are all wet, we'd better take 'em off.' And he sits me down and kneels at my feet and slips them off so dainty that not a toe is disturbed. But he ain't through. He says, 'Darlin', your socks are sopping wet too. I'll relieve you of them too.' He reaches for my socks and tickles my skin and I jump up and say, 'Imagine you.' Well, he has the nerve to look puzzled, but boy did I get out of there fast."

"Scary," I said.

"She knew what he was after," Dor said.

"I never want him poking into me," Lor said.

"Course not. Psychologically very troubling," I said. "I shall bring that awful man up before the Iowa State Psychology Association, Triple A Division."

Lor squealed in horror, "Oh, don't do that, he's so nice."

"What? I thought you hated him."

Dor's tone dripped with scorn. "He's just typical. They can't help themselves."

She settled back, but her lips were straining to confide. I leaned forward to catch the latest Willey-foolery. "Today I saw Clint with only his briefs on."

"Dor!" Lor and I screamed in tandem.

"Yes I did," Dor verified. "Today when I went to his office to unlock the window so's we could get in tonight, he came out unexpected from his toilet and, oh, it was all bunched up to one side of his shorty shorts."

"Maybe it was broke," Lor gasped.

Dor nodded grimly. "Maybe Eddie broke it."

"If it's broke," I said gently, "then you don't have to worry about it."

They seemed a little disappointed, but did indicate agreement.

"Now," I cleared my throat, "let's go over what happened in the office tonight. The old beat-up case you found … "

Lor waggled her head, perhaps to clear away thoughts of sex. "We recognized that case right away. It's what Betty Jane brought to the ballpark on her last day. She stowed it in her locker."

"What time of day?"

"Late afternoon. About 4:30 like always for a night game."

"Was it stuffed full or limp?"

Dor's head jerked up alertly. "Was what?"

"The briefcase, of course."

Spots of color appeared on her face. After a moment, she said, "Something was inside it. It looked kinda full."

"Fleshed out," Lor added helpfully.

"You have any idea what was inside?"

Head shakes. They didn't know.

I pondered. Probably Betty Jane had had the case with her when she left that last time and the murderer took it after he killed her. Maybe he or she killed her for it. A cache of antique jewelry? Was Betty Jane involved in jewelry theft? With Leroy, or, a dreadful thought, with Yegg's organization? That would destroy my opinion of her. Who else did I know with a penchant for baubles? Eddie.

I kept my voice level. "After Betty Jane's death, did you tell the cops about the briefcase?"

A sly grin sneaked onto Dor's face. "Why? Didn't mean nothing to us."

"Besides we mighta been able to use it for our own benefit later on," added Lor.

"Oh, don't tell everything," Dor remonstrated.

I repeated an earlier query. "How about the revolver? You bring it with or find it in the office?" I focused on Dor.

She'd had time to think that over and now reached the conclusion that it was better to have found the gun in the briefcase, to which Lor said gratefully, "That's the truth speaking. Thank you, sister."

Laying my .38 beside me on the davenport, I said pleasantly, "I'm calling a truce. After all, we're one-for-all Hornettes, to the very spriggy core. I'll forget all about tonight if you'll help me improve my ball-playing skills. I may be only a psychologist and, you know - " I was too weary to pronounce "slash kinesiologist" one more time that day, "but I really want to get into a game. I've been practicing hard with a guy, but he went north."

Seeing I held their attention, I spelled out conditions. "One hour a day starting tomorrow, you help me with fielding and hitting and I forget all about your felonies." I didn't believe this pair had murdered Betty Jane, although they certainly had been frightened of her influence. Sneaking around undercover, or underground, as they put it, was more their game than outright blowing somebody away close up.

So I'd observe the Willeys, determine if they had it in them to boil over with murderous rage at the prospect of livelihoods stripped away. At the same time, I'd train with them. Although by splitting my detective duties with becoming a passably good, spit-in-your-eye, ballplayer, my PI career might get sidetracked a bit. So what? I was young; I could handle both.

29.

After some discussion, the twins agreed that taking action would hurt least, so they rushed back to the office, to clean and trash it again, Mr. Delicious style.

As for me, I drove to the Hotel Burton City and caught a quick nap. At 8:00 a.m., I handed over the revolver, locket and briefcase to Chief Shupe, who didn't seem thrilled about connecting Betty Jane's murder to Yegg Washington's business associates.

"I feel the same way," I responded crankily, "so don't rag on me about it. And don't bring in the Willeys for questioning. In return for their information, I promised they wouldn't be bothered. It could ruin my investigation."

"Hell, Wendy, doing what you and Mr. Washington want is the most important thing." He ended the conversation by stomping from the office.

I returned to the hotel and again hit the sack. About 2:00 p.m., the phone jangled. Shupe notified me that I had found the .32 that killed Betty Jane. Scratches on the bullets used in the killing matched flaws in the gun barrel. "Lands and grooves," he elucidated, to which I added, "Holes and ridges." I was proud I knew a little gun science.

After only a brief pause - the chief was getting used to my knowing something - he said Clint had no idea how the briefcase had found its way into the office. He'd never seen it before, or the locket either.

I bypassed Manager Clint's characteristic declarations of utter ignorance. "We have to determine when the case was left in the office. I mean, did Clint bring it in?

"No," he said. "Weren't you listening?"

"Gee, I'll bet when we ask, everybody will say the same thing, and with a straight face too."

"Oh come on, the guy's as baffled as we are."

"He had possession of the gold charm necklace, Chief."

Very patiently Shupe carried forward his own train of thought. "Clint knows somebody was in his office because he can't find the shaving brush that goes with his Burma Shave soap mug. And he asked what you were doing in there anyhow. I covered for you, no, don't thank me. I told him you were following the Willeys as part of your job as psychologist."

"What? Come on, Clint knows I'm a detective. Don't you remember? He was sitting right beside you when you hired me."

"Lord, my nerves are shot and now I got two more suspects to deal with. It's late. I gotta think this over."

My support team was getting goofy. Okay, so he wasn't exactly my backup, but really, dealing with this man was like living with a recalcitrant teenager. Oh well, he thought the same of me.

I'd not told him about Leroy recounting Betty Jane's supposed last words. Fantasy or real, I had no proof either way.

Shupe went on to inform me that the .32 was going to the Des Moines morgue to be tested for blood traces under the assumption that the weapon had been used to bludgeon Millicent Tubbs. "The tough job will be tracking the gun to its owner, particularly if he's a mobster. Wouldn't get my hopes up there." Shupe changed to a related subject. "Maybe the briefcase was hidden the same time the gold necklace was left there. Stuck behind a file. My men could have missed it. Robinson said they did a thorough job."

"Bad police work," I summed up.

"Damn cow-dung cops," he muttered. He raised his voice. "Someone's got easy access to that office. Eddie McLaine's my choice. We know she's not very stable."

"I doubt it's Eddie. Of all the players, she's the one Clint most wants to keep out."

"Well then I don't know." His voice knifed through the phone as he banged down the receiver. There wasn't time for more chitchat anyhow. Although the team had the day off, I was due at the ballpark at 2:45 for my first blackmail practice with the Willeys.

On the field we tossed the ball around while they criticized my technique. "What's wrong, you got back trouble? Follow through, you throw like a girl. Whyn't you just roll the ball back." After that nastiness, Dor spit in the dirt and clarified with, "Spit on you."

But in that hour my play improved and as we stowed our gear, I thanked them. They accepted by giving me their backs.

Although I had decided the Willeys were not killers, when the three of us went to shower together, I kept an eye on them. Nothing violent happened except one flung soapsuds in my eyes. I didn't get which one because I couldn't see. Otherwise, I emerged unscathed. Even after showering, the Willeys still looked dirty.

I dressed in bright colors, and avoiding the Tabu perfume, I walked out front to meet Sid.

Leaning against the front fender of his automobile, ankles crossed, cigarette drooping, he looked natty in a polo shirt and freshly pressed gabardine trousers. My pulse quickened upon seeing him. I only hoped my outfit, the traditional sundress, was spiffy enough to entertain him.

We drove to the river. I had treated my skin with Coppertone, and soon the car was saturated with a coconut smell. As we strolled along the riverbank, Sid slipped his hand in mine and we reveled in the sunny day, moving past grotesquely twisted, wizened trees, their roots exposed by the tides. It was inevitable that we were drawn to the place where Betty Jane had been slain. The police had long since removed the rock with "JUSt" written on it. I kicked some dirt in desultory fashion, but the scene had been gone over both by Shupe's cow-dungers and the Des Moines homicide detectives, so there was no chance of a new discovery.

We stood for a moment of respectful silence. I said a silent prayer that the star pitcher was somewhere happier than here. Then we removed ourselves from the presence of death. While sauntering beside him, I thanked Sid for sending the telegram, explaining how it had led to turning the tables on the Willeys. It wasn't until we were seated on a boulder by the cliff, his masculine warmth against me, that I mentioned the battered briefcase.

His eyes widened. "Whoa, let Shupe handle that."

"He won't do anything. Afraid. But you could help."

He took his time lighting a cigarette, then took a pencil stub and notepad from a pocket. "How?" he said, his eyes roving the horizon.

"I need to get in touch with Mr. Washington, tell him about the new leads I've developed. Find out if he wants to take action himself."

"What do you mean?"

"The Turkish briefcase and the murder weapon. It's somewhat likely that his henchman, the silver-haired man, was involved in her death. Give Mr. Big Shot a chance to decide if he wants to deal with the guy himself. You have a lot of sports contacts. You must know how to get in touch with him, or can find out."

"No, I don't know how to get in touch." His voice was edgy. "It's dangerous implicating a Yegg Washington associate. And don't make light of his influence. You're not taking his power seriously enough." He flipped the just-lit cigarette to the sand and ground it out with his heel. "All I'm saying is, Wendy, that you should consider the ramifications."

"Okay, I'll merely hint that he might check out Mr. Kramer's alibi for that time period."

"Oh," Sid groaned, "extremely ill-advised." I opened my mouth to object, but he was going right on, his hazel eyes riveted on mine.

"I suppose I'll have to help you because I love you. That is, I care about you a lot. I mean I'd love to see you do well on this case. Love to see you get credit for catching a killer, but this isn't smart. No, not smart at all." His voice had risen and he was talking fast.

"You love me?" I asked, returning his concentrated gaze.

"Mmmm," he said, but didn't nod. He leaned in to nuzzle my cheek, a diversionary tactic.

I lifted my brows, non-Groucho, because this was serious. "This is what I do, Sid," I said firmly. "It's my job. I can't worry about consequences."

He didn't have anything to say to that. Instead he stuck the writing tools in a shirt pocket, kicked off his shoes, and stretched out on the scrubby ground, drawing me to him. I rested my head on his shoulder. I slipped my shoes off and snuggled into him. He let the sun soak us for a while before he leaned over and kissed me.

An hour later, with only the cries of songbirds and crows interrupting the calm, he said, "You know, I feel kinda funny about enjoying ourselves so close to where Betty Jane died. Do you?"

So I gathered my handbag and we floated back to his car and onto my big soft bed at the Hotel Burton City. I had longed for his touch with a hunger that left me breathless. That night I was left breathless again. Sid was something special.

30.

The next day the Hornettes travelled by team bus to Cedar Rapids for three games against the Starlets. Arriving about 6:00 p.m., we unloaded in front of the latest dingy hotel. The following morning, after breakfasting on biscuits and sausage with roomie Kay Brock, I joined the Willeys on a march to the local ballpark. Actually I walked across the street from them, since they refused to be seen in my company on their own time. You would have thought some gratitude would have been in order for being spared the breaking and entering charge. We chose sport shoes for our hike and not the heels prescribed for glamour-girl ballplayers when appearing in public because we wanted to reach the ballpark while it was still light out.

On the diamond, after we'd discarded skirts and blouses and changed to shorts and t-shirts behind a fence, we worked out, the Willeys berating me for precisely one hour not counting a ten-minute break. At the conclusion of the session, we retrieved our lady-clothes and went to shower. At the clubhouse door, Lor looked toward the vacated field and said, "Sis, there's hours before game-time, let's get us some extra throws in." Sis agreed and they dropped their apparel next to a concession stand and started back to the field.

"Wait up," I said, tossing my clothes and spinning to join them. "I should do that too."

"Oh, no," the mole-marked one, said, "you got your time in."

The lesser of the nasty said, "Take off, creampuff. Shower room door's unlocked, or at least it was when I used the toilet during break. Hall's got some dead ends but you'll find it soon enough. Gal like you never quits, no matter how hopeless you are, you taught us that."

Wow, a compliment sort of. I'd have gotten teary-eyed if Dor hadn't added, "You'll recognize the visitor's shower room because it's got showers in it."

I gathered my clothes and entered the building alone. The visitors' showers were at the farthest end of the squat brick structure, or so it seemed. I admit to getting lost twice, traversing the narrow, dimly lit, winding passageways, finding dead ends around corners and retracing my steps, thinking grudgingly that illumination must be limited to ten watts in this town. Finally, purely by accident I stumbled across the showers. Entering the moist room gratefully, I heard from a far corner of the loony building the bangs and clatters of a dedicated cleaning person, a Darrell Moeller type unleashed in Cedar Rapids. Either that or Dinah Timberlake was strolling down the hall.

I stripped quickly, turned on the shower spray, tested the temperature, and stepped in. Gathering a used cake of soap from the dish, I luxuriated. As sweat, hot water and soap rolled off me, I rendered an operatic version of "Take Me Out to the Ballgame," complete with tremelo. I stopped in mid-lyric because my mind drifted to thoughts of my ball playing chums: Who were the Willeys underneath that veneer of sliminess? Did they feel any kindness toward others? Were Joanie and Twyla really faithful to each other? I mused upon those and other pressing questions, as well as wondering where I'd eat that night.

I reached to the high bar, grabbed a towel, covered my head, and stepped out of the shower uttering a theatrical "Brrr" at the drop in temperature. A stack of towels lay at the end of a short bench. "Ah," I sighed, unlimited clean towels, the epitome of high living. As a child, I'd had been granted a single towel that I laundered once a week. I seized two off the pile and then one more, piling all on top of my head making a mound of turban. I took another to wrap around my torso.

I heard a metallic bang behind me as if an irritated someone had kicked a locker. Turning to see who was there, I was hit hard on the top of the head. My skull went numb and knees buckled. The most searing pain followed as the world dimmed. My last thought as I hit the floor was deep regret at trusting the Willeys. Then I hit the floor, and that's the last I remember.

I drifted in and out of consciousness hearing the faraway bangs of the cleaning person, a jumble of thoughts about warning her that the Indians were coming over the hill with tomahawks and arrows, but I couldn't get my mouth to cooperate. Time passed painfully before my eyes were willing to open. When they did, I saw green trouser cuffs and scuffed slippers consuming the space in front of me. I seemed to be able to step back and see it was my dad gazing down at me, pistol drawn. The purple welt on his cheek had spread to his mouth. I studied him as he placed a cautionary finger to horribly swollen lips and started to speak.

But the voice I heard was Dor's. "S'pose she needs help? Looks like she passed out from practice."

"Did you do her?" Lor's voice trembled. "If you did, we should get outa here."

"Didn't do nothing. Anyhow she ain't dead. Look, she moved."

Mole-face didn't hit me hard enough, I thought murkily. I tried to cry out for help but the word didn't transmit through my mouth. I tried to raise myself to get away but my arms had no strength.

A blurry brown eye came down to my level and Lor said, "What happened to you?"

"Got hit," I whispered. She took hold by my armpits and wrenched me up as I moaned.Staring open-mouthed at me, she recoiled, loosening her grip. I listed until she firmed up her hold and dragged me to a bench where I collapsed onto the slats. I tried to raise a hand to touch my head but the desired impulse didn't seem connected to my brain.

She whispered, "Your neck's all bloody."

My hand worked then, flying to my neck and ricocheting away red. "Gee-zuz," I said.

"Throat's been slit," Dor's foghorn voice noted.

"Get help," Lor said. "I'll stay with her."

Dor moved to the door and stepped into the hall. "He-e-lp," she croaked. She stepped back in and said, "I'll stay over here while you check if anybody's hiding in the lockers."

"Check it yourself," Lor retorted. "Now Winkie's the one who's down. We're falling like flies." She scooped a towel off the floor and handed it to me. "Cover yourself," she directed. I used it to pat my neck. The white terrycloth came away smeared with red. Bracing my hands against the bench, I made it to my feet and veered toward a steamy makeup mirror. Squinting through the mist, I could see my neck was bathed in red. Don't say a word more, what if your voice box gurgles?

I approached the wound with the towel and patted further. What a relief to see that most of the color toweled off, leaving pinkish skin and no knife slash. I'd been conked and decorated. Head throbbing, I looked around the room. A baseball bat lay on the floor about a yard from where I'd fallen. Next to it was a pile of bedraggled towels.

Lor was pointing at the mirror. "Look," she said.

I obeyed, and noted groggily that on the left side of the mirror, scrawled in red, were the words, 'JUSt lay OFF." It registered dimly that "JUSt" had been written on the rock near Betty Jane's body using the same combination of capital and small letters. That clue had not been publicized for fear of a serial confessor taking false credit.

I dropped the paint-smeared towel and wavered back to the bench. Collapsing onto the seat, I cradled my pounding head in my hands.

A sweet, heavy scent lingered in the room, familiar, but I couldn't think why.

Lor approached with a towel. "Cover yourself up," she said again, more gently.

Dor had disappeared into the hall.

After Lor and I arranged the towel, I said, "That explains that."

Lor sat down beside me. "What?"

"The part of speech. The word 'JUSt.' Its usage here is as - whatchama - at any rate it's not a noun." I closed my eyes and slumped.

"I'm very, very scared," Lor quavered, "so don't say no more that's nutty. Just tell me you passed out from practicing too hard and cracked your head on something. Like Milly Tubbs did."

"Just like Milly," I assured.

"Yuh, yuh."

She grabbed my hand and stroked it.

I pulled away carefully when I remembered that she and her sister had written the first mirror message, in red, like this one.

In the Cedar Rapids hospital, I dozed, dimly aware of a uniformed guard sitting watch by the window. At one point through the fuzziness I heard Sid say, "Honey, you have to give up this business." It seemed like an excellent idea so I nodded internally and once more gave myself to slumber.

Later a growly voice said, "Lucky you never listen to anybody so you grew a thick skull."

"Towels saved me," I mumbled. I opened an eye until a piercing pain forced it closed again. The speaker had been Chief Shupe. Beside him, Clint's jaw worked, tobacco juice trickling from his mouth. A guy who'd let his chaw dribble like that shouldn't be teaching spitting technique to others. I returned to dreamland.

Much later, or so it seemed, a cheery female voice cut through the haze. "Breakfast." A plump nurse hoisted me into a sitting position. As it turned out, I was feeling rather well rested and the pain was only a dull ache all over my body. Taking my pulse, she asked, "Do you feel up to having a visitor?"

Sid appeared around the side of the bed and brushed my cheek with a kiss. I experienced a pang of joy at his presence. Ah, to be alive and have someone love you, maybe.

"Did you contact Yegg Washington?" I asked hoarsely. "Did they do this?"

"Wendy," he said, "you have to quit this case. It's too dangerous. Let me finance you from now on."

I licked dry lips. "Is that a proposal or a job offer?"

"Could be if your answer's yes."

I let my head fall back into the plushy pillow. "Sid, I hurt so much I can't think straight. Don't ask me serious questions now."

He stroked my hair. "Okay. Fine. I'll ask you later. If I remember."

The nurse came back, plopped down a tray and shoved a steel spoon in my mouth. The tepid oatmeal on my tongue was delicious. It was good to be alive.

That knock on the head was the hardest I'd taken. I vaguely remembered a white-coated figure materializing during the night and telling me I'd sustained a lump the size of Cleveland. Doctor humor. Now, exploring my crown, I encountered a sizable bulge.

The door burst open and Chief Shupe was back, carrying a file folder and a paper sack. "Sid, how'd you get here so damn fast?" he said. With a look and a nod and a well-placed hand to the back he pushed the nurse out of the room. After setting the folder on the bed, he drew an enormous sweet roll, slathered with icing, from the bag. He held it against my lips and I took a sticky bite.

"Wowzer," I said mushily. "Thank you."

Between bites, I told Shupe what I remembered of the attack. A metallic bang, a crack to the skull, and oblivion.

The chief said tempera paint had been used to decorate my neck and write the red warning. "A paint bottle, wrapped up in a sopping wet, red washcloth, was found in a cleaning cart."

"Dinah use tempera paint?"

"Nope, only oils, and those are still at the station, booked as evidence."

"You came clear from Burton City to tell me that?"

"You bet. One of my investigators sustained a nearly fatal wound, after all."

I had enough spunk left to respond, "If I live, I'm still not working for you."

"But there's another reason I'm here," he hedged, "another thing to discuss."

"I'm listening," I said, although I knew.

"You haven't contacted Mr. Washington yet, about Ankara and the briefcase and the gun, have you?"

Sid jumped in. "I think she should keep quiet about that, for a while, at least. Do not involve Washington's men. That's about the worst thing she could do."

Shupe couldn't have agreed more, and there followed such back and forth about my health and wellbeing that, finally, I had to interrupt. "Please don't discuss me like I'm out to lunch."

"We're pretty sure who attacked you," Shupe said as he separated a packet of papers from the white folder. "At about the time you were assaulted, a hot dog vendor was setting up right outside the club house." He patted sweat off his forehead. "Goddam hot in here." He resumed, "That time of day, only one door is unlocked, right by the vendor's stand, so he can get in for supplies. He remembers you as the perky one. Says the twins picked up their clothes one at a time, right by his stand, and went through that door separately, minutes apart from each other, maybe twenty minutes after you picked up your duds and went in. We questioned the Willeys one at a time. Lorena admitted right off that Dorena went in first, maybe two or three minutes before her. She didn't seem to realize she was implicating her sister. Now that she's got it straight, she says the first story wasn't right. Now she says they went in together and found you at the same time. The other one of course agrees with this latest version."

"I think Dor came upon me first," I said. "By herself, because of what Lor said. She asked Dor if she'd done it. There's no doubt they'll stick together on a story."

"This is the second incident where they've been involved," Shupe continued, "and we've only got their word that they found the murder weapon inside the briefcase. It may have been theirs. In fact, this is the third instance, because they wrote the 'jailbird' message about Pepper McLaine. And now comes a warning in the same color and same arrangement of letters as was on the rock after the Wadlow murder. That ties it all together. Are you keeping up? You must be feeling pretty dopey."

"No problem. I've hit a sugar high, so I'm keeping up quite well."

"Okay. It's our belief Dor clobbered you and that both the sisters are complicit in the Wadlow killing. But we're not 100% sure because there is a complication."

He paused to take an enormous bite out of another sweet roll that properly should have been mine. I reached to grab the remaining piece but he held it away.

"The hot dog vendor says two cleaning ladies arrived about twenty minutes apart, before any of you three went in. He knew one of them, the gal the Starlets hire, but the other one he wasn't familiar with. So we got an extra cleaning lady to account for. He described her as wearing a long skirt and a scarf wrapped tight around her head and pushing a cleaning cart. She was bent over the cart so he couldn't tell her height, and hurrying the cart along, her face turned away from him."

Shupe consumed the rest of my roll.

"Might it have been a silver-haired goon in disguise?" I asked.

"I doubt that!" He became more conciliatory. "I'll check how sure the vender was of gender."

With the chief actually agreeing to one of my suggestions, it occurred to me that we might just be establishing a grudging respect for each other.

I closed my eyes and they flew open when I recalled the cloyingly sweet smell in the shower room. Tabu perfume, the kind worn by most of the players. That eliminated Eddie. According to Kay, she wore the expensive Parisian stuff. And the Willeys, too. Having just come from practice, they were not yet perfumed up; I'd have smelled it on them. Despair overtook me. It had become depressingly obvious that the killer was one of the Hornettes, a baseball girl who rode the team bus right alongside me.

31.

There weren't enough fingers on my shooting hand to count all the evildoers on the Burton City Hornettes. Cocking thumb was for Pepper the convicted felon; trigger finger for Clint: possesser of the stolen baseball necklace; obscene gesture digit saved for Eddie the klepto; ring finger for the breaking and entering Willeys, pinkie reserved for Man Mountain Dinah, a vengeful bad girl.

Considering the league's lily-white reputation, the list was astonishing, but taking into account the man bankrolling the league, it wasn't so surprising.

At 5:15 on Monday, after the third and final game with the Cedar Rapids Starlets, Clint greeted me at the team bus. Sid had driven me from the hospital, where I'd been kept those three days for observation. My boyfriend and I (yes, he was my fella, for now anyway) exchanged hugs before he sped off to Bettendorf for a YMCA boxing camp.

The bus sat rumbling by the hotel entrance, its bluish fumes spreading over the scuffed luggage sitting by the hold. The yellow bus looked like an upside down bathtub. The sign above the windshield, DESTINATION PENNANT, was depressing to consider. A huge, splayed out black wasp with yellow bands around its body was painted on the bus front, its six prickly legs gripping crossed bats, ball, glove, and catcher's mask. On both sides of the bus, tiny wasp silhouettes flitted around a black stripe that ran the length of the bus.

Clint, in knit shirt and denims, stood beside the vehicle, clipboard dug into a hip. The bags under his eyes were packed with misery.

Eddie stood a few feet away, close enough to observe, and far enough to avoid contact with Mr. Very Undelicious. She was clad in an elegant purple suit, a white scarf tied at the throat. No jewelry, antique or otherwise. Sturdy and thick through the trunk, she was no match for her statuesque sister, who shared a joke with pals Joanie and Twyla by the hotel's revolving door. I heard Clint's name in the laughter.

Pepper was attired in a tight black skirt with a slit in back in case she wanted to move forward, and a red silk blouse that looked like she'd bought it, then gained weight. The outfit was completed by a strand of pearls, black net nylons and high high heels.

A few players approached me with purpose, causing Clint to drift toward the hotel entrance. Apparently he had only braved the heat to check if I was on two feet.

The scouting party got quite near before Connie spoke. "What happened to you? We hear you have a big goose egg on your head."

"Yeah, wanna feel?" I didn't encourage by removing my Hornettes' cap.

There were no takers.

"Bad luck, you seem to draw it," Twyla said.

I stopped smiling.

"We're all under the gun these days," Joanie observed.

"Lord protect us," Connie said fervently. She seemed more spiritually advanced than the rest of us.

More players drifted up until I was surrounded. "You see anything?" Letta asked. "What did you hear?"

I shook my head. "Nothing. Somebody sneaked up from behind."

"They say Millicent Tubbs died accidentally," Connie said, "but with you getting conked, it does make you wonder, doesn't it?"

"Beings as you was the last to see Milly alive," Joanie added.

"What's the connection?" I said.

"What's your opinion?" Joanie fished.

"Killer seems to be focusing on the new people."

"They should post guards around us," Molly said.

"Yeah, why don't they?" Bobby was in my face, inquiring. "You could get them to do that."

"Because you're a dick," Joanie stated.

"Aren't you?" Twyla asked, adjusting her glasses.

"Who told you that?" I asked.

She looked away.

Pepper stepped up. "Why do we have to keep playing ball anyhow? We could get killed doing it."

"Because it's our job," Dor retorted. Sure, she had someone she could trust, a sister who had lied for her.

Deep in her own thoughts, Dinah spoke slowly, "Dor, you was there when Winkie got clobbered, so was you the one who done it?"

Dor jumped away to protest. "No! It was sis and me who saved her life."

"Yeah," Lor said, "M&M, go back into your coma."

Dinah licked her lips. "Okay," she said, "just saying you got good reason, what with her being after your job."

Joanie spoke directly into Dinah's face. "Winkie is a dick, a detective, you understand? She doesn't want a regular job with us. She's here to nail one of us for killing Betty Jane and you're especially included in that. Once that's done she'll get on back to her own dick-dom."

Dinah's one-track mind didn't let up. "Winkie's working awful hard like she wants a Willey's infield job."

Eddie was heading toward us, clapping her hands. "On the bus everybody, we got games to play."

"If we live long enough," Twyla said, moving to board. I hung back to take a few breaths of air untainted by fear and blame.

Eddie strode past me to pose by the steps until all had boarded.

She helped me up the first high step of the bus. From there I grasped seat backs, feeling a mite unsteady as I moved along the aisle. Girls were milling and the few already seated pretended to be busy or stared out the window as I passed.

While I'd been incapacitated, the team lost three straight to the Starlets and sank to fifth in the close race. Yesterday Kay had been lit up for ten hits in the four innings she'd lasted - final score of that one: 9-6. With two weeks left in the season, it was obvious we weren't to be part of any pennant drive.

The driver, a slim, bearded man in his fifties, boarded and questioned Eddie, "All aboard?"

Eddie ordered, "Go!" and he slid into his seat and started the engine.

As the bus rolled, I sensed Eddie following me to the area over the back wheels where the rookies were stashed. I took a seat by the window and said, "Hiya," to Kay across the aisle. She hadn't been part of the welcoming committee.

The Kid bit her lip and didn't look up or answer.

Eddie was in my face, saying, "Without you, The Kid went into the tank yesterday. Poor thing didn't know which finger to milk her cow with." She glanced at Kay. "Did you, baby?" Kay's brow puckered. "Milked the cow but not a squirt," Eddie emphasized, in that delightful way she had of ragging on a player who was already down. She had informed me once that this helped the girl realize the seriousness of her situation. She bent in close to me. "Pay attention to where the rest of the girls are sitting, as far away from you as possible. Guess they don't like bad luck riding on the bus with them. We think you got a bulls-eye on your back."

I leaned past Eddie to peer down the aisle. My stomach took a dip when I realized that everyone except Kay was crammed together in the very front of the bus, in some cases three to a double seat.

Joanie and Twyla were among them, although the way they were entwined spoke of joyously acceding to the apartheid. Only Kay sat nearby and she wasn't speaking.

Eddie droned on. "Talk is spreading that you're a detective. True or not, you can't stop gossip."

Either the unmasking had come from the Willeys' notion that I was like Cousin Ernie the cop, or Clint blabbing to his closest confidant to get her speaking to him again.

"Where'd you hear that from?" I asked, but Eddie had started back down the aisle where she stumbled into Clint going the other direction. They growled apologies and proceeded on their separate ways. He was selling lottery chances for a dime each and marking the donations on his clipboard. The winners got coupons for free soft drinks and potato chips from Burton City groceries. I never won. The drawing probably was rigged to deny me even a semblance of team-hood.

When Clint reached the dividing line between good vibrations and mine, he reversed course.

"Hold it, Clint," I said. "We gotta talk."

He looked toward Eddie's retreating back for permission, after all, he still felt like her property. She shook her head ponderously. He came anyhow as she continued toward the front of the bus.

I waited until he was abreast before asking, "You tell Eddie I was a PI?" I glanced toward Kay, fearing she'd heard, but her attention was riveted in a magazine.

Clint scratched his five o'clock shadow, and snapped the clip on the board. "Had to," he confessed. "She was on me all the time, ever since you sat in on my session with Duane. She saw you coming out of his office afterward. She's my sidekick and darned important to the whole ballclub so she had to know."

"She probably told Pepper and Pepper told Joanie and Twyla and now everyone's heard. Thanks a lot. Don't you remember you promised to keep that a secret?"

"I never counted Eddie in on that. She can keep quiet."

I was disgusted at the man. He had an explanation for everything, from justifying late-night sessions with Betty Jane to possessing her gold necklace. I was sick of his veneer of ignorance, his oh-shucks blamelessness. I had found him to be an intelligent man, aware and calculating in his desires.

He loped back to sit alone in the front seat directly behind the driver. Once there, he'd install earplugs to block out all the female "twittering and nattering" going on behind him. That was not to be a problem this trip; the atmosphere remained spookily quiet as though every woman were concentrating on the wording of her last will and testament.

That night the bus rolled through the northern half of Iowa, destined for Mankato in southern Minnesota. When the driver pulled in to gas stations the girls piled off and flirted with the local boys and tried to get free hot dogs. Pepper, displaying shapely legs and well-turned ankles, did particularly well, cavorting with two college-age men in crew-neck sweaters who posed by a roadster. From an aisle seat, someone noted that Pepper should play baseball in heels.

"Yeah," a friend agreed, "it's when she dons cleats that all skills vanish."

Reboarding, Pepper shared her snacks with Joanie and Twyla who hadn't bothered getting out. Eddie, ever the dutiful chaperon, brought me a hot dog and Korn Kurls.

"Trying to keep me alive, are you?" I said.

"Until you can be repatriated with your own kind."

Soon my tummy was burning from the transition of hospital oatmeal and jello to the floor leavings and sawdust that constituted hot dogs, or so a fourth grade teacher had imprinted upon our receptive minds years ago.

I glanced at Kay, whose head had been stuck in a *Seventeen* magazine for the past hour, staring at frilly things she ordinarily thought were dumb.

"Want some Korn Kurls?" I asked. I tossed the bag across the aisle. She caught and tore it open, took out a couple chips and chewed open-mouthed.

"I guess I'm on the outs with you too," I said.

She bounced across the aisle and plunked into the seat beside me. Her face was pained. "I took a ball to the hospital so's you could rub it for luck but they wouldn't let me see you. You coulda left word to let me in."

"Jeez, kid, I was out cold most the time."

"Well, I lost big yesterday because I didn't have the angels with me. Pop walked out in the third even though I was still out there trying. I mean my winning puts food on our table."

"Your family counts on you for eating money?"

"Yeah, rent too, sometimes."

"Don't you see anything wrong with that? Instead of coming to your games, why doesn't your pop go out and get a job?"

"He's shepherding me out in the big world so's I don't meet with no evil fate. It's the way we do things."

"Look, Kid …" I wasn't about to criticize family tradition, but I could strike elsewhere. "Angels or seraphim or whatever you think I bring you by rubbing a ball, it's …" I settled for, "not realistic."

"The angels are on our side," she said obstinately.

"Sure they are if you get out there and pitch like it's in you to do. The winning magic is in you. Kay, you got twice the talent of anybody on this team. I'm doing myself out of a job telling you this, but, darn it, you have to know I'm no lucky charm. You must have heard the real reason I'm on the team, didn't you?" I coaxed.

"You said you was a doctor-healer." Unless she was a great actress, she hadn't heard the latest, that I was a PI. Absorbed in her own troubles and segregated because of age, maybe she hadn't been in on the gossip.

Cheeks aflame, she bolted across the aisle to reclaim her seat and the opened magazine. The bus traveled on. I dozed. After the second gas station stop, the Willeys climbed into the seats immediately ahead of me and leaned over their backs. They began by saying they hoped I wouldn't accuse them of committing a violent act against my person. What would crime-fighting cousin Ernie think?

"I know Dor came into the shower room first," I said. "You're lying to the cops about that." I directed my attention to Dor. "I remember Lor asking you if you done it. Hit me, I mean. I wasn't out cold, you know."

Lor's little finger dug into an ear. "Yes you were. You were out of your mind so you couldn't a heard nothing. Shoulda just left you laying there and went out for popcorn." She paused. "You tell the law about our visit to Clint's office? You said you wouldn't."

"The cops don't know, unless they found out on their own, which they might have after you insisted that you entered the shower room together. Cops catch you in one lie," I 'tsked' twice, "they'll investigate you further."

"We think Pepper was the one attacked you," Dor said.

Lor nodded. "Gal's a criminal, been to jail for it. You watch out for her. She'll try it again."

"Good thinking. Prior crimes often indicate future misdeeds. Of course, you're guilty too, of stealing, black-mailing, and breaking and entering."

"You tell any of that," Dor said, "and that'll be it for you because the whole team is against you already. You'll really get mud in your eye then. "

"Sticks and stones may break my bones, but mud will never hurt me."

"Far worse will, and shit on you," Dor flared.

"You two mean to off me as a team project?"

Dipping below the seat backs, the twins made a swift departure.

Not a moment to reflect before Eddie moved up the aisle, punching girls' shoulders in comradely fashion, and spouting, "Cheer up, there'll be a better day tomorrow if you klutzes stop slopping it up on the field."

She ignored her sister on her way past, and Pepper mouthed, "Blow it out your ear."

When Eddie reached me, she fell into the adjoining seat.

"Back again? For what?" I said.

"I'm gonna say something you won't like, but just let me say it without getting into a big argument."

I was quiet.

"You asked for the terrible thing that happened in that shower room. I mean, here you are, sneaking around, misrepresenting yourself, barging in where you aren't wanted. You put yourself in harm's way."

"You're doing some pretty upsetting things yourself. Stealing jewelry and interfering with sacred spitting rites."

She went silent, thinking up her next salvo. It came: "Let me be clear. I am the chaperon of this team. As such, I do not want to be in charge of you. I do not want to be responsible for you. You are not a good player. You are a detective who's supposed to be protecting us and you're no good at that either; you should go home right now, immediately. When you get off this bus. You're making us very uncomfortable and wasting everyone's time." She paused. "There is no killer on this bus; I know my girls."

Another one who wished I would vanish. A film of sweat had appeared on her face. It hit me that she was afraid. Was it that, if a Hornette player were guilty, Yegg Washington might shut down the team, if not the entire league?

She sprang up and went back down the aisle, clapping her hands and rooting for brighter days ahead.

Dinah was next, bursting into speech as soon as she hit the seat next to me. "Wasn't me tried to do you in, even though you and the coppers are set on nailing me."

Ever the paranoid. I said, "What a bunch of baloney."

"Yeah? I'll baloney you." She blew into my face and gave me lots of baloney, its fumes anyhow. "You lay off me. If you don't, this team'll give you baloney and a lot more." She burped and bolted away.

Have mercy. I was being threatened by the Willeys and Dinah on behalf of the entire team. To think I'd be the one to unify their spriggy core.

Next to drop by was Twyla Ziegler. She had a different message and spoke softly delivering it. "We waited for you to come to us, but you must be shy. Excellent using Sid Dobrotka as a cover up."

"Huh?"

"You mean you like it both ways? A couple of the girls are bisexual too. Okay with me. Long as everybody has a good time."

"Wait a sec. You don't think I'm, uh, atypical, do you?"

She grinned jauntily. "Go ahead, say it, it doesn't hurt. Queer. Yes, of course I do. Joanie saw you and poor Milly Tubbs hugging, and the way you cling on to Kay and all of a sudden you're rooming together. But, through Joanie and me, you can meet some really nice, mature dykes."

"No. Not interested. Sorry. I'm everyday normal." My response sounded as discombobulated as I felt. Aware that, across the aisle, Kay might be listening in, I lowered my voice. "Although in other ways I'm quite odd." I never wanted to be thought homosexual. A blacker mark was hard to imagine.

As Twyla stepped into the aisle, she kept an eye on me. "What a gutless wonder you are," she said icily. She left rapidly.

What indicated more than mere friendship with Kay? Was I sprawling, not crossing my legs? Engaging in a mannish sport? Hey, so was everybody else on this bus.

Thankfully no one else visited during the remainder of the journey. When, at 1:00 a.m., we pulled up in front of our next unpretentious hotel, most everyone was greasy and slumbering.

Quickly to bed, and the next morning, awakening when I saw roomie Kay dressed and on her way out, I propped myself up on an elbow and said, "Wait a few minutes and we can eat together."

Her eyes were swollen and upper lip ravaged from chewing on it.

"What's wrong? You're not still mad at me?"

Silently she took ball and glove from the bureau and moved with athletic grace to the door. Kay's inner world battled. I turned over on my stomach and clutched my head. Kid, release me from mentorhood, I don't know how to handle it. Or maybe there was another reason. Maybe someone had filled her in on my so-called sexual depravity.

In any event, The Kid walked out on me, shutting the door firmly on some rough innings of growing up.

32.

When you're on the road, each mid-size town is like the one before, but each ballpark is unique. On the Mankato diamond, the infield grass was left to grow long so a hard bunt would disappear and dart out an instant later in an unexpected spot. You can't excavate what you can't see.

The Mankato field was also special in that it was one of the few with actual dugouts; ours was another. In most of the parks of the Star-Spangled League, rival squads sat on benches down the first and third base lines. During afternoon games, the heat of high summer and the turpentine-like smell of insect repellent might make the benchwarmer queasy.

We were about to engage the Mankato Maulers in a three-game series. It didn't help our morale that the Maulers held first place where we had expected to be, assuming Betty Jane was still taking her turn on the mound. Omens were rife for disaster in this series. Kay's pitching had gone in the tank, the lackluster play, and a losing steak extended to five.

Newly frightened by my assault, the Hornette women assured each other that they were in no danger because the private cop was the target and they were simply ball playing innocents caught in the crossfire.

As I whiled away the hours on the bench with nothing to do but swat mosquitoes and brush away gnats, I checked the stands of whatever ballpark we were in, hoping for a sight of the three mobsters Sid had described. Dressed fit to kill, they'd be set up in a row like bowling pins, just begging to be knocked over. In my alley dreams, I'd deliver the ball. But in real life, they never appeared.

In the opening game, we were simply outmuscled. Our starter, Molly Powell, was fast but with little of Betty Jane's ability to hit the corners with changing speeds. That night, Molly's fastball zoomed straight down the heart of the plate. By starting a level swing as soon as the ball was released, a batter could be sure of colliding with something.

In the sixth with one out and two on, and the score 6-2 against us, Clint replaced Molly with Letta. Letta immediately reinforced her recently acquired nickname of "Lost Cause" by allowing a barrage of hits and three more runs. Between pitches, no infielder went to the mound to offer encouragement, and no manager shouted wisdom from the third base coaching box. Even Eddie, usually the soul of optimism during a game, uttered only half as many, "Letta baby, let's go babes," as usual.

Top of the eighth, score 10-2, the small crowd of eleven hundred began heading for the exits. Several shouted that the milking contest beforehand had had more ups and downs. Joanie sputtered at that and kicked Twyla, next to her on the bench. "It's hilarious," she gasped, "the hicks come by and say the same dad-gumb thing about cow-titties going up and down and are so dad-dumb happy they thought it up."

"Shakespeare on the plains," Twyla deadpanned, running a shoe up Joanie's calf. Caught in the spirit, Pepper rose and hopped on Joanie's toes.

Eddie lumbered over in full gear. "What is so darned funny?" she asked. "Have some respect or get some sense." No reply except faces struggling to be serious.

In the locker room after the stinging defeat, Eddie became nurturing, applying oodles of salve on strawberries on Connie and Twyla's thighs, gotten from sliding into bases. She treated the players caringly, almost as if they were her own sisters, although not a sister like Pepper, who whirled in a gaudy full skirt and heels, and clip-clopped to the door where she swiveled and stared fixedly at Eddie. Slowing the massage, Eddie faced her and the two exchanged looks of pure poison.

Lifting a foot slightly, Pepper brought it down with a sharp tap to the cement. She squared off as though challenging Eddie. Eddie stalked to her locker, slipped on heels. She clopped into an open space and did a little dance. Pepper grinned and executed a series of fierce taps, causing Eddie to join in furiously. It was a footwear fight, and developed into a whirling dervish of a dance: spins, hops, stomps landing so violently it seemed they would gouge pits in the cement. Dashing toward each other, whirling, avoiding contact by a hair; there was more competitive fire than in the game.

The racket of feet drummed into my ears and recalled something horrid. I started for the .38 that, since confronting the Willeys unarmed, I carried in my purse. Pepper spun toward the exit and Eddie slowed her mad derring-do. The besieged feeling left me as Pepper flung open the door and disappeared down the hall. What had caused my panic? We had witnessed open hostility and even naked hatred, but that wasn't new. And really, what was at stake? Surely Clint wasn't the prize. Only Eddie truly wanted him.

The team studied the door, their faces alert for Pepper to burst in and reignite the battle.

But nothing happened and, finally, Joanie said to Eddie, "If those'd been bullets, you'd both be laid out on the floor."

Eddie issued a hollow cackle. "Don't talk like that. Pepper's having a hard time lately. It'd help if you'd go easy on her." Eddie didn't want us to be as down on her sis as she was.

She moved back to the rubdown tables. Connie climbed back onto one, saying shakily, "Lord Jesus, that was beyond the pale."

"Another thing," Eddie's tone sharpened as she regained composure. She directed her comments at a wooden locker. "The other day Winkie and Lor and Dor set out on their own to practice and Winkie got really hurt. From now on, you need my okay for any extra baseball activity. That clear?" She glanced over to where I was sitting on a bench, armed handbag beside me. I nodded acquiescence. Eddie began kneading Connie's shoulder muscles with order-affirming vigor.

Twyla jumped from the other rubdown table. She and Joanie dressed quickly and slipped from the room.

"You be careful," Eddie yelled after them. She drew a pained breath. "That's two more headed for an evening of unwholesome entertainment."

Dinah said, "That whole gang, including your sister, is darned irritatin'." She swung her arms and looked for something to launch. Settling on a couple of bats, she tossed them perfunctorily against the same locker Eddie had addressed.

Bobby brushed away one of the glancing bats as of no consequence while her eyes became increasingly haunted. Other players avoided the ricocheting projectiles and, with blank expressions, shrank into themselves.

The space around each player grew so wide that no girl was able to reach across it and console a teammate. Nobody trusted anybody. Each player stood alone, even the Willeys. I believed everyone in that locker room, at that moment, came to the stark realization of how far the team had fallen since Betty Jane's murder.

In the late morning before the second game, the Willeys and I worked out in glum silence. We had informed Eddie of our plans, of course, and she squatted just outside the visitor's dugout, elbows on knees, palms pressed to chin, protecting us by expression alone. During the practice, my skills didn't improve. Perhaps I'd caught the losers' disease, because I felt more floppy and uncoordinated than usual. Eddie's critical observance wasn't exactly an invitation to excel.

When the team took the field two hours later, we were greeted by a large banner draped over the fence to the right of home plate. It said, "The Hornettes has lost there stingers." Some trouble-making teenagers were yukking it up as they pointed middle fingers at it.

The 3:30 p.m. crowd was large, everyone glorying in their winning team and looking forward to seeing it act out its Mauler name.

Clint had rearranged the batting order to spark things up. Dinah was leading off to get her more at-bats. The Willeys were disgraced to batting eighth and ninth, after Bobby Bied, the pitcher.

The home team sent Whitfield, their ace, against us. She mowed us down in the first, no chance. With one out in the second, Dinah slugged a rope to right for a double. Prowling off second, she cussed Twyla for grounding out, and the next girl up, Connie, for ducking away from an inside pitch that otherwise would have crushed a cheek bone. For some reason, Connie felt intimidated and tapped out to the pitcher, leaving Dinah stranded. Her high-pitched complaint caused tittering throughout the crowd: "Can't count on none a you dainties to drive me in."

The top of the ninth, with the Hornettes behind 11-0, Eddie approached Clint. "There's no hope. Let's get some of the reserves in there."

I jumped up. "Yes, yes!" There is a bright spot in any loss. Kay watched, dreary-eyed. Scheduled to start tomorrow, she was on her own. Even if begged, I'd have refused to rub any more baseballs or play catch or whatever she deemed the magic fix for the day.

The first two outs in the top of the ninth were made by reserve outfielder Helen Sanders and pitcher Nancy Grant. After they lived up to no expectation, Clint pointed my way. "You're up, darlin'. Grab some lumber." I hustled to the woodpile and hefted my favorite cudgel, the little number weighing thirty ounces. I took a practice swing that ended with my arms practically wound around my neck.

"Don't strangle yourself beforehand," Eddie advised. "Wait till after."

Clint trotted over from the third base coaching spot. "Watch the ball. Be cool. Wait on the pitch, don't swing at the bad ones." He paused. "Crouch down real low, maybe she'll walk you." He clapped his hands. "Now let's go get 'em!"

I heard my name reverberating mushily over the P.A. system with absolutely no interest from the few fans remaining in the park. At least my at-bat won't be widely discussed, I reassured myself.

With all that advice to ponder, and pitches to deal with too, I whiffed on three outside throws, each further from the plate than the one before.

Running with Twyla for the showers, Joanie called back, "I believe the fans were nearer that last pitch than you were."

I was dazed. "Everything happened so quickly."

"Aw, we woulda lost anyhow," Pepper said, passing me. "Somebody's got to be at the bottom. It looks like us."

But Eddie clapped me on the back and counseled, "Keep the bat up, you're dipping it. You play golf? That swing'd be about right for golf."

In the locker room before the third and final game against the Maulers, Eddie had us form a circle to sing the team song. I hated to sing it when we were down because the words sounded even sillier than those rare occasions when we were up. Eddie had penned the lyrics to the tune of "Frere Jacque." Most of the Hornettes weren't able to hit a pitch any better in music than they could, lately, in the batter's box.

Every player stood with head hung low and fingers loose in her neighbor's hand. I even felt a couple of exploratory pats to my fingers.

We were almost at the end of the first verse, "All for one—all for one—one for all—one for all—Keep your eye out—Keep your eye out—for the ball—for the ball," when somebody stifled a sob and mewled through the entire next phrase before quieting at the end. In the throbbing silence that followed, I peeked around to spot the weepy one before becoming aware that no one else was having a look-see.

I lowered my eyes. This team that constantly ribbed each other had reached a line of privacy not to be crossed. I squeezed my neighbors' hands and one squeezed back.

Eddie cleared her throat noisily, giving the whimpery girl time to recover. Then she screeched into the last verse with us dragging along behind.

"One for all—one for all," we squalled, "all for one—all for one—Let's go out there, let's go out there—'N' have some fun—'N' have some fun." With those last words, so at odds with reality, the sound thinned as choir members dropped out, gulping and choking and honking into collars. Only Kay and I and the old tunesmith finished off the song. Kay's voice was taut and trembly and I didn't quit because I was darned irritated. After the final garroted word, almost everyone collapsed into someone else's arms, even cynical women like Joanie and Twyla. Actually they fell enthusiastically into a fond embrace. Eddie threw back her shoulders and stuck out her bosom, viewing the devastation proudly. Kay turned away from the whole sniveling mess with not a tear shed. The Kid was focused. I only hoped it was on the game.

In the corridor, heading toward the field, players conversed in low tones. "Let's stay together. It's safer."

"You wanna walk with me?"

"No."

Bobby caught up with me. "You got a gun on ya?"

"See any lumps?"

"Maybe in your panties?"

"Good idea. Not today. These shorts aren't that blousy."

"You ever shoot anybody?"

"Scads," I said dryly. "In the restroom mostly, where I can get to my weapon." I moved ahead. The rest of the way, I trotted beside Connie, her lips moving silently in The Lord's Prayer.

The team was emotionally drained by the time we reached the field. The ridiculing sign was gone, as well as the students who accompanied it. Presumably they were in summer school learning to spell.

It was a breezy afternoon. Free Popsicle Day had produced a large crowd.

On the mound, stony-faced Kay battled for outs the first three innings. She didn't have her peak-Winkie stuff and her control was sometimes off. There were some hard hit balls, but right at fielders. No matter the threat, she didn't resort to mumbo jumbo between pitches. The performance wasn't pretty, but gutsy and grim, with cool brainwork and a mighty grunt hurling each pitch. I didn't see her father in the front row of the stands. Maybe he was out shooting squirrels for his next meal.

In the fourth, the Hornettes broke their fifteen inning scoring drought. A well-placed bunt by Joanie, Dinah's single, a run-scoring error, and a walk left the bases loaded and forced a pitching change. After that, the first batter up, Eddie, hit a long single producing two runs.

The bench wasn't quite ready to move out of the doldrums until Eddie screamed, "Let's hear some noise," as she crossed the plate on Kay's single. We were happy to oblige, the score at 4-1.

The bottom of the fourth, Kay had trouble. After walking a burly outfielder, she plunked a wimpy shortstop who had no business getting on. Still, she worked through it with no runs scoring.

Trotting in from the catcher's position, Eddie observed to the bench, "Kay's partway to growing up."

But suddenly, in the eighth, a Mauler hit a home run with two on and the score was tied at four. Us benchwarmers wilted into postures that said, "We knew it. Here we go again."

But on the first pitch in the top of the ninth, Dinah hit a rocket that cut its way through a stiff wind over the centerfield fence. "You can't think big enough to get by me," she mousie-squeaked as she moved leisurely around the bases. We all met her at the plate cheering.

In retaliation for Dinah's deliberate strut, the Mauler pitcher plunked the next hitter, Twyla, on the forearm. After that display of temper, she shut us down and got out of the inning.

At the start of the bottom of the ninth, the score was 5-4, our favor.

The first Mauler hitter, sixth in the original batting order, stepped to the plate. The crowd yelled and stomped, the Willeys chattered so their dusty tonsils showed. A passel of "Baby, Babe's" flew from Eddie's mouth. Joanie tapped her glove twice with an index finger.

I perceived dimly that every one of us Hornettes, including me, was totally out of her head about playing baseball.

To the waggling batter, Kay threw: a fastball in, a curve down and in, a fast ball up and away. With the count 3 and 0, she tossed a low change up. A hard bunt driven into the high grass toward third base. You can't field what you can't see, but Joanie's feet spun, zero to fifty, as she charged the place where the ball was last seen. Coming up backhand with white in her glove, she whirled and threw in one motion.

"Yer out!" the umpire jerked his thumb, hips and entire body toward the Mauler dugout. Face contorted, their manager dashed from the coaching box to confront the ump with frenzied gestures and outraged yells.

We reserves pounded on the dugout roof, Hornettes on the field jumped up and down in glee. Outraged fans rained popsicle sticks onto the field. Being light, only a few made it past the foul lines.

Kay strutted around the mound. "You are hopeless shits," she mouthed in the home team's direction.

Joanie wiped her hands on her shorts to clear away grit. She rubbed the webbing of her glove to cleanse it of grassy debris. She drawled, "Lez go, baby Kay."

After the argument at first base ended and the game resumed, two routine outs followed, and we had our first victory in nine games.

Intercepting our pitcher as we raced for the clubhouse, I yelled over her whoops of joy, "Tonight you gave yourself a gift and me a bigger one." The Kid stopped yelling and her mouth clamped tight and she stared right through me. But when she reached the clubhouse, she lagged so I could catch up. Side by side, we clattered down the hallway, letting our spikes do the talking, making up.

33.

Leaving Kay to celebrate with the rest of the team, I returned to the hotel at 5:00 p.m. Finding a note in my box to call Sid at a Des Moines number, I dialed the phone on the bed stand in my room.

"Hi, Wendy." His voice was richly welcoming. "How are you?"

"Fine, Sid. What you doing in Des Moines?"

"Covering the Polk County Canoe Derby. No headaches or anything?"

"Nope, I'm fine. What's up?"

"Well, I was sitting around without much to do, given the speed of the average canoe, so I called the Women's Reformatory in Helena to see what I could find out about Betty Jane, or rather, Lois Magic. The authorities were very helpful. Her hometown was listed as Butte, Montana, so I called the police there and made inquiries about her parents. They were named in the jailhouse records as Vera and Teddy Magic. Those are different names from the Hornette records where Betty Jane named her folks as Al and Marge Gibbons."

"Oh what a tangled web."

"Right, so, these latest parents, Vera and Teddy, left Butte right before Betty Jane - Lois Magic - was released from the hoosegow."

"Pepper told me that. Said they were actors or in the circus and had to travel around to get jobs."

"Not the case. The Butte police say the Magics were bakers, not members of a theatrical or circus troupe, even part-time. My guess is that Betty Jane told people that to excuse their absence. Betty Jane was a proud lady, probably didn't want people feeling sorry for her. Anyhow the cops said her folks owned a small bakery in Butte, in a neighborhood called McQueen's addition, where a lot of immigrants settle. Croats, Montenegrans, Russkis … "

"Hold it. Russians? Ukrainians?"

"That I don't know." His tone had become shaded, and he hesitated dealing with a possible Yegg Washington connection. Continuing, he said, "I also spoke to a guy who wrote an article for the Butte paper. Wait a sec, I got notes." I smiled, pictured him yanking the notepad from his shirt pocket. Mumbling under his breath about Croat miners and Russian Jews, when his finger landed on the right spot, he brought up his voice. "Bakery specialized in a certain kind of pastry that was popular in that area. Poppy seed bread or what they call 'makhovic,' Hey. Betty Jane told me she loved makhovic bread, missed it in Iowa."

"Wonder if it's an ethnic bread, eastern European, maybe." I couldn't make myself specify "The Ukraine." I remember the word "makhovic." It had appeared on Sid's vocabulary list in the purloined notebook.

"Don't know," he said. "Anyhow, my journalist buddy put me in touch with three of the Magics' neighbors, who I called on my own dollar, I want you to know." Translated, did that mean, "You're the one for me, hearts and W's?" or was I reading too much into the outlay of a few quarters?

"The neighbors insisted the Magics had nothing to do with show biz," Sid resumed. "They were bakers from sun-up to sun-down."

"I'll reimburse you for the phone calls."

"No, no, I did it for you."

"Very nice of you." My voice remained businesslike, but I was back-pedaling like mad, running for the hills like I always did when relationships threatened to become long term. "Were the Magics born in the U.S.? Did they have foreign accents?

"Don't know. I'll check. Two of the neighbors I spoke with had thick accents. The other sounded native born." Hesitation consumed his delivery. Who needed Yegg Washington mixed up in this? Not me, and certainly not the ever-cautious Sid.

I asked if he knew when the Magics left Butte.

"Yeah. Ahh, here it is. March 15, 1950, the bakery didn't open for business. Still hasn't. It took about a week before the police came and discovered that all the furniture and equipment were gone. They must have snuck away in the dead of night. Funny, huh, to take that much trouble to get rid of a troublesome daughter."

"It can't be easy having a convict for a daughter." I knew it wasn't easy having a convict for a Dad. "Hey," I went on, "I wonder if they ran out before or after Betty Jane's father asked Pepper for help in getting her a tryout with the Hornettes. Maybe that was to be his final kindness."

"I bet Pepper can give you the date because wasn't it the same day she got out of prison?"

"Right. She'll probably remember that."

Betty Jane's folks had not appeared at the funeral. Did they know of their daughter's death? The murder hadn't been widely publicized. Sid's reporter pal in Montana hadn't heard. The Star-Spangled League's fame was pretty much limited to the Midwest. Vera and Teddy Magic still might not know of their offspring's demise.

I asked Sid if he had a description of the parent Magics.

"Even better. I have a snapshot. Fuzzy, taken with a cheap camera. While the canoeists were awarded their medals, I ran to the Des Moines library and found an article concerning recent missing persons. It included that photo. I tore it out, kind of borrowed it. That's what you do with libraries, right?"

Wow. I had a beau who would mutilate library materials for me.

"I needed the photo," he justified.

"Right."

"I plan on replacing the newspaper," he added.

"I should think so."

"Anyhow, Betty Jane's old man looks like a wrestler, muscles bulging through his T-shirt. He's wearing a baker's apron. He's got a big grin on his mug and he's shorter than his wife, who's standing next to him. She's husky, fair and unsmiling." I imagined Sid scrutinizing the picture, hazel eyes squinting to master every detail. We had grown close so quickly. If I'd had higher standards I'd never have gotten involved with a man who was a bit of a coward and self-serving to boot, not wanting to take on Yegg Washington and his subordinates for fear of derailing his career. My dad would have engaged them, pistol in hand. That's the trouble, that's why he's dead.

Sid was saying, "The mama's got whitish blonde hair, not much of it, pulled back tight. She's got a good set of biceps herself. Between the two of them, they could have built that bakery with their bare hands."

"Now we know where Betty Jane's athleticism comes from."

"The shape of the mother's shoulders is similar, sort of sloped. Otherwise, not much of a resemblance."

I processed the new information. "A mysterious disappearance. Unsettling, don't you think?"

Sid murmured assent.

"I'll get to work on this right away and I'll see you soon." I started to hang up without waiting for a reply, then clutched the receiver. "Sid, are you still there?'

"I never hang up before you do."

"Great," I said brightly, determined to hold him at bay with shallowness until I grasped the inroads he had made. Okay, so a percentage of me might be in love, but how much? I was never good at fractions.

"We're due back tomorrow morning around eleven," I said. "Will you be back by then? If so, you could give me that picture. The cops have a couple photos of people I'm trying to identify." A frail young woman inside an expensive locket found in a briefcase from Ankara, Turkey and a snotty dude under a bench leg on the floor of Millicent Tubbs' death scene. The hardy looks of Vera and Teddy Magic didn't seem to fit, unless the pair had undergone severe hardship or a weight-lifting course in the passing years. "Thanks, Sid," I said again, allowing tenderness into my voice. "I'll see you tomorrow."

"I hope so," he responded softly.

"Okay. Yes." I hung up quickly as if I were one very busy detective.

Remaining fully dressed I climbed into bed and pulled the covers over my head. I concentrate best where it's dark and quiet.

My mind drifted to the eternal question for all girls from grade school until the walk down the aisle. Who would I marry? Who was the man for me? Would I be able to give myself, in the manner of a Doris Day, and share the rest of my life with one man to the exclusion of all others? Come to think of it, Doris had been married more than once.

My mind wandered further. What of makhovic bread? Of course Betty Jane had eaten it; her parents baked it every day. Were the Magics immigrants? Had they known Washington and his goons in the old country? Unlikely, I hoped. I had hesitated pursuing the matter with Sid, since, with discussion, extreme coincidence could grow to absolute likelihood.

I had to do some serious sleuthing. I surprised myself by feeling energized by that. I had spent an inordinately long time invested in ball playing, trying to be one of the girls, sharing victories, being part of a great game. Somewhere along the way I'd mislaid who I was: a devoted career PI.

With the matter settled, I closed my eyes and let my thoughts drift further until I became fully lost in the past.

Had my father cared for me?

We'd had an indifferent Mom and a charismatic Dad who manipulated his kids for his own purposes. My brothers and I fell for him. Where was the proof he loved me? A goodbye hug, and an offering of beans, snatched away. No, traded for a philosophy: "If it's yours and you ain't watching it, then it's mine."

34.

The day Dad planned to escape, my assignment was to take him a pistol, ammunition, and supplies. In the early morning, Norris dropped me off at the old shed where Dad and I had emerged by the highway after our "camp-out."

Following the twisting path, hours later I broke through dense foliage to arrive at the pond, which lay as brackish and inert as the day we left it. Dad was not yet there. I slung a backpack of clothes and beef jerky to the moist earth and seated myself on a stump, where, surrounded by woods, I could watch for him and be unseen by others. I broke open the food sack and ate raisins and Hershey bars and peanuts. I drank water from my canteen.

By the end of the second day, when I got around to the cheese sandwiches, they were moldy so I threw them away.

The silence of the woods was unnerving, but worse, were the creepy noises that kept me awake and hanging onto the pistol. I moved frequently in the dark because no place seemed safe. The pond was in the open where humans could spot me and the woods were where the wild creatures prowled.

I was always ready for Dad to part the brush and step into the clearing, so he could note with a slight smile, "Even though I'm all purpled up with bruises I can see you ain't scared of me." And then, because I'd saved him, he'd invite me to come along with him.

The fourth morning, I ate the rest of the chocolate and peanuts and there was no other food that I could identify as such. No juicy persimmons on the ground, that season was past. An empty stomach led to extreme resentment. Dad should have been there to provide food. He knew what could be eaten in the wild and what was poison, I didn't.

I kicked the stump. "Goddammit, goddam you," I yelled, waving my fists, kicking some leaves before I sank into foliage, afraid that I'd told every creature out there my exact location. The fifth morning, stomach rumbling, mind black, I decided to abandon my position. Leaving the backpack by the stump in case he showed up (probably he'd be happy to find it without the extra baggage alongside it), I stuck the pistol in my raincoat pocket and began the trudge home.

I never allowed myself to think something had gone wrong. To my mind, my dad was the best, the smartest, the strongest, and yet he had not come for me. Either he hadn't cut through the bars quick enough, or he had ditched me, as before.

Reaching the old shed, I started to walk beside the highway, peering back frequently for any sign of him, while hoping for a quick pick up. Shortly, a vehicle came from the rear, and stopped.

"I been driving by for days," a voice said, "hoping you'd come out." It took a second to realize it was Norris.

I dragged around to the passenger door as he leaned across and opened it.

"He never came," I said.

"Wendy, they shot him right inside the jail. He's dead."

I hauled myself up the step. Comprehension came an instant later. I screamed, "No, not my dad."

He said exhaustedly, "Little sister, let's go home."

We had turned into the rutted road to our farm before he spoke again. The vengeful tone cut through my sobs. "That sonofa bitch that killed our daddy. Someday I'll pay him back."

For a week I drifted, either numb with grief or cold with rage that Dad hadn't shown up. I never saw his body, so where was the proof that he was even dead? It was only what people said, and they always said a lot of things, mostly exaggerated, about my dad.

Night burglar Norris cautioned, "No one knows we're related to him so don't let on at school. We can't do him no good now."

"Where's he buried then?" I asked.

"Some Boot Hill, I don't know. He's dead, he don't know the difference."

Every day I rode the school bus on its route past the shed. Every day I imagined Dad's stooped frame moving within the trees, the purple bruise standing out among garishly colored leaves.

I persuaded a reluctant Norris to take me to the library in Lead Hill, to check the newspaper of November 3rd, the morning after Dad had supposedly been killed. "Because otherwise how do we know he's gone?"

We found it in the stacks, among the smell of newsprint. Norris punched open the state section. "Now you believe it?" In the narrow aisle we read silently, the paper making crisp sounds in Norris's hands.

CONVICT SLAIN
Because a jail guard wouldn't be fooled,
a convict's desperate attempt at escape
ended with his death. William Winkworth,
serving four years for theft, surprised Guard
George Byers in the corridor of the Boone
County jail about 4 a.m. Friday. Winkworth
pointed a gun, later determined to have been
fashioned from soap and tinfoil, at Guard
Byers, and warned, 'Stay put or I'll shoot.'
Guard Byers drew and shot Winkworth in
the head, killing him instantly.
Police said that Winkworth had sawed his
way out of his cell with a small carpenter's
file, which was found on the body.

The accompanying photo, with its caption of GUARD GEORGE BYERS, was of Dumb Cop, the twitchy lawman with a daughter just like me.

Later, in horrid dreams, I crouched at the end of a long dark corridor. At the other end, that jumpy guard shuffled and stewed, and somewhere in there, his police special came out aimed directly at me.

The worst part was that I'd awake in a sweat knowing that if I hadn't left the file, my dad wouldn't have been in that hall.

35.

I uncovered with an effort when Kay came in. The sheets were stubborn vines tying up my legs and torso. While washing off in the bathroom, I reflected on the fate of my brothers. Norris, a homebody, married with two kids, living in Chicago. During a visit a year ago, I had squirmed on the upscale sofa while listening to his new Admiral console FM radio. The unit featured a 10-inch TV and two-speed automatic phonograph. Where did he get that kind of money? Not on his part-time mechanic's job and he hadn't mentioned winning the Irish Sweepstakes.

Had time dimmed his rage? "Oh, yeah, I don't think about it," he said. But a surliness remained in Norris, along with the need to prove himself. In the past, it had surfaced as the desire to be the best damn burglar in the business. Getting up nerve and getting up early were hard for him. I recalled two times when he rose in the dark and I accompanied him to gas stations where we stole motor oil and other car products. Those occasions reminded me of the adventures I'd had with Dad. And they cemented a lasting closeness between my brother and me.

Years ago, we had lost track of brother Jim and his quest for something more lasting than guns or Twinkies.

Presently I tuned in to Kay's account of post-game activity. She and Molly had gone to the malt shop where they met two extremely sophisticated young men. The comely lads were waiting in the lobby to escort the girls to the movies.

"You be careful," was my motherly advice.

"I can take care of myself," she retorted with a deprecating snort.

The rest of us went to a restaurant called The Century Club, a low brick building situated on the banks of the Minnesota River. While dining, you could gaze out an enormous window at huge boulders that littered the slope down to the water's edge. The club's interior was maroon, from upholstered chairs to pleated draperies.

The team had not called ahead for reservations, so when we arrived around eight o'clock, the dining room was quite full. A hostess seated us at widely scattered tables, too far apart to attempt the team song, thank heaven.

I had come alone and stopped by a table that Pepper shared with a handsome fellow in his early twenties, curly blond hair, and clear blue eyes that had seen many a ski slope whooshing by. Whether he was out tomcatting or acting a proper suitor, I did not inquire.

Instead I asked to speak with Pepper privately. She responded, "Thought I was the one talkin' here," after which she caught herself being difficult and tried to win me over with a smile. Her date sprang from the starter's block to pull out her chair. As she, in dirndl skirt and gay peasant blouse, and I, in sundress, walked toward the drapes, she towered over me in the highest of heels.

I tilted my head to meet the tall girl's eyes and began, "I assume Eddie told you I was a detective." The news didn't startle her so I went on. "You said Betty Jane's dad asked you to get Betty Jane on the team. When was that? You remember the date?"

She jutted out a hip while concentrating on the problem. "That was a long time ago. Let me think on it." She returned to her table. I believed she could have responded immediately but chose to keep me waiting. I mean, you remember your birthday, your high school graduation, and your prison release date, don't you? A milestone is a milestone.

I went to a table where Joanie and Twyla were smoking and sipping drinks. Standing behind one of two vacant chairs, I asked, "Mind if I join you? These seem to be the only seats available."

"If it isn't the most normal gal in town," Twyla said.

Joanie nodded cursorily. "Sit." I sat down. She offered me a Viceroy from a pack. To my refusal, she said, "Got any bad habits at all, Winkie? Guess not."

"You think we can be ourselves sitting with the gumshoe?" Twyla said.

I glanced behind me. "You mean me?"

A commotion erupted across the way as Dinah bullied her way through standing-room patrons. Reaching our table, she punched my shoulder and said, "Be at my room, number 58 on fifth floor at 10:00 p.m. for a nightcap and some 'teat a teat'."

"Is that French for milk and mooing?" I yucked, thinking I was pretty funny except that a curious stillness had enveloped our table. I sobered enough to say, "You should know, M&M, that I'm not queer."

That set my companions guffawing.

"Winkie is awful gullible though," Joanie said when the laughter died.

"Ten p.m., or we'll hafta come getcha," Dinah sing-songed. "You fairies better be there too," she added, casting a haughty glance at Twyla and Joanie. She swayed back to the table she was sharing with Clint and Eddie. Diners bending over their plates gazed after her with a mixture of awe and revulsion. Clint and Eddie, sitting together following the victory, had apparently declared a truce.

I reckoned this was to be the night of my funning. Swell. A perfect opportunity for me to observe the team's penchant for violence, except it would be inflicted on me. And with Kay, the one gal who might support me, away at the movies.

At our table, when sizzling steaks were served, cigarettes were snuffed and my teammates dug in, too nonchalant for words.

"You think I better get the chaperon's permission to be out after curfew?" I asked. The pair didn't seem remotely interested, so I spoke to my fork. "What you think? You know what a beast Eddie can be." The fork nodded in my hand and shrieked, "Oh do I." I shoved back my chair and followed in Dinah's wake to Eddie. I asked if she'd mind terribly if I was out after 10:00 p.m. curfew.

"Tomorrow's a travel day so I'm extending curfew to 2:00 a.m.," she said. Clint, next to her, busied himself with his clipboard. Across from him, Dinah spread her elbows out and spooned up meat, mashed potatoes, gravy and peas heartedly.

Returning to the lesbians, I lost my appetite and could only pick at the food. Bad for the mission if I held myself separate, good to be one of the team, but I'd take along the handbag with the .38 inside just in case. Early in the investigation I'd been confident that I'd learn more about the team than they'd ever know about me, but they were gaining in that respect.

I decided I needed a partner to walk in with me. Connie seemed the least malicious of those available with the additional positive that she hadn't attended Betty Jane's funning. I caught up with her outside the restaurant. "I think tonight will be my funning," I said. "Will you walk in with me? I need company, I'm awful nervous."

Being the kindly Christian soul she was, she agreed.

The Hornettes occupied all the rooms on the top floor, the fifth, of the Pink Duster Hotel. As light faded into dark and hall lamps glowed, I scouted the old building for escape routes. There was one hallway per floor with rooms opening onto it, and a stairway at each end, one wide and carpeted, the other narrow, leading to the kitchen. The stairs were in the usual back and forth pattern with landings in between. There was also a halting, creaking elevator where every trip seemed to challenge fate.

Dinah's room was the last one in the hall that led to the narrow staircase. At 10:00 p.m., I rapped on her door, and Connie and I were admitted by a cheerfully cordial first baseman. I had previously seen her this effervescent only after crushing a baseball over a fence.

As the club's remaining star, at least in her own mind, Dinah had a room all to herself. It contained a single bed and a bureau strewn with sodas and beer bottles, paper cups and a few spotted glasses. An armchair, lamp table and two wooden chairs added to the furnishings. A closet was to one side of the room, a lavatory and mirror on the other. Full bathrooms for all residents of the fifth floor were at opposite ends of the hallway.

Connie divested me of my handbag, saying cheerfully, "You won't need this." She set it on the carpet next to a wooden chair. She sat down, crossed her legs, lit up, and prepared to witness my fate. After pushing a beer on me, Dinah gripped my arm and tugged me to the lamp table where the phone, radio, and ashtray had been set on the floor to make room for heaps of Ritz and Graham crackers, strewn over several facial tissues. They had been pretty well crushed in transfer by a heavy hand. To be sociable, I selected a couple fragments. The perfect hostess said, "Aw, come on, grab a bunchful, I brought plenty."

"Looks like enough for a whole team," I commented.

A gleeful inhale came from behind the armchair so I wasn't too surprised when Kay jumped up and Molly crawled from under the bed, and the Willeys and "Lost Cause" Letta burst from the closet. I pretended amazement, flinging cracker shards in the air and screaming giddily right along with them.

"Thought you were on a date," I yelped to Kay.

"Fooled you," she said joyously.

In the midst of the commotion, Pepper, Joanie and Twyla flew through the door and other teammates followed until the room was packed.

"Wow, look at all the people," I screeched. "And I didn't think you guys even liked me."

Eddie wasn't there, nor had I expected her to be. From what I'd been told, she avoided these events. Besides, the room she shared with Pepper was right next door, so she could tune in and stop the good times on the dot of 2:00 a.m.

I assumed wherever Clint was bedded down, he had inserted earplugs.

The fun couldn't wait to begin, with one Willey jumping on my back and riding me to the floor while the other grim creeper pushed from the side. Ever more bodies piled on and after a short gut-wrenching onslaught, people began to climb off. Last to rise were the Willeys who did so stiffly. After two dizzying attempts I made it to my feet and, catching my breath, surveyed the scene.

Most of the assaulters had changed from dresses and heels to jeans, shirts and sneakers. Pepper was still in her gypsy outfit. Judging by its pristine condition, she hadn't joined the pummeling. The Willeys, clad in army surplus khaki, bony arms sticking out of short sleeves, clumped around in desert boots.

"Ready for dessert, Winnie?" Dinah squalled. Before I could request a menu, I was gripped from behind, arms pinned, and a scratchy blindfold tied over my eyes. I grunted when my mouth was pried open and something was inserted. It felt chunky, like a cork. I bit into the ropy texture to keep it from going down my throat. It wasn't oatmeal and I began to get worried. Someone bopped my head forward and, in the act of expelling the stuff, I caught a whiff. A plug of tobacco.

"You idiots, I might have choked."

"Aw come on. Be a good sport," someone said.

Realizing my outburst had revealed how cranky I get when my life is in danger, I tried to rectify with, "Funny, very funny."

Rough hands stripped away the blindfold and I glimpsed a soggy tobacco chaw by my foot. I wiped dribble from my chin.

Dinah loomed in front of me. "Winnie Winkle, I declare your funning to be ended officially and I declare you officially now and forever to be an official member of the Burton City Hornettes, and don't spy on us no more."

"'All for one,' like the song says, even if it's not true all the time," Joanie said.

Talk declined to near silence. Everyone seemed to be waiting for me to express gratitude for the high honor bestowed.

When nothing of the sort transpired, Dinah grunted and said, "Somebody go hunt up the napkins. Time for us to celebrate our new member." The conspiratorial tone set off warning bells. I made sure I knew where my handbag was: in the same spot, next to the wooden chair that was presently unoccupied but not for long because Dinah had just sunk into it. Retrieving her beer from the lamp table, she slugged it back, then said, "Whoo-ah! Hard work, huh, kiddos?"

Meanwhile, others were making an enormous deal of searching for the napkins, overturning cushions and pillows, looking around everything in the room, but not a napkin to be found. Another stupid trick upcoming.

I did the Stan Laurel bit, scratching the top of my head with an index finger. "Oh where can those napkins be?"

Dinah joined in. "Where can them cloths have gone to?"

"I think I seen 'em in that top drawer over there," Kay said innocently. "You wanna check it out, Winkie?"

"Oh, sure," I said, "let me fetch 'em."

The room froze. I wended my way to the bureau and opened the indicated drawer. Nothing jumped out at me. The napkins were there, bright white in a back corner. I sniffed. Nothing redolent hit my nostrils. The room was silent as a grave. My breath caught when I saw tips of bloody fingers protruding from underneath the napkins. I glanced around. Twyla was sucking her lips. The others looked on eagerly. I nudged the napkins aside until a severed hand was exposed, its orange hue too unnatural and shiny to be real skin. Red paint was clumped in its palm and had run down the fingers and onto the drawer. Watercolor was the medium this time. In some department store, there was a manikin that couldn't button its blouse and pick its nose at the same time. Most disturbing were the noodles draped over the severed wrist. No doubt they were meant to resemble tendons.

I had the choice of exploding, "You tasteless idiots," or gushing, "Wonderful. You scared me half to death." Of course, I chose the latter, to which the merry-makers giggled, relieved and maybe a little disappointed too, that I hadn't passed out.

But when I asked who was responsible for the cool art work, smiles disappeared and faces became suspicious. No one answered because here was Detective Winkie plying her trade again.

I lifted the "gory" hand, causing the noodles to slither downward. "Anybody missing this?" I said, tossing it into the group. Everyone screamed and jumped back to avoid the horrid thing, but soon they quieted and ate and drank and laughed in relief that my detective self had retreated under its cloak.

Crimson oil paint, red lipstick, and red tempera paint: messages written with vicious intent on previous occasions, but perhaps the watercolor employed here was not meant to be cruel. I was learning that these baseball girls turned sad events into crude jokes, toughening their hides to take whatever fans and sporting fate dished out.

I retrieved the hand from the floor and dropped it back in the drawer. Dinah stuck a beer in my hand. "Joy duh veever," she articulated. "Means enjoy yourself while you can."

I sipped while waiting for the excitement to subside. I wanted to show those tough baseball babes that I was tough too, in my real profession.

36.

During a lull, I spoke up. "I appreciate the great honor you've bestowed upon me tonight." Gushy enough? After all, it wasn't exactly the Distinguished Service Cross. "You're like family to me," I went on. I didn't say whose. The Addams family was a possibility. I raised my beer in tribute. There had been enough beer guzzling that the moment seemed right for reminiscing. "Here's to you girls, and to my hero, Betty Jane. If only she could have been here tonight toasting along with us."

"Yeah, everybody wishes that 'cause then you wouldn't be here."

Thanks, Pepper.

"Remember how Betty Jane'd come in swinging that greasy old glove of hers?" Twyla said, slurring her words. "And how she'd get mad at people sluffing off?" Her tone saddened. "Wish I'd appreciated her more."

"Me too," Kay said, the melancholy catching. "Sometimes she'd bawl people out. 'Tone it down,' she'd say, or 'save your spirit for the game. Don't leave it laying in the locker room.'" In tipsy imitation, Kay trilled the "r" in "spirit," like a stage actress.

Inspiration hit and I jumped in. "It was an accent, wasn't it? Betty Jane had an accent, didn't she?"

"Oh, I don't think so," Kay responded, but the question bothered her. She grew pensive before saying, "Guess it coulda been. I 'spose. Yeah. Never thought of it that way though."

"She talked funny is all," Dinah said. "Put on airs, because her folks was in the 'theatuh.'"

No, they weren't. They were bakers of poppyseed bread. Betty Jane had an accent because she was from far across the ocean, where to the backwoods child I had been, there were many raggedy-edged countries packed together in shades of black-and-white.

Twyla confronted me. "Winkie, are you on the team to pin her murder on one of us?"

"Come on." I spread my hands. "That guy Leroy Williams did it. The police will keep at him until he cracks."

"Please don't let them search through our stuff again," Bobby pled. "I get sick thinking about strange men pawing through my private things."

With some acquiescing murmurs and no one making light of the comment, I said, "I'm sorry, ladies. I don't have any control over the cops."

There was drifting toward the bureau for fresh beers and sodas. Empty bottles filled the small wastebasket and littered the floor beside it.

Twyla observed, "If Betty Jane had lived, we'd be toasting with champagne because we'd be the champs instead of the stupid Mankato Maulers."

There was quiet assent until Kay said, "You think there's a heaven when you die?"

Connie came alert. "Most certainly. If you want to talk about it …"

"There's a heaven for dykes," Joanie interrupted. "It's a reward for not bringing any more pukey snots like you into the world." She gave Kay a friendly dig in the ribs. Soda-drinking Connie couldn't compete with the beer-drinkers, so she sank back.

"Hey," Kay said, "I want to know what y'all believe."

Pepper blurted, "How can anyone believe in God with the pay scale like it is?"

"You just want to buy more dirndls," I said. Then I became solemn. "I think Betty Jane is looking down on us right now and remembering the good times she had, out there pitching with you backing her up. It was probably the high point of her life." From what I had gleaned of Betty Jane's existence as Lois Magic, I did truly believe that.

Dinah belched. "Yup, she was a good ol' overpaid kid."

"I felt sorry for her no matter how much money she made," Kay said, her words increasingly slurred, "'cause her family never came to see her pitch."

"You rube," Pepper squawked. "Betty Jane's parents ran out on her. They left her high and dry."

Kay's face flushed. "I'm sure they did not! They loved her. She showed me the rooshnik they give her when she graduated high school. It was a family treasure. First it was her grandmother's and got handed down to her mother and then it got passed to her." Kay's voice rose. "You're a dumb rube yourself, Pepper. Bet you don't even know what a rooshnik is."

Pepper laughed spitefully. "No, but I know what a snivelly kid you are with a daddy who can't stand your miserable pitching."

With a roar, Kay leapt at Pepper and punched her in the gut. Pepper howled and doubled over, but retained her high-heeled footing. She feinted toward Kay, but since she didn't want to get messed up, that went nowhere. Other players grabbed Kay's arms.

"Calm down," Connie gasped between efforts at hanging on as The Kid struggled to get at Pepper.

Someone said, "Hey, you won today, so ease up," which finally quelled her enough that people could let go. Their hands stayed close so they could grab on in case of another lunge.

Pepper went to the mirror where she checked for damage. "That hurt," she muttered. "My stomach hurts when I touch it."

"Kid, what's a rooshnik?" I asked Kay.

Still in the spirit of the fight, Kay's voice trembled. "A towel with hens and chicks on it. Handed down by the women in the family, from grandmother to mother and then on to daughters. It's for when the girl marries."

I remembered seeing Betty Jane's rooshnik while searching her apartment. A flimsy gray towel, embroidered with red chicks and hens, neatly folded in a drawer between a washrag and some cotton underwear. Hand sewn next to factory-produced, I'd decided at the time, nothing beyond that occurring to me.

A Willey stepped out of shadow. "No blood relative was at Betty Jane's funeral. Only Leroy Williams was in town and he was kept in jail for killing her."

From another part of the room, Twyla added, "She was buried in Burton City like there was no better place. I mean, didn't she have a home town?"

"Nobody appreciated her more than us and the fans," Kay said stoutly.

"The city fathers are collecting money for a headstone," Connie noted.

"I gave some," Kay said.

Enroute to a refill, Pepper sneered, "I bet you tithe in her memory."

That started it again. Kay grabbed Pepper's hair and yanked her backwards. The tall girl's heels slipped out from under her and she went down hard. Kay was quickly on top of her, punching repeatedly. Screaming, writhing, Pepper brought her knees up to protect herself as Joanie and Connie tried to pull the feisty pitcher off. Kay struck Joanie's arm with a solid right and that brought Twyla in, clutching at Kay's fist and receiving a knock for her trouble. Meantime Joanie had succeeded in pulling Kay off Pepper at the same time Pepper was kicking at Joanie which really ticked Joanie off because, as she pointed out, she was only trying to help.

I withdrew to a straight chair to sit it out.

The latest brawl ended fast when, from across the room, Dinah entered the fray and began tossing around bodies like kitty cats. All concerned took the opportunity to quit, having satisfied some aspect of their character: vengeance, pent up frustration, undirected anger, or simply fun-seeking.

In the aftermath, players roamed about, talking too loud and licking their wounds while downing more beer and crackers. Remember-when stories were told to the accompaniment of staticky radio country music.

About a quarter of two, with cigarette smoke making the room hazy and close, and girls acting sillier and drunker than they could possibly be, a series of raps hit the door and Eddie blared, "Ants! Back in the anthill. And don't any of you insects think about crawling away."

After failing to stuff more empty beer bottles into the already crammed wastebasket, we clinked them together in a corner and loosely covered them with a blanket.

Most of the team cleared out right away, with Connie congratulating me on surviving with such noble composure. The Willeys remained, squatting in a corner, scarfing down every last scrap of free food they could find. Kay also stayed and became Dinah's Girl Friday, darting around, picking up fallen items as Joanie and Twyla deliberately got in her way.

There was no chance that Pepper would obey big sister and leave. Eddie remained at the door, watching as Pepper posed at the mirror, fluffing her hair to restore the part. After clasping twenty-five cents worth of necklace around her neck, she took lipstick from her purse and wielded the tube as Matisse must have his brush. Was it force of habit to apply makeup at all hours or did she have a really really late date? I was running my tongue over my own lips when the glamour girl's eyes strayed to me. "What's your problem?" she challenged.

"You sure know your cosmetics."

She smiled vaguely. I moved closer and dropped my voice to a whisper. "Have you thought about what I asked?"

Her expression became blank. "About what?"

Boy, was she irritating. Too bad Kay hadn't left marks. "About Betty Jane's dad. Come on, Pepper, I know you can pin down the date when he asked you for the favor."

She shrugged. "The day I got out of the reformatory. No trouble remembering that, March 24th."

About nine days after the Magics disappeared.

She went on. "I walked out to the street a free woman, and here's this guy waiting in a big black Caddy."

"What did he look like?"

"Short. Lumpy. Big muscles."

Teddy Magic? Could be. But a baker driving a Cadillac? "What color hair?" I asked.

"Jet black, looked dyed. All slicked back. He had a square face, lots of lines in it. I'd put him near fifty. I hear he's a missing person now. Is that right?"

"Mr. Magic currently can't be located. Did the guy have an accent?" I was digging for the Ukrainian connection.

"Yeah. New York, like Noo Yawk when he said, 'I'm Lois' fadduh.' You know, how Letta talks." She laughed humorlessly. Letta hailed from New York City. "He was dressed up in his Sunday best, looked like a rassler stuffed into fancy clothes for a joke. A regular orang-gootang."

"Wanted to impress you."

"Yep, they all do. " She paused, then confided, "Look here, after all my troubles, I want to keep square with the law. I never knew you were a detective. The truth is Mr. Magic paid me $500 to get Lois a tryout with the team. It was no big deal, I'd a done it anyhow, out of friendship."

"But you took the $500, I can understand that. Did he give you a ride in the Caddy?"

"Nah, he lit out fast. If he'd offered, I'd a said, I'm outa here, forget it. I mean I needed peace and quiet, not no muscle man could throw me across a bed. He said I could earn another $500 if I kept the secret from Betty Jane. Said she was an independent cuss, always had been, and that them, him and her mama, didn't want her tracking them down. Best let her make her way by herself, he said. Well, I had that same line shoved at me by my nearest and dearest." She cleared her throat of anguish that I hadn't seen from the volatile woman. "If it wasn't for Eddie," she finished, "I'd be outa luck."

"You might show a little gratitude occasionally." She stared daggers at me. Sensing I'd meddled too strongly in family affairs, I asked, "So did Betty Jane's father make the second payment?"

"No, I never seen him again." She picked viciously at a hair on her chin, found it was still growing.

"You did see him," I said flatly, "and he threatened you."

Her hand dropped. "None a your business but I didn't go near him that next time. It was in Cranston Park after a game. Sid warned me not to have anything to do with him or I'd get thrown off the team for consorting with the criminal element. Well, I'd already consorted when I took the $500. I mean how'd I know Betty Jane's dad was a mug? And," she faced me, "I'll deny everything if you go to the cops, so just don't."

"I won't tell," I lied. I glanced in the mirror to see who was witnessing this. A Willey was tramping away from us in her desert boots. From the doorway, Eddie, in her housecoat, posed sentry-like, the hall light falling on her face made her look haggard and spent.

After sweeping a glance over me, she mumbled a perfunctory, "Good night," to whichever Willey brushed past her into the hall.

I recognized Lor as the one who remained. Liquor flask in hand, and apparently unaware that her worse half had departed, she was backed into a corner out of Eddie's view. Since the twins rarely parted company I decided that Dor must absolutely have had to get to the john.

Kay appropriated the two remaining sodas and handed one to Lor who poured some into the flask. The Kid was adapting nicely to the ways of her world.

When I checked the door, Eddie had vanished, so there was no need for secrecy except it was the Willeys' stock and trade.

I was rocky on my feet from the arduous evening. A bitter realization hit with dreadful clarity. If the three gangsters were involved in murder, this case might be too big for me. I retrieved my purse and dropped into a chair. I sat for a while. I had to chew on that ugly possibility before continuing. I decided I couldn't stop now.

When I lifted my head, Pepper was prancing out the door with Joanie and Twyla following, their mirthful expressions saying they would not be heading for their quarters any time soon.

With those departures, all the guests were gone and Dinah and I were left alone.

The circle of light from the table lamp illuminated a carpet strewn with cracker crumbs, ground-in tobacco chaw, a Hershey bar wrapper, and a mottled scarf. The room looked forlorn and abandoned.

I rose and moved to leave. If Dinah were a murderer and an assaulter, it was not wise to remain. "Thanks for the fun evening, M&M," I said. "Even though I didn't barf or pass out, I'd consider my funning to be a major success."

With a swoop she was to the door. Kicking it closed, she blocked my exit. In her baby voice, she spoke slowly, "You're a cop, out to get me and seduce my boyfriend in the bargain."

What a strange thing to say. I didn't get it. Had to be too much overwrought partying. Nerve ends twanging, I replied, "I'm glad you know I'm a private detective because honesty counts among teammates." I always try to remember that those skeptical of dicks are criticizing the position and not the person.

She was not deterred. "I had a bellyful of you feeding lies to my man Sid."

"Huh?"

"Lies like I killed her. I done no sucha thing."

"I never said that to Sid or anyone."

Her lower lip pouted. "Did so."

"Did not."

"Did so!"

I didn't have time to play games with an overgrown kid. Instead I offered a nibble of conciliation. "I do see your point though."

She blew out a breath. "So somebody else sees it too."

"You need a friend," I placated further, "because from the very start of this investigation, someone has tried to make it look like you done it."

She banged a fist against the bureau. I fell into a chair. Clinging to my purse, I adored the heft of the .38 inside. She stalked past, whacked my knee with hers and sat down heavily across from me.

Heart thudding against my shirt, I played the one-upmanship card. "M&M, you are a teensy bit tipsy. Let us meet tomorrow when we're feeling more like ourselves to discuss further the salient points you have expressed. We may explore your unresolved anger. Or," observing her expression, "we may table that."

"Stop it," she peeped, "I only went through grade six. Listen, I know you got looks I can't match. I see how people cheer for me on the playing field but out in the world they say, 'looka that freak. Ain't she ugly.'" Her peep darkened. "Except for Sid, he recognizes my woman-ness. He writes I'm everything a man can want."

"Sure, I agree. You're everything a baseball fan wants."

"Betty Jane was like you just. Acting friendly and all the time seducing Sid from me with her beauty. That girl was as pesky as a paper sack that blows under the wheels of a car. No matter how you try to squash that old bag it shows up on the other side."

"Until one day she didn't make it to the other side. Were you responsible?"

"I didn't kill her!"

I changed my tactic. "You say Sid is your boyfriend?"

"Dern tootin'. My Sid calls me 'power-packed' and he writes that I'm …" she blushed and her expression lightened, "… womanly. He writes, 'When Dinah swings, she takes a woman-size stride into the ball.'"

"Well put."

She was gaining fervor, volume, and tempo. "He wrote, 'Dinah's hips sway like Miss America's would if she batted cleanup.' Sid loves me like I'm Miss America."

"He loves your abilities."

"A course, that's natural in any matchup of the heart." Longing was in that childlike voice. "I get a different feeling thinking about Sid than with any other fella."

"Sexual stirrings?"

"Yeah," she clapped her forehead. "And you got 'em too."

"No no," I spread my hands, "Sid's just a friend. I mean, we may have gone out a couple of times …"

Anger flared. "I know you're trying to win over my boyfriend. Sid courts me through the sports pages, the only way he knows how. He's shy." Her gaze roamed around the room, the eyes held that need-to-toss look. In case I was eligible, I was half out of the chair before she grabbed it, sending me off balance and the handbag spinning to the floor. Hoisting the chair above her head, she swung it against the bureau, breaking off a leg. Her eyes cleared and met mine.

"If you wasn't a cop," she said thickly, "your funning would a made Betty Jane's look like a cakewalk."

"M&M," I said, my voice seeming to come from a long ways off, "I can tell that you go for the intellectual type like Sid is. But out there in the big wide world there's some other deep thinker, a guy who uses words ever so much better than Sid, and much better looking than him too. A big, gorgeous hunk of a man that'll carry you over the threshold like you're no heavier than a butterfly. Right now this lonely man is just pining away for a woman like you."

The chair and its separated leg relaxed a bit. Dinah's forehead furrowed. "What's his name?" she inquired.

Two sharp pops in quick succession came from the hall. Dinah and I both jumped and I used my down cycle to grab my handbag. Waving her off with the .38, I hurried to the door.

"Fraidy cat," she sneered, eyeing the gun. "It's just them dykes setting off firecrackers."

"Joanie and Twyla have firecrackers?"

"Yeah. Guess your funning's not over yet. Here's hoping you're in for lots more pain, you Jezebel."

I eased open the door. "You follow me, I'll shoot you," I said.

She dropped the chair parts. Her face sagged and suddenly she looked worn out. "I had enough a you," she said. "I gotta get my sleep in for tomorrow's game. You're a dope thinking I done it. If I had of, I never woulda handed you a reason for it like I done tonight."

37

I peered both ways down the hall. Connie was coming out of the bathroom to my left. Several other players were also in the hall, looking around apprehensively. I stuck the pistol in the front of my waistband and dropped my shirt over it. After strapping the handbag across my chest, I stepped into the hall and closed Dinah's door behind me.

Connie saw me and said, "You hear that noise?"

"Firecrackers. I'm supposed to check it out. More funning for me before I get to rest." I raised my voice to address the others. "You better get to bed before Eddie comes out and lands on you." Connie went two doors down and into her room. The others, after considering, followed suit.

I moved the long way down the hall toward the closed fire door and the wide steps beyond. That was where I believed the firecracker reports, or gunshots, had come from. Letta poked her head out of a room at that end of the hall. I spoke sharply. "I'll handle it, Letta. Don't give Eddie a reason to stomp on you. It's my night to suffer." She liked the idea and retreated into her digs.

Glancing back, I saw Dinah's door opening very slowly. "Let it go, big gal," I said under my breath. After several seconds, the motion stopped, leaving the door slightly ajar. I waited briefly before deciding to continue on my course without regard to Dinah's passel of grudges..

Eddie and Pepper's room was right next to Dinah's, but the chaperon hadn't shown her face. Probably waiting for the entire ant colony to collect so she could wipe it out with a single stomp.

Now the hall was empty, dimly lit by sconces at regular intervals. I continued in the direction of the sharp reports. Nearing the stairway, I heard guttural moans coming from beyond the fire door. A shiver ran up my spine. This was major funning.

Drawing my weapon, I pushed open the door and, hugging the wall, stepped into the dark stairwell. The overhead bulb was out. Faint light from the doorway played down wide steps. I let go of the door and it closed with a soft thump, leaving only streetlight illumination through a small square window, under which a Willey sat moaning into her hands. It seemed we were alone.

I moved to her and touched her shoulder. "What's wrong, Willey?" The eerie moaning stopped and she stiffened. "Willey, what happened?" I bent to her but she seemed to be in a stupor.

"Where's your other half?" I looked around. It was then I saw a desert boot sticking out where the wall of the next landing stopped and steps continued down to the fourth floor exit.

I flipped my bag behind me, and crept down the stairs to where the other Willey was sitting on the top step just off the landing. I smelled blood. I bent and poked her shoulder gently. Her head fell forward and her arm dropped onto my foot. I recoiled, but caught myself quickly. Reaching forward, I tilted her chin up. Her clouded eyes passed momentarily through a shaft of light.

I ran a hand over her face and located the mole. Dor. I ran one hand down her front and the other down her back and I encountered a thick wet substance. Blood was oozing from her back. In the dimness my hand was sticky with dark blood.

I felt her wrist and located an erratic pulse. From the stairway below, I heard a single sharp metallic click. It was the same sound I'd heard in the shower room before I got whacked.

A bullet snapped by my ear. I ducked, raised my weapon and fired around the corner, a slim chance of hitting anyone, but I sure wanted them to know I was armed. The smell of gunpowder competed with the strong odor of Tabu that filled the enclosed space.

A rapid clack-clack-clacking of retreating footsteps sounded from below. A distant door thudded open and the sharp footfalls were deadened by carpet. But I already knew I was hearing high heels, and I knew who had murdered Betty Jane Wadlow and Millicent Tubbs, then trying for a homicidal trifecta by shooting this poor Willey. Not to mention conking me and now firing at me. For sure, the fleeing steps were those of a woman who ran in heels better than in baseball spikes.

I tucked the .38 in my waistband. Grasping Dor around her waist, I hauled her up the steps, no easy job since she was dead weight. My thought was to get her out of the kill zone. On the arduous climb, another thought took over, that I shouldn't be doing this, moving her, but Pepper was so wild - you never knew what crazy thing she'd do next. I feared she'd bust back in and finish the job. But too late to return Dor now; I was halfway up the steps.

As I reached the top, Lor flew at me, bony hands clawing. I let Dor go.

Lor cuddled her critically wounded sister. How I regretted moving Dor, but at least if she died, it would be in her sister's arms.

I observed that Lor's right bicep was bloody. "Are you hit?" I asked but got no reply. Lor's teeth were clenched and her jaw worked. She muttered, "Dor, say something, please say something."

"Who did this?" I asked. "Did you see?" Again no response for me.

"We have to get a doctor for Dor," I said. I hurried up the steps to fifth floor. By the fire door, I said, "Come on, come on," each word rising with the necessity for action. Lor didn't budge. All her life she had stuck with her duplicate and she wasn't going to be torn asunder now.

I had to go, to save Dor's life. I drew my gun. My right palm was bloody. I wiped it on my shirt. It still felt sticky. The enemy would have a hell of a time prying this .38 out of my sticky hand. At times like these a PI needs a little humor.

Edging open the fire door, I entered fifth floor. No one was in sight. I assumed Pepper was the killer, although upon reflection, I saw how it might be Eddie, equally adroit in heels, cleverly spritzing on that very identifiable Tabu instead of the more delicate Parisian perfume. Eddie wasn't that devious, was she? She wore her heart on her sleeve for all to see. Besides, at last sighting she'd had on socks or slippers with that housecoat. Surely I'd remember the incongruity if she'd worn heels. But Eddie was another who balanced perfectly in heels.

Either way, there was a good chance the killer had fled to her room, in this instance, the same room, because a blood relative waited there, and where, later on, she could seek to blend with teammates. Assuming neither Willey was able to identify her.

First I ran to Connie's door and tapped insistently. "Who is it?" she whispered so softly I hardly heard.

"Winkie," I said in a low tone. "Open up."

The door opened an inch, no farther because of the security chain. I said, "Call the police and an ambulance. The Willeys have been shot. Lock your door and stay in your room. Don't let anyone in."

I closed the door to her gaping mouth. Immediately she shot the bolt. As I sprinted to Pepper and Eddie's room, I saw that Dinah's door was still open a crack. No light flowed beneath the McLaine door, but inside voices argued in low tones. I knocked. Half-whispers swelled to hysteria, forcibly shushed. I knocked again. "Eddie, you there?" I had to draw her out of the room, separate the pair, then I'd have one less to deal with. "Two of your girls need help." I spoke with urgency. "They're injured and down on the wide steps."

Hesitation before, "What?" came from Eddie.

"Someone took a shot at me. Maybe it was blanks, I don't know." I continued speaking softly so no one else would join us and turn the thing into a melee. I noticed a sizable bloodstain across my shirtfront, from hauling Dor up the steps.

"You're past curfew," Eddie said.

"Please come help," I urged. "I know it's after hours, but you've always protected us." This was a woman with a desperate need to feel valued.

A weak light appeared beneath the door.

The door opened slightly. Barefoot, clad in a mussed gray nightie, Eddie squeezed out. I couldn't see that she was armed, but kept my hand near the pistol under my shirtfront. Her eyes widened, seeing all the blood on my front. She shut the door and pushed me in front of her down the hall. I complied but way too slow for an on-duty chaperon, so she couldn't help but chuff past.

I drew my gun, spun around, raced to the room, and flung open the door. Pepper made for the open window.

Eddie struck from behind with the force of a locomotive. She knocked the gun away. She rode me to the floor. I had no a chance in hell of retrieving that weapon, with my shoulders pressed to the floor and my breath squished under her solid weight.

Grim as the world, she said, "You shoulda stood in bed."

Pepper was thrashing around the room like a caged animal. When the door slammed and the lock turned, I sensed that she was still inside. Eddie released her pressure and lumbered to a standing position. I rolled over, stared up. Pepper was advancing, a tiny pearl-handled pistol in her hand, eyes glittering.

I raised up on my elbows but before I could make a likely fatal lunge for the .38, Eddie leapt in front of her sister and shoved her backwards. "Don't even think of doing one in front of me. My purse, it's on the dresser. There's money in it."

Pepper was to the dresser, rooting in the purse, pulling out bills. She stuck them in a dirndl pocket.

"Go out the window," Eddie urged. "Take the fire escape to the roof. Get out! You're on your own."

"No. I can't be." Pepper's voice shook. I saw that her face was mottled with red lumps as if Eddie, or Dor before she was downed, had landed a few.

Eddie turned her back on her sister and picked up my .38. Pepper, pearl-handled peashooter in hand, advanced toward me.

The murderer's white teeth caught her lower lip. With all the mayhem she had committed, her perfectly applied lipstick was chewed off. She whined, "Cop, I told you to just lay off. Betty Jane wouldn't listen either and now you're gonna pay too."

Eddie smacked her fist to her palm. Swooping by me, she stuck her face in Pepper's. "Get out fast, baby baby baby PEPPER!" she chanted, as if she were behind the plate urging on a besieged pitcher.

Pepper blinked. Hearing the patter put her on the ball field where Eddie's word was law. "Pepper, sweetie," Eddie begged brokenly, "get out while you can."

Pepper lowered the tiny pistol. Eyes large and dazed, she backed to the window, turned and stuck her head out. The whines of several sirens came from a distance, rapidly increasing in volume. Pepper ran to the door, snapped the lock open and disappeared into the hall. As soon as she was gone, Eddie banged the door shut and slammed home the dead bolt. Her eyes sought mine. There was so much pain in them, I didn't think they'd ever calm enough to be ordinary eyes again.

The sirens cut off and pounding footsteps accompanied by clipped male voices soon came to our floor. I wriggled to a sitting position as Eddie sighted my .38 at me. "You got anything in that purse to kill me with?" she asked. "Go for it. I'd just as soon take you out as live another day." We measured each other. She was not going to allow me to chase after her sister and I wasn't about to give up the hunt for the sake of McLaine family reunions.

I heard two male voices going from room to room, accompanied by sharp knocks on doors. The lawmen worked their way down the hall.

Eddie broke the stalemate, talking to the wall as much as to me. "Pepper stole the jewelry. I covered so there'd be no reason for the police to single her out. With her record, I was afraid for her. I never dreamed she'd done all this." She waved the gun to include a world of felonious possibility.

Eddie continued directing her comments to the wall. "Tonight I heard two shots. Then another shot. I stayed put thinking it was the girls popping caps or something. But when Pepper came running into the room with a heavy pocket, that's where I found the gun. It was mine, a family heirloom. I smacked her around until she admitted what she did. I didn't know till then, honest, that my sister was a cold-blooded murderer." Eddie's anguished eyes met mine and her voice rose slightly in hope. "The Willeys, are they still alive?"

"They were when I left them."

Her face lengthened.

"Did Pepper say why she shot them?"

"Got scared. Something about her and you talking about a $500 bribe she took. Dor overheard. She told Pepper she'd tell about her running with criminals if she didn't pay up. Where would she get the money? I didn't have any extra to give and she knew it." Eddie sighed. "My sister. She tries to grab onto the brass ring, but somebody always knocks it away. She's so beautiful. Most girls'd be happy to have the looks she was born with."

The policemen's voices were very near. I heard an increasing number of people talking in the hall. Expelling a breath, Eddie stepped to the side of the door and slipped to the floor, beefy legs sprawled in front of her. She laid the .38 at her side. "I'm tired of this world," she said. Her face dropped into her hands and her shoulders heaved with silent weeping. I moved quickly to the weapon. Tucking it in my handbag, I grabbed her elegant purple jacket that lay neatly over a chair back. I slipped into it, wanting to cover the smeared blood until I had a chance to explain. Didn't want some overzealous cop drawing his weapon and snarling, "Fee, fi, fo fum, I see blood on the guilty one."

I opened the door and stepped into the path of a red-faced police sergeant.

Pointing to his tin shield and touching his holstered firearm, he said, "Ma'am, just getting to your room. One more to go. That door's closed too."

"Sound sleeper," I said. The big girl must finally be getting her beauty rest.

"Why didn't you come out before now?" the cop asked. "You musta heard us."

I said nothing because there was no explanation I was immediately willing to advance.

Nodding toward the room I'd just exited, he raised his voice. "Anybody else in there?"

A distraught Eddie appeared.

"Sergeant Ruggle," I said, reading his nameplate. "I'm Private Investigator Wendy Winkworth." After so long, I felt some pleasure in pronouncing my real name. "My ID and weapon are in my purse."

Keeping hold of his holstered weapon with his right hand, he unsnapped the handbag with his left, withdrew the pistol, and after some rummaging, allowed me to fish for the credentials. Knowing the palm of my right hand was still bloody, I used my left.

Once he'd confirmed my identity, we shook hands, I with my left. I said brightly, "This lady beside me is the Burton City Hornettes' team chaperon, Eddie McLaine. She's also the catcher, and mighty fine at both jobs." I was stalling.

The charge is harboring a fugitive, I couldn't quite bring myself to say. I had to think out how the allegation would damage her further. But all those implicated in a crime must be punished. Give me time and a blanket to crawl under while I sort that out. Eddie had protected her sister until there was no use any more. I'm my father's child. Don't expect perfection of me. Maybe I'd just give her a good talking to like she'd done me so many times. On the other hand, I'd lose my license if it came out that I knew her complicity and didn't turn her in.

Marking Eddie's haunted appearance, the cop said, "What's the story, ma'am? You in trouble?"

I spoke for her. "Trying to keep these ballplayers in line just saps a person's strength. Our chaperon's altogether too conscientious."

The cop and Eddie shook hands. She still didn't say a word. "Rough time, eh?" he presumed.

I became official. "The killer escaped, but we know her identity. Send an all-points bulletin …" I have never understood what that included but Broderick Crawford on "Highway Patrol" seemed to know, "… for Pepper McLaine, middle twenties, five foot seven, 120 pounds, red hair, wearing a full skirt, bright colored blouse, and heels. She's armed, she's killed two people and tonight she wounded two more and took a shot at me."

The sarge assessed with a squint the validity of my dictate and moved off to consult with a broad-shouldered uniform who had taken up duty outside the one remaining closed door, that to Dinah's room next to the narrow stairs. Practically the whole Hornette team was in the hall, clustered together in bunches. Rumpled nightclothes, frazzled hair, gave evidence that all the noise had produced a restless night.

Abruptly the last door swung open and Dinah poked her head out. Her lips seemed unnaturally full and her face was as fat as if she'd just cleared the bases.

"This what ya looking for?" she piped. Reaching back into the room, her fat paw reappeared with a clump of red hair to which Pepper was attached.

38.

At 12:30 p.m. the next day, in front of the Pink Duster Hotel, the team bus sat rumbling in its smelly fumes, as a depleted troupe of ballplayers wandered nearby. The bus's departure had been delayed so the Mankato police could conclude their investigation.

I had spent the night with the police, detailing my role in the case and in the subsequent arrest. At noon, I'd been driven by squad car to the hotel with a half hour to spare before the bus was due to depart. No longer a part of the team, I'd remain with them for the ride back to Burton City.

Lor and Dor were in the local hospital, Dor in intensive care. Clint and Eddie were missing. "About 4:00 a.m. we saw them coming down the stairs in the hotel lobby," Joanie said, Twyla nodding in affirmation. "On their way out, they were hand in hand."

"Tender," Twyla observed.

"Young love," Joanie added acerbically.

At 12:10 p.m., the Mediapolis, Iowa, police reported Clint's Buick, very recognizable with the hornet logo on the door, was parked on the street opposite the Mediapolis Inn. No one was inside the car. He, or more likely the pair of "young lovers," must have caught an express Greyhound from Mankato.

I would not rat out Eddie. I'd never told on my brothers or on Dad. Blood loyalty kept Eddie from realizing the truth about her sister. That I understood. Leave it to someone else to clarify Eddie's role.

Team members were discussing Pepper's arrest. I caught fragments.

"What a relief."

"I'll sleep good tonight."

"I'm not surprised. She was always very hard to get along with. And she couldn't hit for squat." Like those failings led to murder.

Joanie fixed me with an accusatory glare. "Winkie, you have virtue-lee wiped out the Hornettes."

"What? All I did was nail a killer."

"Beg pardon. M&M caught Pepper."

"Well …" I said, at a loss to for words to grant me a little credit.

By my side, a puffed up Dinah said, "Little podner, you did the right thing sending her to me." That was all the appreciation I was going to get. The big gal went on. "Dum-dum stopped right in front of my door, waving that peewee pistol like she couldn't think straight about which way to run."

I moved away from the ball-playing clan to grouse off by myself. I had expected a pat on the back for a job well done, or, even a chatty, "So you're a PI, what's that job like?" Instead the girls either blamed me for rendering the team impotent or bestowed credit elsewhere. Maybe things would have been different if I'd been able to hit even a little bit. Anyhow, because of my one at-bat, I would forever be in the official records of the Star-Spangled League. Maybe I'd check in at its fiftieth reunion to see if sentiment had changed.

But for right then, I had to be content with my seat over the back wheels. I slept fitfully, developing a headache during the trip to Burton City. Not even Kay came to sit across from me. She remained with boisterous pals Dinah, Helen, and Bobby up front. I tried to be happy for her at last fitting in with the old-timers.

Late afternoon the following day, in an interrogation room in the Burton City jail, Chief Shupe perched on a corner of a square table, next to a stenographer wearing a business suit and horn-rimmed glasses. I sat at the opposite end of the table, around the corner from Pepper who was in a light green prison dress. All the furniture, including the chairs, was bolted to the floor.

Pepper looked drained. The first half hour of questioning, she'd been defiant to Shupe's relentless interrogation. "I ain't saying nothin'. Figure it out yourselves," she'd responded, but after the same questions were drilled over and over, she wore down. A cigarette waggled from her lips as she said, "I don't give a flying crap what you think of me, but, okay, this is how it went. B.J. had this case that the gray-haired man had gave her and Leroy said she was gonna dump it in the river."

Shupe inserted, "Why'd you care?"

Her eyes widened. "10,000 bucks was in that case. Small bills, easy to pass."

"Instead of shooting her," I said, "you ever think of just breaking her arm or busting a kneecap? Did Leroy know what you did?"

"Yeah, after. Cried like a baby when I told him what her last words were, how she said, 'Why you doing this?' all innocent like she didn't have no idea."

"I'm surprised he didn't kill you right then. He told me many times how much he loved her."

Pepper flared. "Wouldn't a dared. He's afraid of me."

"Tell us about the silver-haired man," Shupe said.

"A guy, had a rat's chin. Leroy seen him once from a ways away, not to talk to."

"Why did the man give Betty Jane all that money?"

"Ask Leroy. Didn't make no sense to me."

"Yeah?" Shupe seemed less than convinced. "Tell us about the night Betty Jane died."

Pepper ran a fist across her nose. "That last game? Where Betty Jane run off after throwing the lousy pitch? Leroy tried to stop her when she came out of the park but she ran right through him. He found me after the game and said you gotta stop her, she's got the case and she's going down to the river to think it over, but I know she's gonna end up throwing that money in the water. Well, on foot Leroy'd never catch her but in my car, I might.

"So I said I'd take care of it, and I ran to my car and got my gun that I keep under the back seat and I drove like a maniac to the river." She looked significantly at each of us in turn so we'd know that what came next was very meaningful. "Once in a lifetime," she stated, "a chance comes along to somebody like me that I had to take full advantage of."

None of the listeners seemed impressed. The noisy fan blew on. The steno wrote some final hieroglyphs and waited with pencil poised.

"Feel free to continue," Shupe said.

Pepper shrugged at our lack of understanding. "At the river, there she was holding onto the case. The moon was out and it lit her up like the star she thought she was. When she saw me she started talking crazy, yelling that her father wouldn't let loose of her. I says right back, 'Who cares about your daddy, he don't mean nothing. We want that money, you can use yours to buy some wheels for Leroy.'

"But she turns away from me and raises her arm like to throw that case into the water. 'I gotta do this,' she yells at me. 'This is how I get free of him.'

"I yells back, 'Don't be a damn fool.' I write a word on a rock, coulda been any word. The idea was to get her up close to me, I'm a lousy shot from a distance. I yell for her to come over here and take a look like I had found something really neat. But up goes her arm again and I know that case is gonna go far out in the water where we'd never find it, she had a world class throwing arm. So I shot her. She fell forward and reached out and the case flew out and floated off down the M-I-S-S-I-S-S-I-P-P-I." She gazed disingenuously at Shupe. His expression was skeptical. I doubted there'd be even a bite of a Baby Ruth bar for her after this session.

"But," she resumed, "if she didn't try to get up onto her feet, face all pinched and sand on her nose. It was weird watching her trying to get at me, all smart assy like she was. And right near me was when she said, 'Why you doing this?' like she had no idea." Pepper gazed around the bleak room. "The gun went off again. This time she stayed down."

Shupe loosened his tie, rubbed his jaw. "Why'd you take Dinah's paint jar along?"

"I wanted her to get blamed in case I had to do it up royal. She's such a tree, and we all knew she hated B.J. and already went off half-cocked about her. So on my way out of the clubhouse, I grabbed the paint, with the feeling that something was going down tonight. Taking it wasn't hard to do. The idiot left her locker open. I'd been taking stuff all along, jewelry, gimcracks the girls got from their steadies. They all thought they were better than me."

"You let your sister take the blame for the thefts," I said. "That's really low." "Where's the ten grand now?" Shupe said.

Her voice rose. "I told you, it floated away down the damn river!"

"No!" he leaned across the table. "We have the briefcase from where you hid it behind a file in Clint's office, and the murder weapon that you stashed inside it. That revolver had Millicent Tubbs' type-O blood on it." First I'd heard of that, but not surprising.

The chief lowered his tone ominously. "It's clear we have the case and it's not in the river, so where's the money?"

She paled, suddenly realizing we had the evidence. "I want a lawyer."

"I'm sure that's not the first time you said that," Shupe responded. "Sure. Who do you recommend?"

Tears seeped into the corners of her eyes. "I can't pay," she whispered.

I hadn't an ounce of sympathy for her. The image of Betty Jane, bloody in the moonlight, was too vivid.

Shupe leapt to his feet and crashed around the table. "Girl, I'm tired of dancing with you." He grabbed the front of her dress and yanked her up. Her arms flopped and head jerked like a ragdoll's.

"Where's the money? Don't bother lying. You'll never be free of this mess anyhow."

"You proud of yourself, beating up on a defenseless girl?" Pepper cried.

Shupe shoved her down into the chair. She grabbed the table to prevent tumbling to the floor.

"Robinson," Shupe shouted, "get in here!"

The enforcer banged in.

"Winkworth, Blanche, go powder your noses." Shupe spoke softly, but his grapeshot eyes told me he meant business. It was Shupe's town, Shupe's police station. If I interfered, I'd land in a cell before I knew what my wink was worth.

As the door closed behind the two of us, we heard Pepper shriek, "You can't get away with this. My sister will - " A horrendous shriek cut off whatever her sister would do.

I waited in the hall with the functionary. I didn't need a glass pressed to the wall to hear the cries, demands, weepy protestations until, finally, all subsided into silence.

Shupe opened the door. "Blanche," he said to the cowed stenographer, "we're ready."

Pepper was huddled in the chair, weeping, her mouth dripping saliva onto an arm. "Leroy said he'd bury the money out near the ballpark," she blurted between punches of breath. "Please, that's all I know."

She brought her head up and I saw red marks on her face and arms. I pulled out my hanky and dabbed at her wet cheeks. I still didn't feel anything for her. She'd survived, her victim hadn't. I did it simply because I didn't care for the passivity I'd been forced into.

The woman was terrified to the extent that Shupe saw there was no more to be gotten from her that day. He said, "Detective Winkworth, you got anything more to ask?"

"Where did you go after you shot the Willeys?" I asked.

"You know."

"I found you in your room. Was Eddie hiding you? That's a crime if she was."

Mouth squinching, she worked through a tangled relationship with a controlling big sister. Finally she said, "Eddie told me to turn myself in." I breathed a sigh of relief. Let Shupe figure out any complicity.

"When you ran out of your hotel room why'd you pause outside Dinah's room like you didn't know which way to go?"

"It was them damn thin stairs. I'd turned my ankle on them once already. But if I took the long way down the fat stairs, I'd a had to see the Willeys again."

"You might say it was your shoes that did you in."

She shot back, "You might say you're an asshole."

"Why'd you take the ball-charm necklace off Betty Jane's body?"

"I wanted it. She had everything. I didn't have nothing even though we started out the same."

"Why did you kill Millicent Tubbs?" I asked.

"She was in the way."

"How, exactly?"

"I was hanging around outside the clubhouse waiting for everybody to clear out so I could get in and get the case. It was eating at me that my revolver was in that case. I was sure that Eddie knew I owned such a gun and after the cops found it, she'd ask me where was my gun that was like that one.

"I had stuck the case in a locker after Leroy was too scared to keep it. It was good luck seeing you coming out the back door with the box of laundry. After you loaded up your car and left, I just sashayed in since you left the door unlocked. Damn, the new girl was still in there and hanging onto that case, was I surprised. So was she, but I smiled so sweet and she relaxed and said, 'Look what I found. Is it finders keepers here?' Well, I got up real close and said a sweet thing or two and rubbed against her and she got hot real fast, I knew her type, I'd been around Joanie and Twyla enough. Fairy queens." She made a face.

"I told Tubbs to strip quick and get washed off and I'd meet her in the shower. She hopped to it and I whacked her some and down she went but she was still blinking, so I grabbed her head and cracked it against the tiles. That was it for her. I had to be safe, sorry she had to be part of the party."

Everyone was stunned at Pepper's ruthlessness.

I broke the silence. "Never say 'finders-keepers' to you. So you took the case from Tubbs and hid it in Clint's office."

"First I took it home and wiped all of it down and then hid it under the porch. But I got scared when the cops wouldn't let Leroy go to B.J.'s funeral and then they found out about me and her being cell-mates, and that Leroy was married to her. With Leroy being such a limp dick he'd let the cat out of the bag for sure. Cops been on my tail all my life; I never get a break."

The steno was gaping. It was obvious this was one crazy killer.

"The gun and the locket inside the case just weren't worth it," Pepper went on. "I decided Eddie didn't know about the gun after all, so let the cops prove it was mine. So one night I snuck the case into an almost full equipment bag and lugged it over to Clint's office. Eddie was so happy when she saw me. She said, 'What's with you being a help for once?'"

"Why'd you hit me with the Louisville Slugger?"

"'Cause you weren't playing fair, pretending to be a player when all the time you were a stinking cop."

"Lesson learned. One more thing: why did Joanie and Twyla alibi you for the night of the Wadlow murder?"

"Oh, we always covered for each other. I was the hetero- who went places with them, making them be all right. You know it's a scandal if queers are found out. And they knew me well enough to know I'd never kill anyone."

Joanie, Twyla, join the ranks with Eddie on that one.

39.

The front-page headline read, "MURDERER CAUGHT IN BASEBALL KILLINGS." It was the top story nationwide. Dinah was interviewed. "Ragglehead couldn't decide which way to go. I filled her in." I gave a modest quote: "Just did what I'm paid to do."

The Hornettes were put on a three-day hiatus by the league office. They couldn't field a complete team and the manager was still unaccounted for.

Sid returned from Des Moines and handed over the photo of Betty Jane's parents. We celebrated that night in my hotel room. Later, in bed beside him, I was too on edge to sleep, thinking about the case and how it was almost over.

An all-points search was conducted for Leroy Williams.

On the third morning, a call came in to the station that a lumpy young man had tried to hop a train in the Fort Madison freight yard. A worker had pulled him off and was left with a five-dollar bill flurrying around his feet as the man escaped in a peculiar jiggling and joggling gait.

On that gray, drizzly day, Shupe and I headed out immediately for Fort Madison, a small town twenty miles southwest of Burton City. The chief had agreed to my wish to accompany. Of late, he had been awfully congenial as I strolled through the station feasting on donuts, candy bars, and homemade cupcakes. Scanning the daily reports, I left frosting on their margins.

In fact, all the local cops were relieved, excited even, that the case was wrapping up. Even Officer Robinson came to me, saying, "Good job there, Winkworth. Uncommonest thing." He shook his head in wonderment, gave me a thump on the back and wandered off.

"That you under there, Leroy?" Shupe boomed, aiming his police special at the fugitive who cowered behind heavy equipment in a track-switching shack on the outskirts of Fort Madison. With small bills hidden all over his body, Leroy bulged all over. He was as breasty as Tarzan and as fortified as Nijinsky. $9829.36 was recovered in a private session that Shupe and Leroy had behind the massive machinery. The ex-con had spent little. He was a small-timer all around, except in physique that day.

It was 8:00 a.m. when we nabbed him. After stomping on the gas pedal, Shupe blared the siren for no reason; on the return trip to Burton City, we met only a hay wagon on the road. Arriving at the jail about 8:30, we found the cop contingent waiting on the steps to greet us. As Shupe and I half-carried the bedraggled prisoner up the walk, Sid arrived with a screech of brakes and a twin lens reflex camera swinging from his neck.

Pencil pointing, he asked Leroy, "Why'd you let Pepper get away with it? She killed your wife." Leroy wilted even more.

An hour later two cops brought the suspect to the third degree room where Shupe, the steno, and I waited. They shoved him onto a bolted metal chair and departed. Handcuffed, hunched over, the pasty-faced suspect declared he had nothing to say.

I shoved a bag of potato chips at him. He made no move to accept; he was not subject to blandishment, at least not right away.

After balancing a stogie on the edge of the table, Shupe drew his billy club. He rounded the table noisily and came up right next to Leroy whose dumb-animal eyes prepared for punishment. I got ready to retire to the powder room.

But the chief thwacked his own thigh, causing Leroy's knees to react by bumping the underside of the table.

"How'd you like this crushing down on your skull?" Shupe threatened. "You better open up fast or I'll open you up. You and Pepper McLaine decided to kill your wife and steal her money, didn't you? I'd love to hear your side of it. Rather use this instead, though."

"My wife died bad but I didn't do it." The declaration was so weak it was almost covered by the whirring table fan.

"You helped."

"No sir, huh-uh." Leroy shook his head. "I want a lawyer."

"You'll get one first chance I get." Shupe grinned.

"How'd Betty Jane come into all that money?" I asked.

"Ain't saying, else I'd have lead up my ass."

"Afraid of the silver-haired man?" I said. "He followed Betty Jane home and gave her the $10,000, didn't he? But now he'll get most of the money back, won't he, and you can owe him what's left. His name is Kramer, right?"

Leroy's chin trembled. "I'm dead if we keep on with this."

"Oh, we're keeping on," Shupe said. "Tell us about the ten grand or we won't protect you. In fact, I'll pay your bail right now and tell the world that you told us everything and then I'll push you out the door where you won't last 'til nightfall."

"All I wanted was for her to keep the cash."

"What did the guy want for his money?" I asked. "Why was Betty Jane going to throw it in the river?"

Leroy shook his head and refused to answer.

Resuming his seat, Shupe said, "Pepper's confessed. If you aren't equally responsible for the murder of Betty Jane Wadlow, you'd better speak up now. Otherwise, like Pepper, you'll never walk in free daylight again."

"Jesus help me." Leroy's chin wobbled.

Shupe sneered, "You're pathetic. Be a man."

I urged, "Tell us about Kramer, Leroy. Is he a professional hit man working for Yegg Washington? If he is, you should be frightened."

The snuffling abated. Leroy sat up, drew his shoulders back and seemed to have decided on a course of action. The steno had been writing busily, now she slowed to a stop. The room became still except for the whirring of the fan.

Leroy moved his cuffed hands to the tabletop and, with an index finger, drew the potato chip sack toward him. He tore it open and stuffed a handful into his mouth.

"You got me by the balls," he said, rubbing salt and oil off his lips as the recording of testimony started again. "I let Pepper get away with murdering my one and only because I needed that money to escape with. I knew the silver man would blame me for her death and come after me. He is one stone-cold killer."

"Was the silver man Betty Jane's daddy?" I asked.

A barely discernable nod from the prisoner. "Before I tell," he said, "I want five bottles of Coca Cola and a bottle opener and a pack of cigarettes. Make that two packs. And a book of matches." There was utter weariness in his tone.

Shupe delivered the demand to the hallway. "And step on it," he growled, "I don't have all day." He clomped back to his seat.

After Leroy was supplied, he arranged the chips, drinks and cigarettes neatly in an evenly spaced arc in front of him. In spite of his fear I sensed the guy liked being in charge, probably hadn't had many such moments in his life. He used the bottle opener to flip off a Coca Cola cap that he placed in the ashtray.

"Leroy, you've always been honest with me," I said, "so I'm expecting you to tell the truth now."

He locked eyes with me. "It'll be the truth," he said. He lit up a Chesterfield and took a deep drag as if it were his last.

"Betty Jane was in reformatory in Helena when her folks who raised her, her aunt and uncle, disappeared. She thought something bad had happened to them. She thought the silver man was hunting them down and would just as soon kill 'em as beat 'em up to teach the lesson, that's what she said. It was their entire family history, this man, he was her tato, that means 'father' in Russki, had killed her mama, and how he was forever after them and her too. It's why she made up the story about her family being actors, to cover for moving all the time."

Shupe shifted restlessly. "You got some proof of this?"

"Leroy's never lied to me," I reiterated. "What he's telling us now is what really happened."

Leroy resumed in his bleak tone. "After her aunt and uncle disappeared, she changed her name to throw him off the trail, in case he had, you know, offed the folks. She was born in the Ukraine, with the last name of Mejic. Spelled 'M-E-J-I-C'.

"We swore we'd never speak that name again. Her name was gonna be Wadlow, Betty Jane Wadlow, and I always honored that and I always will. Pepper forgot that one time but she's a stupid bitch."

"Got that right." Shupe creaked back in his chair. He clasped his hands behind his head and stretched. "When you get to the part about the bad man and the money, wake me up."

"Take your time, Leroy," I encouraged, "enjoy your treats."

The ex-con extracted another cigarette from the pack. He laid it in the ashtray for the future. "After Betty Jane joined the Hornettes, she began wearing a lot of makeup to disguise herself. She hated being caught in crowds, skipped out of parties early.

"A couple of weeks here and we breathed easier when the bogeyman didn't show up. At night she laid in my arms and said, 'I'm free of him, I hope. Probably it was all in my mind that he's still hunting me. Maybe my folks just gave up on me.'

"But then, the shock of her life. One night after a game a tall silver man followed her home. She couldn't make him out quite, it was dark and he stayed back about a block. But his walk. Even though she ain't seen him since she was a kid, she knew it was her tato's strut. He didn't try to catch up, so she made a run for the house and made it safe inside. The next day she told Sid Dobrotka about him. That he was dressed in a gray suit under the streetlight, and had ashy-colored hair. Sid said right off he was a gangster, one of three who came to games, mostly when she was pitching."

I advised Shupe: "His name is Kramer. He's a thug who works for Yegg Washington."

Shupe chomped on a fresh cigar and said through the smoke, "Nobody's proved Mr. Washington is a bad man."

"You got that wrong but I'm not about to argue," I said.

"Mr. Washington is a wealthy individual who's done a lot for Burton City and female athletes in general."

"Please continue, Leroy," I said.

The suspect cleared his throat. "This man killed Betty Jane's mama because she run off from him."

"Where? In the Ukraine?"

"Yup. She ran because he beat her to an inch when she didn't like him screwing with the whores. When she ran, she took Betty Jane with her. She was eight years old at the time. They made it to another town where they hid out with the aunt and uncle. Betty Jane's *tato* sent his goons to hunt them down."

Shupe clucked. "Damn savages over there."

"I heard the story a hundred times so I can see it as it happens," Leroy went on. "Auntie and uncle lived in a white building in a courtyard covered with cobblestones. Wide open area. The fourth day of hiding, Mama went out like she did every day to get water. She carried a jar, a beautiful porcelain jar. That jar had blue cornflowers hand-painted all over it; it bulged in the middle and tapered off at the ends. It was the most beautiful jar."

Shupe slapped the table. "Goddamn, why are we hearing about a jar?"

Leroy jutted out his chin stubbornly. Resuming, he gave each word the same ponderous weight: "It. Was. A. Very. Beautiful. Jug." Shupe restrained himself even after Leroy paused further to let the effect clear. Then the ex-con said, "Betty Jane was watching from the attic in the house where they were hiding. Mama started across the courtyard lugging that jar. Two men came out from behind a little thatched hut. One of 'em grabbed her mama and the other one threw the jar onto the ground where it exploded into a thousand pieces. Then he pulled out a pistol. Killed her with one shot."

The steno and I recoiled; Shupe just stared. I imagined Betty Jane's powerful presence in that room, in her Hornettes uniform because that's the only way I knew her, guiding her husband through the sad story of the climactic moment of her childhood and perhaps in all of her short life. Leroy's eyes had swelled with tears.

"Mama was shot in the head, wasn't she," I stated.

"Yuh." He lowered his head to mask the emotion.

I spoke to Shupe. "The funning in the graveyard, when Dinah pressed the toy pistol to Betty Jane's head, she got sick and passed out." Shupe's lips tightened as Leroy grunted in acquiescence.

"What happened after that?" I asked.

"The killers ran one way and Betty Jane and her kin ran the other. They hid out with different friends in a bunch of places. Finally they made it to Paris, France, where they took a boat to Ellis Island. Immigration wrote down their names as 'Magic', since that's what they thought it sounded like. Anyhow, they finally ended up in Montana."

"Story of America," Shupe opined. "Is it time yet for the tale of the ten thousand? Kramer gave it to Betty Jane. Why? Because he murdered her mother and felt sorry for her?"

Leroy took his sweet time dragging the cigarette down to the nub, then lighting a fresh nail off the old.

Exasperated by the delay, Shupe exclaimed, "Oh, for Christ's sake."

Leroy shrugged. "Nothing you do can make it worse. I'm dead anyhow." He dragged, exhaled and watched smoke spiral before saying, "That last afternoon, she came into my room carrying this old case. There she was, standing in the doorway, pulling fives and tens and twenties out of the case and tossing them all over, screaming she can't keep the money because it's her mama's blood money.

"I'm begging, hey, close the door, don't let the whole neighborhood in on this. She shuts the door. She says she found the case sitting on the coffee table in her living room. 'He's been in my apartment,' she says. I hold her and rest her head against me. 'It's a lot of money,' I say.

"She shows me this note she found in the case. It says something like, 'Dear daughter, this is for you. We will meet tonight after the game underneath the - ' I can't remember, some kind of special tree in Cranston Park. Then there's some crap about how much he loves her and he ends it with 'I am so proud of you.'

"She turns the case over on the bed and dumps it out. A locket falls out with the rest of the bills. There's two photos inside. She says her *tato* is sentimental, wants her to have these pictures of him and her mama. 'I can't keep any of it because he touched it,' she says. She shoves the locket back in the case. She yanks it out, puts it on, then rips it off. She jams it back in the case. She is acting nuts. I say, 'Jesus, honey, all this money, we'll be on easy street and maybe we can get more if you go along with him.'

Leroy's eyes got big with astonishment. "Well, what did I say that starts her yelling all over again, I was being practical. I start picking up the bills. I figure somebody's got to calm down to get her through this and convince her to make the right decision for both of us." He drew on the cigarette. "She gets quiet and starts mumbling so I have to listen real close and it seems like she says, 'The worst part is, he owns the league.'

"I say, 'Who? Will you repeat that?' and she does, louder and madder, and she says, 'I checked with Sid and he called him Yegor, not Yegg. His real name is Yegor and he's a very bad guy who's from Ukraine and he owns the league and now he's here to get me back,' she says. 'So Leroy you better get out before you're dead too.'

"'Well, no,' I argue, 'that doesn't fit. Mr. Yegg or Yegor, whoever, still loves you, so nobody's gonna end up dead, right? And in the Ukraine he was rich and powerful and he still is, so it's all good news, right?' But she doesn't take it that way and pretty soon we're yelling things in sailor language that we never said before, and she takes up the case with all the bills in it and slams out. She goes to the ballpark and she pitches in her last game." His voice had dropped in resignation.

Shupe's mouth hung open, the cigar dangling by loose strands. He leapt up so violently that the bolted-down chair came loose. He rushed to the door, flung it open and yelled for Robinson. When the cop showed, he yelled softer. "Officer! Take this boy back to his cell and don't allow him no visitors!" Robinson hauled Leroy out.

Shupe barked to those of us remaining, "Owns the league, that's bull. No one heard that, that's enough of that fairy tale. Everybody out!"

He dashed to the stenographer, snatched the steno pad from her and ripped out its pages. He squashed them into tiny balls he stuffed into his pockets. The steno headed for the door as he ranted on. "That lying S.O.B., I never want to hear anything so ridiculous again. What God-awful crap …"

I got out of there.

40.

My job was finished. There was no way I was going to bring to justice a man who, years ago in a foreign land, had ordered the murder of his wife.

Before I headed back to my home base, I had to know how I'd left certain people. I visited the Willeys in the Burton City Hospital. They had been transferred from Mankato by ambulance, sustained travel that indicated Dor must have improved a great deal. As I paused outside their sick room, I saw through the glass panel a baseball wafting past. In adjoining beds, the twins were tossing a ball back and forth, Lor used her wrist and lower right arm, the bicep being thickly bandaged, and Dor, upper body swathed in wrappings, flipped it back. Perhaps three yards apart, they were doing what they loved. I smiled. I was happy to see Dor alive and flipping a ball after my medical mistake on the stairway.

I entered the room. "Hey, Willeys, you're looking good."

They stopped chucking and withdrew into a fortress of two.

"Thought I'd check on you before I left for home."

"You ain't coming back on the team?" Lor asked.

"Naw, I'm through."

"Best thing," Dor said, flipping the ball to Lor.

"Yeah, cause we want to win a few," Lor said, catching and returning the toss. "But thanks for being a good dick."

"Such a dick as you was," Dor qualified, laying the ball on her stomach. She reached out a hand to me, stiffly, because of limited movement.

"Can I bring you anything before I leave?" I said.

Dead quiet. After a moment, Dor withdrew her hand, located the ball and looped it to me. I arced it across her bed into Lor's waiting hand.

Dor sort of smiled. "You can bring us our friggin' gloves," she said.

The next day, an announcement appeared in the Burton City Gazette that the remaining games in the Hornettes' season had been cancelled.Putting a happy face to it, the season had ended with the apprehending of a killer, something to draw upon in case there was another season.

The article went on to say that a service was being held the following afternoon, to pay tribute to the murdered and wounded players and close out the season.

Subsequently, Clint phoned Shupe to say that he wouldn't be at darts and that he and Eddie would be totally unavailable now that the season was officially over.

Shupe responded that he wanted more detail from Eddie. He said he'd wait until things quieted down, but he needed to talk to her.

Eddie's mood at our last encounter had been so bleak, even suicidal, that I had to know for sure that she was safely with her man so I drove the short distance to Mediapolis. In speeding by Dave Madison's farm, I saw him in his bean field. He recognized my car. Neither of us waved.

The telltale Buick was parked on the street in front of the Mediapolis Inn. "John and Jane Case" had taken a room on third floor, a "Do Not Disturb" sign on the door. Shacked up. Not available.

I knocked.

"Don't want any," Clint shouted.

"It's Wendy," led to his admitting me reluctantly.

They were in bathrobes, his hair tousled, hers neatly combed. The freshly applied makeup didn't make her look any less haggard.

The desk was cluttered with cinnamon rolls, coffee cups, bananas, pizza crusts, aspirin bottles, and a pitcher of water. Today's paper lay open to the article.

I closed the door and stood just inside. "Thought I'd drop by to bring you up to date. Pepper has made a full confession. Leroy's caught too. The Willeys will pull through; I visited them in the hospital. Pepper will go down for two murders, Wadlow and Tubbs. Chief Shupe will want information from you, Eddie, but I doubt anything will come of it.

"I see you know about the service," I continued. "Wouldn't you like to meet with the team, have a chance to say a proper goodbye? Bet it would mean a lot to them to say goodbye to you." Oops, did that come out right?

"I'm skipping it," Eddie said, nodding toward Clint. "He hasn't made up his mind."

"You gonna show up, Clint?" I asked.

His face came alive with thoughts of the publicity that an appearance would bring. "I'll decide later," he waffled. "Eddie doesn't want to face the girls after what Pepper did. I think I'll probably stay right here with her."

"I shoulda done more," Eddie said sorrowfully.

Clint reacted, "An elephant sitting on her couldn't have kept that girl down."

"You could go to the service hand in hand," I said, "get hitched while you're at it. There'll be a minister present. Be a nice touch, put a positive cast to the day."

Eddie's expression brightened, guilt feelings temporarily surpassed.

That firmed up Clint's decision. "We ain't coming out."

"Okay," I said, "just thought it'd be good publicity for next season."

"You can just shut up," he said.

Eddie dabbed at her eyes with a hanky. She squared off in my direction. "You got a nerve coming here after what you did," she said, hardly able to squeeze the words out. She added in a more normal tone, "Okay, you did what you had to do and it rocked my socks, but still, so soon after, to come here and rub my nose in it."

"You're fired," Clint said to me. He moved past to get the door.

The service was held in the sultry air of the ballpark. Although the gray, overcast day already had a forlorn aspect to it, many townspeople stopped by to honor and grieve with the remainder of the Hornettes. Led by a Methodist pastor in an opening prayer, the group then joined in singing "The Star-Spangled Banner" to squeeze box accompaniment. There was no follow-up team song; our music director was absent.

Connie stepped forward and introduced each team member to great applause. After my name was announced, I got additional kudos as the PI who had sent the killer Dinah's way. The burst of applause that followed made me blush and I bowed slightly as I took my place of honor among the girls. Of course, Dinah got the ultimate ovation for clobbering a killer and a baseball equally well.

After that, people came onto the field from the stands. They shook our hands and expressed appreciation for the chance to watch highly skilled females playing a sport they loved and getting paid for their abilities. After an appropriate interval, Connie signaled the ballplayers to retreat to the clubhouse for final, private goodbyes.

In the locker room, some of us had a last chaw away from the public eye. Girls came to me in small groups saying, "Glad you were here. Thanks for watching out for us."

There were parting hugs and kisses, addresses and phone numbers exchanged, and promises to remember forever. I hung around for a while, participating, listening, watching, enjoying. The

Willeys' gloves had been returned and lay on the bench in front of their locker. I picked up them up on my way out.

Most of the fans had left when I stepped from the path into the gravel parking lot where Sid was waiting to take me out on his new motorboat. Impressing the girlfriend was costing a few bucks.

It had turned steamy hot, mist floating up from the stones. As I walked toward my beau, I basked in having become an honest-to-goodness successful dickless dick.

It was then I saw a tall, slim, silver-haired man emerge from a black limousine into shimmering heat. I wiped my eyes of reflected glare to see clearly the middle-aged fellow dressed in a flawlessly tailored gray suit heading toward me with a graceful stride. The man's skin was sun-cured, his eyes protruded slightly, and when he turned to address the muscular little man by his side, I saw that his receding jaw line was a trace of Betty Jane's.

I went to meet him. "Mr. Washington," I said when I was near enough. I let the Willeys' gloves drop to the gravel and stuck out a hand.

At that motion, the short, square-faced fellow of the same description as the thug who'd bribed Pepper, slipped a hand under his suit coat. His attire, though expensive, would never fit well over his orangutan body.

Kramer, or Yegor Washington, because I was sure it was he, said, "Miss Winkworth, we meet again." He looked me over. "It was difficult, your task, and you are proved successful." He had a heavy accent. He took my hand, his wore a showy ruby ring, and squeezed with just the proper pressure for a business relationship. He drew a business envelope from an inner pocket in his suit coat. "I bring this for you. Bonus to show how happy I am in your success."

I caught sight of Sid by the parking lot entrance. He was making the barest of gestures for me to scram out of there. I decided it was best to ignore him.

Puzzled, I said to the silver-haired man, "We meet again?' Have we met before?"

"You do not remember?"

I shook my head. "I can't place you," I said.

"Long ago, in jailhouse in Harrison Arkansas, we pass very near each other." He winked, one huge, exaggerated wink. "Your father say, 'If it is yours and you are not watching, it has become mine.'" He cleared his throat. "A funny joker was your tato."

I stepped back. I had hardly noticed the other prisoners that day, but I remembered the wink, how frightened I'd been that someone had seen me hide the file and would tell. I needn't have worried.

My voice was dry as crackers. "Did my dad - did he ever talk about me?"

"Yes. To me he talks; he says you are the smart one. I am sorry when I hear how he died. But did I not choose well a detective to solve my *donechka's* slaying? Almost I keep it in the family." Satisfied lip smacking led to a despairing sigh. "My murdered daughter, she inherit athletic skill from me as you inherit know-how in crime. At age of eight, my child run, jump, outwit in football the teenage boys of the village. I train her, so happy in her skill. Here I watch her pitch, a blessing. A dream filled. An angel returned to me."

For a second I saw Betty Jane on the mound, on top of the world, flipping back her golden hair, proud, triumphant. Baseball prowess was practically all I knew of her. But that was before the *tato* came to town and destroyed the one arena where she dominated.

Washington's voice hardened. "Angel taken from me by devil."

"It's terrible when loved ones like her mama and my dad are suddenly taken away from us."

He took a moment to ponder that before favoring me with a smile. His predator's teeth were yellow and imperfect from poor dental work in the Ukraine. "So we must to leave the past and move on," he said. He bent slightly and took me in as a whole. The intense scrutiny was at first disconcerting, then downright unsettling, like I was a slave for sale at the market. He straightened and pronounced, "*Ty moya donechka.*" He went on less portentously. "Miss, you are strong and with courage, and you have brains to work for me on permanent basis. In such a way, you follow in your father's footsteps."

I was no good at translating the three-word Ukrainian phrase, but guessed at its meaning when I heard the yearning behind the offer. Replace a daughter with a daughter.

"What did you do with the aunt and uncle who raised Betty Jane?"

The challenge caused his brows to lift in surprise. "Ah," he said, "you have courage to ask this. The false parents were good Christians and so they are in heaven now."

I studied him. A handsome man clad in a Savile Row suit, creased hanky in a pocket, silver hair neatly parted. A powerful man, moneyed. Except for the jagged yellow teeth, the ideal catch for any woman. Who wouldn't want to be kin to such a man?

But I'd had one dad. Didn't think I could survive another. And what I'd accomplished in this case was my own. I'd keep it that way.

"I must decline your offer of employment," I said. "I'm an independent cuss and prefer doing my business with the silk and pearl trade." Humor save me, please. He caught his lips tipping up and directed them to their proper position of arrogance.

Only a polite remnant of the smile remained when he spoke. "Your decision is your own. I know, except for her murder, my dear daughter would come to me in the end. It is her Mejic background, and mine, to make compromise and live well. Her last thought in last game was of me. Her last pitch, she threw at me."

"You were at that last game," I stated.

"Yes. In casual dress of crowd, so not to be recognized when meeting with her. She had spirit, fire, and proud. I hunt many years for my child and so close to meet with her, to see her smile for me again. I wait that night until dawn, beside linden tree. I wait for you too. In time, you may wish to accept my job offer."

"Thank you for the bonus," I said. "No strings attached, otherwise you can have it back." Bodily weakness and shock had receded and I was regaining courage and pluck and all that I was famous for. I dug into my handbag, causing the muscle man to jerk his gun into partial view. Yegor/Yegg struck the guy's elbow so he noticed. I brought out the envelope slowly and held it forward. I had the remnants of chaw curled between cheek and gums that I could have let loose on the big boss's wingtips, but, hey, there's a limit to a bold heritage.

He slapped the envelope aside. "Never do I renege on reward." The trills were fierce. His voice degenerated into weariness and something passed across that smooth face, perhaps regret. He said so softly I could hardly hear, "Your *tato* said you are the smart one. Maybe he was right." He turned on his heel. Striding toward the limo, he made a backhand gesture at the hoodlum, who kowtowed after him as the driver started the Caddy with a smooth purr.

I walked over gravel to Sid. My shirt was sticking to me, and the purse and gloves felt sticky in my hands. It was over. I had won; I'd beaten back Yegor Washington and my fears. If they came back to intrude on a later case, I'd be more prepared next time.

Betty Jane Wadlow, Lois Magic, I hoped I served you well.

Later on, I'd go sit by the lollipop marker at the base of that stately and durable elm and tell my dad that he was right; I am the smart one.

The End

Photo by Peter Barta

About Marilyn Bos

Marilyn Bos, Emeritus Professor at Minnesota State University, Mankato, is the author if three books on violin playing.

As a child, she wanted to join the All American Girls Professional Baseball League, but the league folded before she got the chance. Nothing personal, apparently.

If you enjoyed *The Stray Pitch*, turn the page for a sneak peak into Wendy Winkworth's next case: *Bubbles, Roses, and Rump*, available March, 2013.

In "Bubbles, Roses, and Rump," Wendy Winkworth, Private
Eye Extraordinaire, is visiting her brother Norris in Bern,
Illinois, when a hot case drops in her lap. A man wants to find
his real mother before she gets in the way of him marrying his
sweetheart. The year is 1951. The weather is hot. The talk is fast
and furious. This delightful period mystery is a frothy romp of a
book—the language good enough to eat. And when the bananas
flambé go flying, watch out!
    —Mary Logue, author of the Claire Watkins mysteries

Bubbles, Roses, and Rump

I'm Private Investigator Wendy Winkworth, the dickless dick.

One bright September afternoon in 1951, I was sitting in a high school classroom chatting with a former teacher of mine when a tall, well-built man burst through the door and aimed his fist straight at me.

If I were the reflective type I'd dwell on what might have happened if I'd not been in that room at that very moment. Maybe lives would have been saved.

The man glanced off two student desks in his haste to get at me. I was almost to my feet when he stuck a scrap of paper up to my nose. "Did you leave this?" he demanded.

I sank back down. "Surely not."

Miss Bubbles Baumgartner, thick glasses quivering, rose from her swivel chair. "George, what in the world …" Bubbles wasn't her real name. Fourteen years ago in Lead Hill, Arkansas, our sixth grade class had dubbed her "Bubbles" for her habit of reaching under her blouse and tugging on a brassiere strap, irrefutable proof, we decided, of a past as a bubble dancer. She didn't look much like Gypsy Rose Lee now.

The big guy stepped back and I saw fear in his eyes rather than anger.

I crossed my legs, smoothed my slim-line skirt. "What's the deal with you?"

He scowled at Bubbles. "Who is this woman?"

"Now you ask?" she said. "This is Wendy Winkworth, a former student of mine from Arkansas. Wendy, meet George Fullerton, our Biology teacher. Please forgive him. The school lunch must not have agreed with him."

"Chocolate cake turned out to be made of peanut butter?" I wisecracked.

Fullerton yanked at his collar. His complexion was stewing like a tomato. Middle-aged, tousle-haired, he had deep worry lines running between nose and mouth. He wore a navy blue suit, shiny with wear, a white shirt with a pen sticking out of a pocket, a bow tie on crooked, and dark-rimmed eyeglasses. The room where we contested smelled of dense wooly heat and sweet apple cores.

Waggling the paper, he said in a throttled voice, "This note was on my desk when I returned from lunch. The woman is a stranger so naturally I thought she'd left it."

Bubbles responded, "Where's the logic in that?"

"Well …" he hesitated, "… she's out of place like the note, so she must have brought it in."

A corner of Bubbles' mouth rose disdainfully. "What's in the note? Is it dirty?"

George Fullerton shuddered. Whatever it contained, he could not speak it.

Slipping fingers under her blouse, Bubbles pondered her bra strap and the problem. "Twenty minutes ago I saw Paul Rump in the hall. I called to him but of course he ignored me and went clodhopping down the steps." She turned to me. "Paul's in his first year of junior college." Bubbles had already explained that the Bern, Illinois, high school and its small junior college were housed in separate sections of the same building. "He's a wastrel and had to repeat his senior year," she went on. "After he finally did graduate, he took last year off to work for his father. Now he's back and thinks he's the toughest guy around. He's on suspension, shouldn't even be on school property, much less in the high school area. I'll bet Paul left the note, George, particularly if it's dirty. It doesn't actually threaten, does it?"

"Only the rest of my life," he said gloomily.

She made a face. "Aren't you being over-dramatic? If it's that serious, Wendy here is a private detective. You can hire her to bring the culprit to justice." Bubbles giggled.

And there you have it. What happened after was all Bubbles' fault.

George Fullerton's large torso leaned toward me. "A private detective. Then she must have paid you to leave this."

Non sequiturs accumulating, I fought back with the weaponry of the English classroom: grammar. "And who is this she of whom you are speaking?" Peripherally I saw my old teacher roll her eyes and knew I had lost the battle of the who-whoms, which I usually fight in dense fog.

With an exasperated breath, George Fullerton bolted from the room. As the sound of footsteps diminished, I thought that was the last I'd hear of him. Boy, was I wrong.

My PI business is located in Burton City, Iowa, where I moved after solving the murder of a star baseball pitcher. The folks in that Mississippi River town had a pretty high opinion of me and I expected business to be good. But murder, suspicion of adultery, and the various other detritus of life that are bread and butter for a PI were in short supply there, so I left my mobile home in care of my boyfriend and took the Greyhound southeast to visit my brother, Norris, and his family in Bern, Illinois, also on the Mississippi, about fifteen miles northeast of St. Louis. Bern was a town of 13,000 mostly working class folks who had not fared well since the depression.

Three days into my visit, Norris had said sideways, (his normal delivery, like his life, was somewhat askance) "I forgot to tell you, your favorite teacher from Lead Hill lives here now. What's 'er name - Bubbles - I saw her in the market. She stared at me through those fish-eye glasses and then she started in just where she left off." He trebled his voice into an unstable squeak.

"'Norris Winkworth, I hope you got yourself straightened out.' I said, 'Yes'm,' grabbed a can of pork and beans and got the hell out." Norris jittered a hand through his greasy hair; he was a part-time mechanic, full-time jitterer, and who knew what else. Part of the reason for my visit was concern, even dread, over the "what-else".

In Lead Hill, Arkansas, my brother had dropped out of school in tenth grade so he could spend the day sleeping and the night burglarizing. Of an evening, he'd swill black coffee and read Captain Marvel comic books until the alarm clock blasted, notifying him it was time to start robbing people. But often he'd respond by heaving a sigh and, having met part of the obligation, that of waking up, he'd fall back asleep.

At one point in my hour's conversation with Bubbles, she interrupted, "Oh, go ahead, call me 'Bubbles'. It's on your lips every time you force out 'Margaret.'" I stifled an embarrassed smile until I saw the corners of her mouth twitch and then we both chuckled. She was never one to bear a grudge. There was one other delicious moment when she toyed with a lapsed bra strap, but didn't follow through on pulling it up. That may have been designed to amuse.

I returned to Norris's home about 4:00 p.m. He was at work, his hours as an auto mechanic irregular. His wife, Kathy, had probably taken their two kids to the park.

I'd leave for Iowa tomorrow. The visit had been five days, that was enough.

The time of gabbing and hanging close had passed. Today, with no kin paying much attention to me, I knew everybody longed to get back to normal, and that included me.

Gazing out the front window, I saw a tall, broad-shouldered fellow crossing the street with a slightly pigeon-toed gait.

George Fullerton was hustling down the walk to the Winkworth front door.

Inside, after directing him to the sofa, I said, "I hope you've got a new question to ask." Still in the frayed suit and lace-up shoes he'd worn at school, he refused the offer of a Dr. Pepper, so I went to the kitchen and opened one for myself that I took from Norris's hummingly new GE refrigerator. Returning, I sat at the other end of the sofa. The sofa looked new, as did most of Norris's furniture. I didn't see how my brother could afford such expensive stuff on his part-time mechanic's pay, but wasn't about to ask. I wanted to end the visit on a high note, not discover he was still a thief and have to huff out.

"Margaret Baumgartner told me where you were staying," George Fullerton said. "After I saw you, I tracked down Paul Rump—the student on suspension." I nodded.

"He denies being in school today," he went on. "Of course I don't believe him. He's a liar and a hothead. Good family, but adopted." He spread his ham hands. "Not that that means anything. Harland and Birgie Rump own their own business; they work all the time. Good people. Pillars of the community." Whenever anyone used that expression, it brought to mind two vertical marble columns lacking any indication of gender. Maybe that's why they adopted.

"Paul's on suspension because he stole a car, went joy-riding, and wrecked it. Drunk at the time." Fullerton shook his head. He picked up a statuette of a female Olympian from the coffee table and studied it. A ribbon was diagonally across the lady's chest and she held a victory wreath above her head. Norris's wife loved such gewgaws. She checked them out of the library.

Fullerton gazed at the idealized figure without, I felt, really seeing it. "You must have thought I was crazy this afternoon. It's just that I was convinced only a stranger could have brought in the note. I realize now that I wasn't thinking clearly. Miss Winkworth,

I've come to ask you to find the person who wrote the note. You see, it's from someone I haven't seen for years, someone whom I thought I'd never see again this side of heaven. My mother." He pulled the scrap of paper from a shirt pocket and handed it over. It was a lined sheet, about three by five inches, torn from a tablet.

Scrawled on it, in pencil, was one word: "Roses." I looked at Fullerton and waited. And waited. This must have been his idea of tempo in a classroom—a pacing to heighten drama.

Just as I was about to prod with, "I charge by the hour," he took an agonized breath and began. "My mother walked out on us, my father and me, when I was six. Thirty-six years ago. I haven't seen her since, and I've talked to her only once. That was when I was twelve and she phoned to tell me that 'Roses' was going to be our secret code word. She said every January 5th, on her birthday, she'd write 'Roses' in the Personals of the Bern Morning Sentinel to let me know she was all right."

So it had not been pacing after all, but building up courage to begin a painful story.

"There's a memory behind that word," he said. "One day when I was just a small child, I grabbed a rose from Mother's hand to claim her attention. I was very demanding at that age. As Margaret pointed out today, I can still be quite rude and then, later on, deeply regretful. "

"Uh-huh," I said. "Keep going." Ignoring people's bad manners is required of one whose occupation involves Basic Buttinski.

"Well, I pricked my finger snatching the rose and blood bubbled up. It scared me half to death and made me cry. Mother took back the rose and said, 'Never grab on tight to a beautiful thing, Porgie.'" He blushed. "'Porgie' was her pet name for me. When she phoned that time, she called me 'Porgie' so I'd know it was really her." His eyes glazed in remembrance of the sweet voice that had once been the center of his world. Then they cleared and his tone became matter-of-fact.

"But the messages stopped when I turned eighteen. I guess she considered me old enough to look out for myself. I was heartbroken. I had loved the secret communication. Had she returned, I might have been disappointed." He laughed self-consciously. "No, no, I'm joking, of course."

"I'm sure it was awful when the messages stopped."

"Yes. I felt low, like I wasn't even important enough to be remembered once a year." He cleared his throat to rid it of emotion. "Over time, I've set my mind to the fact that she's gone - dead or where she doesn't need me any more. That's why this note comes as such a shock."

I said, "Instead of sending a note, why doesn't your mother just drop on by?"

He shook his head. "Oh, no, no, she wouldn't dare after what she did. I think she's putting out feelers, wants to see if I'll accept her back. That time years ago when we talked on the phone, she felt so guilty, crying for abandoning us. After she left us, my father explained that she wasn't meant for the happy housewife act, that we could never match her flair for the dramatic. Sometimes I pictured her having a grand career under a stage name, like a movie star or a royal princess."

Since it sounded like the child's fantasy of a runaway mom, I cracked, "Wallis Simpson is your mother?"

"Very funny. Look, Miss Winkworth, I'm certain my mother's alive and close by. I've called all the hotels in the area, but the desk clerks say that no single woman in her sixties is registered. I really want to meet with Mother and show her I'm a success despite having a pretty rough time growing up. Terrible things can happen to kids who run around unsupervised and I'm proud I made it through. I mean, look at Paul Rump and what a mess he is. And a youngster died just last month falling off a ladder in the middle of the night. Where were his parents? What was he doing on a ladder propped up against a third floor window of the historical museum?"

"Climbing in to steal something?" I speculated. George Fullerton was evidently another of those rosy-brained teachers who tried to see the best in their students. Thank heaven Bubbles had been that way.

The deadly example of neglect having served its purpose, Fullerton continued, "I can't have Mother invading my life right now and dropping off secret code-words. I'm to be married in five weeks to a lovely woman, Maragay Massman, you know, of the kitchen cabinet Massmans - the company that makes the fashionable kitchens."

It sounded like a royal title. I tried it on for size: Wendy Winkworth, of the trailer park Winkworths. Shucks, just didn't have the same resonance.

Since I make a habit of calling potential clients by their first names, on the theory that coziness breeds confidence, I led with, "George. Your mother's sudden reappearance might disrupt your wedding plans."

He gnawed on a fingernail, caught himself and stopped. With that careworn expression, the ruffled hair and little-boy pout, not to mention the wide shoulders, I'd have bet there were some young ladies' hearts broken in biology class the day he announced his engagement.

He said, "Wendy, my fiancée is thirty-six, I'm forty-two. She and her family are a staid and proper lot. Translated that means they don't like abnormal backgrounds, or surprises of any sort. What would they do if they found out I'd been abandoned as a kid? They might not want me as part of their family. Look, I'm in love with a beautiful woman and she loves me. But this note might mean bad weather ahead that no one can control. I don't mean to sound heartless, as if I don't want my own dear mother around, but she's been gone for such a long time and I want the chance to tell her how things stand."

"What is your dear mother's name?" I hoped that didn't sound sarcastic. I understood too well how love and hate can crowd together, one assuming dominance, then the other.

"Emma's her name - " He paused. " - of course she'll go by an alias."

"Why?"

"W-W-Well," he stammered, as though trying to come up with a reason, "because there are people in Bern who'll remember her, and may despise her for running out on her family and community." Jaw thrust forward, he looked and sounded a figure of Biblical probity.

His reasoning surprised me. In a town of 13,000 that hadn't done well for thirty years, surely there were stories worse than hers. This guy seemed to have inherited his mother's flair for the dramatic.

And I wondered if the old folks who remembered could hate her any more than he did. I suspected I was looking at the person who hated her most, as well as the one who loved her most.

"After you grew up, did you search for her?"

"No." Many headshakes. "I wouldn't have known where to start."

"George. Take a time out. Consider. Do you really want her back?"

"Well, yes. Sure. But I want her reappearance to be civilized and not some sort of surprise thing in the middle of my wedding. Surely I have the right after what she did."

I agreed. Parents popping up unexpectedly can be trying. My dad had been a travelling thief who occasionally dropped in on the family. He'd had impact enough to drive me over to the side of the law. Not so with my brother Norris, or so I feared.

I asked George if his father still lived in Bern.

"No. He's passed on. Died seven years after she left. Anyhow, he immediately sent me to Quincy, to be raised by my Aunt Mae, his sister. She gave me her married name, Fullerton."

"Ah, so the people here don't know you're the little kid whose mother walked out. Do you have a picture of her from way back then?"

"Father destroyed all photographs of her. Some even had me in them. Not long before she left, she had her portrait painted by a local artist. After she'd gone, I remember Father raving and weeping as he slashed the canvas with a knife. He cut her face to shreds."

I grimaced at the brutality of the last rites. "Did she have distinguishing marks? Moles, dimples, scars?"

"I was only six, and pretty myopic even then." With his middle finger, he slid the thick glasses further up his nose. "To me she looked perfect. I remember that, side by side, she was a lot smaller than my father. As I recall, she had light colored wavy hair, clear eyes, blue or even purplish I think, often sad. Wistful." He smiled deprecatingly. "Maybe I'm imagining that. I dream about her sometimes. I do remember her eyes opening wide when she cuddled me. There was a smell about her, I can't describe it. I guess I associate it with being motherly. And when she was outdoors, she wore a white cap with a bill."

"She probably won't still have that cap. I'll speak to Paul Rump about the note. Maybe the threat of the law will have some impact. How old would Emma be now?"

"Sixty-two. Sixty-three on January 5th."

That would be about Bubbles' age. The Bubbles I had known fourteen years ago had given way to a rather dilapidated elderly English teacher with washed out, close-cropped blond hair, and pale blue eyes over which spectacles had thickened. As a child, I had thought her tall. Today I'd been surprised at how much she'd shrunk. Or was it that I had grown up? After meeting the current

Bubbles, I tried conjuring up the former: erect, solid, with an explosive laugh. I failed. My beloved Bubbles, I hated losing her to the mists of the past.

I found myself nodding at the new client. This would be simple. Somewhere in Bern a remorseful old lady sends out a "Roses" feeler, and is working up the nerve to reunite with baby-boy-Porgie. I'd pick up a few extra bucks, sorely needed, to locate her; I mean how hard could that be? She probably wasn't all that speedy at fleeing anymore.

Then, in short order, I'd be back home with my beau in Burton City.

Uh-huh.

Order From

TITLE	COPIES	PRICE	SUBTOTAL
The Stray Pitch	_____	X $12.95	= $_________
Bubble, Roses, and Rumps *(pre-order, available 03/13)*	_____	X $12.95	= $_________

TOTAL $_________

(shipping and handling included)

NAME:

ADDRESS:

CITY: STATE: ZIP:

EMAIL:

Enclose a check or money order payable to **Winks Books** and mail to:

Winks Books
PO Box 1827
North Mankato, MN 56002

Please allow 2 weeks for delivery.

(also available as ebooks at amazon.com or barnesandnoble.com)

CPSIA information can be obtained at www.ICGtesting.com
Printed in the USA
BVOW010636110912

300037BV00001B/5/P